THE CENSOR'S HAND

A. M. STEINER

BOOK ONE OF
THE THRICE-CROSSED
SWORDS TRILOGY

A Ptolemy Publishing Book
First published in Great Britain in 2017 by
Ptolemy Publishing UK, 32 Stanhope Road, London, N6 5NG

Copyright © Adam M. Steiner 2017
Cover © www.patrickknowlesdesign.com
Design and typesetting by Jakob Vala

A catalogue record for this book is available from the British Library
Source ISBN: 978-0-9957229-0-3
Ebook Edition © April 2017 ISBN: 978-0-9957229-1-0
FIRST EDITION

PTOLEMY
PUBLISHING

TABLE OF CONTENTS

3

4

PRINCIPAL CHARACTERS

DANIEL MILLER,
aspiring censor and younger brother of

JONATHAN MILLER,
honest tradesman, husband and father.

MIRANDA,
a ward of the 'Dowager Duchess'.

ALSO APPEARING:

Of the Honourable Company of Cunning, manipulators of magic,
(principally at the Convergence, 'the Verge')

Chairman Gleame,
grandmaster and founder of the Convergence.

Master Pendolous Bolb,
formerly his apprentice.

Master Riven Gahst,
hekalogist and theoretical magimatician.

Master Allum Somney,
recruiter of demi-masters.

Of the Brotherhood of Censors, enforcers of justice,
(principally at Bromwich Seminary)

The Chief Constable,
leader of the Brotherhood of Censors.

Magistrate Campbell Lang,
commander of Bromwich Seminary.

Prosecutor Corbin,
an experienced investigator from Cruithin.

Brother Adelmus,
resident censor at the Convergence.

Various denizens of Bromwich, the second city of the Unity,
(the district of Turbulence and its environs).

Peacock Matthew,
gangster and brothel-keeper.

Big Shark and Littleshark,
his enforcers, greatly feared.

Gilbert Gordon,
a powerful moneylender.

George Barehill,
dissenter, leader of the so-called 'Freeborn'.

Laila,
his lover.

Other notable figures and institutions of the Unity.

The Rational Pantheon,
the gods, higher and lower, who dream our lives. We pray for their favour.

The godsworn,
their servants and temple-keepers.

The Wise Council,
the government and its ministers, noble by birth and in spirit,
who rule by their mutual consent.

Her Grace,
the 'Dowager Duchess' of the Wrekin and the North.

"We rarely hear, it has been said, of combinations of masters, though frequently of those of the common man. But whoever imagines, upon this account, that masters rarely combine, is as ignorant of the world as of the subject."

—"The Wealth of Nations,"
Adam Smith (1776)

PROLOGUE

The master needed more time to decide. Having none, he went to his bastion window and sought an answer from the night. Far below, waves maddened by the autumn tide lashed the flanks of the island. He considered hurling the device he had created into the void; imagined it spinning, bouncing and tumbling down the colossal masonry of the Convergence to sink beneath the surf. He waited for a sign. The cold damp of the sill slowly numbed his fingers.

A shearwater flew by, a black arrowhead against the starlight. It swooped across the endless walls, folded its wings and dived for the ocean. Moments later, it returned with a squid trapped in its beak. The master grimaced, uncertain of the omen, and withdrew into his bedchamber.

He lifted his robe from its mannequin. Countless embroidered bells of silver and gold jangled as he wormed his corpulent body inside. The air around him crackled with an unseen energy as the magic of the Convergence sharpened to his senses.

He clicked his fingers and the garnet lid of the casket on his vanity sprang open. The device nestled within; a hand fashioned of wire and tarnished brass, engraved with morbid symbols. Three taps on the contraption's base with a chubby, oil-stained finger and it twitched into life, uncurled slowly as if a spider released from a glass. He scooped the device into a small sack, which he tied tightly, unperturbed by how it bulged and writhed from within.

When the Convergence's celestial clock chimed the ninth part of the night the master half opened the door to his bed-chamber. Satisfied that the corridor was deserted he hoisted his hem and set forth, scuttling through windswept arcades and wall walks towards the Voyeurs' Gallery.

Sooner than expected, he found himself standing by the broad, arched window that overlooked the Flagellant's Garden, and took some satisfaction in having arrived first. The meeting place had been chosen wisely. The sound of the waves below and the creaking of the breaking wheel would drown a hushed conversation.

A tall, thin shadow broke loose from a corner and revealed itself as a man. A whalebone corset strangled his waist to the width of a child's neck and his thorn-wood skirt scratched the flagstones like a witch's broom. He breathed desperately.

"Master Bolb."

Bolb offered his most lopsided and idiotic grin, an unnecessary formality. "Master Gahst. If I had foreseen a need for stealth, I might not have chosen the Path of the Ludicrous."

Gahst, who was always smiling because of the tightly drawn wires that hoisted the sides of his mouth towards his eyebrows, considered this briefly. His wheezing filled the barrel-vaulted gallery.

"The Way of Pain also presents its challenges," he said, his tongue-spike clattering wildly against his teeth.

Bolb flinched as a third man strode silently into the room. The newcomer was dressed from head to toe in midnight blue. A silvered riding sword swayed under his hooded cloak. Despite his age and his battle wound, he moved with the lithe muscularity of a highland cat.

"Censor," Bolb said. He opened his mouth to continue, but found no words and gawped like a fish in a bowl. The fascinating lethality of the censor did not diminish as he drew closer. The man fixed Bolb with his grey eyes and reached out unnaturally quickly. Bolb untied the sack, his nervous fingers struggling with the knot, and held out the device reluctantly. The censor tucked it deftly into the sleeve of his cloak. Bolb's brow furrowed. His emptied hand dawdled in the air.

"Adelmus, do not fail us." Gahst's spittle flecked the perfect blue uniform.

"I serve no master but justice," the censor replied, and departed silently through the trapdoor that led to the postern gate.

"Now everything is with the gods," Bolb said.

●

The censor crept down the winding, sea-soaked steps to the small dock. There he had hidden his coracle under some old fishing nets. Soon he had cast out into the bay and fallen into a rhythm of hard rowing. The Convergence receded into the distance. Against the false dawn, it looked once alive, like the blasted stump of some vast and ancient tree.

He wondered what perils he would face on his journey. As a young man, in the days when the censors had been the soldiers of the godsworn, he had fought the barons to a bloody stalemate in the War of Edicts. This was no different, just another honourable battle. Once on the highway, he could make it to Lundenwic in less than ten days. He hastened his paddling and turned his attention to the shoreline, searching for signs of danger.

He crouched low as his coracle glided towards Seascale's gravel beach and, just before landfall, slipped over its side. Waist-deep in the breakers, he hoisted it onto his back and crawled across the exposed foreshore like a great sea turtle. He placed the craft in a hollow between gently waving grasses and buried it, scooping sand quickly with his paddle.

He searched out his next destination; the faint light of the lanthorn that hung in the courtyard of the stable master's enclosure. Two ambushers were waiting for him, hidden amongst the dunes. He killed the first with the stiff edge of his hand, a blow to the neck that brought swift and silent death. The second, he strangled with his bandolier. Moments later, he was in the stables. He grabbed a well-worn saddle pad, a saddle, girth and bridle from the wall, and picked out a bay-coloured mare — the most inconspicuous animal and the least likely to fuss. He led her from the stalls and checked her hooves, stroked her flank and set to harnessing the beast.

Without warning, the mare reared backwards, her nostrils flared with fear.

The censor drew his sword into a high guard and spun, to find the bit of a woodcutter's axe plunging towards his face. He reacted instantly, beating the heavy blade aside. Momentum carried his assailant forward and for a moment the man's neck was exposed. The censor wrenched a backhanded blow that should have sent his head tumbling into the dirty hay, yet somehow the assassin ducked the riposte and pitched into a forward roll. He returned to his feet like an acrobat, in defiance of his considerable size, and faced the censor with eyes full of anger and disbelief.

"That axe is no match for my sword," the censor said calmly, and pulled back his collar to reveal his badge, the Thrice~Crossed Swords. He stepped forwards, his blade levelled at his opponent's throat, its polished edge blazing in the torchlight.

"Shitarse!" the big man bellowed, looking frantically from left to right.

"Lay down your weapon," the censor said. "Tell me who sent you."

The assassin shook his head and wielded his axe menacingly, but the knuckles wrapped around its haft strained white. He took a step backwards.

"You won't live, if you resist me." The censor spun his sword impossibly swiftly. Its tip whistled in the air.

"Right," the large man said, dropping his axe to the dirt, "you win." He raised his hands high. "But hold fast, there's something you need to know."

"I'm listening."

"You won't like it."

"No?"

The night was broken by a flash and the deafening crack of a gunshot. A plug of flesh spat from a hole in the censor's neck, trailing a cloud of fine red mist. He staggered sideways; saw the stain of his blood on the stable wall. Smoke and the acrid scent of black powder drifted across the courtyard. He dropped to his knees and bowed his head. His vision began to fade.

"I'm not alone," the assassin said, his voice becoming distant.

The censor heard the assassin spit, then the scrape of metal on stone as he retrieved his axe. Footsteps crunched across the gravel, moving closer. Death came quickly.

●

The large man inspected the censor's corpse while his companion kept watch, his long arquebus at the ready.

"Hurry up," the lookout hissed.

"You took your time, didn't you?" the large man drawled as his hands moved systematically from pocket to pouch.

"You'd rather I'd missed?"

"What about the others?"

"Dead."

"Saves us some bother. If I'd known the mark was a censor I'd have asked for more, at least double." The large man removed his victim's cloak, flipped the body over and pulled down his trousers.

"Who'd be a censor nowadays?" his companion said.

The large man prised the fine riding sword from the censor's stiff, gloved hand and stood up. "I've searched him proper. There's nothing on him, and the Verge is a long way to come for nothing. It'll be dawn soon. Let's grab our horses and make haste before the stable master finds his courage."

"Do I have to search him myself?"

"Take all night if you fancy, but I'm not waiting for you."

The two men disappeared into the stables. A moment later, they were thundering away, at full gallop.

●

Seascale Bay was a forsaken place, and if the stable master had heard the fracas, he must have decided that there was no need to investigate before sunrise. Soon the only thing to disturb the corpse was a sea breeze.

Turning as imperceptibly as the century dial of the Convergence's celestial clock, and then with some urgency, Pendolous Bolb's creation, concealed within the censor's left glove, unscrewed itself from the dead man's wrist, raised itself on bent fingers and scuttled into the undergrowth.

I

THE ASPIRANT

By the time Daniel had finished in the bathhouse, the quadrant had been swept clear of straw and the fighting posts stacked neatly in the cloisters. His battered colleagues trudged towards the refectory or the infirmary, complaining of the day's hard training. He headed for the main gate, watched over by dusty gods and trailed by the scent of lemon soap.

There were no mirrors in Bromwich Seminary so he checked his reflection in the slab of obsidian that bore the names of censors fallen in duty. He meant no disrespect to the dead and was sure none would be taken.

His thick blond hair, freshly cut as short as a boot brush, was hidden under his metal hat, but the eyes that peered from under the brim were a dangerous kind of lively. His uniform, the light-blue leather buff coat and weighted cape of an aspirant, glowed with the bright hue that would be lost forever in a first wash. His black bucket boots shone. A cudgel and a set of manacles hung menacingly by his hip. He looked good. The only thing missing was the badge of office that he craved; the Thrice~Crossed Swords of a censor.

The seminary's armoured doors, two great triangles of oak and iron, stood open to the city, ready to receive its detritus.

"Six hours' leave," the guardsman said. "Get back any later and you're sleeping on the street." Daniel grunted affirmatively, artlessly scrawled his destination in the gatehouse's logbook.

As he crossed over to street-side a patrol of censors were hauling a man towards the receiving room. The prisoner's hands were striped with fresh cuts that drizzled blood onto the flagstones. Daniel wondered at the cause of the wounds. The prisoner was shouting drunken obscenities about the Dowager Duchess and proclaiming the rights of the people. *A dissenter.* That was a new breed of trouble for Bromwich, though all had expected it to arrive eventually.

First Temple Row then cut through Needless Alley and on to New Street. That was the best route to Turbulence. Not the quickest, but the Row had a good pavement and a few lime trees, which had not yet surrendered their last few yellowing leaves. The clerks and merchant adventurers of High Town tipped their hats as he passed. He accepted their politeness with a nod and tried to catch the eyes of the housemaids returning from the great bazaar carrying panniers stacked with vegetables and game. Most stared demurely at their feet, but some met his gaze with a blush or a look. He smiled at those as if they would be remembered.

At the edge of High Town, a team of roadsmiths were installing a lamp-pole shaped like a palm tree. It was uncommon to see men working on an Enday, but the authority of the godsworn waned with every passing year. The men's efforts didn't bother him, nor the gods from what he could see.

He thought the device pretentious and a marvel, and stopped to look at it for a while. Glow-stones moulded as coconuts hung from its ferrous fronds. It had cost a fortune, he reckoned, and been positioned for show alone. Its magic was destined to illuminate nothing but the guards hired to prevent its theft, but the wealthy of Bromwich would not be outshone by relatives and rivals in Lundenwic, Alchester, Ebarokon, Aldergrove or any other city of the Unity that might have the means for cunning.

He had been living away from Turbulence long enough to notice its stench. Few rode horses in the narrow, cobbled street that passed through the shadows of derelict mansions and the tenements crammed between them. Without horse manure to collect for fuel or fertiliser, scavengers could not make a living — and so the shit, animal or otherwise, was left where it fell. To keep a tidy heel you kept to the middle of the streets.

To show that he was not afraid, he slowed his pace to a measured and heavy stroll. It was a walk that claimed dominion. A warning to vagrants and cutpurses that he would not be moving on anytime soon. He had practised it in the seminary's cloister until his feet had blistered and then bled. It was essential, Lay Brother Hernandez had told him, that before he entered a dark alleyway or rounded a street corner, men knew what he was. Attention to detail, the instructor had said, would one day save his life.

He hoped it was true. Daniel was conspicuous in his bright uniform. That said, there was no reason for street pirates to trouble him — he wouldn't pay them for passage and they knew it. If an aspirant was assaulted the Brotherhood of Censors would perform an inquisition, use the sight to take confessions. Nobody wanted that. The men who lounged in doorways or on street corners — peekers for the gangs — averted their faces as he approached them, or sidled into shadow. He didn't know why they bothered. He knew most of them by name or to which gangs they belonged. He wondered how many would recognise him in his finery.

It was sundown when the mill came into view. It was in better shape than he remembered, freshly painted, the brass finial of its curved cap polished bright. The sails were locked, despite the flaccid breeze. Daniel stopped in dread as he spotted his father perched halfway up one of the frames, repairing a sailcloth.

That was impossible. Father was long dead, his ashes on the wind. Daniel had lit the funeral pyre himself, watched the bastard's body burn under the indifferent glare of the midday sun.

Not Father. Jon, standing in Father's old spot. His brother had grown a beard. Daniel wondered why and whistled his relief. He wanted his brother to notice him but the mill was too far for a shout or a wave, so he stepped up his pace.

He was sweating when he arrived. Jon was at the loading door, arguing with a sour-faced man in a long broadcloth coat. Jon's strong jaw was locked in restraint, his fists were bunched and his face was pained. A scraggy stevedore waited close by with a handcart, picking at his thumbnails. *Trouble*, Daniel thought, and switched back to his slow walk.

"We agreed two pounds," Jon said.

"I'm making hard biscuit. I don't pay for silk when I need cloth."

Jon flapped his arms like a stork. "What's in the bag is in the bag. If you want middlings, I'll fetch you some."

"I'll take what I've paid for." The baker jabbed his thumb at Jon. He was enjoying this. *Not for long.*

"Belay your yapping," Daniel commanded. The baker rounded on him in radish-faced fury. The man was almost as large as Jon, which mattered not a jot.

"I know who you are. Piss off. Come back when you've got a badge." The baker's anger was real, but lacked control. It was the weakness of an untrained mind.

"What makes you think I need a badge, son?"

Without taking his eyes from the man, Daniel unhooked the manacles from his belt and let the chain unfurl to his ankles. As a censor in training, he was not permitted to make arrests, but the cuffs were of heavy iron and the chain just long enough to swing to good effect. They would do some real damage. He twirled a wristlock in the air and it whistled menacingly. The colour drained from the baker's face. His stevedore got set to run.

"Let's not get carried away. It's a small disagreement." Jon stepped between them, shying from the spinning metal.

"I'm a regular customer," the baker protested over Jon's shoulder.

"Then act regular."

Daniel whipped the iron to a halt and fought to maintain a stern face as a price was hurriedly agreed. After the deal was stuck, he helped to load the flour onto the handcart. The baker paid and left without a word. Daniel bade him a good evening. Jon spat onto the cobbles, once they were out of view.

"I've given that man fair trade for years. Now he picks at me like a piece of carrion."

Daniel grinned. "Did you see the look on his face? I thought he was going to soil his pants."

"You scared him. He might not come back."

"Bollocks. If that flour was as good as you said he got a bargain."

"He'd better." Jon frowned and counted the baker's payment again, as if a second calculation might improve the result. "Come on in, Dan. See the baby. Dinner's waiting."

Daniel embraced his brother, trying to squeeze out the anxiety that bunched his massive shoulders. Jon patted him on the back as awkwardly as ever.

As they entered the great hall of the mill-house, Jon touched the crescent moon engraved above the door. Daniel smiled at the familiar gesture and copied it, for luck. Inside, the fine oak armoire was missing. So was the long floral tapestry from the side of the minstrel gallery, where as kids they had hidden from Father's rages. Otherwise, all was as he remembered. Anna was stooped in the broad hearth, stoking a small fire, her long black braid tucked back into her cap. Her head lifted as they entered the hall and she called Jon over to take her place, wiped her sooty hands half clean on her apron.

"They let you come!" The warmth of her smile demanded another in return. Anna had always been a handsome lady and the hard work of marriage and motherhood had done nothing to diminish her gaiety. She hugged Daniel warmly and gave him a peck on the cheek.

"The grading starts tomorrow; I'm allowed a few hours for family business."

"I've fed the little one already. I'll put her to bed." Anna took the baby from her swaddling hook on the wall and hung Daniel's cape in her place. The baby blinked contentedly.

"Hand her over." Daniel laid his cudgel and manacles by the door and cradled his niece-to-be in his arms, rubbing her tiny nose with his own. It wouldn't be long now before her first smile signalled the arrival of a soul in her body. "Only a few more weeks till her naming."

"I was thinking of Dahlia." Anna said it quietly and waited for Daniel's reaction. He felt a jab of pain and scowled, then a sense of shame as Anna turned away, crestfallen, to light the dining candle. It burned cheaply, with a fitful green-tinged flame.

"Working on the next one yet?" Daniel said to neither of them in particular, trying to restore some jollity. Anna clacked her emptied mug down, tousled Dan's hair and reclaimed the gurgling baby. She had forgiven him already.

"What makes you think we want more kids?" Jon said.

"This place."

"No reason why a woman can't run a mill," Anna shouted as she carried the infant upstairs.

"A maid can't haul grain sacks," Jon grunted from the fire.

They'd decided to keep the girl-child nonetheless. "If she gets Anna's looks she won't be wanting for gentleman helpers," Daniel offered.

"Watch it," Jon cautioned.

"That earned you an extra slice of pie," she said. "Don't wait on my account. I'll check on Mother, feed her some pap." Anna disappeared into the master bedroom.

Daniel and Jon sat at the dining table, a huge slab of oak worn pebble smooth with age. There was no wine and the bread and cheese were no fresher than they needed to be.

"We should pray," Jon said. He raised his arms above his head and began to mumble thanks to the whole of the Rational Pantheon. Dan pretended to do likewise, and thought about his training.

They picked at the food. Daniel asked after the few friends they shared in Turbulence. Jon seemed distracted, gave half answers, looked miserable.

"Are you still upset about that baker?" Daniel asked. "I only wanted to make sure you got a fair deal."

"That tosspot? No. Remember I told you about the manufactory they were topping off on Arkwright Hill?"

"The one with six sails?"

"A pair of eightsails, with ten-foot sweeps." Jon could not hide his awe at the scale of the beast.

"Right," Daniel recalled, "they finished rigging it last month. I heard the slipstream wasn't too bad."

"It wasn't at first, just a little bit more buffeting. I made some changes, ran the mill a little longer at night." Jon already knew how to set the mill better than Father ever had. Daniel regarded him proudly.

"Sorted," Dan said.

"No. Last week I was up in the bin room. One moment the mill was running like clockwork. Then nothing."

"Nothing?"

"A couple of minutes of freewheel. Then it stopped dead." Jon popped his fingers.

"Sounds like cunning to me."

"Right. They paid a master to divert the winds to their advantage. The bastard came down from his glass tower at the Verge, spouted some Mammon-Dagon, and now I'm buggered."

Dan had heard such complaints before, from the mouths of vandals and vagrants. The law was not kind to such men.

"The Convergence is the greatest enterprise of the Unity, the source of all our magic," he warned.

Jon swept the table in frustration. "It was wrong, how they used to treat the Cunning, but there ought to be laws."

"So long as the works were properly licensed they were legal."

"There's a surprise." Jon set down his cup. "I'm finished."

Dan didn't know what to say.

"Cheer up; we're supposed to be celebrating," Anna called out as she returned to the table.

"I'm not a censor yet," Daniel said, still troubled by Jon's words, but his chest puffed out anyway, as if in preparation for the badge.

"Just getting a chance to take the tests is an honour," Anna said. "You've wanted to be one since you were a little boy. You used to make capes out of grain sacks and try to arrest the rats."

Daniel shifted uncomfortably at the memory. "You joined in sometimes — the damsel in distress."

"Until I came and rescued you." Jon picked her up and perched her on his knee.

"You shouldn't tease," Anna said. "He'll be promoted to prosecutor before you know it, be a magistrate some day."

"Gods help us," Jon said, and they laughed together.

"Daniel, we have a present for you. I found it cleaning out your old room." Anna handed him a book wrapped in cheese-cloth. It was his old *History of the Brotherhood*, well-thumbed in familiar places. He remembered the hours spent reading it on the cold metal platform that ringed the mill's bagging floor. As a child, he had skipped over the politics and history, delighting in the tales of justice dispensed, heroic censors and the notori-ous rogues they brought to book or final reckoning.

"Do they feed you well, at the seminary?" Anna asked as she ladled a greasy pottage into their bowls. Some bird meat and a few lonely apple seeds floated on its surface. It smelled better than it looked, but not by much.

"Warm milk and a biscuit before bedtime, every night."

Jon laughed. "How's the studying? You used to struggle with your schooling."

Only because you were my teacher, Daniel thought, but let the comment slide. "Rulings. Precedents. Amendments. You just have to remember them. I took my examination in law last week and passed soundly enough. There's no getting round it. We have to prove we can fight using words."

"It's 'we' now, is it?" Jon said. "You want to be careful with that."

"It's called the Brotherhood for a reason."

"They aren't your family."

"Who would have thought it?" Anna interrupted. "Daniel Miller, a scholar of justice."

Daniel waved his spoon in the air. "Everyone knows what justice is. Give me a squadron of men and half an hour and I'd deliver more justice to Turbulence than any lawyer in history. It's the meditation that's the hardest."

"It must be a wonder, to see with the gods," Jon said, sud-denly solemn. There was no way Daniel was going to be drawn on the details of confession. If he started, the questions would never end. He sipped at the stew. It tasted mainly of water and scalded his tongue.

"We kneel for hours."

"I can't imagine what your father would have thought about Daniel becoming a censor," Anna said.

"Fair point," Jon said, "and for that we should open a bottle — one I've been saving." He vaulted from the table. Anna looked away before Daniel could catch her eye.

"Maybe we should wait until after I've passed," Daniel said. "The grading's a serious business."

"I thought you were going to train for another year?" Anna said.

"I'm ready for it."

Jon returned from the pantry clutching a couple of goblets and a bottle with a peeling label. "Tulip wine."

Anna kissed Daniel on the forehead. "I'm going to bed. Don't drink it all. You've both got work tomorrow."

Daniel pretended to sip at his drink, let Jon top it up a fraction after he emptied his own. The fire dwindled as they talked about life in the seminary. Daniel described the daily routine of exercise, combat instruction, study and meditation.

"It's all order and discipline. That was hard at first. Now I see it differently. There's no thieving or squabbling. Men work together instead of taking advantage. It makes me think how things could be different."

"Different?"

"In Turbulence. If the censors paid more attention. Stopped crime instead of just clearing up afterwards."

"Maybe."

"Maybe we'd still have our sister."

"It wasn't your fault," Jon said.

They stared at embers in silence for a few minutes. Jon emptied another glass. "What's it like being the only Turbulence boy?"

"Easy. Most of the aspirants are much younger. Orphans and foundlings. They don't know how the streets work, and the Brotherhood is their only family. I'm exciting to them. A big brother." He winked at Jon. "Anyway, I'm not the only one."

"Who else?" Jon was already blinking from the booze.

"Lay Brother Hernandez. It's a good story. He used to fight in the pits — had an unbroken record. Wylde's and Gordon's bookies got upset."

"Sounds like he wouldn't take a fall."

"The Brotherhood let it be known that it would be better for all concerned if Hernandez ended up teaching at the seminary."

"Rather than floating face down in the Windrush. What does he do now? He must have been too old to learn the sight. He can't be on the streets."

"He's the master-at-arms. He teaches me how to fight."

Jon snorted and Daniel smiled knowingly. Hernandez had taken him aside after his first week in the seminary. Some warriors, he had said, were talented but lazy. Others were great athletes who lacked patience and wiles. Every student presented a unique challenge. For Daniel, he had promised, it would be finding enough time to perfect what Hernandez could teach, and that had been the truth of it.

"Tell me stories," Jon slurred, "dirty street stories."

"I'd love to, but I've got to head back. Grading starts tomorrow, remember."

Jon planted his elbow on the table. "Let's wrestle. Come on — for old times' sake. The loser finishes the bottle."

Daniel laughed. "There's nothing left in the bottle. Are you sure you want to put your record at risk?"

Jon cleared the table with a sweep of his huge forearms. They bulged under his cloth shirt. Jon was thirty pounds heavier than Daniel, and four inches taller. He might not be a trained warrior but he spent most of his day throwing hundred-pound grain sacks around.

They locked palms. Jon applied pressure slowly, as if the game were a test.

"You're as strong as ever," Daniel grunted. Jon levered his forearm downwards, inching Dan's hand towards defeat. Daniel allowed his mind to enter the still place that Hernandez had shown him, saw himself and Jon from the outside, two brothers bonding in loving opposition. He inspected the angles, how the forces came together in their palms. With bewildering speed, he spiralled his wrist, twisted Jon's hand back on itself and sent it crashing down.

"What was that?" Jon stared at his prone hand, shocked.

"First time for everything," Daniel grinned.

"I'm drunk. Fuck."

"It's only a game."

Jon's face screwed up tight. He looked tired and vulnerable, nothing like the brother who had raised Daniel into manhood.

"How can I take on big jobs if I can't guarantee delivery? I can't stay up all night waiting for a ten-minute gale on the off-chance. I'm losing customers. And if they build another factory I won't get a robin's fart of a breeze." Sometimes Jon got angry when he was drunk — that was why Anna didn't allow it — but not sad, like this. "I go to temple every week, make offerings. I've prayed correctly — to the Father for courage and the Mother for wisdom, even to the Watcher for knowledge of what is to come."

"Prayers can be long in the answering."

"You're right, I should make better offerings."

That wasn't what Daniel had meant, but he held his tongue. "You'll think of something, you always do. You're a man of property, you've kept honest trade."

"I've never adulterated, or sold gone-off as fresh."

"Exactly. How many millers can say that? Let alone around here?"

"All I want is to be able to look after my family."

"I know."

Jon exhaled lengthily, combed his hair with his fingers.

"I'm going to meet the Peacock."

Daniel's face soured. "Why?"

"He used to be fond of Anna."

"Don't borrow from him."

"I won't."

"I know times are hard, but people like that, they can't help us. Once they have their hooks in, they never let go. Wait a while. When I'm ordained I'm going to sort this neighbourhood out. I'll make things better for the both of us."

"You'll fight the gangs and I'll fight the factories." Jon was humouring him, and that hurt a little.

"Promise me you won't do anything stupid. I'm going upstairs to see Mother before I leave."

She was sleeping peacefully in her room, the same as always. Her face was drawn, skin paper thin, but she looked happy. Daniel wiped a few crumbs of dried pap from the side of her mouth and kissed her head. She had been like this for so long. He wondered if she would see out the baby's naming and said a prayer for her comfort. He realised his cheeks were damp and wiped them dry. It would not do, for a censor to appear weak on the streets.

Back downstairs Daniel strapped on his weapons and wrapped his cape about his shoulders. Jon was slouched over the dining table, head on oak, counting out the baker's coins for a third time. Daniel let himself out.

Evening had turned to night and the air was brisk. If he ran back to the seminary, Daniel reckoned he could fit in another hour of training before they locked the dormitory doors.

A STRANGE AND CURIOUS GIRL

"Ladies must wait outside. Who do you attend?" shouted the doorman who defended the Exchange building's portico.

Miranda could barely hear him over the cascades of rainwater that spewed from the mouths of the granite griffins overhead. Their fierce aspects perfectly expressed her growing anger. She was young, but clearly no longer a girl. Her immaculate attire and freshly cut hair, onyx black and scented with ambergris, made her pedigree obvious. A man of her position would be getting more respect.

"I attend no one. This is my invitation." Miranda snatched a card from her handmaid and flapped it in the doorman's face. She jabbed at its extravagant print with a white-gloved finger. "Miranda, Ward of the Duchess of the Wrekin and the North. I am she. Ayrday the 63rd, Malchus III, I think we can both agree is today."

Naming the emperor was a little absurd, but she was trying to make a point.

She jabbed a finger at the ducal crest embossed on the coach-and-four parked behind her. "My maid will wait with my governess in that carriage if she is not permitted entry."

The horses fidgeted in the downpour.

The doorman shook his head, as if she had asked him a question. His behaviour was extraordinary. She wondered if he couldn't hear her or simply chose not to do so. "This is no use at all," she said. "I would fare better in a conversation with the statuary."

The broad brim of Miranda's hat had begun to droop. Equipped with a swan-plumed umbrella, wholly inadequate for the task, her handmaid was failing in her duty to keep it dry. The hem of her silk and velvet skirt would be next. Everything about the situation was unacceptable.

Miranda snatched the umbrella from her maid and shoved it in the doorman's face. As he wrestled with it, she stepped around him and marched into the building.

The Exchange's ornate interior looked like a palace but without the history. Later in the day, it would be crowded with men trading saffron, lead and tin. For now, the merchants were outnumbered by statues of guildsmen heroically wielding ledgers and hand scales. The clattering of Miranda's fashionably heeled shoes turned heads as she sought the meeting room. The doorman chased behind her leaving a wet trail on the marble.

"Milady, the rules of the Exchange are clear and strict."

"Then you are doing a particularly poor job of enforcing them."

"Please desist," he whined.

She turned to face her irritant. "My invitation came directly from Chairman Gleame. I would know your name, sir!"

The doorman mumbled something inaudible.

"I shall mention that to him when I am done," she declared.

The muscles in his jaw tightened. "Come with me, milady. I'm sure I can resolve this misunderstanding."

Miranda followed him down corridors lined with austere paintings of unremarkable-looking, middle-aged men. They arrived in a room decorated with fashionable tapestries displaying stylised images of mechanical marvels from the Convergence and the cunning at work. A trio of young men, students judging by their tasteless suits, waited nervously on small chairs beside a tall oak door. A giant of a coachman in a silver-lined greatcoat watched them discreetly from a corner. His garb was expensive but unkempt. A shortish sword, the width of her arm, hung by his side.

"This must be the place," Miranda said.

The doorman scowled and engaged the coachman in a heated conversation, punctuated with exasperated gestures in her direction. The coachman deflected his rage with nonchalant shrugs. Eventually, tired of the agitation, he drew some coins from his purse and pressed them into the doorman's hand. He left the room without a glance in Miranda's direction. Ignoring the snub, she bade him farewell with a victorious nod and waited to be attended, as poised as a temple dancer. The gazes of the waiting boys crawled her body as the coachman ambled towards her.

"They don't allow ladies in the Exchange," he said, and her heart sank, "but that doesn't bother me any. Big Albert, at your service. May I see your invitation?" He spoke with the thick accent of a Nor-Wester. Miranda thought his smile charmingly rural.

She presented the elaborate card with both hands and the barely discernible dip that she reserved for men of uncertain station. He handed it back with the speed of an accomplished reader and she curtsied more deeply.

Albert gestured towards the row of seats and the three students stood for her all at once, moved away and began a conversation amongst themselves. Judging from their glances it was about her. She smiled at them prettily and tried to appear confident. She guessed they were hopefuls, like her. Only a select few were invited to apply to join the Honourable Company of Cunning each year, the very brightest in the Unity, and even those who received employment would only retain it if they could master the cunning arts. The process was intimidating and humiliating, but for those who succeeded came wealth and power. Not that it mattered to boys like these; they were rich already. Their lives overflowed with choice.

The oak-panelled door opened and a young man exited, clutching a velvet cap in both hands. He looked as pale as if he had eaten bad meat and he left the antechamber without a courtesy. Big Albert took instruction from behind the door and then invited Miranda inside. Surprised not to have to wait her turn, she composed herself and entered.

It was some kind of council room, designed for the long-winded discussion of matters of business. A long walnut table set with silver inkpots and leather writing pads ran its length. The men who decorated its walls looked as unexceptional as those in the corridors, but their portraits were much larger. On the other side of the table sat an odd fellow wearing a silver skullcap and dressed in a richly gilded maroon suit. A thick gold chain dangled between his breast pockets, and he looked exhausted. His lids drooped dark and heavy over blood-shot eyes.

Miranda's head fizzed like a migraine, but without the pain. Specks of light seemed to dance in the air before her, like a swarm of golden midges.

The man stood and bowed, offered a place with his palm. "My name is Master Somney. Please be seated."

Miranda stood trembling, befuddled by the delusion.

"Are you unwell?" he asked.

"I'm fine."

"The business with the doorman — please forgive him. The Exchange has its rules so you can understand his confusion. I didn't realise the invitation . . . I forgot . . ." Somney seemed to lose track of his words. "Shall we press on? You are aware that no woman has ever . . ."

Miranda sat. "Been given the opportunity to interview for the Honourable Company."

Somney seemed a little flummoxed by her interruption so she flashed him a gracious smile.

"Very well then. Let us begin." Somney lifted from the table a thick compendium and opened it to a picture of a monolith notched with a thousand tiny marks. "I don't expect you to know what these squiggles are."

Miranda squinted at the etching. "The romance of Tanit and Baal-Hammon from ancient Qart-Hadath. Unusually it has been transcribed from the original Oenic into Omek. I must say, it is a very beautiful illustration."

Somney stared at her, expressionless.

Miranda scrabbled for something cleverer to say. "I believe this stone now resides at the pleasure palace of Rabat. The sculptor made three errors in translation. Don't you agree?" Still nothing. "I possess five languages, you see, including both of the greats —ancient and archaic. I had to teach myself Omek, but it's relatively straightforward. You start with Eyalet and work backwards."

She walked her fingers along the edge of the table. Somney didn't seem as impressed as she had expected.

"Let us move on to matters more conventional."

"Of course."

"Astronomy. What is your opinion of the heliocentric model?"

"That only a man could conclude the planets revolved around himself. The new theories are far superior. Epicycles are an inelegant solution."

"The distillation of botanicals. What is the preparation for plague water?"

"Um . . . according to Hieronymus Hogg there are . . . two recipes?"

Somney pounced on her hesitation. "Yes, yes, but what are the details?"

"Let me think. Dr Burges's is a handful of sage and rue boiled in two, no, three pints of muscadine, then stained and fired."

Somney's face fell. "Enough! Let us turn to matters geographical."

So it continued. Somney quickened his pace. Miranda answered his tricky questions as best she could. Whenever she tried to elaborate or use a clever analogy, Somney interrupted or changed the subject. He switched without warning from geography to grammar, between mathematics and metaphysic, architecture and astrology.

There was a knock at the door and it opened a crack. Big Albert's substantial head emerged and then disappeared as rapidly. Miranda had no idea how long the interrogation had lasted. It felt like mere minutes.

Somney harrumphed. "What do you believe was the impact of pre-war morality on the development of cunning in the Unity?"

Miranda thought the question dull, like something from an examination paper. "I don't think it made any difference. The godsworn did not prohibit magic for moral reasons. That was just an excuse. Cunning put power into the hands of individuals in a way that threatened them. If men can be like gods, then why make offerings or pray?"

Somney's eyebrows twitched. "An interesting theory, but you present it as a fact. If that is the case, how do you explain our current state of affairs? The existence of the Honourable Company?"

"Cunning is tolerated, for the time being."

"Tolerated!" Somney spluttered. "For the time being!"

"Because the masters are discreet. Because the Convergence is remote. Mainly because the ministers of the Wise Council see how much money there is to be made from magic and so shape our laws accordingly." Somney's sternness finally crumbled. He chuckled and blinked.

"Then I have nothing to fear, because that will never change. It seems we have run out of time. I must admit, you answered my questions superbly. I cannot fault your intellect. What about your judgement?"

"What do you mean?"

"You are a beautiful young woman, a ward of the duchess."

"We are her sorrow and her joy."

Somney coughed uncomfortably. "Indeed. No doubt you have many excellent suitors. Why pursue a career at the Verge?"

Miranda bit on her cheek. Society considered the hundred adoptive daughters of the duchess to be wedding fodder, delicious awards for the greatest artists, merchants and foreign diplomats. Little more than candied fruit. It was foolish to suppose that Somney thought differently. Besides, it was a question that she had asked herself many times. Most of the ward-daughters enjoyed the prestige, the easy life. Some even found love.

"I think my intellect would be of greater service to the Unity at work in the Convergence than listening to a husband discussing the price of sheepskins over dinner."

"Why do you believe that the Convergence is a proper place for a woman?"

"I think that the proper place for a woman is wherever she chooses to be."

"Ah ha! You have a rebellious mind." Somney wrung his hands and grimaced at her. Anger balled in Miranda's throat. She coughed it out.

"I would have thought you'd consider that a positive — after all, it was only thirty years ago that censors were burning the Cunning alive for their rebellious minds." Somney's bloodshot eyes bulged. "With all due respect, Master Somney, you seem to be more interested in my circumstances than my capabilities."

"You are an orphan, yes?"

"You have already noted that I am a ward-daughter of the duchess. Of course I am an orphan."

Somney laced his fingers and stared at them. "Your birth mother abandoned you to the street and now you seek to abandon the flower of your youth to a career. Isn't that a little selfish? What about children?"

"Master Somney, if I may be so bold, that question is so personal and so ridiculous, I must assume that its sole purpose is to dissuade me from applying for this position. If that is your intention then please do me the simply courtesy of saying so. If not, then allow me to ask you a question." He sullenly invited her to continue.

"What happened in the air when I first saw you?"

"What? You saw that?"

It wasn't really a question. She could see he was shocked, though he tried to hide it. He went to the latticed window that overlooked Exchange Square and stared unfocused into the distance, played with his gold chain. Miranda waited patiently while he gathered his thoughts.

"Actually you didn't *see* anything. The phenomenon was mental — imagined but also entirely real. In simple terms, you saw magic. My magic. I cannot explain that to you here. You will learn about it at the Convergence."

"I will?"

"If you choose to go. My questions were not intended to dissuade you from attending, although my presumption was that you would prove incapable. I had assumed that your presence here was solely due to Chairman Gleame's desire to remain in Her Grace's favour. Something to do with our licences." He let out a long sigh, but returned to the table a happier man. "I had not expected you to be so . . ." He flapped his hands in place of an adjective. "I will not deny talent where I see it, though I will have to suffer some painful explaining to my colleagues."

Miranda tried to sound grateful. "Thank you."

"You are a clever girl and it appears you already have a sensitivity to magic that few possess. Far fewer than you might suppose. You should understand that, if you accept a position as a demi-master, many at the Convergence would wish to see you fail. They may do their best to ensure it. Moreover, as a woman, you will be utterly alone. I would think carefully before deciding."

The door opened and Albert's head appeared briefly again.

"I cannot spend any more time with you. Here is a letter confirming my offer of a position. Whether you accept it is entirely up to you. Thank you for your attendance."

●

Miranda was glad of the rain that soaked her face as she crossed the street to her carriage; it hid tears of anger. Her handmaid, appalled that she had not waited for assistance, was nearly run down by a patrol of horsemen as she rushed to shield her mistress with the useless umbrella. Inside the coach, her governess had laid a lace mat over Miranda's bench to keep it dry. She slumped miserably down upon it.

"That was just awful," Miranda said.

"I was afraid of that."

"I argued with the master."

"Oh dear." Her governess rapped on the ceiling of the carriage and it set off towards the duchess's embassy at a pace. "Not to worry, child. Her Grace feared it might prove impossible. If you would like to choose a different gift . . ."

"The Company offered me a position."

Miranda revealed Somney's letter and handed it over. Her handmaid screeched and clapped in delight, drawing a disapproving look from her unflappable superior.

The ducal carriage rolled through the obelisk-lined streets of Lundenwic. The monoliths were new; the style of the First Empire was all the rage, now that people could afford it. Ramshackle half-timbered houses and shops along the river were being torn down by rope and hook, and replaced with symmetrical slab-faced buildings clad in yellow stone. Miranda wondered how many centuries of progress the Unity had squandered under the leaden rule of the godsworn, and how quickly things had changed in the thirty years since their overthrow. One day soon, some mill owner or trader would have the means to commission a pyramid of his own. She considered how odd it would look, towering over the rainy city that the ancients had believed to be the last before the edge of the world.

"And will you accept the offer?" her governess continued, as if they had not travelled for twenty minutes in silence.

"Honestly, I don't know," Miranda said. "The master was a pig at first. He made me feel like a circus freak. I expect he's kinder than most. Why would I want to be part of something that makes me feel so miserable?"

"It's not my place to give an opinion," her governess ventured, "but maybe I could tell you a story to pass the time."

Miranda smiled sideways. "That would be wonderful."

"Once upon a time an infant girl was abandoned in the snowy streets of Urikon. If she had been an ordinary girl, the cold or hunger would have taken her, but she had beautiful green eyes and tawny skin, and so she was delivered to the Royal Orphanage. The moment the duchess set eyes upon the foundling she knew that the child was a blessing."

"I think I know this one." Miranda settled into the soggy comfort of her bench.

"When she was a little older she helped her ward-sisters perform funerals in the manner of the Snake. They were an expensive business, and profited the orphanage greatly. She paraded the ash-urns of nobles she had never known through the streets wearing a crown of white lilies, to symbolise her innocence, and a chiffon robe that displayed her girlish purity."

Miranda remembered the smell of the flowers.

"So pretty," the handmaid cooed. The governess slapped her across the knees.

"When they entered the ancestral mastabas her ward-sisters became fearful and would go no further. Our little girl was not afraid of burial chambers; darkness and the passing of flesh were not her enemies. While her sisters cowered in the gloom, she felt her way, placed the urns in garlanded niches. Then she would disappear underground into the darkness. Why was that again?"

"Looking for hidden secrets," Miranda said. *I never discovered any, though.* She recalled the disappointment of it. *I suppose I never had any real idea what they might be.*

"What an odd little lady. Then there was the stealing. The governess was accustomed to girls with light fingers. When she took them to dance at gentlemen's estates, they would make off with sweets and fruits. The worst of them stole jewellery, hairbrushes and hand mirrors. When they were caught, they had to make good the crime to the client's satisfaction. But there was only ever one girl who stole books."

Miranda winced with guilt and embarrassment. "I never knew she was discovered."

"Maybe the books were just for show and never missed by their owners. Maybe they couldn't imagine a tiny dancer wanting them, but the governess saw everything. Now what kind of a girl steals books?" Miranda blushed. Her handmaid looked confused.

"And there was worse to come. When the girl was old enough, she left the orphanage and joined the entourage on the grand tour. At fourteen, she looked like the consort of a pharaoh, was kept under close guard, for scandal stalks young ladies like a serpopard. One night, in this very town, she was spotted climbing out of her bedroom window disguised as a scullery maid. Where was she going? Her governess was curious. Was it a rendezvous with a handsome cavalryman? Did she plan to watch a bawdy play? The governess followed her through dark streets, every moment in fear for their lives."

Nonsense, Miranda thought.

"What happened?" the handmaid blurted, her eyes bulging with excitement.

"Well might you ask! She went to the anatomical theatre. Paid half a shilling to witness the necropsy of a suicide performed for the entertainment of a crowd of beery tradesmen. Watched a travelling surgeon pull fleshy gobbets from the waterlogged body."

"Ugh!" The handmaid looked at Miranda as if she had just swallowed a live frog.

The organs looked nothing like the brightly coloured drawings in my medical books, Miranda thought, *but I did learn something that night, about the fragility of flesh.*

"And so we reach the end of the story. What do you think happened next to this strange and curious girl? Did she marry a handsome cavalryman? While away her days in peaceful entertainments?" The governess coughed theatrically.

"I don't know," Miranda said. "I really don't."

The coach skidded to a halt.

"Oh," her governess said, her mouth drawn into a tight circle of surprise. "Well, we've arrived."

Miranda surveyed the glorious facade of the duchess's embassy. Through the broad sashed windows of its ballroom, she could see the pastel-gowned ladies of the entourage dancing a stately pavane. They moved with a beguiling grace, swapped partners at the caller's command.

The sight of it made her feel sick.

"She went to the Convergence," Miranda said quietly.

"Thank goodness for that."

THE BELL JAR

There was no telling when the Peacock would arrive. He wasn't the sort of man who kept to a schedule.

Jon perched on an uncomfortable half barrel in a dark corner of the Bell Jar, and peered over the chipped brim of his tankard. The place stank of stale smoke and dried beer. The only other patrons, a pair of elderly drunkards, had passed out across a makeshift table bodged together from two short planks and a stolen waggon wheel. They weren't snoring, but they drooled copiously. That made Jon the only paying customer and he was damned if he couldn't make his beer last the whole evening.

Raymond, the Bell Jar's disagreeable landlord, was absent. Harriet the barmaid, having clocked the impossibility of drumming up any trade was nose-deep in a mud-splattered copy of yesterday's news.

Tossed from a merchant's carriage and retrieved from a gutter, Jon thought. He wondered if she was catching up on court fashions, results of games, scandals or court dispatches. A bit of everything, he guessed. Harriet was sharp enough to care for a read. Most around here would only use a newsletter for toilet rag. He admired her attempt at self-improvement, her unwillingness to rely on smiles and buxom flirtation. She deserved a decent man. He ran a big hand through his thick blond hair, pulled his beard into shape and wondered what he would have made of her when he was younger.

She's swimming against the tide that one, Jon thought, *and the tide is strong.* A deluge of itinerant labourers, beggars and petty criminals, dirty foreigners and the sharps who prey on them. The kinds of people who drank at the Bell Jar.

A cacophony of whistling from the manufactories on the south side of town signalled the end of the working day. Jon gathered his wits and stacked his memories back where they belonged as a gaggle of sail-men and axle-greasers led by an opulently tattooed foreman bundled into the tavern.

"Oi! Wheat belly! Looking forward to the grading?" the foreman called out.

Jon gave him a smile and raised his drink. Daniel's imminent ordination was well known to the denizens of Turbulence. People were starting to treat him warily, to guard their tongues in his presence. He welcomed the respect, felt he deserved it, but tonight he didn't want the attention. He shuffled his stool backwards into the shadows, and wished the Bell Jar more crowded.

If the foreman had noticed Jon's reticence, it didn't cause him to hesitate as he led his trio of wiry young men over from the bar. Beer froth slopped over the sides of their over-sized tankards.

"Alright, Jon? Haven't seen you for years. Not since we last played ball together. Why's that then?"

"I've been busy, Rollo; the mill."

"Times are tough I suppose. Good stuff this. Spiced ale with a gin petard. Your kind of drink." The foreman took a deep swig and turned to his colleagues. "Lads, meet the Lion of Turbulence."

The young men paused talking among themselves, shot dull glances at Jon.

"Looks more like an old bear to me," one said and wiped his nose with a filthy forearm. Jon, equally uninterested in maintaining the conversation, let it pass.

Rollo pressed on. "No, listen lads; before this man became a fat bastard, he was a legend."

Jon flexed his muscles. He might have gone a little soft around the waist since passing thirty, but he was never fat. *Built.* That was a better word.

"Lads, I'm serious; Daniel and him played unbelievable."

"Dan? The one what got taken into the seminary?"

They were interested now, which was not what he desired.

"Daniel was special — he could wrong-foot anyone, swerve tackles that you couldn't see coming." Rollo waved his tankard enthusiastically. His colleagues jumped to avoid the drink that splashed about their boots. Jon glowered.

"Jon was good too — captain once," Rollo added quickly.

"I heard Daniel took heads," said the roughest-looking labourer.

"Violence is part of the game," the youngest observed.

"Daniel wasn't a gouger, but he was righteous," Jon rumbled. "If the opposition played dirty, Dan would happily drop them on their backs."

"Staring at the sky and screaming in pain," Rollo added. Jon shrugged. "Tell 'em about the big match Jon, the Battle."

"It's an old story and I'm no storyteller." Jon craned around his small audience to see if the Peacock had arrived.

"Jon played in it," Rollo said.

"Bollocks. He's too old," the rough one countered.

"It was only five years ago," said the youth.

Jon lost patience, rose from his stool. He rolled back his shoulders and stood at full height.

"Don't be like that," Rollo pleaded, bravado gone. Harriet's head popped up. She had an unnatural sense for trouble brewing. Jon let his shoulders flop and sighed.

"It was a testimonial, against the Brotherhood."

"Real censors?"

"Aspirants. They do it district by district. For once it was our turn."

"You know the score," Rollo said, "the sporting gentry stump up a handful of coins for a feast after the match. Get their jollies watching a bit of young blood being spilt and go home feeling safer than ever."

"Censors got too much time on their hands now they're not collecting taxes and telling people when to worship," the rough one said.

Jon laughed. "You're more learnèd than you look, my friend."

"I'd love to give a censor a kicking," the youngest said. "My uncle spent a week in the stocks after an inquisition, and he told me he'd not done nothing."

"It was training for the Brotherhood, pure and simple, to see how the aspirants coped with pressure," *and to teach idiots like you a hard lesson before they got full-grown and dangerous.*

"Now that censors don't answer to the godsworn, they don't answer to anyone," the rough one said belligerently. Whatever point he was trying to make, Jon wasn't interested.

"They answer to the gods," he said flatly.

Rollo intervened. "Before the Battle the aspirants always won easy."

"Well, this match didn't follow tradition. After the first half, we were bloodied and knackered, but the match was tied. That got right under their skins."

"Up noses," Rollo slurred loudly. His colleagues ignored him.

"They knew that Daniel was our danger man."

"They couldn't believe what they was seeing," Rollo shouted, flailing his arms. "It was epic."

"Shut up," Jon snapped, bringing a cheer from Rollo's mates. "Every time the ball went in the air, Dan caught it — so they tried to take him out of the game. I was his safety. Six of them came for us, all at once. Big mistake. When Dan twigged what was happening he went on a rampage."

For a moment, Jon was transported by the memory and found himself standing on bloody grass. Coils of steam swirled from his mouth and body. He watched Daniel deliver the most dreadful flurry of fists and elbows ever seen in Turbulence. An aspirant ran at Jon. Dan's elbow smashed through his cheek-bone. Jon picked up another and threw him to the ground.

"Everyone was so busy scrapping, they forgot about the ball," Rollo said. "It was lying by the touchline like a dropped purse. The Peacock jumped out of the stands, grabbed it up, legged it down the side-line and scored." Jonathan remembered him, hoisted onto the crowds' shoulders, revelling in the unde-served glory. "Everyone went mad. Half of Turbulence was on the pitch."

"We won! Turbulence won!" the youngest lad said in amaze-ment, though the result was well known.

"Officially the match was abandoned," Jon said.

"No. We won," the rough one asserted.

"Too right," Jon said. He'd drink to that. The labourers clapped him on the shoulders and the one who had not spoken filled Jon's tankard to the brim with his own.

The tavern had filled as the tale was told, and the labourers wandered off in search of female entertainment. Pride in the memories had lightened Jon's mood, and he smiled broadly. *They missed the punchline*, he realised. Afterwards, at the game-feast, Daniel was invited to sit at the high table next to an el-derly censor. A week later, he was living and training in Brom-wich Seminary.

Peacock Matthew entered the Bell Jar in a blur of red felt and kaleidoscopic feathers, his splendid hat an incongruous splash of colour in that dull place. The good-for-nothing was flanked by his muscle, two infamous thugs known as the Sharks. *He walks as if he owns the place*, Jon thought.

Harriet stiffened, put on her brave face and sauntered towards them.

"Let me help you gentlemen with this," she said, grabbed the two old drunks by their collars and dragged them away from the table before the Sharks had the chance to do it more roughly. The gangsters sat down expansively. An imperial of wine and three flagons appeared on their table. Matthew flashed a toothy grin at Harriet and hunched into conspiratorial conversation with his lackeys.

Jon set aside his unfinished ale and made his way over. Five paces from Matthew the thugs got to their feet and fixed him with remorseless grey stares. If they recognised him, they did not let it show.

Matthew flapped his hat. "Easy lads, the Lion approaches. He used to be considered a bit of a hero around here. Even you two might have a few problems knocking him down." Jon doubted it. One was the size of a bull; the other was just massive. There was a story that they had made their reputations in the fighting pits of Glaschu, another that they were heretics from overseas, censors of the Evangelicy who had deserted. The locals called them Big Shark and Littleshark. The good folk of Turbulence were not famous for their imaginations.

"Jon, my son, what can I do you for?" Matthew said.

"I need to talk."

Matthew flicked back a slick black forelock. "Evidently. Pull up a chair." The Sharks relaxed. Littleshark produced a vial of temerarious oil and a pipette from a pouch, pulled wide his lids, set a drop in each eye and hissed with the thrill of it.

"I mean talk alone — business."

Matthew furrowed his brow, but his eyes smiled. He asked the Sharks to give them some space and they made their way leeringly over to the bar. Jon sat down and prepared himself.

"How can I be of service?" The Peacock was grinning like a hog in shit.

"You know what the problem is. I can't turn my sails four days out of five."

"Prayer not working out for you?"

The Peacock was a fool to mock prayer's power, Jon thought, and in no position to do so. He'd bet his mill that Matthew hadn't been to temple since he was a boy. There was nothing to be done for the man if he wouldn't help himself — everyone's soul was his or her own responsibility, as far as the gods were concerned.

Matthew picked at his teeth. "How's Anna and the baby . . . Mother Miller?"

"A little bit hungrier than I'd like."

Matthew poured them both a drink. "You did better than you deserved with Anna. I should have married her when I had the chance." Jon's face reddened. *She would never have agreed*, he thought. Matthew smiled. "If you need money, that's easily done. My girls aren't bringing in as much as I'd like right now, but I'll put in a word with Gordon. He'll lend to you at a reasonable rate."

"I don't want to borrow money from Gordon. I want to pay you."

"Come again?"

Jon hushed his voice. "I need something to make the mill solid again, to move with the times. I need some cunning. I need magic."

"You what?" For once Matthew's surprise seemed genuine. "That's a laugh. You can't afford to feed your family but you want some fucking magic."

"There's got to be something out there. Second-hand or something."

"How would you get a licence? You couldn't even afford the fine for not having one. I thought you was supposed to be respectable."

The little shit was right, and it shamed Jon to concede it. "I'll pay you back. It'll take time of course, but I'm good for my word. You know that."

"Know it? You won't let anyone forget it. Maybe if you was a little more realistic you wouldn't have to resort to begging." Matthew smirked playfully. Jon felt like his head was going to burst.

"I'll be going then."

"Alright, keep your wig on." The Peacock made an act of doing a little thinking. He seemed to be finding Jon's discomfort amusing. "If you want magic, what about Galbraith?"

"Are you mad? First off everything that passes through that witch's hands is stolen, and secondly none of it is any good, or at least not good enough to do more than entertain simple children."

Matthew glanced over to his men, who had started to hurry back towards the table, and raised his hand nonchalantly to keep the peace. He leaned forwards with a stare as sharp as razors.

"Firstly, take that tone with me again, you miserable dung-heap, and I will cut your fucking face. Right. Now that's out of the way, let's look at this objectively. I am trying to help you out. I am known as a helpful man. People respect me. People bring me things. All you are bringing me today is your attitude. If you've got nothing for me then I've got nothing for you."

"Matthew, I'm on the edge. I'm this close to going under. Please."

There was a long pause.

"Your brother is about to become a censor," Matthew said.

"Nobody lets me forget it."

"Is it his ambition to police Turbulence?"

"He hasn't said as much. Actually, I suppose he has."

"He listens to you, does he?"

"Of course — he's family."

"That could be useful for a man like me."

"I suppose it might." It was wrong to say it; Daniel wouldn't be drawn into Peacock's schemes. So long as Peacock was repaid, it wouldn't matter. Jon swallowed his shame and forced a conspiratorial grin, his neck tight with anger and no choices.

Peacock ruminated, this time in earnest. "You understand what a debt to me is worth," he said, gesturing absentmindedly at his heavies.

Jon nodded.

"I just wanted to make sure. Right then. There's this character I know, his appetites run to a little odd. Sometimes I help him get some odd, so he owes me. His name is Stanizlav. He didn't make it at the Verge, not the right kind of personality, but he got far enough to make connections. He understands how the cunning works."

"Can he summon me a wind?"

"No, he's not practising; he deals in artefacts — hear me out — not lost trinkets, proper stuff. He might have something for you. If he does I'll let him know to lend it over." Matthew whipped a pencil from the pocket of his jerkin and ostentatiously scrawled some numbers onto a scrap of cloth. "This is more than you deserve, Jon. I'm being unorthodox on your behalf. You and your family will owe me considerable."

"How much?"

"A hundred pounds a year, to be paid over twenty years, secured upon all of your possessions. Two thousand in all. No negotiation, but you can pay me back early if you like." That wasn't a loan, Jon thought, *more like indentured labour*.

"Visit Stanizlav tomorrow after nightfall, speak what's on this cloth when he asks for a code."

"Where?"

"He lives in the cemetery on top of Spook Hill." Matthew waited for a reaction.

"Funny man."

"The problem with you, Jon, is all those morals and no fucking sense of humour. Go to the bonded warehouse on Canal Street; he's dealing out of the top floor. The bit about after dark wasn't a joke."

"We should make an agreement. Sign and seal."

"No need," Matthew said, "I have witnesses."

Jon finished his drink, left without making pleasantries. He had what he came for — taken a risk and won. That was good, he supposed. So why did he want to punch someone in the face?

When he got home, Anna was waiting for him, stoking a small fire.

"How did it go?" she asked, taking his coat and hanging it by the door.

"I don't know, love."

He kissed her on the forehead and went upstairs, pulled up a chair in front of his baby's cot and watched her sleeping.

THE PATH OF THE RIGHTEOUS

Daniel sprinted the length of the dormitory in a small loincloth, his slippers slapping loudly on the floor. His practice swords were bundled under one arm, his fighting robes under the other. He barely noticed the amazed stares of the cooks, clerks and aspirants as he skipped past, dodging from left to right.

He raged as he ran. To have spent the night, first practising meditation and then nervously staring at the ceiling of his billet was stupid enough. To have been woken by a gentle chorus of swearing from the cloister as the young aspirants performed their morning exercises — that was something else. Five years of training and on the final day of his grading, he had overslept. Sometimes it seemed the only enemy he could not best was himself.

At the end of the bustling passageway awaited Titus. The particularly large aspirant had seen Dan coming and taken a broad stance blocking the exit to the refectory. The idiot was grinning from ear to ear, arms outstretched, knees bent, ready to tackle Dan as if they were playing ball.

"Shift, you fat fuck," Daniel shouted, waving the oaf aside with his head. Titus was unmoved. At the last minute, with expert timing, Dan slid between the aspirant's rooted legs. A passing punch to the balls would have taught the boy a lesson, but Daniel had no hands free. He used his momentum to return to his feet, shouting over his shoulder, "Too slow, loiter-sack."

Daniel had a long way to run. In the days when the censors had been the soldiers of the godsworn, the seminary had been a city within a city, brimming with pedants and clerics. Now it was a sparse maze of long corridors and empty rooms. Daniel pelted through the refectory where godsworn and censors had once dined side by side, then past the counting rooms where tithes of gold or grain had been hoarded. The walls were pock-marked with old bullet holes and the clawing of shrapnel. You couldn't blame the barons for having risen, chafing under the cost of faith and seeing no benefit. The godsworn had become corrupted by wealth. You could see that everywhere you looked. No wonder then, that they had been cast out of their homes. As far as Daniel was concerned, that was all ancient history. As he passed vestries left empty, or worse still converted into classrooms, his chief thought was that he was happy to be done with studying it.

He skidded into the rear axis of the building that was still called a temple. Thirty or so aspirants, those who had pro-gressed to the final day of the grading, knelt on its marble floor, palms on thighs. Lay Brother Hernandez instructed them from behind a box pulpit. Behind them all, a square of reed mats had been pushed together to form a makeshift arena. A burly assis-tant stood at each corner wearing full practice armour. Daniel smiled. He had been beaten by them when he was green, but had returned the favour many times since. He ducked behind a pillar and pulled his fighting trousers to his navel, tried to tie his belt cord with the same hand. He imagined the grotesques in the capstones laughing at his efforts.

Hernandez's gravelly voice rumbled out, "Got lost in our meditations, did we, Miller?"

The aspirants laughed.

He can't exclude me. I'm the best.

Hernandez allowed the pause to hang long enough to let Daniel know he'd cut it fine. "Be so good as to join us." Half-dressed and shamefaced, Daniel took his place, kneeling in the back row. "Now that I have completed my instruction, it is my privilege to introduce Magistrate Campbell Lang."

A murmur arose from the aspirants. "What in the belly of the Snake did we do to deserve him?" whispered one. Daniel cursed and wrestled on his singlet.

A pale man with slicked back hair, dressed in a simple mid-night-blue robe, imposing far beyond his diminutive stature, emerged regally from the inner sanctum. Dan knew that some of the older censors believed Lang would become the next chief constable. He walked as if he agreed with them.

The magistrate took his place at the podium and saluted, bringing his hand sharply level with his neck.

"Justice Advances."

"Justice Advances," the aspirants chanted, and saluted in unison. Their keen obedience was accepted with the slightest of nods. Lang's gaze drifted over the assembly.

"It is only a week since the Mournful Bell sounded at Tiburn, declaring to all that another brother had climbed the ladder to the stars. The Path of the Righteous remains beset with dangers — yet here you are, every one of you willing to risk their lives for justice. You cannot all be chosen. I seek only the best: men with discipline of mind and body, men willing to honour the mission of our Brotherhood with absolute loyalty, men with the strength to bring order to the Unity."

Dan carried a Turbulence boy's natural contempt for politicians, but he felt his spine straighten as Lang spoke.

"You are here today because you have already prevailed in trials of strength, speed and study. Climbing, riding, swimming and running are the skills of the outrider and the scout. History and law are the provinces of academics and scribes. You hope to become censors, to wear the Thrice~Crossed Swords. It is the highest of all callings."

Daniel knuckled his thighs, punched his muscles into readiness.

"Today you must prove your fighting spirit and your mastery of the sight." *Combat and confession*, the test Daniel craved and the one that he feared most, held on the same day precisely because the temperament required for one was exactly the opposite of that required for the other. He had known what was coming and still thought them bastards for it.

"Brother Hernandez will administer the tests of arms this morning. I shall examine those who remain capable this afternoon. The gods will be watching."

Those final words were delivered with the cadence of a judge's gavel. The excitement of the aspirants was palpable as Hernandez returned to the podium.

"I have trained with you for years. I know your strengths and weaknesses as well as you do. In some cases, better." Aspirants laughed nervously. "To be made a censor is an admirable thing, but remember that you cannot all be chosen. There is always another year."

The aspirant kneeling besides Dan wondered aloud, "Blood duels?"

"The first combat will be a free-for-all. You may choose from any of the weapons in the south transept. The swords and maces are wooden. The arm-claws and fist-hooks are blunted. The crooks, staves and singlesticks are street fashion. Nets are permitted. You may strike to the soft and hard parts of the body, but not gouge eyes or nethers. If you are rendered incapable you will be retired, and should not be considered fair game. You may withdraw by surrender. The melee ends when the field is reduced to eight. You have a quarter hour to prepare."

The aspirants around Daniel went pale with a fear that he shared. What the master-at-arms had described was an organised riot. Melee was random. It had taken Daniel a week to recover from the last one. He did not fear any aspirant — though some had been in training since the day they could walk — but in a frenzied mob even the most skilful warrior could be caught out by a wild blow. He imagined a singlestick caving in the back of his skull.

"This doesn't make sense," a nervous aspirant said.

"Maybe they wish to test our luck." Dan's bravado was fake. He would never say so in front of his rivals, but the youngster was right. Censors were supposed to be justice-keepers, not soldiers to be sent into battle. He looked at the sullen and nervous faces around him. A few aspirants were already racing to the transept, trying to ensure they had the best of the weaponry. *Selfish*, Daniel thought, and resolved to hit them especially hard.

Then it came to him. The melee wasn't a test of skill at arms, but of something far rarer. *If eight can win, they can win together.* He quickly gathered men, not the strongest but those he knew would accept him as their commander, at least for an hour. None refused. By the time the more observant had worked out what he was planning his team was complete.

Daniel assigned his men weapons; hooks and claws for the front four, crooks and staves for the three at the back. He armed himself with a singlestick, a toughened ash cudgel with a leather hand guard for punching with, and on his left arm a claw, a thick leather vambrace armoured with metal splints and mounted with raking blunted talons. Other teams had started to form, but compared to his they were pitiful. Most were still arguing over who would lead. Daniel glanced at Brother Hernandez. The instructor did a good job of keeping his grizzled face straight.

Daniel's heart beat hard as straggling aspirants were ordered into the arena. Hernandez blew a whistle and the melee began.

Daniel could sense that his crew were itching to fight but he held them in the corner, watching and waiting. He didn't want to win. He wanted a rout.

The first to be eliminated were those who stood alone. Wise or terrified, they fled the arena with hands raised in the air. One, obstinate enough to stand his ground, was set upon by a team of five and lasted only seconds. What the master-at-arm's assistants dragged from the arena looked like a trampled sack of beetroot. Seeing his fate, a team of three young friends retreated off the matting, and out of contention.

Three teams remained.

Daniel expected the others to unite against him because it was their only chance of winning. To his amusement, they launched against each other. He waited until they were entangled before sounding the charge. His men swept upon them like a tsunami. His back row used staves and crooks to jab faces, beat arms and hook necks. His front row punched, dragged and clawed the opposition to the ground. When the work was done, Daniel's men formed a ring around the opposing captains.

"Submit," he ordered calmly.

"Never."

It was a shame; Lucas was a nice lad. A terrible cut across his forehead was pouring blood into his eyes and he could barely see. Daniel leapt to his blind side, landed in a crouch and unfurled, lifting the boy from his feet with an explosive uppercut that didn't feel entirely fair.

"Submit," Daniel repeated. The remaining captain dropped his axe and raised his hands.

Hernandez's whistle blew sharply. Daniel and his crew roared in triumph. They exchanged smiles and boisterous hugs, wiped the blood and vomit from their fighting robes. The worst of their injuries was a twisted ankle.

Brother Hernandez appeared at Daniel's side.

"Congratulations," he grunted obliquely as he helped one of the fallen aspirants back to his feet.

Daniel grinned inwardly as he returned his weapons to the racks and fell back into rank.

The smell of fresh sweat filled Daniel's battle-flared nostrils. A few of his rivals were gone, taken to the infirmary. The thinned rows nursed swollen joints, delicately prodded the swollen parts of their faces and grimaced from the pain of broken ribs. Hernandez announced that the second test of arms was to be a round robin. The remaining aspirants would all fight each other once, for three minutes, with weapons of their choice. The fighting was to resume immediately.

●

It was nearly done.

"On your guard," Hernandez said. The old war dog had been watching Daniel throughout, noting and judging like he always did. He could not hide his satisfaction — his protégé was unbeaten so far and they both knew that the final fight was unlikely to prove a challenge.

Daniel saluted his final opponent and dropped into a wide stance. He loved fighting. More precisely, he loved moments of perfect action: the crushing blow slipped; the net plucked from the air and sent flying back to envelop its caster; the spiralling parry that sent a weapon pirouetting from his attacker's grasp. Such moments stayed forever, in perfect clarity.

Daniel leapt sideways, narrowly avoiding his opponent's swing and cursed himself for the loss of concentration. It was complacent. Underestimating an opponent was the easiest way to lose. Back in the moment, he circled the lad warily.

Keep distance . . . wait for the mistake. A deftly executed shuffle provoked a clumsy step from his sword-wielding opponent. Daniel beat the aspirant's blade aside and kicked him between the legs, bending him double. Daniel scissored his adversary's neck with his singlesticks and hammered him to the ground with a wicked headbutt. His forehead stung from the force of the blow.

"No, Daniel, duck and lean forward. Use the crown of your head." Hernandez slapped his balding pate in illustration, then flashed a craggy grin, like a benevolent mastiff, took the twin sticks from Daniel and ushered him across the transept. "I'm sorry, Daniel, I should not complain. You fought magnificently today."

Daniel began the long walk to the end of the axis with a victor's pride. He imagined the vast hall to be a street in Turbulence, and that he was patrolling it, feared and respected by all. Then he looked ahead. The entrance to the inner sanctum had been obstructed with a tapestried screen. He thought of what awaited behind, and all at once felt his tiredness and the pain of his bruises catch up with him.

The ritual of confession was not hard to perform once known and understood. The trick was clearing the mind, creating a space for the gods who lived outside of time and saw all things. Daniel reminded himself that he was capable. Only a few days earlier, in the rustic calm of the orchard, he had deduced from which tree his instructor had taken an apple, followed the rituals to the letter and watched in amazement as the ghostly form of his instructor plucked the fruit. There had been a price for that moment of godhood — there always was. Later that day, he had cried blood-stained tears.

Daniel rounded the ornate screen, to find Magistrate Lang waiting at the deconsecrated altar. When the seminary had been a place of worship the altar would have been draped in rainbow silk, the statutes upon it presented with food and gifts; now its mantle was plain white linen and the statues were gone, replaced with thick wax candles. Lang's face looked soft in the subdued light. He stared at Daniel with owlish eyes.

"I am told you excelled at the trial of arms."

"Yes, sir."

"You can be violent without falling prey to anger or malice. That is a rare gift."

He lifted a cloth from the altar to reveal a feather, a juggler's ball and a palm book, laid out in a neat row. Before those every-day objects, lay three open boxes and a stick of charcoal. Lang gestured at the array. To Daniel the arrangement looked like a trap, sprung and baited.

"The task before you is easy by comparison. Please return each of the items to the place from which it was taken." Daniel wasn't paying much attention. He had already figured out what was required of him. He wondered how best to attune his mind, which meditation exercise would be most appropriate to the task? All that came to him was the soporific voice of his meditation instructor talking about his love of fishing, and behind that, the voice of Magistrate Lang.

"To make the past confess is the greatest weapon of the censor. Even the threat of it can prove more powerful than a blade or a law. Confession is how the gods guide our hands."

Daniel felt Lang's impersonal gaze hard on his face and broke into a cold sweat. *Don't just stand there looking like an idiot*, he told himself. He grasped the charcoal and began to scratch out a pattern on the altar cloth.

First, a waving line for the ocean that was once called Nuun, abyssal home of the Dreamer:

He-who-sleeps-in-the-ocean.

Rising from the waves a triangle, the Mound of Creation, domain of the Devourer, eater of souls:

He-who-trembles-the-earth.

An eye inside the triangle, the unblinking gaze of the Judge, the Preserver of Balance:

He-who-sits-upon-the-mountain.

Upon the apex of the triangle, two gentle curves, the wings of the All-seeing:

He-who-sails-the-wind.

Finally above them all, the circle of proud Father Sun, and within it the crescent of the moon, his wise consort, the Mother of Man.

He-who-lights-the-way,
She-who-reflects-his-glory.

A symbol for every god of the Rational Pantheon combined: the Sigil of the Gods was complete.

Daniel knelt, presented the charcoal skywards in outstretched hands and tried to empty a mind that buzzed with anxiety and distraction. He breathed deeply, ran through the stages of the meditation ritual, at the same time knowing that such a conscious act was a mistake in itself. *The sound of my heart*, Daniel thought, *the air passing through my nose. Focus on these things only*. He tried to picture what he wanted. *To be a censor, to help my brother. No!* He screamed inside, trying to stay in the moment. *See this altar in time, through time. Start again. State your belief. The Sigil of the Gods holds the meaning of my intention. Good. Now, believe it. Gods, let me see how this place has unfolded.* He observed the thought, tried to know it to be true, waited for the world apparent to shift.

The world remained resolutely in place. A gulp of hot tears ran down the back of his throat. It was impossible. He was destined to be a censor — he knew it in his heart. He squeezed his eyes tight, to force out the world. For a moment, his vision edged with a ghostly blue light and he felt the calm attentiveness he required. He saw his sister smiling proudly and his heart leaped with joy. Then the divine sight wafted from his mind like the breeze from a dove's wing.

He opened his eyes. Magistrate Lang was looking down on him pityingly, as if Daniel were a cripple. Somehow, he knew. Lang had said it himself. Sight was the essential skill of a censor. You couldn't be a censor if you couldn't take confession. Daniel rose to his feet and, in a blind panic, placed each of the objects into a box. He bowed jerkily. Without looking at the magistrate, he turned and fled the sanctum. By the time he had returned to the axis, he couldn't even remember which boxes he had chosen.

He made his way mournfully to the refectory. His stomach ached as if he had not eaten in a week. He railed at his stupidity, and replayed the test in his mind. If only he had been less arrogant, practised more, waited another year.

He bit on his wrist like a child. What would he tell Jon?

Then the after-effects of his attempt at confession struck. His brow burned and terrible images formed in his mind: the mill-house on fire, his brother fighting the flames, Anna and the baby nowhere to be seen. Gangs of men rioting through Turbulence. His sister being dragged away by unseen hands. The gods were punishing him and who could blame them? If he couldn't protect his family all those years ago, why should they trust him now?

BRIDGES BURNED

It was three hundred miles of bumpy road from Lundenwic to the Convergence. A convoy of stagecoaches could cover forty miles a day until the mountains, then twenty at best. Miranda had expected the journey to be long and tedious. As it turned out, travelling as the only woman and surrounded by men who did nothing but loudly predict the vertical trajectory of their careers, was torture.

There were twelve carriages in the train now. Four had left from Lundenwic; the others had joined later from Alchester, Boudicon and Brightstowe, the best universities in the Unity. Each carried a cargo of rich men's sons, expensively educated. *Nice in theory*, Miranda thought, *but they all look the same*. Despite highly developed grasps of algebra, logic, philosophy and theology, and a shared ability to recite *The Philosophies of Ptah-hotep* without pause, there was not one ounce of charm between them. One wit, one gallant was all the companionship Miranda required. At the very least a rippling wall of muscle, pleasing to the eye. Was that too much to ask? *Really?*

They're not even men, Miranda thought as she watched craggy mountainside crawl past the gilded window of her carriage, *just libidinous boys, giddily excited to have escaped from their parents*. She ran her elegant fingers absentmindedly through her short black bob and tucked it behind her ears, recalled her governess scolding her for doing so and smiled.

She considered today's fellow travellers. Next to him, Bartholomew slouched backwards, a fashionable blue cap laid over his face. She could see little more of him than the underside of his chin and the insides of his nostrils. Portly Lloyd snored by her side, thankfully leaning away. Nathan, who sat opposite her, alternated between concentrating fiercely on his palm book and trying to look up her skirt.

Miranda knew that men found her attractive. She did not demand attention and it sometimes surprised her, but she was not the type to contrive complicated delusions to exaggerate or deny her beauty. She wasn't vain. Her beauty was simply an objective fact, attested to by a lifetime of attention. Compared to the flirtatious knights of the city and the difficult friends of Mother, these bookish squires could be fended off with ease. Her governess had stashed a long pillow knife amongst the bed linen in her traveller's trunk, for emergencies, but there was no need. A slow, contemptuous roll of the eyes was usually enough.

Maintaining her self-respect came with a price, of course. At the beginning of the journey the boys had called her slender, gamine and mysterious. Those same aspects had slowly transformed into skinny, boyish and aloof. Sometimes, when presumed out of earshot, she heard them call her 'the bitch'. At first, she had tried to revel in the transfiguration, to imagine herself a vixen or she-wolf, to accept pettiness as evidence of her superiority. It didn't work. These boys were as bored as she was, and unaccustomed to rejection. Faced with a lady of station they had no other means of revenge. Neither did she, and so many hours of travel were spent daydreaming of happy comeuppances and reversals of fortune.

Miranda imagined the long train of horses and carriages, carrying the best young minds in the Unity to their new home, plunging over the edge of a narrow clifftop road.

"Let's see if rhetoric can get you out of that," she mumbled at the window.

"Pardon me?" foppishly dressed Nathan said, after a confused pause. Bartholomew was asleep or uninterested.

"Nothing," Miranda replied without turning from the mountainous view, and congratulated herself on another teaspoon of cement poured onto her reputation as a distracted oddball.

It was a childish thought anyway. If some tragedy were to befall the convoy, its precious cargo would be missed, and not just by bereaved parents. The Unity needed these brains. The cunning arts had transformed the land. What had once been a modest and constantly threatened trading island was becoming one of the wealthiest and most powerful lands in the Empire. The Convergence was now a priority of state and Miranda had chosen to make herself part of that process.

●

Rain streamed from the grey autumn sky, drummed insistently on the coach's roof. An inescapable smell of damp leather hinted at nausea. Miranda breathed softly on the coach's window, drew a spiral in the condensation with a silvered fingernail then rubbed the pattern away, leaving her fingers cold and wet.

"What's that symbol?" Nathan was intrigued. She smiled at him enigmatically. It was just a childish doodle, *of course*. That was the one thing she had in common with her peers. None of them knew anything about magic. They had trinkets, sentimental enchantments manufactured at the Verge: compasses that always pointed towards home, lockets that concealed animated portraits of families and the like. Magic touched all of their lives, but not one of them possessed the slightest understanding of cunning — the secret to how or why it all worked.

Surrounded by the brightest and best, she thought this a little surprising. She knew that the Convergence guarded its secrets fiercely, but it seemed a little odd that the most coveted profession in the Unity was one held in total ignorance by those who sought it.

The coach shuddered to a halt, skidding on the wet road. It rocked on its springs and a moment later Big Albert's head popped up outside the misted window of the stagecoach like a jack from a box. Miranda flinched in surprise and pulled the panel down.

"Might be a while, lads, milady," Albert half shouted through the rain that poured from the broad brim of his coachman's hat. "There's some bother up ahead. Not to worry though."

He hopped back off the footstep and vaulted onto the box seat, rocking the carriage wildly on its springs.

"Some slack-jaw shepherd has blocked the road," Bartholomew said with a yawn. The tumult had woken him, and now he sat up, his cap still half covering his face. Lloyd snorted, oblivious to it all. Miranda opened the door to the carriage, wrapped her cloak tight around her shoulders, and stepped out into the rain.

"Rather drizzle than drivel," she quipped quietly and smiled at her wit as she made her way towards the front of the train, delighted at the chance to breathe some fresh air and be in her own company.

The first thing she saw was the desolate panorama of Seascale Bay. It was unmistakable. The Convergence itself was obscured by the impenetrable grey of the downpour, but the famously frail causeway that allowed foot-passage from the mainland stretched thinly into the misty distance. She knew that while secure during the day, that perilous path could be submerged in an instant by the command of a master with cunning of the waves.

Her journey was near its end.

Miranda turned her attention to the gathering ahead. Four travelling vendors, stooped under heavy packs, talked nervously among themselves. A man in a white cassock, obviously a godsworn — though she could not see a menat, the sacred collar that would confirm it — stood alone. Further ahead, several of the chaperons gaggled about Master Somney, whose skullcap glistened with raindrops. A man dressed in midnight blue towered above them all, mounted upon a glorious chestnut mare with a terrifying longsword strapped to its flank. A censor.

Miranda thought him a handsome man, but too old and severe to be beautiful. His sky-blue eyes were piercing but his hair was thinning on top, and his close-cropped beard was badger grey. Judging by the steam rising from the horse's flanks he had only just arrived, and at some pace.

"Sabotage, censor?" Somney shouted, pointing towards the bay. Then she noticed. The covered bridge that traversed the last ravine before Seascale Bay had been gutted by fire.

The rider pulled back the broad collar of his greatcoat to reveal a silver badge. "I was elevated to prosecutor some time ago, Master Somney." He dismounted and loped to the damaged crossing.

Within the bridge, he moved cautiously, skirting the side wall, wary of the boards that creaked and cracked under his feet. He drew a hunting knife from his belt and prised a handful of blackened splinters from the scorched aftermath of the conflagration. Back on the safety of the highway, he knelt and carefully arranged the splinters into a pattern on the ground, made the shape of a wave, then a triangle, then a circle in the mud with the point of his knife. Finally, he drew a line around it all.

"Give the man some space," Master Somney commanded. The company drew back reluctantly. The travellers' fear seemed close to panic now. Miranda craned her neck to follow the action. "Will you be able to divine much?" Somney asked.

The censor did not reply, but raised his hands in front of him with his palms facing upwards, seemingly in supplication to the mountains that surrounded them. Suddenly his shadow began to flicker, as if a gigantic invisible candle was guttering behind his back. For a second the charcoal on the road sparked, glowed red and then white hot. Then all was as before except for a few delicate puffs of steam that rose from the embers. The censor rose to his feet with a look of deep concern.

"I held the vision for as long as I could and saw little more than shadows. The fire was set at night by two men. They came from the direction of the Convergence in haste. I imagine the fire was prepared in advance, set to slow pursuers. The damage to the bridge was incidental, but I wouldn't hazard a coach and horses upon it."

"If not sabotage, then what?" Somney muttered. "An attack on the Convergence? Dissenters?"

"I don't know. They were careful to leave no trace behind."

"Is this why you came to visit us?" Master Somney asked. The censor did not reply but began to pace in neat circles, staring at his feet. For a few seconds Miranda assumed this was the beginning of another mystic ritual, then she realised that he was searching the ground for anything that might provide a greater insight. Instinctively she began to look for clues herself. After a few minutes of fruitless searching, the censor replied.

"Maybe. My presence was requested by Chairman Gleame and the Chief Constable. I come to investigate the murder of one of my brothers."

Somney's face fell. "Adelmus? That is grave news indeed." The travellers began talking frantically amongst themselves.

The censor nodded.

"Will you walk with me? And may I have the honour of calling you by your given name, Prosecutor Corbin?"

"You may, Master Somney, but before we renew our acquaintance, that godsworn, the mendicant; I see he serves He-who-sails-the-wind."

"It could be worse."

Corbin frowned at the blasphemy, spat onto the ground. "Have some respect. Ask if he will perform the rites for a brother who has fallen, help guide his soul to the realm of the dead."

Somney spoke to the godsworn in clipped tones.

"Well?"

"He says yes." Somney sighed. "I understand why censors and the godsworn cannot converse directly, but I find the tradition tiresome. It is thirty years since the Great Cleansing. The world should move on."

"The law is the law. In my opinion the Cunning are far too eager for the world to move on."

Somney laughed mirthlessly and the two men shook hands. They walked together, passed out of earshot. Corbin's mare followed by his side.

Miranda felt a heavy leather gauntlet clamp down on her shoulder and jumped.

"I'm sorry, milady," Big Albert said, "but we're on foot from here. I have the honour of escorting you. Your luggage will be brought after-ways." Relieved by his presence, Miranda turned to see Nathan, Bartholomew and Lloyd standing next to him in degrees of sodden misery.

They set off on foot down a narrow seafront track that led towards the causeway. Miranda and Albert walked side by side in the lightening rain. Nathan, Lloyd and Bartholomew trailed far behind, having fallen into a discussion about sports with the occupants of the coach from Urikon. She was glad to be rid of them, and of her fur-lined ankle boots, which were warm and well heeled. Ahead, Somney and Corbin conversed animatedly, arguing or righting the world.

"Are they friends?" Miranda asked.

"They've known each other a long time."

"I presume your name isn't really Big Albert."

"You can call me Albertus if you prefer."

"Albertus, that ritual of Corbin's?"

"Taking confession, the censors call it."

"Was it magic?"

"It's not my place to say, milady."

"Would you rather we discussed the weather?"

Albertus chuckled. "Some believe that the censors are favoured by the gods, that their powers are a blessing. Some of the masters don't believe in the divine — they think the censors use magic without understanding. But I don't want to get ahead of your training."

He's much smarter than he pretends to be, Miranda decided, and took his arm. "What do you believe?"

"I believe in leaving difficult questions to censors."

Miranda laughed at that and they exchanged pleasantries for a while. Albertus pointed out the native sea holly, an ice-blue thistle with purple flowers, and lifted a stone to reveal a natterjack toad. Miranda joked that he was acting like a governess. Embarrassed, Albertus changed tack, asking her questions about Lundenwic. Miranda asked about life inside the Verge.

"That's hard to say," Albertus said. "I suppose it depends if you're a chambermaid or a master. It's become more like a town than a house. Near three hundred workers and servants supporting the twenty-three masters."

"Why twenty-three?"

"Because of the stones." *As if that makes any sense.* "Then there's sixty or so demi-masters — and that number grows by the year. Plenty of visitors from academies and abroad, guests and customers. Two men might abide in the Verge and not meet for weeks."

"Did things use to be so different?"

"In the old days it was a small place. Youngsters came to the Convergence by way of natural talent — sensed its power from afar, did the dirty work, hoping to earn a scrap of teaching. We called them apprentices, jobbers. Nowadays we're sent the sons of the rich, and we're supposed to call them demi-masters. You don't see any of them mucking out the stables."

Miranda smiled wryly. "Surely it's better for everyone if the smartest can devote all of their time to artifice and research?"

Albertus fixed her with a hard gaze. "Well, getting some real work in early didn't do Gleame any harm."

Chairman Gleame, the founder of the Convergence. The only man Miranda had heard Her Grace describe with true admiration. Meeting him should be her first priority.

When they reached the foot of the causeway the tide was low and the sky had cleared. The Convergence squatted boldly in the distance, a brooding dolerite in the dark waters of Seascale Bay. It seemed to Miranda that a haze was rising from the stone, as if it were heated by a desert sun.

Censor Corbin parted ways with Somney and led his horse to the stables that marked the end of the highway. Somney returned to the party, and cheerlessly ordered his chaperons to sort the youthful party into a single file.

They marched briskly along the causeway. Miranda did not need to be told to hurry; after many days of dreary travel the sight of her destination was a tonic. She felt a little afraid as well. The tide was low, but the wind seemed calm and the waves on either side of the causeway unnaturally placid.

At first, the stronghold did not seem to grow any closer. Miranda knew that was simply the illusion of its enormous size, but the effect was startling nonetheless. The Convergence could not really be described as a building; its architecture defied symmetry and its construction seemed beyond the capability of any mason. Its stones looked like the black teeth of giants, and its gigantic teak doors were the height of a temple's dome. Miranda had never seen a construction so huge. Even the duchess's Fortress-Capitol in Ebarokon was less imposing.

Etiquette demanded that a lady, a ward of the duchess, should cross the threshold first, but she insisted on waiting, claimed that she wanted to savour the view of the mainland a while longer. Miranda watched and listened as her colleagues, *her rivals*, stepped through the small wicket door in the corner of the gates, to be swallowed one by one. The rowdy banter of the boys faded away. Soon only she and Albertus remained.

"It's quite a thing," she said.

Albertus took off his hat, tilted back his head. "Yes it is. Sometimes I forget. Are you going to go inside, young miss?"

"Why do you ask?"

"I've been bringing youngsters to the Verge by the waggon-load for a dozen years now. Every year we have a little sport. The night before we arrive, the chaperons place bets on who will become a master. You wouldn't be the only one to have faulted at the first hurdle."

"I presume you're telling me this because you bet on me?"

Albertus raised a finger to the side of his nose and winked. "I got good odds."

Miranda breathed deeply, lowered her head and went inside.

LIONS LED BY DONKEYS

Canal Street was an hour's walk away, on the other side of town. It would be dark before Jon got there, so he took his lanthorn and his iron-cleated walking stick, and dressed warmly against the cooling autumn air.

He ventured into the labyrinthine alleyways that surrounded Bromwich Market. As he crossed Bell Street, he passed a corner-man of Wylde's gang protecting the locals from unauthorised extortion. The gangs had been on good terms lately and Jon felt oddly reassured by the enforcer's presence. He tipped his hat and the gesture was returned in a friendly fashion.

"Where you headed, Jon? I'll tell the pickpockets to lay off."

"Very good, Andro. I'm going down the docks."

"Not sure that's a good idea, mate. I heard some idiots are trouble-stirring."

I have an appointment with a dealer in unlicensed magical artefacts, Jon thought. *Trouble and idiocy are the order of the day.*

He wended his way between passing shoppers to the edge of the great bazaar, found himself somewhere between the spicers and the beast market. It was still bustling, but the traders, shopkeepers and assistants were starting to outnumber customers. The laziest of the stall keepers were already packing away goods. He checked that his purse was secured deep inside his jacket, and made his way through the throng, swiping his stick from side to side to ward away urchins and beggars.

Dusk began to flicker across the rooftops, light to dark and back again. That meant the sun was setting behind the swooping sails of the elephantine manufactories that lined the southern edge of the city. After the long summer, it was easy to forget how tightly the sun held the horizon as winter approached. He reached the centre of the square. Directly ahead of him the gilded spire of the temple of He-who-lights-the-way glowed a magnificent amber.

Nowadays there were men lazy and foolish enough to call Him 'the Sun God'. To name a god after a mortal conception was no longer considered schismatic, not even blasphemous, though Jon's grandmother would have swooned to hear it; but why any sane man would take the risk was beyond him.

"They shall have no names." Jon repeated the catechism three times as a penance for the wicked times in which he lived and implored He-who-lights-the-way to protect him on his journey. Then he made the sign of the greater circle, just to be safe.

He achieved the city end of Canal Street unmolested and started into the commercial district. The working day was long over; the loudest noise he could hear was the rasping of hob-nailed boots on the cobbles as tired dockworkers made their way back home to Coldbath and Smallbrook. Some tipped hats, mistaking him for a foreman. For no reason he could discern Jon began to feel that maybe, for once, the wheel of fortune was spinning in his favour.

A stone's throw from Stanizlav's bonded warehouse, a handcart was parked by the side of the road, surrounded by a small assembly of workers. A fresh-faced young man dressed in labourer's clothes, red-cheeked and curly-haired, was using it as a platform, brandishing a manifesto and pontificating. Beside him, a woman with flowing auburn hair was trying, with little success, to press pamphlets into the hands of the rambunctious crowd. Her simple green gown lay modestly on her immodest body. She was the most comely woman Jon had seen in a long time — far more interesting than the dull sermonising. A weasel-faced man, standing like a bodyguard, but too slight to be taken seriously, guarded the cart.

"New chains and stronger cages!" the pamphleteer cried. "Cunning and machines will be your undoing. What of work for honest men?"

Jon frowned at the polemic. There was more of this flavour of nonsense on the streets every day. And not only talk.

"Listening to you is bloody hard work," a wise-cracker riposted, and the crowd chuckled with rowdy meanness. Jon approved. The dissenter was very foolish or very brave. A crowd could turn quickly on a man like that; he had seen it happen and dockers pulled no punches. Then there was the town guard.

The snippersnapper prattled on.

"The Wise Council misrules this distressed nation. Who possesses more wisdom than the common man? What better rule than by the agreement of the people?" A few of the mob murmured approval. "You toil for pennies while the rich fill overflowing coffers with effortless coin produced by wicked machines. The duchess and the southern barons . . ." There were boos from the crowd.

"Leave the duchess out of it — that's sedition that it is."

Jon approved of the loyalists' outrage. It was good to know that even in the docks men still had sense. What Bromwich needed was more jobs, not an excuse for every man to down tools and rob his neighbour. There had been riots in Brightstowe and in the marshes south of Lundenwic. What good had they done? Jon set his mind to tell Daniel about the disturbance, or a watchman if he passed one.

"Heed his words," the young woman yelled, "the time of the common man is at hand."

"Show us yer tits," a pot-boy shouted, and the crowd laughed and then dispersed, leaving only a handful of desperate-looking men. The firebrand jumped down from his handcart and began to address them, handing out small parcels of bread and cheese.

●

The bonded warehouse on Canal Street had a steel-plated door and small arched windows that had been shuttered against storms and thieves. As far as Jon could tell, the building was deserted. There was no obvious knocker or bell pull, so he hammered on the metal with his meaty fist. He was starting to fear a wasted journey when a heavyset doorman emerged and eyed Jon suspiciously down a broken nose. Jon stated his business, and at the mention of Stanizlav's name, the doorman feigned uninterest and pointed upstairs. Jon reckoned two things: firstly, he didn't look much like one of Stanizlav's customers; secondly, the usual customers didn't much like questions.

He lit his lanthorn with his scissor-flint and climbed five flights of broad and windowless brick. The stairs ended at a stout oak door pierced with a tiny spyhole that shone from within. Jon knocked and after a few seconds heard the sound of shuffling.

"Numbers," a muffled voice requested.

"Two, one, seven," Jon replied. He'd been worrying about this meeting for days, and the code was branded in his memory. He was ushered inside and the door was bolted behind him.

He had expected to enter a dusty warehouse, to be greeted by a majestic warlock assisted by a snivelling hunchback, so he was astonished to find himself in a drawing room, finely furnished with paintings and porcelain and overlooking a neatly hedged garden. His first thought was that he had been magically transported to an imperial palace in some distant sunny state.

A tall, eagle-nosed gentleman, formally attired for a stroll in a pleasure garden, greeted him with a haughty demeanour and curling bow. The popinjay flicked back his long curled wig, raised a monocle to his eye and squinted disdainfully.

"The miller, I presume? Not much silk on you, is there?"

"Is that a problem?" Jon asked, eyeing the man's fitted coat, white stockings and court shoes. "I wasn't told to dress for the occasion."

"I doubt that your wardrobe would have been up to the task. I have spoken to our mutual acquaintance, and we have made an arrangement. Come with me."

Jon followed Stanizlav through a panelled door and, anticipating a parlour or garden, was amazed to find himself in exactly the kind of dusty warehouse he had originally expected. He looked back over his shoulder and realised the drawing room was an elaborate prop, the garden landscapes were lamp-lit paintings.

"You keep a pretty shop."

"Smoke and mirrors," Stanizlav said. "I never cease to be amazed by how many clients are more impressed by the pretence of magic than the real thing."

He led Jon on a winding path between arcane objects and precariously balanced crates. Everywhere there were curiosities that begged for an explanation. As he gazed around in wonder, Jon's foot caught on a dust cover, pulled it from an onyx-framed mirror.

Jon faced his reflection. He was immediately struck by how handsome he looked. His sharp cheekbones and proud chin spoke of strength and authority. His muscles rippled under his clothes. His azure eyes sparkled in a way that would make any woman feel wanted and safe.

Stanizlav pulled him away.

"What you see is not real. Magical mirrors flatter with cliché. The largest are fabulous aids for lovemaking but most serve as slaves to vanity in dressing rooms. One day they will be produced in thousands, if the Convergence has its way."

"You disapprove?"

"They can be a danger to certain types. Put a weak person in front of a strong mirror and they may do nothing but gaze at themselves to the point of dissipation."

"Never," Jon laughed.

"The previous owner of this mirror was thought gone abroad. A strange smell led his neighbours to report mischief to the censors. When they broke into his room they discovered him sprawled naked upon a chaise longue, starved to death."

"Really?" Jon said. "That sounds too good to be true."

"All of my stories are true, or at least partly so," Stanizlav replied, and led Jon deeper into the stockroom.

It seemed that the further they progressed into the attic the more morbid its contents became. Animated paintings, impenetrable caskets and glowing trinkets were succeeded by iron maidens, scold's bridles and other instruments of torture. If there was magic in those things, Jon did not want to know how it manifested. They came to a series of tall cages, like those in an asylum, doors bound fast with chains. Jon paid no more attention to them than to what had come before, but as he passed the last he heard a faint sobbing. He paused and peered into its dark interior. As his eyes adjusted to the light, he could make out a thinly scattered carpet of straw, and beyond that, tucked into one corner, a heap of grey woollen bedding. A small foot poked out from under the blankets, dirty and trembling.

"What's this?" Jon shouted after Stanizlav.

The dealer returned and shone his light deep into the cage. The foot jerked back under the covers.

"Show yourselves," he commanded, and two tiny faces emerged, blinking in the lamplight. "Songbirds. Pretty, aren't they?"

"What will happen to them?" Jon said, and discreetly made the sign of the Mother, for their protection.

"They will be sold."

"To whom?"

"Those who can afford them. Men of status. Princes, bankers and so forth. Now, stop dawdling by the merchandise." Jon bristled with anger. He wanted to leave.

They ascended an iron spiral staircase into the very top of the rafters. Stanizlav was the first to fill the uncomfortable silence.

"I sense that you are still thinking about my caged beauties. I am not surprised. They are an addictive vice."

Jon thought of Dahlia and his stomach knotted with wrath. "It's somebody's daughter in those cages," he said. Stanizlav looked at him sharply.

"You should not begrudge me my trade. Those girls are strays. If their families did not care enough to keep them safe, then what should you mind? Besides, it is your friend Matthew who rescued them from the streets, so in a roundabout way those songbirds have paid for your salvation."

A man so laden with sin was a fool to speak of salvation, Jon thought. Stanizlav would discover that for himself, when the Devourer swallowed his soul.

Stanizlav rapped a small gong and the room filled with the beautiful wordless singing of a castrato. Jon wondered if Stanizlav kept a catamite, and shuddered.

"Have a drink." Stanizlav conjured a decanter of amber brandy from a liquor cabinet and filled two crystal chalices. Jon didn't want to accept the man's hospitality — but he needed it. Stanizlav sipped his drink and sighed in appreciation of the liquor's quality. "Now to business. I reveal the solution to your worries." He seized a crowbar and prised open the crate with abandon.

Straw. That was all Jon could see. Stanizlav stepped forwards and pulled aside the packing to reveal a statue of a horse, the size of a wheelbarrow, made of white enamel and painted with swirling patterns of red and gold.

"What the fuck is that?"

The dealer ignored Jon's expletive. "A toy. An extraordinarily expensive one intended as a gift for the Frankish king. His son was born deformed, you see; too feeble to ride a real pony. He wanted to play carousel, a new game from Arabia. The unfortunate died before it could be delivered. I was able to service the family who commissioned it by relieving them of this embarrassing memento of their grief."

"What are you talking about? How can that thing help me save my mill?"

"The horse is designed to walk in circles. It would do so forever if you allowed it. It requires no food, no care, and by my calculations should run for at least one thousand years, or until it wears through your floor. It is powerful, much stronger than a real horse or pony. Certainly strong enough to turn a grindstone."

Convert the windmill into a horse mill? That's insane. John stroked his beard. If it worked he'd never have to worry about being downwind of the factories again. *No bastard could interfere with my business. I could run the mill all night if I wanted to.* Jon leaned forwards and examined the horse more closely. "Do all of your goods bring death to their owners, or just the two you mentioned?"

"Oh, this toy isn't cursed. Items that guarantee death are far too valuable for the likes of you."

"It's not what I was expecting."

Jon spotted a place on the horse where he could use a short shaft to attach it to the spur wheel, stepped back and inspected the angles.

"You know what, Stan, it might just work."

"I did make it to the Convergence, you know."

"Does it come with papers?" Stanizlav laughed aloud. Jon frowned at his disrespect for the law, and then at his own guilt. Even if there were a licence, it would cost a fortune to have it reassigned. He would have to content himself with knowing that it was the laws of the gods that mattered in the final reckoning, not the scribbled legislature of men.

The horse glowed gold and red in the torchlight.

"There's another problem."

"What's that?"

"Getting it back to the mill."

"You could ride it," Stanizlav suggested.

"Don't be a soggy bollocks. Hold on, I've got an idea." Jon opened a window and looked down into the street. "Put it back in its box and ready the winch."

Jon left the building as quickly as he could, his mind spinning with the mechanics of the mill. He trotted across the road to where the dissenters were still gathered and shouted out to them.

"Oi, you lot." They glanced at him nervously over shoulders. A few got set to run. "You say there's no work to be had for honest men. I have work. I need a cart and men to pull it, to bring some equipment back to my mill in Turbulence. I'll pay a shilling a man." That was three days' pay for a pauper. They accepted without question.

●

Jon led the motley crew, illuminating suspicious alleyways with his lanthorn, and swaggering as menacingly as he could. If Andro were good to his word, Jon would be safe when he reached Wylde's territory. Closer to home he would be a concern of the Peacock's, and Matthew would stand for no man to move against him without permission. That was as close to safety as Turbulence allowed.

When trouble came, it was of the other kind.

A small militia of bill-men, the hooked blades of pole-arms bobbing above their heads, came advancing down the road, led by a squad of border horses, harnesses jangling. A censor accompanied them, assiduously searching for trouble.

A lifetime of respectability, and the first time I'm contrary to the law this happens. Jon chewed on the iniquity of it and turned to the leader of the dissenters, half expecting to see him fleeing down an alleyway. Instead, the man had opened his coat a little. His hand rested on the butt of a tiny flintlock pistol. He made sure that Jon had seen it, then let his coat fall closed. The redhead woman and her weaselly companion moved their hands discreetly behind their backs.

Jon imagined how desperate they must be, to contemplate fighting a censor and his squadron. His stomach sank low.

The censor cried for the bill-men to halt and sent the horsemen cantering towards the cart, lances levelled. Jon waited obediently as the horsemen surrounded them in a raucous, iron-shod clatter. The ragged crew around him raised collars and shrouded their faces with hair or hats as the censor and bill-men hurried to catch up. There was no possibility of escape, with or without the cart and crate.

"Good evening, brother," Jon called out boldly, trying to calm his heart.

"There are rabble-rousers in this area." The censor gazed intently at Jon's stevedores, giving each man, briefly, his whole attention. He rested his hand on the pommel of his cutlass. "An infamous rebel is amongst them. There is a substantial reward for his capture, or information about his whereabouts."

"How much?" Jon asked.

The censor ignored the question. "What is your business?"

"I'm collecting parts from the docks," which was true, in a way.

The censor looked at him oddly.

"Sir, I am no rowdy; I'm a man of property," Jon said, as if it were obvious.

"Is that so? And who are these men who accompany you at the dead of night?"

"Stevedores."

"How long have they been in your employ?"

Jon felt the group stiffen behind him as they waited for his response.

"This lot?" He looked at the young firebrand, weighed the price on his head against his own secret cargo. Betrayal bubbled in his throat. He considered the gun and his illegal consignment. "All afternoon." He said it even before he had decided, and then nothing could be done. What was worse, he was not sure the censor believed him.

"What about the woman?"

The auburn beauty replied for them both, squawking like a drunken slattern, "A man can get himself into all sorts of trouble round 'ere." She grabbed at Jon possessively, as if in fear of losing his custom, and her fragrance enveloped him: perfume and not half as cheap as she pretended. "I'm protecting him — from loose women." She smiled at the censor, lips over teeth to hide their lustre, and slapped her hand onto Jon's crotch, squeezed gently.

Jon leapt in shock. The soldiers laughed. The censor was unmoved.

"Sergeant, inspect that crate."

Jon held out his hands. "Please, sir, I'm in a frightful rush." He played his last card. "Do you not know me? Jonathan Miller? My brother Daniel trains at the seminary."

"Daniel? Daniel Miller?"

"The very same."

Now it was the censor's turn to shift uncomfortably.

"Daniel Miller?"

"Yes."

"Have you not heard?" His eyes evaded Jon's searching stare.

"Has there been an accident?" Jon asked, all thoughts of peril banished.

The censor laced his fingers, cracked his knuckles. "Daniel failed the grading. He was not chosen, though he fought admirably."

"Oh."

"He has fled the seminary."

Jon stood dumbfounded.

"I'm sorry to be the bearer of such unwelcome news," the censor said. He scratched his throat, turned to the militia. "Let them pass. These are not the men we're looking for."

Jon's hired crew hurried down the street towards the market square, pushing him before them. He offered no resistance, lost in his thoughts. Once they were out of the sight and sound of the patrol, they relaxed.

The young leader spoke to him. "That was well done, goodfellow, well done indeed. I owe you my liberty."

THE SOLEMN BEHEST

Daniel slouched over the long refectory table, his fighting robes garlanded with other people's blood. He ignored the excitement all around him, rotated a tumbler of Carthusian in his hand. The liqueur looked like a fairy-tale poison, a lurid green drink that could fell a giant. He made a toast in thanks to the Brotherhood for all it had given him: a cold billet in a half-abandoned monastery, a war's worth of bruises and the disfavour of the gods, then shot it back. He felt his throat burn and tried to ignore the taste.

The refectory bustled with aspirants, nursing wounds or eager to hear stories of the grading, all oblivious to his gloom. Word of Daniel's performance in the test of arms had spread through the seminary like a bad case of the itch. He was the first aspirant to have defeated all comers since George Quicksilver, forty years previous. The juvenile aspirants, who were not allowed to enter the refectory after sundown, crowded in the arched exit that led to the dormitory and jostled to see their new hero. He winced at a slap on his back from an ebullient aspirant.

"You're indomitable — the Qart-Hadian reborn! You trample foes like his war-elephant." It was a history lesson disguised as a compliment from a bookish aspirant with girlish arms.

The room was brought to attention by an ear-splitting clanging — the seminary's chancellor ringing his handbell with metronomic authority.

"The following shall report to the inner sanctum for ordination." An excited hush settled on the room, even the kitchen boys paused to hear whose names would be pronounced.

"Keither, Wolfe, Umberto, Lucas, Flounders." The refectory roared with approval at each call and the jubilant aspirants were lifted onto the willing shoulders of their colleagues. The chancellor rolled up his scroll. Daniel felt the embarrassed disappointment of his colleagues settle on him like a fever. He sat trembling, staring at his tumbler of spirits, transfixed by its glistening green light.

The chancellor's bell tolled again. "Mr Miller is to report to Magistrate Lang in the chapter house. Immediately." Some of the younger aspirants cheered, and were immediately elbowed into silence.

Daniel stood malevolently, jaw and fists locked, glared around the hall, daring anyone to speak. The aspirants standing closest edged away. He left in absolute silence. Aspirants scattered from his path like blown leaves.

●

There was a chill wind in the quadrant and the expressions of the dusty gods that edged the cloister twisted in the guttering light. Daniel ambled towards the soft glow of the chapter house's latticed windows. His fighting robe left him exposed to the cold but the Carthusian inured him against it. He puffed out his chest and steadied his gait. He really didn't need some pompous prick to remind him that he was a failure, especially not when he was drunk out of his six senses.

The chapter house stood between the old temple and the armoury. It resembled a fortified manor house. A pair of censors guarded its iron-banded doors, halberds crossed, in no way ceremonially. They raised their weapons as they saw Daniel approaching and one of them knocked a code on the ironclad door with his gauntleted knuckles. It swung open, and Daniel stepped inside for the first time.

He found himself in a galleried hall, dominated and illuminated by an enormous canopied fireplace. Intricate theological carvings decorated its dark panelling and the walls were hung with gold and silver plates and rich tapestries that depicted the comings and goings of the gods. *The magistrate lives well*, Daniel thought. The warmth of the room brought a prickle of sweat to his brow and he loosened the already dangling strings of his collar.

"Splendid, isn't it?" a soft clear voice declared from above. Magistrate Lang hovered in the gallery. He still wore his simple blue robe, but now it was adorned with an indigo stole trimmed with ermine, held down by a heavy chain of office. He descended the thickly carpeted stairs to the hall. "Of course it was their undoing. The godsworn spent their tithe even more quickly than we could collect it, and far more willingly. But those days are long gone." He approached Daniel using the silent walk, perhaps to show that he still knew the ways. "Now this hall brings respite and calm where it is needed most. It allows for clear thinking. These are challenging times, Daniel. Clear thinking is a most precious thing; to be able to see the world as it is, not clouded by hope or prejudice." Lang's head seemed to glide as he drew closer, owlish, stalking.

Enough bullshit, Daniel thought, *just get it done with*, and wondered why drunken thoughts seemed to slur, even when unspoken. The magistrate paused serenely and cast his arms wide.

"So how do you see things, Daniel?"

He looked the magistrate straight in the eyes, as straight as he could manage.

"However you decide."

Lang's mouth curled dolefully. "If only life were that simple." He looked at Daniel in a peculiar way and beckoned. "Follow me."

Daniel tried to will himself sober as they climbed the stairs together.

"Do you know what a solemn behest is?" Lang asked. Daniel knew it well from his studies of the Brotherhood's history; *an undertaking never to be admitted or discussed, even upon pain of death.*

"Do they still exist?"

"Oh yes."

They continued their ascent. Dan tried to match the silence of Lang's walk and failed. Lang halted, turned to him and made the sign with his hand. It asked a simple question of him: '*Do you accept my solemn behest?*' Daniel's heart lurched. There was only one possible answer.

He dropped to one knee, gave the censor's salute and then ran his finger across his throat, making the life-pledge. He expected some kind of affirmation, but when he looked up Lang had already reached the top of the staircase. He hurried after him to a door on the landing gilded with the magistrate's name and engraved with the Thrice~Crossed Swords of the Brotherhood. Lang unlocked the door with a heavy iron key.

"My office."

It was as opulent as the entrance hall, its shelves laden with leather-bound tomes of history and law, its thick oak floor carpeted with rugs from the Orient. An expansive tapestry of the Unity and a smaller one of the Empire covered one wall. Both were dotted with tiny flags of many different colours.

In the centre of the room was an enormous desk. It bore a gemstone globe, a rugged travelling case and the strangest device Daniel had ever seen, a giant brass seashell mounted on a squat wooden pedestal. A glass alembic was fixed to the device's side, a ticking clock in its base. Its purpose was unimaginable. It reeked of cunning.

"This is a hekamaphone, a gift from the Convergence. It allows for conversation over any distance."

"Like a beacon, or the flags they used to mount on windmills."

"No. Voices are transported instantaneously — outside of time."

"How can a machine talk like a god?"

"The difference between cunning and miracle is a question that troubled the godsworn terribly; the idea that a man's invention could surpass the imagination of the gods was unthinkable to them. Thankfully, it is no longer our duty to worry about such things." Lang opened a small drawer in the side of the pedestal. It contained rows of tiny phials, each labelled with a name. Lang selected one and poured a drop of pale red liquid onto a small spoon.

"Is that blood?"

"Greatly diluted. Now we wait. Whatever you hear, you will remain silent. Do I make myself clear?" Lang spoke forcefully for the first time, and his tone was iron. Daniel saluted.

When the clock chimed the hour Lang lifted the lid of the alembic and tipped the drop of blood-water into it. Immediately a faint whistling began to emanate from the shell-horn. It became a crackling noise, like the crunching of snow under a sledge, and slowly resolved into speech.

"Magistrate Lang? Can you hear me?" the horn said. The howl of unnatural winds cut across the disembodied voice.

"Reporting," Lang confirmed.

"You have chosen your man?"

"Yes, sir. The aspirant."

"Did he pass the tests?"

"At combat he is a new invincible."

"And how was his sight?"

"He performed well enough."

"I am surprised. It is rare to master it so quickly."

The voice changed in tone, turned patrician, superior.

"I am now speaking to the one who has been chosen. In accordance with our methods I do not wish to hear your voice or know your name." Daniel nodded and then remembered that the voice could not see him.

"There has been a murder at the Convergence. A most worthy censor's life has been cut short, Brother Adelmus. We suspect a plot."

"I suspect treason," Lang clarified. "The workings of the Evangelicy."

Evangelicals? Daniel had heard of the deluded worshippers of the prophet Abjemo and his one 'true' God, knew that their skirmishers harassed the eastern army of the Empire, but it had never occurred to him that their heresy had reached the Unity.

The voice said, "It is possible. I have already dispatched one of our number to the Verge, Prosecutor Corbin from Whitehaven. No doubt you are aware of the quality of his work, his reputation for thoroughness." Daniel wasn't. "The Brotherhood requires you to perform a secret service. You will travel to the Convergence and, while Prosecutor Corbin carries out his formal investigation, you will spy on the demi-masters and the masters from within their ranks." The voice paused to let that sink in. "Only Corbin, Gleame and I will be aware of your mission." Daniel had no idea who Gleame was either. "Ensure that you have memorised a credible legend by the time you reach the Verge. Magistrate Lang is very good at that sort of thing. He will assist you as required."

"We should discuss contingencies," Lang suggested. A distant cough became a discordant squeal that shrieked from the machine.

"The situation is delicate. Given the sensitivities, a censor spying at the Verge is unthinkable, but Lang considers it essential in the circumstances. If you are caught, both the Brotherhood and Gleame will disavow any knowledge of your mission. You should attempt a disappearance. If you are unable to escape, you will allow yourself to be tried and executed as a foreign spy. A full confession will be provided at the appropriate moment." Daniel stared at the horn wide-eyed. "You are to depart this evening. Justice Advances."

"Justice Advances," Magistrate Lang returned, but the hekamaphone had already fallen silent.

Daniel wetted his dry lips. His mind whirled with questions. "Who is Gleame?" he said.

"A grand master of the cunning art, and the chairman of the Honourable Company of Cunning. He founded the centre of all their works, the place we now call the Convergence. You could not fairly say that the Cunning report to him — he struggles to control his protégés at the best of times — but he represents their interests. He is a very powerful man. Leave discussions with him to Corbin."

"The man in the machine, the Chief Constable . . ." Daniel knew it was a good guess, because Lang did not deny it. "He doesn't trust Gleame."

Lang sighed. "For five hundred years it was the Brotherhood's task to keep watch over the Cunning. The law was severe, and we were efficient in its enforcement, often with good reason. Old habits die hard."

"Should I trust Gleame?"

"The first duty of a censor is to trust nobody. Nonetheless, Gleame has arranged much for us. He is as keen as I am to uncover what happened to Brother Adelmus. He allows this deception." Lang handed Daniel a leather-bound dossier.

"Deception?"

"Of his colleagues at the Convergence. In order to spy on the masters you will take up the guise of a demi-master called Edmund Sutton, and be presented as a late arrival."

"I understand."

"Do you? I have prepared some materials for you." Daniel flipped open the dossier. Several pages of dense writing detailed the Sutton family for three generations. The last sheet was a beautifully painted manuscript passport.

"Memorise this legend, then burn it. It might be easier if you were from more noble stock, but mannerisms are more easily faked than brains and training. You will need both at the Verge. You are now the son of a successful merchant. New money. The passport bears the stamp of a prosecutor. It is unimpeachable. The travelling case on my desk is sealed and can only be opened by Prosecutor Corbin. Deliver it to him at the earliest opportunity."

"Why me?"

"That is an impertinent question. I would rather send a more experienced man, but an ordained censor could not work undetected in the midst of the Cunning. You do not appear on the register of censors and have never ventured outside Turbulence. You are nobody."

You mean expendable, Daniel thought, and stared at the floor to hide the anger that flushed his cheeks.

"Do not be so proud, Daniel. That is not the only reason. You must learn to hide your emotions better."

"Yes, sir." On that count, Lang was correct.

"You are nobody. More importantly, you are the right man for the task. The other aspirants are too young to pass as demi-masters, or have too little experience of the real world. You are a solid student and a tremendous warrior. Hernandez tells me he has never seen your equal. You have trained with us for five years and beaten your colleagues at every test you have been set." That was almost true. "And you desperately want to become a censor."

"Yes, sir." Daniel wondered who had told Lang, and how he knew it to be true.

"I am the only person who can grant you that wish. This is your opportunity to earn my appreciation. I reward obedience." *Yes, you do*, Daniel thought, *and you prefer your loyalty baited, and with a hook on the end*.

"So am I made censor?" Lang seemed surprised by the presumption, but more impressed than annoyed.

"For now you are made a country squire, but if you complete this behest to my satisfaction I will ordain you."

"The grading? I passed the tests?"

"That remains to be seen," Lang said, and Daniel wondered if the gods had somehow guided his hand without his knowing.

"May I patrol Turbulence when I return?"

"You may choose your first beat, as tradition dictates."

"I'll do everything I can to warrant your faith in me."

"That is what I expect," Lang replied. "We have a few more things to settle before I send you to the stables."

The magistrate pulled on a cord beside the wall-map, and it slid smoothly upwards, exposing a cabinet. Displayed within was the finest assortment of weapons that Daniel had ever seen. Needle-pointed rapiers, broad-bladed hangers, riding swords and cutlasses. A two-hander as tall as a man. Strange exotica as well — cinqudeas from Etruria, tulwars from across the Middle Sea, gently curved blades from the Orient with patterned edges that swirled like mist or frost.

"My personal collection," Lang explained. "Most of the weapons have provenance."

"What's that?" Daniel asked pointing at one shaped like an elongated sickle.

"A khopesh, from the time of the First Empire."

"The Cradle of the Gods!" Daniel's mind filled with images of desert lands far to the south, the vast pyramids at the heart of antiquity.

"It was forged long before the union of Kemet and Qa-rt-Hadath. Ptolemy pronounced it to be the perfect shape for a sword, mathematically speaking. It is the most ancient in my collection."

"May I?" Daniel asked. Lang nodded. He expected to heft the bronze weapon but found it surprisingly light and fast. He twirled it around his head in a deadly arc, and imagined what it might do to an unarmoured man. Then he replaced it in the display.

"Tradition dictates that when an aspirant becomes a censor he selects a companion weapon that he will carry for the rest of his life. You are not yet a censor, but I do not want to see you sent to the North poorly prepared. Choose a weapon."

Daniel bowed deeply in true gratitude. He had already seen what he wanted, a sword with a chiselled hilt, three-foot long and sharp as a razor. Delicate vines decorated the fullered grooves of the blade, and its curved half-basket guard was en-crusted with overlapping leaves of orichalcum set around the face of Melchior II, the previous emperor. A mortuary sword. It balanced exquisitely in his hand.

"A clever choice," Lang said. "Ornate enough to be mistak-en for a dress sword, but perfectly deadly. The stamp on the tang claims 'D.M.', a Tartessian smith of no small renown. The blade itself is genuine, the trappings are more recent." Lang took the weapon. "Hold out your arm."

Daniel did so without hesitation. Lang raised the sword over his head. The blade swept down with intractable speed.

Daniel did not flinch, nor feel a thing. Lang caught the few drops of blood that trickled from the nick in Daniel's forearm in a glass phial.

"For the hekamaphone. I want to know everything that happens in this investigation. Everything. The Convergence falls under the jurisdiction of Magistrate Clovis in Whitehaven, but matters affecting the Unity's security fall to me. Assist Corbin as best you can, but reporting back to me must always be your primary concern." There was the rub. Lang did not trust the investigation to Corbin. *Or is it Corbin himself that he does not trust?*

Lang handed Daniel a purse of coins and an unremarkable-looking locket. "That piece of jewellery contains a small phial of my blood. When you get to the Verge find a container and mix it with no more than one hundred parts of water. Gain access to a hekamaphone and report every development. I will be here to receive your reports on the sixth hour of the night."

There was only one thing Daniel wanted from his dormitory, everything else he needed he would take from the storeroom next to the stables. He took the travelling case from the desk and saluted.

"I'm ready," he said. Lang shuffled papers on his desk impatiently.

"Daniel, my years of service have made me an excellent judge of character. The true qualities of men are as visible to me as their raiment is to others. I can see the qualities in you. You have been trained well and you deserve a second chance. Now go forth and do as I command."

CHAIRMAN GLEAME

Miranda perched contently upon the windowsill, legs dangling safely inside her room, and marvelled. The Verge's vast octagonal atrium, two hundred feet below and open to the elements, was so crowded with multi-coloured canopies and people that she could not tell the colour of the dirt beneath their feet. The sound of their labour drifted up to her as a soft murmur. A sea view would have been romantic, but this was more interesting — a circus in miniature for her entertainment. It was a long way down, enough to make her feel dizzy.

Her accommodation was small but dignified, one of several chambers the Convergence maintained for wealthy customers and the foreign scholars who were often its guests. It provided a bookshelf, a chest and a child-sized writing desk that nestled beneath the generous window she presently occupied. She wondered what great minds had previously slept in its unfamiliar bed.

Throughout history, all the big ideas, everything that really mattered, had come from the lands to the east. The gods, cunning, literature and philosophy, coffee, all had been discovered in deserts or the cities that somehow thrived within them. The Convergence was changing that, pivoting the world on its axis, shifting power northwards towards the frigid extremities of the world.

Now I am a part of that change. At its centre. A fulcrum.

She laughed at herself then, her tendency to sift for meaning in everything. It was so self-absorbed, and so unlike the boys with whom she had arrived. She pictured them twelve floors below, unpacking belongings, comparing their bunked accommodation to the luxury of family palaces, bemoaning designated roommates. No doubt, her boarding privileges would be seen as another reason to ostracise her.

She had three more days to settle in, then her contract would come into effect and she would become a demi-master. It was an opportunity to explore the Verge, to study and prepare while her rivals drank and played at games of chance. *An opportunity to get ahead.*

Duty to Mother came first.

Miranda slid from the sill to her desk, laid out her remembrance candle, an inkwell, a copper-nibbed quill and a sheet of fine paper, then set a ring on her writing hand — a fire opal surrounded with diamonds and engraved with the crest of the grand duchess.

She had seen that symbol nearly every day of her life — saw it in her dreams, imagined it as the first thing she had witnessed as a baby, being carried through the arched gateway of the Royal Orphanage.

That was a fantasy, of course. At the age she was adopted she would have been unable to focus past her hands. Her first real memory of it must have been the carving on her headboard in the dormitory. She remembered staring at it at night, terrified that she would be sent back to the streets as the nursemaids sometimes threatened. That had been a cruel threat to wield at a small child.

Miranda began to write. Mother would be distracted by her politicking; all of her attention for the last year had been focused on trying to convince the ministers of the Wise Council that the Unity needed a supreme leader to represent its power, the elected equivalent of a prince of the Empire, so Miranda decided to keep things brief.

There was a knock at the door.

She hissed in frustration. Interruptions always came just as the words began to flow. She placed her hand over the letter, pressed down on the opal of her ring and watched as the sentences rearranged themselves into a tangle of incomprehensible gibberish.

"What is it?" she called out.

"A message, milady, from Chairman Gleame," came the muffled reply.

She opened her door to a messenger boy standing attentively in a crisp uniform. He pressed an ivory scroll case into her hand and she instinctively reached for her purse.

"No coin, milady; it's not allowed," he said. "If runners got paid by the delivery I'd be richer than a master by now."

Miranda smiled. In Lundenwic, one was expected to tip a chimney sweep for blowing his nose.

"You need something delivered, there's a whistle-tube next to your desk."

"I was wondering what that was. Thank you for your service." The boy performed a marching turn and sprinted away.

The cylindrical scroll case was a seamless whole, carved with cosmic runes. Miranda pulled hard at each end, but they were stuck fast. She tapped her foot on the floor as she pondered, examined the symbol. Gleame had obviously sent the scroll as some kind of test, but how was she supposed to break the spell with no training in magic?

A cracked voice rasped from the corridor. "May I?" Miranda turned and shrieked. The shadows in her room sparked and popped before her eyes. In her doorway stood a man wearing what appeared to be a black leather pincushion, complete with pins. His face was pierced with hooks and wires.

"I . . . err . . . this," she babbled holding out the scroll case.

The man took it in both hands and, by way of demonstration, twisted it slowly clockwise. He handed the half-opened tube back to her and shuffled away, exposing a pair of flabby lashed buttocks that protruded limply from holes in the seat of his trousers. Miranda snapped her jaw shut. Master Somney's cape and skullcap were eccentric enough. To clear her mind of the shocking image she turned her attention to the scroll.

Ward Miranda, Chairman Gleame requests an interview in the Gallery of Decadent Art upon the eighth hour of the morning. By his word.

That was no surprise. She was a ward of the duchess. Etiquette demanded a summons. She leafed through her wardrobe. If she dressed too plainly she might be taken for a maid, too prettily and she would not be taken seriously. *I should have brought more clothes*, she thought, and cursed the boys who could get along with two suits.

●

Up close, the bustle of the atrium was extraordinary. A constant stream of messengers, butlers, porters, chambermaids and waiters weaved between the stalls of metalworkers, tanners, fishmongers, bakers and jewellers.

Miranda ducked underneath a stretcher of mysterious objects being brought from the workshop. She had seen bigger markets in Lundenwic and Urikon, but they were filled with the stink of animals and the clamour of traders competing to hawk wares. Here there was banter, and money changed hands all around, but the buyers and sellers seemed to trade with a sense of common purpose. There was no pointless haggling — every good and service had a set price; every transaction seemed effortless and efficient.

She looked for a break in the crowd, to find her bearings. The sides of the atrium were a crazy mix of ladders, stairs and elevators. A squadron of waiters wheeling a roast bull on a thick steel platter emerged from a vault, hotly pursued by a dozen waitresses carrying casseroles, tureens and crystal condiment caddies. The place that could spawn such a marvel was worth investigating.

Smoke and steam battled for supremacy in the high-ceilinged cookery. Sea light refracted from the ocean windows sparkled on the walls. Chefs and cooks in spotless white worked in serried ranks along bench tables. Through openings in the seaward wall, Miranda could see the flames of ovens and the shadows of the men who worked them.

"Lost?" asked a plain-looking serving girl by a service hatch. Miranda's governess would have been appalled to hear her addressed by a menial without invitation, but the rules in the Verge seemed different and her governess was not here.

"Why all this food in the middle of the morning?" Miranda asked.

"The masters keep odd hours. Some of them don't keep hours at all. Breakfast time for one is supper for another." Someone slid a laden tray into the girl's hands.

"What in the world is that?"

"Naga chillies from the southern peninsula for Master Bohapemetys, so spicy you can't touch them with bare hands. Flavourless gruel for Nohapness. It took the cooks years to come up with a recipe that didn't taste of water. Poached badger eyes for Master Bolb."

"Are all of the masters so peculiar?"

The girl eyed Miranda suspiciously, but her mouth got the better of her. "Half of them won't answer the bloody door when I come calling. They get lost in their work, haven't finished lashing themselves or whatever. They keep me waiting and then they have the cheek to complain that their food's cold, or gone sluggish, or died in the waiting."

"Man trouble?"

"What? From that lot? I get more attention from the chambermaids. There's a handful of masters that way inclined, but they're served by a special crew. Not my problem."

"Do you like it here?"

"It's a job."

"Is that all?"

"The pay's good. Otherwise, it's like everywhere else. The ones up top think they know more than they do, and fool themselves that we at the bottom know less. Secrets don't stay secret for long. Your arrival has raised a few eyebrows. A lot of the men say it's unnatural — most of the women too."

"What about you?"

She laughed. "If you're the sort who worries about what's natural and what ain't, then I say you're working in the wrong place."

❋

The glass-panelled doors of the gallery were opened for Miranda by two men of broad shoulder and inscrutable face. She swept past them into a stately room floored with intricate mosaics and lined with gaudily painted statues.

The man who waited inside seemed not to notice her entrance. *Chairman Gleame.* Miranda recognised him immediately. His walking stick that glittered with a thousand tiny crystals, his shock of hair the colour of shredded paper, the white silk robes that lit up his umber skin. He held himself with all of the quiet dignity that Her Grace had described, stood motionless, examining a statue of a muscular hero who wielded a club and held a lion skin.

Miranda called out, "This place is fascinating. I had no idea that the Company of Cunning maintained such a magnificent collection of antiquities."

He turned with a subtle bow. "These works of art represent the systematic veneration of vanity by two irredeemably corrupt cultures. Notice how the gods are represented as idealised human beings. Absurd. The exaggerated softness of the women, the infantile penises of the men." Gleame used his cane to point out examples. "No wonder those degenerate empires fell. Imagine a world of Attican values enforced by the brainless militarism of the Tiberians."

Miranda curtsied broadly as she reached him. "It doesn't bear thinking about."

This was comfortable territory for her, and for him, no doubt. Miranda knew vainglorious men were fascinated by history, *probably because they see themselves as part of it.*

Gleame said, "We should be open-minded. The Atticans believed that beauty and intelligence were inextricably linked. I had always thought the idea ridiculous, but maybe you are the proof."

Miranda laughed gaily. It was expected of her.

"Flatterer."

"Nonsense, you are delightful and I am very pleased to meet you. I trust my chaperons ensured you had a pleasant journey."

"I was well looked after. There was some excitement on the last day."

Gleame's thick eyebrows furrowed. "An attempt to sabotage the bridge. The ignorant are frightened of that which they do not understand, and very few people understand what we do here. There is no reason to be afraid. We are well protected."

Miranda had not supposed otherwise and something in his tone unnerved her.

"Her Grace relies upon you for my protection."

"The duchess has been a great friend to the Convergence since the beginning. I am delighted that one of her own is finally participating in our works."

Miranda cleared her throat, adopted a formal tone. "The Honourable Company's monopoly has brought considerable wealth to the North, and elevated the duchess's standing in the eyes of the Wise Council. She instructs me to inform you that she never expected her union with you to be so fruitful, and encourages you to build upon what has been accomplished already. Your licences remain assured."

Mother's message had been delivered word for word, and it seemed to please Gleame greatly.

"And here you are. It is excellent to see the fairer sex represented in these halls. I fully support the idea. We must be progressive if we are to advance our art. But tell me, who proposed it? Your mother?"

I did, Miranda thought, but the point was better left unsettled.

"My mother believes that to employ both sexes within the Convergence will lend the Unity an advantage that other less enlightened realms do not enjoy."

"Your mother insists that you have a mind as sharp as any man's."

Miranda thought that self-evident and could not think of a reply. They faced each other in silence, eyes locked. Gleame seemed to be searching for something to say. Eventually he just nodded. "Is there anything you would like to ask me before you begin your career?"

Why am I the first, when the legends are full of wise women and witches who used cunning to heal and charm? Miranda had hundreds of questions, but her years at court had taught her that powerful men preferred deference to challenge, particularly when they claimed otherwise.

"Any advice would be helpful."

"Of course. I've never been in quite your position . . ." He waved his cane at her dress. "But I can try to imagine. I was just an apprentice once, you know, and even less before that. Maybe you should give the men some time to get used to the idea of a woman being in their midst. Don't rock the boat. Begin by focusing on areas where the fairer sex have excelled in the past. Healing, love potions, amulets to ease childbirth and so forth."

"Anything else?"

"Work hard, and don't let others take credit for your ideas." Gleame said it profoundly, as if in appreciation of a wisdom hidden deep within the comment.

"Master Somney suggested that some of the masters oppose a woman in their midst."

A frown flickered across Gleame's brow. "Did he now? Somney exaggerates, but forewarned is forearmed I suppose. Master Talon is supremely talented," Gleame chuckled, "but he can be a little rough. Try not to antagonise him. You should be fine as long as you remain discreet."

You mean so long as I keep my mouth shut. Miranda curtsied and forced a smile.

CAROUSEL

The leader of the dissenters cupped his ear and looked up.

"What now?"

Jon leaned over the curved iron railing of the reefing deck that ringed the mill's bagging floor, pointed to the loading-bay door thirty feet below and hushed the youth with his finger. That didn't stop his ragged followers from puffing and groaning as they wrestled with the creaking handcart. Its wheels had buckled on the two slow miles from Stanizlav's warehouse. Jon observed with worried eyes. A breakage would wake the neighbourhood.

Inch by inch, the handcart reversed into the mill. Jon watched the folding doors slide closed behind it and took a moment to savour the empty silence of the street. He looked to the north, across the rooftops of Turbulence and beyond to the occasional lights of Bromwich's outskirts, and wondered where his brother might be.

Daniel would never flee without a parting word or a message of explanation. Failing the grading would have been hard on him, especially after his boast about fighting the gangs, but to run away? That made no sense. Dan was family, loved and needed. There had to be more to the matter than Jon knew. For now, a quick prayer for safe travel to He-who-sails-the-wind was all that Jon could offer. He hoped it would be enough.

Sailcloths cleaved the air perilously close to head height. For once, Jon had a breeze when he needed one. He ducked instinctively as he entered the mill and climbed the stepladders to the mill's peak two rungs at a time, first into the stone room where grain chutes fed into the well-worn grindstone, then to the bin room where two huge empty hoppers sagged forlornly like the tits of a crone.

He inspected the mass of spinning shafts and wheels in the cap room with a glance, pulled and released a gear lever to disconnect the grindstone and switched the drive to the sack hoist. A tug on the rope that hung from the ceiling opened trapdoors on every level of the mill, creating a vertical shaft the height of the building. Peering down it, Jon could see the handcart and its cargo, positioned perfectly, five floors below.

He lowered the hoist chain until he heard the hollow thump of its heavy hook landing on the crate, then slid two-handed back down the stepladders. He paused at the storage floor, listening at the door that led from the tower to the mill-house, but heard only the riotous snoring of his mother.

If anyone's going to wake the neighbourhood now, he thought, *it'll be her*.

Holding the rope that controlled the hoist in one hand, he lowered himself through the final trapdoor to balance on top of the wooden crate.

The handcart cracked horribly as it took his weight. He looped the hook through the ring of the crate's lifting band and heaved the crate a few inches into the air. It swung slightly to one side and he heard the unmistakable thwack of wood on flesh. A man swore loudly. Jon rapidly raised the crate to just above the level of the storage floor, hopped off it with the ease of a disembarking sailor and descended to the loading bay.

The red-headed woman was holding a wet cloth to the forehead of the weasel-faced man. "What happened?" he asked woozily, and then vomited spectacularly over the loading-bay floor.

Jon had bumped his head enough times in the mill to know how much a knock like that could hurt. He felt sorry for the man, but he still resented the mess he had made.

The youthful leader of the dissenters laid the injured man down while redhead made a pillow of a folded cloak and tucked it beneath his head.

"The crate rattled your brains," she said plainly. "You'll be back to yourself in a few minutes."

"I should have warned him. Let me help," Jon said.

"Don't worry yourself, goodfellow," the curly-haired leader replied. "Laila is a capable physician." As if to prove the point, Laila tore an even strip from the cloak with practised ease and bandaged the injured man's head. As she wrapped, the youth took a long clay pipe from his jacket, stuffed it with blackwort, and sparked it with a rubbing flint.

"Kareem will live to fight another day. We all will, thanks to you. I don't know why you saved us, but I'm sure you had your reasons. You seem like an honest man, and an educated one. I sense you have some sympathy for our cause."

Jon was incredulous. Could the youth not see the mill that he was standing in? That Jon was a man of property.

"You are in my house because I paid for your help. I have nothing to say for your cause," Jon said. Laila's nose wrinkled in disapproval.

"The Wise Council misrules the land. The people have had enough. The system buckles under the weight of its tyranny. There are men like me in every town preparing. When the time comes, every man will have to choose a side."

The man was a pompous goose. His prattle would be boring if it wasn't so extraordinarily dangerous. Jon looked around nervously. It wasn't simply that he disagreed; who knew which of the poor men from the dock might be a spy or informer for the duchess?

"I don't want such talk in my house," he said. "It's well past midnight — time you made your way back to whatever you call home."

The youth was unperturbed; he smiled in the way men do when they have you at a disadvantage and are about to tell you something that you do not wish to hear.

"I know your name but you don't know mine," he said. "George Barehill, at your service."

Jon looked at him and the woman called Laila in disbelief. Everyone in the Unity had heard tales of Barehill the Breaker, the sworn enemy of machine and magic. Fools said he operated from a secret camp in the Thelney Marshes, or a pirate ship, or a flying castle. Jon had believed the man a myth. The idea that this beardless youth with his red cheeks and curly hair could be the most hunted dissenter in the land was laughable.

Then again, the censor had said that the reward was 'substantial'.

Jon looked at Laila, her thin pale lips and eyes as brown and light as ginger wine, and wondered if such a woman would fall for the nonsense of a charlatan.

The man who claimed to be Barehill leaned forwards and confided, "When you wish to speak with me again, tie a red cloth around the railings of your mill, and I will send someone."

His men opened the folding door and they dragged their lopsided cart outside. Laila whispered something into Barehill's ear and closed the door behind them as they trailed outside. She faced Jon alone, her hands clasped behind her back, chest proud.

"You should listen to what George says. He's a visionary."

"He's a lunatic. Your man will be hanged before the year is out."

"He's not my man and I'm not his woman. We are the Freeborn. We believe that no man or woman belongs to another."

Jon was confused; did she declare herself a whore? "What George is doing is important."

"Fighting the rich to feed the poor? Then what? After the factories are broken and the prisons emptied?"

"You could help us."

"I don't think so."

"You're brave; I saw that today."

He looked at her with pity. He could tell by the way she spoke and held her face that she was not from the streets. A rich man's pretty daughter had been lost to rebellion and licentiousness. It was a terrible waste, and the law was harsh on wayward women. When she was caught, she would be put to the flame and the cheers of a mob of fools would drown out her screams as her beauty burnt away.

"Just leave," he said.

She stepped up close and whispered, "I know you're a good man; you saved us for a reason," then pulled herself against him, her chest flattening against his, and kissed him lightly behind the ear. He was speared like a fish, left gasping for breath. In that instant, he was aware only of the musky smell of her perfume and the feeling of her hands on his back.

Laila ran to the folding door, turned with a smile, and slipped out into the night.

Jon's anger was tinged with shame. What Laila had done was disrespectful to Anna and himself. He would not let himself be drawn into some madman's schemes like a child tempted with candied ginger, but he could still feel her kiss on his skin.

He made the sign of the crescent and prayed that Mother Moon would guide his mind to virtue. Then he made himself busy.

It was bad practice to leave the crate hanging from the sack hoist, dangerous and hard on the pulleys, though the chain could take the weight and more. As he checked the hook and clasp, he heard the door to the mill-house open behind him and turned to see Anna in her nightgown, shielding a candle-stick in her hands.

"What's the noise, Jon? Who were you talking to?" she muttered drowsily.

"I got what we needed, but Dan — he's gone north."

"I don't understand. I thought I heard a woman." He worried then that the conversation would end in an argument and a flood of tears, no matter what he said.

"It's late, flitter-mouse. Just give me a few minutes to finish up, then I'll come and explain."

Anna held out the candle and peered around. "What's in the box?"

Jon stepped into the mill-house to block her view and took the candle from her.

"Something from the docks. It's part of my plan."

She yawned. "Well, at least you didn't wake the baby. Come to bed and tell me about Dan."

"Yes, love," he replied, amazed to have survived the conversation and kissed her cheerfully. Her body went rigid.

"That woman I heard below. You stink of her." She raised a palm to slap him, then her face flooded with tears and her arms dropped.

"You've got the wrong idea," Jon said, and rubbed his temples tiredly. "You've got it all wrong. Just go to bed." Anna's face twisted. The baby cried out. She stormed away.

Jon glowered. He would have to wait for her to fall asleep before he attempted to share the bed. He was too angry to sleep anyway. *Trying to keep the family fed and all Anna can think about is other women.* Anna only got jealous when she was miserable, and then there was no stopping it. Had she always been this way? He'd had his fun as a lad, but it wasn't as if she'd been a wallflower before they'd married. He couldn't remember, and there was no point talking to himself in her stead. He said a quick prayer to He-who-sits-upon-the-mountain for forgiveness, and got back to work.

He activated the sack hoist and stood atop the crate as it rose through the mill, guided it by hand through the trapdoors. When it reached the stone room, he swung the heavy container into the room and bumped it clumsily to the floor, grabbed a crowbar and attacked the side of the box, violently levering planks away, revelling in the noise of splintering wood. The side of the crate off, he took handfuls of straw and dumped them through the trapdoor. A few well-aimed kicks sent what was left of the crate crashing down the shaft.

The carousel horse stood exposed. He dragged it from the crate, set it on the floor and wondered how an object that weighed no more than a man could possibly power his mill.

The horse's eyes were red-veined quartz, with a lustre that looked almost wet. Its billowing tail and mane were gilded, as was the star on its forehead. Its white enamel body was as smooth as ice and patterned with red and gold ribbons of paint that reminded Jon of snakes or smoke. He blinked and had the eerie sensation that the pattern had moved a fraction. He shut his eyes for a few seconds. When he opened them again, the ribbons had rearranged themselves around the animal's body. It didn't bear contemplating.

A brief illustration of how to activate the strange device was tied to its saddle. Jon placed his finger on the horse's forehead and circled the golden star clockwise. The cap room filled with a soft hum and the horse's eyes began to glow with a dull amber light. Jon had never really doubted that the horse would work — the oddity of Stanizlav and his lair had been perversely

reassuring in that regard. Even so, to feel magic actually operating in his mill was a fearful thrill. He traversed the circum-
ference of the room with comically obvious steps, and although
the horse's eyes did not move, he could feel them following
him. Finally back beside the horse, he tapped the star on its
forehead once again.

The carousel horse shuddered, lowered its head and raised a
jointless foreleg. It took a step forwards and its wooden hooves
clacked onto floorboards with surprising heft. Jon had expected
that the horse would float through the air, as was only natural
for something magical. He laughed in childish amazement as
it began to trace the path that Jon had walked, moving more
stiffly than a real animal but with the same thumping gait.

Running behind it, Jon grabbed its tail and dug his heels
into the floorboards. He weighed two and a half hundred
pounds, but the horse dragged him as if he were a silk rib-
bon. He laughed again, this time with joy. It would power his
mill with ease. He let go of the horse's tail and straddled it.
He looked ridiculous, a man well over six feet tall riding a toy
made for a crippled child. His feet dragged along the ground
on either side of him, but the carousel horse did not slow or
buckle. Satisfied with his purchase he tapped the gold star on
its forehead once again and the beast shuddered to a halt. Jon
applied the brake blocks to the mill's sails. He would probably
let them turn in the future, just for show, but their working days
were over.

He returned to the reefing deck to catch a minute of sol-
itude before facing Anna. She would worry about the risk of
using magic without a licence, but she knew how few choices
they had left. Now that the anger had passed, he pitied her
misunderstanding about the perfume. Circumstances had been
precarious for so long that he could not blame her for being

on edge. He looked at Mother Moon and thanked her for the wisdom. Maybe the gods did listen, sometimes.

He glimpsed a flash of light, a hand lanthorn swinging gently in the street below. Its bearer was walking purposefully towards the front door of the mill-house. Jon was halfway down the stairs when the hammering began on the front door.

"Daniel?" Jon called out and flung the door open.

Peacock Matthew stood on the threshold flanked by his shark-eyed thugs. They had pickaxe handles in their hands.

"Hello, Jon. I thought I'd drop by and see how you were getting on."

"It's not a good time."

"Never is for you, is it?" Matthew stepped past Jon and sat in his chair by the fire. The Sharks took position on either side.

"You know this town has turned into a right shithole since we were kids," Peacock declared. "This afternoon, one of Gordon's patrols caught a young lad scratching slogans into the wall of All-Gods." Peacock mimed a knife stabbing into the temple's stone. "Smash the rich, smash the machines, smash this and smash that. Not very witty. Turns out it was one of Barehill's mob. Must have come up from Lundenwic."

"What did they do to him?" Jon asked.

"Took him to the bridge, beat him. One of my lads fucked him with a stick before they threw him over the side. Made sure everyone got a good look. I don't think we'll be seeing any more troublemakers for a while."

Peacock's thugs laughed meanly.

"You're in a talkative mood tonight."

"We've got a lot to talk about. Care to bring me up to date about your brother? I've been hearing stories."

"Then you know as much as I do. When I heard you knocking, I thought it was him."

"Well, it wasn't him, was it? If it had been, he'd be of no use to me anyhow, seeing as how the boy marvel failed his grading. Family of losers, you Miller boys are. Lose, lose, lose . . ." The Peacock conducted the brief melody with his fingers. "I've no idea what Anna saw in you. You were handy at sports, mind."

"So what do you suggest?" Jon asked, staring at the floor.

"Suggest? I suggest that you are in the shit. I suggest that you pay me two thousand notes to put this right."

Two thousand pounds. Jon had never seen that much money in his life. In a good year, when there were good years, the mill had made less than three hundred.

"I'll give the horse back," Jon said, his heart sinking. "I'll get it ready."

"No you fucking won't. Stanizlav doesn't take returns. I don't take returns. That wasn't the deal. The deal was for Daniel, but I'll take two thousand. I'm giving you the chance to pay me back. You should be grateful." Peacock Matthew grinned as if he was retelling the best joke he had ever heard. So did his men.

"Matthew, I didn't know you were our guest." Anna descended into the hall, still wearing her nightdress. "My silly husband hasn't poured you a drink. How rude." Peacock Matthew stood sharply, removed his red hat and bowed.

"Anna, milady," he said, straining to sound genteel.

"You do me great honour, my Lord," Anna said in a parody of nobility, and curtsied extravagantly, "but none of us Turbulence girls will ever be a lady." Anna sashayed to the pantry and poured out three glasses of sweet sherry. Her nightgown was translucent in the hearth light and Jon watched Matthew's gaze trace the curves of her body.

"I hear we owe you some money," she said innocently.

"I'm afraid so," Matthew said, rolling his hat in his hands. It was the first time Jon had seen him look embarrassed. He hadn't thought the man capable. Anna went to Matthew, handed the Sharks drinks. They thanked her in unison, "Mrs Miller." Then she gently pushed Matthew back down into the chair, her finger on his chest and handed him the last glass. Jon felt a pang of horror as she perched on his knee. She looked at Jon with fierce, defiant eyes. *I shouldn't have shouted at her*, Jon thought, and hoped that she knew what she was doing.

"How much?" she asked sweetly. Something hardened in the Peacock's face.

"All of it. More than you've got. I'm a businessman, Anna. I can't let this go. I've got my respect to think about." Anna's lips pursed in concentration.

"Why do you want the mill, Matthew? What use would it be to you without a miller? We'd have to leave Bromwich." She brought Matthew's face close to hers. Their gazes met and she looked deep into his eyes. Matthew gulped.

"What do you suggest?"

"That we work for you. My husband has told me that you've lent us something that will turn the mill around. We'll live here and we'll pay you a rent."

"Ten pounds a week," Matthew said.

That's impossible, Jon thought. *We'll be slaves until the profits run out and then they'll take the mill anyway.* Problem was he didn't have a better idea.

"Three," Anna said. "There's no point in making an arrangement if it can't be kept." She cupped the Peacock's hands in her own, as if she were a pilgrim seeking a blessing. Matthew pondered this, looked at Jon quizzically.

"Five it is. Starting a week today," Matthew declared. He took Anna's waist and lifted her from his lap, clicked his fingers. "Lads, it looks like we'll have to find our entertainment elsewhere tonight."

"Thank you, Matthew," Anna said softly.

After they had left the mill, Jon and Anna stood awhile in silence. What she had done was necessary. It had saved them. But that didn't make it any less humiliating.

Jon sucked on his teeth. "Five pounds a week. It's impossible."

"We'll find a way — together." Anna reached out her hand and he took it.

"Together," he said.

"Now tell me about Dan."

A NEW MAN

Daniel rehearsed his new identity as he rode north. Passing travellers took him for a madman as he babbled to himself astride his horse, but by the time he had reached the inn at Lymm, he was sure he could answer to the name Edmund Sutton without hesitation.

Lymm was a weaving town, and so the following morning he bought several cases of gentleman's attire from a fashionable outfitter. Lang's coin was plentiful, but it still pained Daniel to accept the prices that he was offered without haggling over every button and stitch.

In the fortified tavern at Carus, another two days up the highway, he practised a moneyed accent as he played a game of dogs and jackals with a bored notary. He wagered shillings for the first time in his life, and enjoyed it less than he expected — until somehow, between tipsy and intoxicated, he got lucky on the last round of the game and threw four tails. He treated the house to a barrel of scrumpy with his winnings, delighting the farmers, merchants and mercenaries who drank there.

As the evening wore on, he was called from table to table to join in idle banter, asked to sympathise with common concerns and answer questions about affairs in the South. There was no denying the conversation, and it was good practice, but every slip of his accent or word of Bromwich slang felt like a stab to the chest and he prayed that the lapses in his fakery had gone unnoticed. Later that evening, when a farmer stood on a bench and called upon the assembly to give thanks to the 'young lord' he looked about to see who they meant and blushed with pride when the realisation came. The drinkers mistook his confusion for intemperance and roared in approval. At the end of the evening, glowing by the fire, he felt confident enough in his new persona to burn Lang's notes in the tavern's hearth.

Daniel expected to reach the Verge in two more days, horse and weather permitting. He had read that the roads north of Carus were lonely and dangerous; there were still wild animals in the North, and men who lived in the lakes and forests who had never known honest work. They would not hinder an armoured carriage but a young esquire, dressed in new silks and travelling alone, would be a tempting target. Lang's well-crafted traveller's case felt like a bullseye strapped to the back of his horse.

He rode tall with his hand resting on the pommel of his mortuary sword, and ate in his saddle. The travellers he had met at Carus claimed that the northern countryside was the most beautiful in the world. He would have preferred a featureless plain. He put the scouting techniques he had learnt at the seminary to hard use, inspecting every patch of waving grass, rock or tree for a hint of hidden villainy. When he reached the shore of Vinands' Lake, the longest in the land, he perceived it only as a natural barrier to protect his left flank and hoped that the light reflected by its fish-scale waters would blind observers to his presence.

After two long days of watchfulness, he was overcome with fatigue. He had barely the energy to tether his horse in the stables at Galava. It was a prosperous market town for the local wool trade, so its inn was both expensive and flea-infested. He noticed the subtly different posture of the northerners, the hangdog expressions of the men, and the way the women held their heads back and high, as if in readiness for a rebuke. Feeling tired and unwelcome, he ordered a private room and supper in his rich man's voice and watched the innkeeper's wife suddenly become more smiling but less friendly. He fell asleep before his food was brought to him, and was not even roused by the serving girl's clamour at his door.

Dawn the next morning it was raining lances, which pleased him greatly. The criminal fraternity were unfamiliar with early rising, and lacked a fondness for foul weather. He signed his new name in the inn's guestbook, paid the innkeeper an undeserved and memorable tip, and set out upon the final stretch of highway.

The man who emerged through mist and horizontal rain at Hardknott Pass, his riding hood pulled tight around his head, was Edmund Sutton Esquire — and there was not a soul within two hundred miles who would claim otherwise.

SECOND BEST

The Verge's library was legendary, reputed to encompass more tomes and manuscripts than every other in the Unity combined. Some claimed that its collection equalled that of the maze-like Library of Rhakotis, destroyed by fire in ancient times. So when Miranda arrived at a room little larger than a reception, with the appearance of a ticket office, and apparently devoid of books, the only logical conclusion she could draw, despite the sign outside that clearly stated 'Library', was that she had made a mistake.

Its occupants were a stiff-faced couple who sat behind an oil-smooth slab of black rock. If it was not for the woman's lace bodice Miranda might have taken the couple for twins. Their grey hair and wrinkled faces were peaked with tall hats, from the brims of which hung a multitude of differently coloured lenses.

Miranda knocked and entered. The lady rotated the brim of her hat until a clear glass monocle dangled in front of her, and plugged it into her face. The gentleman beside her mounted a pair of clouded onyx spectacles on his modest nose and his expression blossomed into a crude leer.

"I seem to be lost," Miranda said. "Could you direct me to the library?"

The man pointed to the ceiling and then the ground at her feet.

"During the day I am the librarian and this gentleman is my assistant. At night our roles reverse," the woman said.

"Thank you for explaining," Miranda replied. "Where are the books?"

"Safe and sound," the librarian said, and pointed to a barely visible rectangle etched into the wall behind her. It looked like an engraving of a letterbox. "This is not the sort of library where anybody can borrow anything. Gods know what that would lead to."

"Or what gods that might lead to?" her assistant added.

"I wish to impress the masters. I can read Unitarian, Oenic, Hesperian, Imperial, Old Imperial and Omek. My Frankish is passable."

"You wish to learn another language?" the librarian asked.

"No," Miranda said, struggling to maintain her gracious smile, "I wish to learn more about the cunning. What would you recommend for a beginner?"

"That would depend very much upon the beginner," the assistant said.

"The best books about cunning are the thin ones," the librarian added.

"Short, easy to digest. That sounds perfect."

"No, not short, spread thin. Voluminous but with very little content."

"I don't understand."

The librarian adopted the tone of a teacher at a school for the hard of learning. "Books about cunning cannot be like ordinary books. If they were, who would believe in their power? A passable grimoire has maybe six ideas in it, described over five hundred pages of incomprehensible jargon."

"The very best are the size of a serving tray and five inches thick," the assistant said. "They contain maybe half an idea. Nothing practical."

"Coded messages and enigmatic diagrams. Misleading pictures of plants and animals."

"Red herrings," the assistant chuckled, "Yarmouth capons, golden hares."

"I don't . . ." Miranda started.

"Obscurantism," the librarian snapped. "A person can hardly be considered an expert if everybody can understand what they are saying. The same applies to books."

The assistant adopted a kindlier tone, although still patronising to Miranda's mind. "Nothing inspires confidence and respect like an accurate quotation from an obscure book."

"From the masters?"

"From the magic."

Miranda was baffled. She decided to change tack. "Is there a compendium, maybe? A list of recommendations I could choose from?"

The assistant rotated his hat and donned a pair of lenses the colour of summer grass. He rifled about under the desk and eventually produced a huge scroll, which he unrolled before her.

"This is a list of the books that have identifiable titles," the assistant said.

"Or authors," the librarian interjected.

"Or can otherwise be described pictorially."

Miranda scoured the scroll for texts that might be of use to her, without the first idea of which those might be. Most were denoted by little more than strange symbols. Of the names she recognised, none were available. Duauf and Kagemni were on loan to demi-masters. Alhazared had been withdrawn. Merikare was a good choice, the librarian explained patiently, but had been borrowed five years previously and neither the book nor the master who had loaned it had been seen since. Voynich was forbidden.

In the end, Miranda chose three at random: a bestiary, a guide to alchemical marriage, and an encyclopaedia of fairy pageantry. They appeared out of the strange portal behind the librarian as soon as she mentioned their names. She left the small room with her small selection of second-choice writings and absolutely no idea what purpose they might serve.

"Lady Miranda."

She nearly ran into the tall man, long-necked and sharp-nosed — had to swerve to avoid scattering his clutch of books.

Adrian Lavety.

He composed himself and bowed stiffly. Miranda curtsied deeply — however little Adrian deserved the politeness. The Lavetys were one of the oldest families in the Unity: southern barons, distant cousins of Her Grace. A Lavety had been the high priest once, a long time ago, which explained why Adrian's smoking smock referenced the stitching of a god-sworn's cassock. Etiquette aside, they had studied together at Alchester.

"I did not see you amongst the carriages," she said.

"Gods, no. I travelled here upon my own convenience, direct from our estate. I have little appetite for the chatter of these university types."

That was a lie. His father's opinion of the transportation was a more likely explanation. Adrian had probably been delivered to the Convergence in an armoured carriage accompanied by a squadron of horse.

"Do you find your fellows boorish?" Miranda asked.

"Frivolous. They care more for entertainment than advancement."

"I know what you mean. I'd expected to be dazzled by intellects. It was terribly disappointing to find myself still to be the cleverest in the class."

"We are no longer at university, Miranda, and you seldom were." Adrian was trying to make some point about her private education, the tutors that Mother had provided to help her with examinations, *as if he had grounds for true complaint!* Miranda's results had been unsurpassed, yet he had been the one to win first honours. As a woman, Miranda could not even hold an ordinary doctorate.

"A ward of the duchess could hardly be expected to live amongst so many young men," she said. "The innuendo would be ruinous." She smiled at him gamely.

"Whose idea was this anyway? What do you hope to gain by your presence here?"

"I am here by Her Grace's command."

"Of course," he said, meaning 'nonsense', though whether that applied to her attendance or her explanation of it was unclear.

"Do you disapprove?"

"You're a very clever girl," he said, and she strained to find the insult hidden in the compliment.

Finding none, her attention turned to the stack of books he carried. They looked promising; she had already spotted Kagemni tucked into the middle of them.

"Are you returning those?" she asked as sweetly as she could manage. Lavety looked closely at Miranda's small collection and compared.

"I was about to, but I think I've changed my mind." He bowed again, even more grandly than the first time, and departed, his books clasped tightly to his chest.

FINDING A WAY

Pigeon pudding was Jon's favourite meal, so he tried to enjoy the taste of it. He glanced up between each joyless spoonful, hopeful that Anna might say something to calm his mind. A small bone caught in his throat. He coughed it out and balanced it on the edge of the table.

"We can't afford this. We should stick to soup."

"Dan wouldn't go without a reason," Anna said. "Maybe he's gone soldiering in the North. Plans to send us his wages."

"A pound a month? How would that help?"

Anna stared at her bowl, shuffled some food around its edge with an iron fork. Her cheeks reddened and the energy of her anger reminded Jon of when she was young. She had been the prize that every man in Turbulence had fought over, with fists and flowers. He still thought her beautiful, especially when she was angry. Maybe that was why she won all of their arguments.

"You did well, love, to get him down to five pounds a week, you really did. You always drive a hard bargain." He tried to smile but it came out as a smirk.

Three floors above, the mill's grindstone turned ceaselessly. The carousel horse was working better than he could have hoped. The mill's hoppers bulged with the grain he had bought with the last of his savings. The problem was there were no customers. Sacks of unsold flour slouched in the storage room, slowly going off. Jon would lose more money this week than he had the last. In a few days, Peacock Matthew would send one of his men to collect the first payment and there were no valuables left to sell.

"What are we going to do?" Anna said, shaking her head, staring at her food.

"I'll find a way, I always do."

"Peacock's just playing with us." She pushed her plate away, food uneaten.

She might be right, Jon thought. It would be just like him to warn off the bakers, to try to speed things along. Maybe it was for the best — a quick death rather than a slow one.

"Then why did he agree to a deal in the first place?"

"Isn't that obvious?" Anna looked at him as if he was mad, or a fool.

"No it isn't," he shouted, pushed back his seat, threw his napkin over the remains of his meal and stalked out of the room.

When his head had cleared, he found himself on the reefing deck, the city at his feet, gulping down deep breaths of cool evening air. He rested his chin on his thick arms and looked out over Turbulence's half-tiled roofs and rickety chimneys. Maybe one window in five was unbroken. He shut his eyes and let the sinking sun warm his face.

A memory came to him. Once, when he was a small boy, he had come home weeping, with a black eye. Father, sober for once, had sat him down and explained that Turbulence had not always been the roughest part of Bromwich, that before the factories it had been a middling sort of place where merchants built substantial houses with the profits from workshops. Back then, it had possessed another name, something leafy-sounding. Jon couldn't remember it any more. Father had told the story by way of an apology, as if Turbulence's genteel past could somehow make his face hurt less.

It was all bullshit.

As far as Jon could work out, his father had been lured to Bromwich, the middle city of the Unity, by the once-in-a-lifetime opportunity to buy a windmill from an imprisoned debtor at a distressed price. He hadn't stopped to think why the man might be in debt, of course. Now the mill was as much a burden as Mother was. If Father had made one good decision in his life, it was marrying such a forgiving woman. Until Dahlia was taken. Until Mother's body had shut out the world to protect her from the misery of it and Father had hanged himself in shame.

Jon had been the one to find the body, swinging naked from the minstrel gallery, harmless at last. How many times had he punched and kicked that corpse before he had cut it down? *Too many to remember.*

Jon gripped the cold, pitted iron of the railing.

You promised Anna a plan, and she deserves one, so think of one. He dragged his fingers through his hair and pulled his beard into shape. There was no use in trying to fight the gangs, especially without Daniel's help. Maybe Dan wouldn't help anyway, if fighting were contrary to the law. Jon's debt to Matthew was legitimate — as far as anything that happened in Turbulence was legitimate — and Daniel had warned him not to get involved.

He heard footsteps on the platform. Anna took a spot beside him, her back against the railing.

"We can't be like this," she said.

"Maybe you should stay with your family for a while, till I get things sorted. Country air might do Mother some good."

"I'm not leaving. If the worst comes to the worst, I might be able to persuade Matthew to let us keep something."

"Peacock will never have this mill. I'd rather see it burn."

"That thing upstairs, the carousel — it wasn't a bad idea."

He touched her hand gently.

"So what are we going to do?" she said.

"If Daniel had made the grade, everyone would be buying from me. They'd be afraid not to."

"It's not our fault, or Daniel's. It's theirs." Anna pointed towards the vast sails that turned lazily on the horizon.

"Here's what I want you to do," Jon said. "Start visiting temple every day, not just on Endays. Pray for us and for the mill, and to all of the gods, not just to the Mother. Wear your best shawl. Dance inside the temple."

Anna stared at her feet. "Do you really think that the gods are going to help us?"

"Could it do any harm? Pray for greater luck. For a successful enterprise."

She looked at him quizzically. "You've thought of something then?"

He smiled at her as reassuringly as he could and she went back inside the mill a little happier.

It was a lie. He didn't have a plan. *Maybe they do*, he thought as he looked over the distant domes of the temples. There had to be a reason why the gods were so cruel to him.

Dahlia.

He discarded that thought quickly, fearful of where it would lead.

Something had to be done, and the only answer he could see lay with the dissenters. Barehill and his roughshod army. The substantial reward that the censor had mentioned. *To collect it I need only learn where they hide, inform the censors and live to tell the tale.*

That was a terrible risk, and not much of a plan. On the other hand, a stand-up fight with Peacock was no kind of plan at all. Jon considered his choices and whistled in appreciation of their poverty.

Poverty. The dissenters he had seen were the poorest of men. They followed Barehill out of desperation, not conviction. If Barehill were captured, they would end up branded, enslaved or killed. He told himself that they would have brought that upon themselves anyway, that they shouldn't have got involved with the man, but it didn't feel quite right. He couldn't pretend that they didn't need money, food or whatever else Barehill provided them with.

Family must come first, always. Family and the mill.

He fetched an old red scarf from the rag box in the loading bay, tied it tightly to the platform's rail. The wind had gone flat again. The pennant hung flaccid, like a dead man's tongue.

2

PROSECUTOR CORBIN

One last hill was crested and then Seascale Bay revealed itself, desolate and magnificent in the middle distance. Daniel's journey to the Verge was nearly complete, without incident or mishap, and even the heavy rain could not dampen his triumphant spirit. The mountain bandits would have to stay poor and hungry. He whooped and dug his heels into his horse's flanks, set off towards the Verge at a gallop, scattering clods of wet earth in his wake.

Just before Seascale Bay, he took shelter from the deluge in a covered bridge. It was being repaired by a team of carpenters. One of them sang a song of lost love as the crew chopped, hammered and sawed to the rhythm of the tune.

"Is it always like this?" Daniel asked, after the song had ended.

"It's rained two days out of three since I've been here," the closest said, his Lundenwic accent undiminished by the nails clasped between his lips, "but I only come up for the summer money. Ask Thomas." He hammered down a board and gesticulated at the saw-man with his hammer. Daniel didn't bother. He had only been making conversation, and he was already thinking about what lay ahead.

Peering out from under the bridge's awning, he watched the Convergence sharpen into view as the rain subsided and the clouds lifted from the hillside. He rode his horse down the gently sloping highway towards the Verge's stables. A crucifix had been raised on the last hillock before the dunes and a body dangled from it. Daniel cantered to the grisly landmark.

He guessed that the corpse had been exposed for about a week. It was tied by its forearms and ankles, naked apart from the small cloth that covered its modesty. The sea air had desiccated what the funeral birds had not eaten. A solitary seagull picked unenthusiastically at the leathery remains. The left hand of the corpse was missing, but Daniel could tell from the way the bone had healed that the injury was an old one. The Sigil of the Gods was carved into the head of the cross and, underneath, the name of the deceased, with a circle drawn around it to denote eternity. It was a sky burial, performed with all of the correct rites, offering the empty body of Adelmus, the murdered censor, to He-who-sails-the-wind.

The crucifix had been placed facing across the bay, and the hollow eye sockets of the deceased seemed to stare reproachfully at the Convergence. Daniel doubted the macabre exhibit could be seen from that far away.

He dismounted and tied his horse by its reins. Adelmus's neatly folded uniform lay at the foot of the cross, weighed down with a small rock. There was only one glove, which made sense. The censor's weapon, which should have been broken and placed on top of his clothes, was missing. There were few greater sins than grave robbing, and no man would risk the wrath of the gods for a useless sword or axe. The weapon must have been stolen when the censor was killed.

The theft angered Daniel more than the murder. The censor should not have allowed himself to be beaten in combat or caught unawares, but the theft of his companion weapon was an affront to the entire Brotherhood. Daniel hoped he would have the opportunity to hear the culprits howl with pain.

●

He left his horse at the stables that marked the end of the high-way. Carriages embossed with the livery of academies were being serviced, cleaned and repainted in the yard. He demanded assistance and was provided with a porter who escorted him along the causeway to the Verge.

Daniel watched guiltily as the man struggled under the weight of his luggage, balanced on a reed pannier mounted high on his back, but his moneyed persona forbade the possibility of lending a hand.

The scale of the Convergence was a wonder. In a way, it reminded Dan of the factories of Bromwich. It was as if every one of them had been shoved together into a great pile by a clumsy giant. He tried to guess where inside the sprawling compound Prosecutor Corbin might be and how far advanced he was in his investigations.

He entered the Convergence through the wicket door built into its tall teak gates and reported to the small-windowed porters' office that was located immediately within.

"Sutton. I am expected," he said nonchalantly and leaned against the counter feigning boredom. An elderly porter retrieved a scroll from the rack behind him, checked for the name and frowned. Daniel's gut clenched.

"I'm sorry, sir," said the porter, "but I have no resemblance by which to confirm you."

"My papers," Daniel said, giving a calm smile to hide his apprehension and offering Lang's forged passport. The porter put on a pair of thin white gloves and unfolded it with care.

"Edmund of Sutton, son of Walter Sutton, twenty-two years of age and near six foot of height. Blond." He looked Edmund up and down. "Lovely penmanship, sir. I shall escort you to your room."

Daniel was led through broad service corridors to the demi-masters' accommodation. He half expected goblins or flying carpets, and was disappointed to see only a press of hurried scribes and a youth in a shocking hat.

"You can go where you please, apart from the Masters' Quarters. They're strictly off limits, and you'll have to leave that beauty in your room." The porter pointed at the mortuary sword hanging at Daniel's side. "Unless you're headed back out, that is."

Daniel shrugged indifferently.

He was given a twin room on the ground floor with a neatly made bed set against each wall. He could see no roommate's possessions. The room was grander than a prosecutor's chambers back at the seminary. He wondered if the luxury was ordinary or if it had been arranged by Gleame. He did not want to stand out. He stowed his blade on top of the wardrobe and directed the porter to put Lang's travelling case and his own luggage on the spare bunk.

There was an envelope waiting on his pillow. The porter turned discreetly away as he unsealed it. A letter of congratulations from an imaginary relative. He ran a finger down the edge of the paper and felt for the tiny cuts that would spell out a message in the battle-code of the Brotherhood. Meet. Dusk. Fight. Room. The message was straightforward enough. In a few hours, he would meet Prosecutor Corbin in the fencing court. Daniel whipped a clean singlet, pair of trousers and slippers from his luggage.

If there is luxury here, he thought, *I might as well enjoy it.*

"My journey has been long and hard — I fancy a bath."

●

It was buried deep within the island, although how far and in what direction Daniel could not tell. The porter led him from the oak panelling of the Verge's inner corridors to tunnels of granite embedded with tiny crystals whose milky radiance con-fused his sense of time and place. The gently winding corridor seemed interminable. The only feeling of progress was an un-natural sensation like a soundless buzzing or drone that grew with every deepening step. Lang's notes had given Daniel no guidance on how to react to manifest strangeness and so, while his mind boggled, he casually asked the porter if the long walk would be worth the effort. The spectacle that awaited him at the end of the stairway gave the answer.

The bathhouse was a natural cavern, open to the ocean and hidden from the bay. It was high and sheltered enough to avoid the sea spray and strong winds. Steam rose from the clear wa-ters that filled the cave to the brim of its mouth. Beyond, Dan could see a horizonless grey where distant breakers met ashen clouds. The only sounds were wind and slowly dripping water.

A solitary swimmer shared the cavern — a splendid man who carved the length of the pool with elegant strokes. Through the swirling vapours, Daniel could discern the pool's floor, an ages-old mosaic depicting He-who-sleeps-in-the-ocean. The primordial god was surrounded by men of all colours. The un-lucky ones were being devoured by creatures of the deep.

Daniel smiled with joy. He had thought the bathhouse at Bromwich Seminary a luxury, even in winter when the ice on the tubs had to be broken with a hammer. Any water was preferable to the buckets and flannels of Turbulence. This was another world. He dismissed the porter and undressed quickly, piling his clothes onto a marble bench on the raised platform that served as a changing area.

He gasped at the stinging heat as he lowered himself into the water; it could have been freshly poured from a kettle. He could not tell whether it was heated by an underground spring or by some unnatural device, nor did he care.

Jon won't believe this, he thought as he pushed off into the centre of the pool and felt the sweat and travel grime flush from his skin.

When he was done, Daniel dried and dressed in his fighting clothes by the light of a setting sun that painted the changing platform with a rosy light. The rocks around him cast strange shadows, and he had the unsettling notion that before it was a bathhouse this pool and platform had served a different, darker purpose.

●

Daniel could hear the clash of wooden wasters, practice swords, through the paper screen that divided the deserted armoury from the fencing court. There was some boisterous repartee and then a yelp, maybe from a strike upon a knuckle or a knee. It sounded more like child's play than combat. He picked out from the racks the waster that most closely resembled his mortuary sword and tested it for balance. It wasn't bad, for a piece of wood.

"You two. Out. Now." A man had entered the court. His accent lilted but his tone did not allow for the possibility of dissent. There was a pattering of hurried footsteps and then a moment of silence. "Mister Sutton, lock the armoury and join me in the hall." The accent was Dalriadan; it had to be Corbin. Daniel did as he had been instructed, then slid aside the screen.

Corbin was nowhere to be seen.

The fencing court was a rotunda, high ceilinged and edged with painted columns that depicted warriors performing the nine lines of attack, and the nine wards that could defeat them. *Not ordinary warriors* — the martial legends of the world, from the bright lands of the Empire to the foggy shores of the Six Kingdoms, all made gloriously real: Ramesses locking swords with King Lud; Hannibal, the indomitable one, wrestling with

Setanta; Gwydion dodging Moraltach, the unstoppable sword of Diarmid; Wayland and Kaveh hammering it out in a battle of blacksmiths. It was truly a hall fit for heroes.

Daniel realised he stood agape. He knew the Cunning had made fortunes from their craft, but he had not expected them to spend it so munificently. He placed Lang's travel case by the wall and subtly tested the parquet floor as he made his way to the inlaid star that marked the centre of the room. It was gently sprung. Perfect.

"My regards to Magistrate Lang." Daniel pirouetted to face the voice, saw only shadows between the pillars, then a flicker of movement to his side. He was balanced and ready, turning and batting away the objects hurled at his face with ease. A handful of practice daggers clattered to the floor around him.

The lesson had begun.

Daniel held his waster in a neutral guard, protecting his face and body, and edged slowly towards the side of the hall from where the missiles had flown.

"Judgement, distance, time and place."

It was confusing; the same soft accent had called out from four different places. *The bastard is throwing his voice*, Dan realised.

"The four principles of the true fight," he said, listening hard.

"The fifth is the most important." The voice seemed to breathe from the empty air above.

"Deception," Daniel said. "'When you are least certain, return to the centre of things — from there you will see most clearly'," he quoted, and edged slowly back towards the star in the centre of the hall.

"The *Tactics* of Wilhelm Von Basqueburg," Corbin said. "Have you learnt your fighting from books?"

Keep talking and I'll show you what I've learnt, once I've worked out where you are.

"The sound in this room is deceptive," Daniel called out.

"The Convergence is like that."

"You've worked here before?"

"A long time ago, and with some success, which makes me wonder; why does Magistrate Lang burden me with an aspirant in this investigation?"

"I've brought a package for you," Daniel replied.

"A deflection! You have some skill with words. Lang wouldn't send a fecking idiot, though, would he? Your instruction begins."

Prosecutor Corbin emerged from behind a pillar and in the same casual movement flung a javelin at Daniel's head. Daniel concentrated on the arcing missile, far easier to deflect than a handful of daggers or throwing stars. He took his time, beat it aside neatly and was pleased with his work. Only at the last instant did he grasp that Corbin had silently charged him down, his sword held back and low, and that its wooden blade was now wrenching towards his neck in a resolute arc.

Daniel ducked and pitched himself at the prosecutor's shins. Without breaking stride, the prosecutor drove the tip of his sword into the floor and used it to vault high over Daniel's head.

He barely made a sound as he landed on his feet and switched his guard high, to the executioner's stance. Daniel grinned from ear to ear. It was an extraordinarily athletic move for an old bastard. Corbin's hair might be greying but his eyes were smiling, and he wasn't even out of breath. *I can learn from this wolf*, he thought as Corbin slid backwards out of distance and rested his sword across the hollow of his shoulder.

"If you tried that leap with a metal blade you'd ruin it, but it can be done with a staff," Corbin said. Daniel nodded and tested the grip of his weapon. "Return this message to Lang. I have taken confession from the scene of the murder. Brother

Adelmus faced four men. He slew two of them; local roughs. Another two survived. Big men, well trained. He was arresting one of them when the other shot him with an arquebus, from behind a bush twenty yards distant. Hit him in the neck."

Dan kept his guard up as Corbin walked back and forth in a semicircle, changing direction with unpredictable speed.

"And then?"

"The villains searched his body, took his sword and fled by the highway. They attempted to slow any pursuit by setting fire to the covered bridge."

"Why haven't you gone after them?"

Daniel readied himself.

"That's not the . . ."

As Corbin answered, Daniel jumped forwards and feinted a jab at his hands. The prosecutor parried it easily, sidestepped the remise and drove the point of his longsword hard towards Daniel's chest. He jerked back to avoid the hit and stumbled. Corbin chuckled.

"It happened at dead of night and the men wore conceal-ments. I spied only their eyes, which were as black as dried shit. I was lucky to divine as much as I did. The fire at the bridge was their mistake; it illuminated their passage."

"Horse thieves?" Daniel suggested. "Smugglers from Ravenglass?"

"No animals were stolen from the stables and I found no contraband abandoned."

Daniel lashed his waster at Corbin's head. The prosecutor blocked the blow above his shoulder, and replied with a hori-zontal swing that Daniel was barely able to duck.

"They might have panicked."

Corbin advanced behind a flurry of interweaving blows that drove Daniel dancing backwards from foot to foot.

"Fled-when-they-saw-whom-they-had-killed."

Corbin's attack finally ended and they drew apart again.

"It's possible. I suggest you return to Lang with your conclusions and help him track down the felons, assuming they are still in the North."

Daniel's chest heaved. He circled Corbin warily and considered how to get the bastard to take him seriously. "The attackers' motive," he ventured. "That's not the real mystery."

"Go on."

"What was Adelmus doing at the stables in the middle of the night?"

Corbin leapt sideways, wrong-footing Daniel, and swung a cut upwards into his body. The blow was too strong to deflect, too fast to dodge. Daniel grabbed the tip of his waster in his free hand and held it in front of him like a bar. He heard the wood crack as it caught the force of the blow.

"That's the one."

The two men strained against each other, weapons locked.

"If I can answer that, the rest will become clear." Corbin reversed his grip and twisted the pommel of his sword into Daniel's face. Dan tried to jump backwards, felt a jarring pain in his knee, and found he couldn't move. Corbin was treading on his foot. The bastard tapped him gently on the tip of the nose with his pommel.

"Lesson over. We can't have you going back to Lang with your handsome face all bashed up, can we?"

It was a dirty move, but effective. Daniel committed it to memory.

The fencing court echoed with the sound of applause. Daniel and Corbin spun to face it, weapons ready. A distinguished-looking black man in white robes appeared from behind the pillar of Ramesses and Lud. He seemed both old and young. He walked with a stick and the eyebrows that dominated his speckled brow were thick and white, but his eyes sparkled like those of a youth.

"Chairman Gleame. I didn't know we had an audience." Corbin's disapproval was unconcealed, and Daniel was surprised to hear the prosecutor speak to the grandmaster so brusquely.

"No matter," Gleame said, waving his sparkling cane in the air, "I found the sport and the conversation most entertaining. It seems to me that Lang has provided you with a valuable asset."

Corbin glanced incredulously at Daniel, as if he were a horse with three legs.

"Why are you here?" Corbin asked, still unsmiling.

Gleame turned to Daniel. "I wanted to see Mister Sutton for myself. If there are dark forces in our midst, they must be rooted out. Furthermore . . ."

Corbin cut in loudly, "Grandmaster, I share your desire for justice, and will do everything within my power to solve this mystery. Nobody is above suspicion."

"Of course, Prosecutor, please continue. Your reputation precedes you."

Gleame left the hall by way of the armoury.

"I told you to lock the door," Corbin said.

"I did, sir."

Corbin sighed like a scullery maid after a banquet.

"How did he just appear like that?" Daniel said. "Was it cunning?"

"It doesn't work that way."

"Oh."

"I reckon he used a secret passage. I daresay the secret passages in this place outnumber the known ones." Corbin rubbed the stubble on his chin. "Shite."

"I'm sorry, sir."

"Too late for that. Sutton, bring me the package."

Daniel brought Lang's travelling case. Corbin placed his hand on its lid and its complex seals split open with a crack.

"What have we here? Some important-looking papers. A wheel-lock puffer. A bandolier of powder and shot. And a fistful of gold coins."

"I thought wheel locks were prohibited throughout the Unity."

Corbin placed the miniature pistol back into the case. "A good thing too. The weapon's only fit for an assassin — I want nothing to do with it. Lang only sent it to rile me. It's yours for now; keep it safe."

"What are the papers?"

"Dispensations from the Wise Council. Lang really has gone to town. Unlocked the top shelf, you might say. This one's for you." He dropped a sheet back into the case. "It bestows the right to bear a pistol in exception to the law. Don't lose it or I'll have to arrest you."

Daniel wasn't sure if he was joking. Corbin pulled out another scroll. "This one bestows upon the bearer the right to perform an inquisition and trial at the Convergence. I'll keep that." He rolled it tightly and slid it into one of the leather tubes on the bandolier in which he kept his laws. "And this last one . . . permits a censor to communicate with a godsworn for the duration of the investigation. I'm not even sure the Wise Council has the power to grant such a right. That's something to look into when all of this is over. I wouldn't do it anyway, dispensation or none."

Corbin stood to leave.

"My orders are to stay and assist. What do you want me to do?" Daniel asked.

"I don't need your help. Lang only sent you here to keep an eye on me. That wretched man can't stand the idea of not knowing." Corbin waited for a response, so Daniel gave none.

"If watching is what he reckons you're good at, let's put his judgement to the test. Keep your eyes and ears open and pointed away from me. Observe the demi-masters and let me know if anything comes up."

"Prosecutor, the demi-masters arrived after Adelmus was killed. It would be a waste of time."

"Luckily your time is less valuable than mine," Corbin grinned. He hoisted the wooden two-hander over his shoulder and headed for the armoury. "I'll send for you when I require your assistance. Scratch a code on your door."

Daniel imagined the expression on Lang's face souring as Daniel reported nothing after nothing back to Bromwich. His last chance for ordination turning to vapour.

"I can help you," he pleaded.

Corbin said nothing. The acid of exercise pooled under Daniel's tongue. He wanted to spit it at the old man's back. The grey bastard had no idea of what he was capable. He swallowed his pride and saluted, hand across neck.

"Justice Advances."

"One funeral at a time," Corbin replied.

INDUCTION

"Stop blocking the corridor!" Albertus shouted, and slammed the ornate door in their faces. The new arrivals formed a disorderly queue outside the demonstration hall and began to chatter in cliques like conspiring tradesmen.

They buzzed with confidence and ambition, as if they had known each other for months. Miranda waited in the background, alone, feeling sick with nerves and underprepared. Academia had always been easy for her yet the books of cunning from the library had left her feeling nothing but a dull confusion. After three days of cross-referencing, she'd discovered not one paragraph of good sense. They had forced her to consider the possibility that she was not quite as clever as she supposed.

An endless traffic of scribes, butlers, illuminators and serving maids flowed past, punctuated by the occasional master. The crowd hushed in their presence, out of curiosity as much as respect. The first master strode past dressed like a king, in a glorious violet turban crowned with jewels. The next wore grey rags and stumbled under a pannier full of rocks, his back bowed double like an old woman's. The last was transported by a stately chair with pseudopodal legs that moved with a languid, alien beauty. It was like an extraordinary costume party whose theme was a mystery, even to the guests.

Not one of masters so much as glanced in the new recruits' direction.

The doors to the demonstration room were unbarred, and an ungainly wave of young manhood poured through them. Miranda drifted in its wake. She had no appetite for the childish, sharp-elbowed scramble that securing a seat at the front would require. Those who fought for one were pathetic, more concerned with prominence than education — or so she told herself.

The demonstration hall was functional; it was no opera house or coliseum. It could seat a few hundred souls on the steeply banked rows of seats that curved like a horseshoe around a raised platform that was more of a pier than a stage. It reminded Miranda of an operating theatre. Its one extravagance was an enormous chandelier, brass and copper verdigris, moulded like the drooping boughs of a tree and studded with an outrageous number of glow-stones gathered in bunches, like greengages.

Albertus grabbed Miranda's elbow.

"If I were you I would be discreet, stay at the back, sit with a friend." Her face darkened at the suggestion — the room was barely a third full, and she had no friends at the Verge.

She scanned the amphitheatre for a promising pew. The centre of the hall was already crowded. The unoccupied seat next to Nathan was out of the question; she could live with his wandering eyes, but not with the prospect of an entire lecture spent warding off his hand from her thigh. Her gaze fell deeper into the room, the wings and the back, and she tried to reconcile herself to a place amongst the mediocre and antisocial.

Sitting in the shadows at the very back of the hall was a man she did not recognise, a pale-skinned blond dressed in hopelessly provincial attire, his hair cut oddly short, like a jousting knight from the previous century. The sort of man who might wear a codpiece in public. He had his arms stretched out, resting across the tops of the empty seats to either side of him.

No manners, little prospect of genius and no style, Miranda thought, *but then again, he has neither ignored me nor insulted me, which is more than can be said for the rest of them.*

She edged her way towards him down a sparsely occupied aisle, navigating an assault course of legs and bags. Most of the boys shifted sideways in their seats to let her pass, one stood and she smiled courteously in thanks, and then scowled furiously as he pinched her bottom. The last pretended not to see her approach and stretched out his legs to block her way. She ground his toes into the floor with a crunching twist of her boot heel and pretended not to hear his yelping expletives as she parked herself nonchalantly beside the blond.

"Nicely done," he said, slowly withdrawing his arm from behind her back, "he'll be limping for a week."

His voice was deep and self-assured, his accent hard to place. It was the first time she had been complimented by someone of her own age in a month. She granted him a sly smile as she retrieved her commonplace book and balanced it on her knees. The blond hurriedly copied her, pulling an extravagantly bound folio from his bag. It was very large and unsullied by study. *Like him*, she thought, and giggled.

He looked at her quizzically. Up close the blond looked more like an athlete or a herald than the perpetually inebriated petty nobleman he undoubtedly was. He was handsome, beautiful even, with thighs like pistons and a broad chest. The sort of man her ward-sisters swooned over. In a funny way, he reminded her of the guards who stood watch outside Her Grace's embassies.

From beneath the stage came an unbearably shrill noise, like the slow turning of a rusted drill. The assembly fell silent as a trapdoor opened and a costumed man was lifted into the room. He wore feathered robes, all angles and edges, a brimless conical hat and a mouthless mask with a long beak, like that of an ibis. The elongated fingers of his gloves tapered to stiletto points. His costume reminded Miranda of the plague doctor from Erdinberg whose tales of the terrible sickness had intrigued her, and given her governess nightmares for weeks.

Why do all the masters dress so oddly? she wondered.

The strange figure inspected the audience, head bobbing and eyes wide. He had brought a gurney with him. Its wheels screeched diabolically as he pushed it to the front of the pier. Once in position, he pulled a lever at its base and the bed flipped upright to reveal a withered husk of a body strapped to its surface with leather braces and bands. Everyone leaned forward to get a better look. It looked like the corpse of the most dangerous inmate in an asylum.

Its eyes flicked open.

Miranda jumped in her seat. The hall filled with nervous tittering. The feathered man took ahold of the gurney and revolved it, displayed the cadaver to the entire room. It remained immobile apart from its eyes, which swivelled derangedly.

The grating noise became louder. After a minute, an imperious voice called out from the front row.

"I think we've seen enough."

The gurney was spun to face in the speaker's direction. The feathered man stepped out to the edge of the pier, identified him with a gloved finger that quivered an inch from his forehead.

"Out," the corpse rasped. The young man said nothing. "Out. Now." The corpse's voice had a sibilant echo, as if a desert snake had made its home in the desiccated cavity of his lungs.

"I'm terribly sorry. I presumed you were dead," the young man quipped with the haughty confidence of one born to immeasurable wealth. He laughed insincerely and the audience laughed with him.

"Out. Now," the corpse hissed.

"I beg your pardon." The youth raised his hand in apology.

"Not pardon. Not sorry. Out."

"I am the first son of Count Orison!" the youth exclaimed, his face turning rosy with indignation.

"And your offer of employment with the Honourable Company is withdrawn. Pack your belongings and return home."

There were gasps and exclamations from around the hall.

The feathered man perched on the edge of the stage and hooked his feet over its edge, ready to pounce. Suddenly he seemed more prey-bird than human. The young noble scrambled to his feet and shuffled his way towards the aisle, not averting his eyes for an instant. "I have every right to be here," he shouted, cheeks moist with rage. "You have not heard the last of this."

When he reached the exit there was a porter waiting for him.

The corpse scraped its lips with its tongue, leaving them no wetter than before. "Good. Now that I have your undivided attention, we can begin. I am Master Talon Turon. Understand that in this place you are nothing. Your presence here is tolerated only because of the very small chance that you might one day turn a profit. Some of you dream of becoming masters, one of the Twenty-Three. Know that far better men than you have tried and failed. The truth is that most of you will prove useless."

Miranda wondered how many times Talon had delivered that miserable introduction. *It was nonsense, of course.* If the recruitment of demi-masters were that fruitless, it would have ended long ago.

Master Turon cleared his throat, a sound like paper tearing.

"What is magic?" he said, and the room fell silent. "Come now. The question will not answer itself. Anybody. Somebody? Anybody."

Men looked at each other, willing others to speak first. An uncertain hand lifted near the stage, and the silent birdman swirled the gurney to face its gangly, bespectacled owner. "Go on," said Talon.

"The art, um, the science of causing change in conformity with will?"

"Everything a man does bends the world to his will to some small degree."

"I meant directly, just . . ."

"I did not ask for a clarification," Talon squeaked, and then belched dustily. "Your answer was incoherent and irrelevant, which is a good start, but also incorrect, which is less promising. What you are attempting to describe is cunning, the manipulation of magic by a person. That was not what I asked. What is magic? Anyone else?"

Talon ignored those who suddenly had found the courage to raise their hands.

"I didn't think so. Answer. There isn't a man, woman or child in the world who doesn't know what magic is. Other-worldliness made manifest. That which trespasses the threshold of reality."

The answer made perfect sense, Miranda thought, yet was utterly uninformative. She wondered if Talon really wanted to share his secrets.

"Question. Does magic work?"

A chorus of affirmative noises filled the room.

"Incorrect. No. Magic does not work. No more so than a flame or the wind or tides. In its natural state, magic serves no purpose; it is a whore without coin. It only becomes useful when it has been structured, invested. Dim the stones," Talon commanded.

The hall faded into half-light. The birdman flapped to the back of the stage and retrieved from behind the gurney an object the size of a hatbox, draped with a cloth. He displayed it eagerly. Even the most apathetic ceased doodling. Miranda set aside her commonplace and leaned forward in her seat, eyes riveted on the stage.

A cube of flawless crystal was unveiled with a flourish worthy of a sideshow conjurer. Thousands of infinitesimal points of light swarmed within it like agitated insects. Rarefied lines of razor light flashed between them, like fissures opening in breaking ice, and then were gone as quickly. As Miranda's eyes grew accustomed to the light, she began to discern a pattern to the movement. It was contained within a delicate cobweb, an arcane geometry of translucent edges.

"What is it?" the blond asked.

"Magic as a thing unto itself," she said in wonder.

"This box has been enchanted so as to make the invisible visible," Talon said. "The phenomenon you see stirring within it is magic. The magimatical structure that contains it is what we call a construct. Magic does not like being constrained and so it expends a great deal of energy trying to escape. This tension, the energy expended, is captured by the construct, which in turn powers the enchantment of the box. A circular process." His jaw clicked in a horrible parody of a guffaw.

Talon's smugness was grating, but Miranda shared the excitement of the room. This was the first real secret of the Convergence she had been shown and she was not disappointed.

"In order to structure magic, first we need to find it. Where can we find magic?"

Lavety's voice rang out. "Here."

"Yes, here. Why here?"

"Because it is a sacred place."

"Yes. Good."

It's not as if that was a difficult question, Miranda thought, and imagined the far more insightful answer that she would have given.

"The Convergence is a place of power," Talon continued. "Whether it is sacred or enchanted, and what the difference is between the two, is a question for the theorists. It always has been. Nevertheless, we, by which I mean the Honourable Company of Cunning, have enhanced it. We have created a limitless reservoir of other-worldliness."

Talon sucked air noisily through his rotted teeth for an unfeasibly long time. Miranda wondered where it all went — his chest did not swell an inch. "We have added to the flow of magic through this place, its liquidity, through an accumulation of ritual, mainly incantation and sacrifice."

"Which is better?" a man called out.

"The particulars of an act are irrelevant," Talon replied with irritation. "What matters is the conviction and skill of the practitioner. As I was saying, to derive a useful effect from magic it must be structured. Magic does not like to be trapped and so we are presented with a battle between the cunning of a master and the wildness of magic. A construct must be formed in the mind of the master and imposed on the magic. That is what you must attempt to achieve in the coming weeks."

Miranda nodded in agreement. What Master Talon was saying almost made sense. She was not alone in that thought. The audience welled with excitement.

"Structured magic, derived magic, can be used in diverse ways: as a source of power, to animate, to imbue properties, even to project the senses. The applications are limited only by our imaginations. As an example, consider the hekamaphone, a recent innovation. The device amplifies the sympathetic connection between the bloods of two persons. It is effective to such an extent that they can communicate over any distance as if they were present in the same room."

The audience gasped at the idea. Miranda's thoughts spiralled sideways as she grappled with the implications of communication without delay.

"Let us speculate. If a man arrived in the Unity from a land without magic, what would he make of the hekamaphone? Anyone?"

"He would believe it impossible," someone declared excitedly.

"Idiot. Do you actually understand what impossible means? Get out. No, stay. Anyone else?"

Miranda twitched. She scanned the room, hoping somebody else would answer first, but she couldn't help herself. Her hand shot up like a firework, stood solitary.

The birdman pointed at her. Talon appeared to not notice.

"Anyone?" he asked.

The room remained silent. The birdman squawked and jabbed a cloth-clawed finger. The whole auditorium turned to look at her. Her heart beat so strongly, she could hear it. There was no question of lowering her hand; her pride would not allow it.

"I see the girl, Geoffrey," Talon said. "Is there no man in the room who can answer the question?" He sighed a thousand little deaths. "Go on then, if you must."

"He might assume that it was a machine which transported the messages in accordance with nature," Miranda ventured confidently, "by wind or light, or some other means. Perhaps the vibration of ropes or wires?" A hush fell over the assembly. The only sound was the grinding of Talon's teeth.

"Nice," whispered the blond. Miranda knew it was a good answer; her interest was in Talon's opinion of it. The master said nothing, just stared at her with his dead eyes.

"There are two key requirements for the successful formation of a construct," he continued. "The first is that the practitioner is able to visualise a coherent and lucid structure, a pattern within which magic can be trapped. Choose one today and start practising it immediately. I recommend something simple. A cube or a sphere."

Miranda had an idea. She scribbled it frantically into the margin of her commonplace.

"The second requirement is that you make yourself visible to the magic. To structure it you must be able to relate to it, and likewise it to you. We achieve this by making ourselves otherworldly, like the magic. How? There are infinite paths. You could choose to speak only in a language of your own invention, or backwards, or never at all. You might never sleep, like Master Somney. Dress ridiculously. Grow a beard to your feet. Wear a pointy hat and cultivate eyebrows that extend beyond its brim. Indulge constantly in perverse and loveless acts of sexuality. Flagellate. The specifics of the method you choose matter less than its scope and extent. Be original. What you are attempting to achieve is simple. You must become unnatural. The more extreme, difficult and consistent the path, the more powerful you will become."

That explains the odd costumes.

The room quieted as the audience considered what was being asked of them. Miranda thought it pathetic that Talon could only think of ways to become unworldly that were cruel or silly. She imagined a beauty as irresistible as gravity, so powerful it drove men and women to worship and despair.

Talon broke the silence. "As you can see, I have chosen the Path of Complete Immobility. I have not lifted a finger for twenty years — spent every minute strapped down or tied up. The sores on my back weep for my sacrifice, but I can work miracles. It was not easy. Many turn from the path after a short while. Others waste health or sanity without achievement."

Miranda wondered how many had been destroyed by the process, and began to see Talon in a more forgiving light.

"Is that why magic was forbidden for so long?" someone asked.

"What the godsworn and their censors failed to understand was that our ancient predecessors, who gained power by bathing in the blood of innocents under full moons, were not necessarily evil; they were simply doing the best they could with limited resources. The Convergence does not dabble in magic. We research, structure, invest and sell — and we must be careful not to upset our customers. I fear that virgin sacrifice is no longer on the agenda."

The auditorium filled with mean laughter. Talon whispered something to Geoffrey, and was turned to face in Miranda's direction.

"Of course anything that brings you closer to the practical, the mundane, will rob you of ability. Romance, children, domestic work. That is why the mind of a woman is not equipped to achieve any significant power. Her maternal instincts and gentle nature prevent it." Talon waited for a response. Miranda's brow knotted at the baiting but she resisted the temptation to dignify his provocation with a response. Talon addressed the blond.

"You at the back — the lumbering one next to the chatterbox lady." The blond raised an eyebrow. "What is your name?"

His nervousness made him hesitate. "Edmund, Edmund Sutton."

Sutton? There was no bloodline of that name that Miranda was aware of, no heraldry and no armigers. Miranda knew them all by heart. *New money.*

"Sutton, is it fair that some bright young man has lost the opportunity to work here in order that a woman without qualifications could take his place?"

The audience murmured in agreement and Miranda hated them for it, the way they already thought as a pack. The blond glanced at Miranda, and she gave him a look of ice, dared him to concur. He coughed into his hand to clear his throat, and as he did so, winked at her slyly.

"Could I deny it?" he replied jovially. It was an evasion culled straight from semioticians of Alessandria and if only two people in the room knew he had not agreed with Talon, then at least that was something. Maybe he was not quite as stupid as he looked.

If Talon noticed the equivocation, he did not press. "An apprenticeship at the Convergence is a resource not to be squandered. To award one to a female is idiocy. It is impossible for a member of the weaker sex to become a master. If it were up to me she would be sent back home to her needlework and gossiping — but nothing can be done; Grandmaster Gleame insists because she is a ward of the duchess." A murmuring of disapproval spread across the room and a few cast glances in her direction. "No matter. As much as her presence might vex me, she will at least provide the rest of you with some entertainment."

The audience laughed again.

Miranda rose to retort but the blond put his hand on her thigh and pushed her firmly back into her seat. She glared at him in indignation. He released his grip.

Without further comment, the gurney was reset and Talon was fixed horizontal like the effigy atop an emperor's tomb. The birdman wheeled him back to the trapdoor and they both sunk slowly out of view.

Miranda and the blond waited as the lecture room emptied around them. She ignored the glances of the departing and glared at Lavety as he sauntered towards the exit, as stiff as a lamp-pole. To her astonishment, he turned at the last moment and made his way towards them.

"Lord Lavety," she said.

"In fairness I thought your answer was not at all bad."

"Thank you."

"I would have you for dinner. A formal invitation will be forthcoming."

"Of course," she replied, thin-lipped.

Lavety bowed again and departed. The blond stared at her incredulously. Oddly, he seemed more distressed by her good manners than the dishonour of being ignored by another gentleman.

"Friend of yours?" he said.

"Sir, you forget yourself!" The blond stepped back as if bitten, then made a very straight, almost military bow, most unlike the gestures she received at court.

"Edmund Sutton of Bromwich, at your service."

"I know who you are."

"I apologise unreservedly."

She realised that he had not meant to mock her, and almost regretted losing her temper.

"A formal invitation is well within his rights, but I shall arrive at least an hour late, with a chaperon twice his size, and leave early with an upset stomach." Apologising to the blond was impossible but she curtsied a full inch lower than his station deserved and offered the back of her palm. "Miranda, Ward of the Grand Duchess."

He stared at her outstretched hand uncomfortably. It was very strange. Mr Sutton had shown no fear of Master Talon, yet now he seemed on the verge of running away. Clearly the poor boy knew nothing of the intricate rules of invitation by seniority, or curtsies for that matter. It was understandable, she supposed; his noble obligations probably went no further than leading the first barn dance of his estate's harvest festival. Maybe his father had seen no value in courtly ways. There was only one thing for it — to keep him talking.

"We are all equals here, according to Talon Turon. Apart from me, of course."

"The master was vicious, but has made his point," Edmund said. "I doubt he will feel the need to do so again."

"Maybe." Miranda was not convinced. Gleame had warned her about him, but she had not expected something so brazen. If Talon was willing to humiliate her publicly maybe Gleame's support was less of a protection than she had supposed. Sutton bowed again and turned to leave. Miranda felt uncharacteristically lost for words. "How do you find your lodgings?"

"Comfortable. I am lucky enough to have a room of my own."

"I have one in the Masters' Quarters," she said enthusiastically and immediately regretted the boast, which seemed to confirm all of Talon's prejudices. "It can feel lonely there." That was even worse. What would he think she meant? She felt her cheeks redden and sucked them in.

"Of course," he said, looking more confused than ever.

The introduction was a disaster, but she was feeling fragile after Master Talon's remonstrations and Mister Sutton was at least pretending to be friendly. She racked her brains for a suitable subject of conversation with a Bromwich merchant's son and found that her brains were not at her service. *I'm overthinking*, she decided, and gave up.

"Would you be so kind as to escort me to the Masters' Quarters?"

"That would be a pleasure."

Edmund Sutton smiled broadly, and his smile was delightful.

THE HOLT

The red pennant had been flying from the railing for less than ten minutes. Twice already Jon had decided to take it down and had climbed the stairs to the minstrel gallery, only to change his mind and return to the mill hall. He cursed his resolve and poured himself a large sherry. His hand shook as he drank it, so he poured himself another and went to the spice rack for a mint leaf to chew on.

How was he going to convince Anna of a plan he was so unsure of himself? He realised that he couldn't, and that her reaction would change his mind in an instant. The first she would know of it would have to be when he returned — if he returned.

There was a hammering at the door. *Barehill must have had someone watching the mill the whole time.* The realisation pulled at his gut.

"Who's there?" Anna called out from the gallery, the baby crying in her arms.

"A customer — at last." Jon closed his eyes and thought about the price on Barehill's head. *A substantial reward*, the censor had said. *It had better be.*

"I found some coloured string, to offer at temple," Anna said.

"Well done, love. Bolt the door behind me."

He gathered his courage along with his coat and stick, pulled his hat low over his brow and slipped out of his own house like a burglar.

Kareem was waiting for him. He was taller than Jon remembered. A wiry sort of fellow, younger too. The wispy moustache he was growing failed to make him look any older than the twenty years Jon guessed he had. The clash with the crate had left a bruise the size of a gull's egg on his forehead. He still looked like a weasel.

"Follow."

They went south, through the nameless alleyways of Turbulence, then across the great bazaar and on to Moor Street. Kareem moved swiftly but discreetly, led Jon through a hole in an alley wall, later through a mercer's shop and out the back door. It was done out of habit, or maybe to impress; Jon saw no sign of pursuers when he glanced over his shoulder.

"Where are we headed?" Jon asked.

"You'll see."

The sun was setting as they approached the temple district. The factories on the horizon towered over their neighbours like mausoleums between tombstones, pompous and immense. The hundreds of windows that flanked their sides burned with reflected light.

"How's your head?" Jon asked.

"Clear enough to see through the likes of you," Kareem replied.

Jon halted, heart beating guiltily. "What's that supposed to mean?"

Kareem squared up to him. "It means keep your trap shut, Miller. I don't trust you, or any of your sort. So shut the fuck up."

Under normal circumstances, no Turbulence man would allow an affront like that to go unpunished. Today, Jon had no choice, and both men knew it. Kareem turned his back and set off with a swagger.

Jon's mind chewed on the insult. What did the vagabond mean by his 'sort'? *Men who worked? Men who made something of themselves?* He was arguing with himself again. That was pointless. When it came to naming names, Kareem's would be the first he gave to the censors.

Jon was still brooding as they crossed through the slipstream of the factories. The unnatural, constant breeze stuck their clothes to their skin, as if they were suddenly wet.

At the foot of the temple district they passed by the squat black pyramid that was the temple of He-who-sits-upon-the-mountain. A jackal and cat-like mafdet guarded its entrance. The two faces of justice; mankind's laws in life and the gods' laws in death. Jon focused on the obsidian pyramidion that capped the building and made the sign of the eye.

"You don't believe in that rubbish, do you? It's just fairy tales, told to keep the people down." Kareem looked at him in disgust and spat at the basalt statues.

Jon shook his head in disbelief and imagined the stone animals springing to life, pinning Kareem to the ground and tearing out his faithless throat. The sun glinted on the gold leaf that surrounded the statues' eyes and in that moment, it seemed to Jon that they winked at him.

"You want to be careful," Jon said.

Kareem scoffed, "I thought I told you to keep your mouth shut."

They came to a temple of He-who-trembles-the-earth. All that was visible above the ground was an alabaster cupola, very old and in poor repair, in the curling shape of an enormous snake burrowing from the earth. Its apex was its frightful head, wedge-shaped and grasping a crimson heart between its fangs. A godsworn with a shaven head, wearing a green cassock and a menat in the shape of an adder, stood outside the temple's iron-grilled entrance.

Jon had never visited the temple before. He rarely worshipped the Devourer. Its virtue was honesty, and he knew the world could do with more of that, but its negative aspect was sloth. It was a complicated god, but the truth was, Jon just hated snakes. He looked around, got his bearings. The temple's location was easy enough to remember.

The godsworn swung open the grill and led them into the cupola. The only feature inside was a pit, twenty feet wide and as deep as death. Rough slabs of stone embedded in its walls formed a stairway into darkness.

"Is he to be trusted?" the godsworn asked.

"No." Kareem looked Jon over, proffered a dirty strip of hessian. "Surrender your stick — and you're wearing this."

I'm already at their mercy, Jon thought, and closed his eyes in submission. His logic couldn't hold back the panic he felt as Kareem tied the blindfold tight.

An arm looped around his own, pulled him forwards. Kareem was half his weight; if Jon tumbled, they would both fall. With faltering steps, he made his way down the stairs, his free hand grasping at the wall's rough masonry.

He tried to count the corridors that they passed, to make a map of the place in his mind. The stones in the wall became slippery and warm to his touch. Jon imagined giant scales, and shuddered.

Deeper, he was led from the stairs into a maze of passages. Kareem spun him at every turning. Soon he had no idea how many lefts and rights he had taken, or in what order. It was impossible. He felt as sick as a dog and cursed himself for imagining the Freeborn to be fools. There was no way he could describe the route he had taken to the censors, or find his way back.

●

"Remove your blindfold."

Jon was blinded by the glare of a lamp.

"Where am I?"

"A long way from home. Keep up, big man, or you'll be lost for all eternity." Kareem turned his lanthorn away and tramped off into the darkness. Jon blundered after him, half blind, suddenly more afraid of losing his guide than of reaching his destination.

They travelled tunnels of red earth, always downwards sloping, surfaces greasy with slime. They were barely tall enough for a man, and if they had once been part of a mine or catacombs, no tools or litter lay beside the paths and no engravings or alcoves decorated the walls to prove it.

Jon wondered how deep they walked and felt the pressure of tons of rock and soil overhead.

The corridor widened into an open space where footsteps echoed. The floor was pockmarked with sandy rivulets, and wet underfoot. There was a faint sense of a breeze but no stars. Droplets of water fell all around. Jon tested one that splashed on his hand, tasted minerals and acid.

Two lanthorns swung in their direction. A thick Glaschu accent called distantly from the darkness. "Who goes there?"

Kareem grunted his name and followed the lights. A small rowing boat appeared in the gloom, lying lopsided on the gravel. A rope rose from its prow to a small wooden pier that extended from a bank of clay. Jon realised that he stood on the bed of an underground river.

The guards on the pier wore drab workingmen's clothes but their chests were crossed with powder belts and they were armed with swords and arquebuses, wheel locks of recent design, which they trained on Jon. It was the first time he had faced a man down the wrong end of a barrel and it made his skin crawl.

One of them helped Kareem to clamber onto the decking.

"Where's the general?" Kareem asked.

"Giving a sermon." The guard thumbed over his shoulder as his colleague helped Jon onto the bank.

Jon followed Kareem along the subterranean riverbank to a wall of thick stone. There was a culvert at its base, surrounded by a litter of iron bars and recently chipped rock. The ends of a rope ladder were tied to the remaining stubs of black metal that protruded from the ground like a hog's teeth.

Kareem gestured with exaggerated politeness. "After you."

Jon squeezed his bulky frame backwards through the small opening. His legs dangled in the void beyond. His feet groped for a surface. Feeling one, he dropped down, and stumbled as it slewed underfoot. He held out his arms to keep his balance, saw that he stood on a pontoon floating in the waters of an arched tunnel. Kareem laughed and scurried down to join him, nimble as a monkey.

A punt and pole were tethered to the side of the wooden platform. Kareem untied the flat-bottomed boat, slid it into the water and steadied it. Jon climbed gingerly on board, half-expecting it to flounder under his weight and huddled at the front of its small square-cut prow as they cast off into the underworld.

Tall columns loomed out of nowhere and passed silently on either side of them as they glided across the water. There was no light save for Kareem's lanthorn on the dank walls, no sound but the dripping of water. For a moment, Jon fancied that he was in the land of the dead, being ferried to He-who-sits-up-on-the-mountain for judgement, who would weigh his sins in the scales, against the tear of a child.

"What is this place?" Jon asked, hoping for a clue that he could pass onto the censors, should he make it out alive.

"A cistern. We've fixed it up so it doesn't fill. The water's only a couple of yards deep."

Jon heard the distant chatter of voices and assumed that by some trick of amplification the sounds of the city had been transported by well or sewer. As they grew louder, he turned from side to side in confusion, trying to understand their source.

They drifted around a corner and a hundred lights came into view. He saw strands of lanthorns hanging from ropes that looped through the air like the rigging of a ship, a score of campfires that burned in braziers suspended in mid-air. The shadows of men moved amongst them and the air stank of people, the water or worse. He jolted, startled, as a bucket flew overhead, speeding along a high wire, suspended from a whining pulley.

Jon slowly made sense of what he could see: a shanty town made of platforms and bridges, pontoons and old rowing boats that hovered just above the water, lashed to the columns that supported the roof of the ancient underground reservoir. It was as if an absent-minded shipwright had decided to construct a galleon from the top down, and then forgotten to build the hull.

"This is our home," Kareem said. "We call it the Holt."

THE DREAM

It is a blazing hot day. The stamping boots of grown-ups fill the air with dust. It doesn't bother them, but it makes Daniel's eyes sting and Dahlia is coughing up a storm.

He drags his sister from the vintner. The quicker they can bring home the bottle of wine, the less likely a beating from Father. They hurry across the street, deep into the crowds.

"Stop pulling me, Dan-Dan," Dahlia complains. It's not her fault. She's only little; she doesn't understand. Dan is ten years old, nearly a man. Responsible.

A path opens up between the legs of the adults, like a tunnel or a forest track, and at its end sits the man with the painted face.

The crowd freezes mid-stride, motionless, like statues in a memorial. It's as if time itself has deferred to Daniel's destiny.

The painted man beckons Daniel over with a wave and a smile. His golden tooth glints, and in the dream it makes a noise like a chime.

Daniel and Dahlia stand in front of him.

"What are you doing?" Daniel asks, staring at the man's lap. He has a tray balanced between his knees and upon the tray sit three cups, inverted. It's some kind of game; one that Daniel has not seen before. The painted man licks his lips. His teeth are rotten; his tongue is serpentine. Somehow, in the dream, Daniel doesn't notice the danger.

"You can keep the gold, if you can follow it," the painted man says, "but you must concentrate, boy — real hard."

He sets a coin spinning with a casual flick of his wrist, *a crown*, covers it with one of the cups. He shuffles them slowly. Daniel's eyes, as sharp as an eagle's, track every move. The cups move faster and faster, flicking from hand to hand, but for Daniel time slows. He can see everything. *The game is easy.*

The cups stop. Daniel picks out the one that covers the coin, tries to peek under its lip as the man lifts it from the tray. There is nothing underneath. Daniel realises that he has been tricked.

The painted man makes a sad face.

Daniel feels dread, rising through his legs and into his heart. He turns. Dahlia is gone. He screams her name into the crowd, turns full circle, searching desperately. She has disappeared as completely as the coin. Snatched by sleight of hand. He runs into the thicket of men's legs, pushing and screaming as they tighten around him. They become a cage. He is trapped. She is gone, forever.

Somewhere far behind him, the painted man begins to laugh.

●

"Fuck!"

Where am I?

Daniel's mind whirled. Reluctantly his faculties returned to his head, some semblance of sense returned. *I'm in bed, in a dark room and I'm still drunk,* he realised, and sat upright.

His head throbbed viscously. Waking up drunk was just about the only thing worse than waking up with a hangover. Apart from that dream.

Actually, the dream wasn't so bad in remembrance. He could almost forgive himself when he was awake: blame it all on Father's drunkenness, remind himself how young he had been, that he was a victim, not the criminal.

Almost.

There was no forgiving the tightness in his face or the taste in his mouth.

"Fuck."

A passing night-maid cast a hush towards his door. Daniel barely noticed and did not care. His mind was still locked inwards. He groped about for his tinderbox and after five minutes of swearing, incompetence got his candle lit.

Three years spent perfecting my knowledge of law and the martial arts in order to listen to the flatulent gossip of idiots. He sat on the edge of his bed, head in hands, and totted up the evenings he had wasted eavesdropping at Corbin's command, the hours spent watching dissipated demi-masters stuff their mouths with quail and biscuits, quaff wines from every corner of the globe. Not just any wines, obscenely expensive bottles normally reserved for name days and funerals. They spilt almost as much as they drank. They were unworthy of investigation. The greatest danger that they posed was to the carpets.

He had begun to detest their careless hands and rowdy banter. In the taverns of Turbulence, you guarded your tongue and listened for the threat in every spoken word. The demi-masters hadn't the brains to hide their thoughts. Some delighted in causing offence, as if doing so could have no consequence.

And I have learnt nothing, despite their ceaseless yapping.

All the while Corbin, the grey bastard, was searching for clues, solving the mystery of Adelmus's murder without Daniel's help. It was worse than having to help Mother clean the mill-house while Jon and Father worked the sails.

He needed to piss.

The house of office was several corridor lengths away. He reached for the chamber pot under his bed and emptied himself. As he looked down at his manhood, he noticed a softness about his stomach that looked suspiciously like the beginnings of fatness. He cursed Corbin to the land of the dead and back and launched into his drills. He worked his way through the Brotherhood's system of grips, wards, evasions and flourishes. Every punch and kick felled an imaginary prosecutor.

Sweating and exhausted, his temper subsided. There was no point in going to bed; broken sleep was worse than getting none at all, and it would be dawn soon. He knuckled the sides of his eyes and watched the geometric mouldings of the ceiling blur. A thick envelope lay on his writing desk. Its seal was the colour of dried blood and stamped with the henge icon of the Verge.

My contract.

He supposed he ought to read it, however pointless that might be. It would start to look suspicious if he left it uninspected forever. He broke the wax and withdrew a loaf of papers inscribed on the headed paper of the Honourable Company of Cunning.

The letter of welcome from Chairman Gleam was banal. The conditions of his new employment were lengthy and printed in a type almost too small to read. One detail stood out; his stipend was two hundred pounds a year, less the cost of his materials and lodgings, to be held on account at the Convergence. It was a ridiculous sum of money. Daniel doubted a magistrate earned so much. He would lend it to Jon, after the mission was over, if he was allowed to keep it. Finally, there was a schedule of employment.

It said that he had been assigned to the workshop for his first week of paid work, making votive offerings and the like.

He knew that already, had spent several days working with some of the more hopeless demi-masters. Was it a punishment for something, he wondered? His carousing? Maybe his chivalry towards Miranda? Had Gleame arranged it to keep him out of the way of the real talent? It didn't matter either way. He wasn't at the Verge to learn the cunning arts; he was there to solve a crime.

The problem was, the way things were, that wasn't going to happen.

Corbin be damned, Daniel thought. If the bastard wouldn't let him help, he would have to find his own way to prove himself. Where to start?

I must think like a censor. Nothing was forthcoming. *I should pray to the All-seeing for insight, trust the gods to guide me . . . Gods help me! I'm turning into my brother.*

Daniel raised his hands and brought them together like a pair of wings. As he did so two ideas combined into one, gripped him. He smiled wryly and thanked He-who-sails-the-wind. If that was providence in action, it was a subtle thing indeed, but wherever it had come from, he now had a plan.

I am not yet a censor, and that gives me one advantage over Corbin, he thought. The Verge's diminutive temple with its conical glass steeple lay in the mess of the atrium, confined to a corner like a wayward child. If Corbin could not talk to the godsworn then that was a rock left unturned. When the week's work was done, Daniel's investigation would begin.

He changed his mind about the value of short sleep, and buried his head under his pillow.

TERMS OF ENGAGEMENT

The Drowner's Finger looked like a land for the dead, Miranda thought, albeit a pleasant one. Some driftwood, the sun-bleached skull of a whale and the blackened ribcage of a longship decorated the small promontory that cowered under the Convergence's leaden walls. They helped to keep the salt and sea spray at bay.

The garden's centrepiece was a natural spring ringed with stout oak posts and bedded with smooth pebbles of Blue John, purple and gold. According to Master Somney, it was the work of ancient men, each stone the culmination of a hazardous pilgrimage. The purpose of those journeys had been lost in time but the slow accumulation of ritual and superstition had made the pool a superior source of magic. The greater part of its power had been drained in the construction of the walls that towered above them. Now it served, like a retired warhorse or obsolete artillery piece, as an instrument of training and practice.

Every place at the pool's edge was taken. Miranda waited impatiently for her turn.

It could be worse, she thought. *It was more crowded yesterday.* Of the forty or so demi-masters who had arrived with her, only two dozen remained. Lloyd was gone, Bartholomew as well, neither one expelled but rather having gone of their own free choice. A few days of manual labour, the indignity of shared accommodation, and the revelation of what mastering the cunning would entail had been enough for them.

Miranda was mystified by their irresolution. What had they expected? The Convergence was a place of industry, not a school. Every day that they received a stipend and did not invest magic, the masters were losing money. It was a state of affairs that would not be tolerated a moment longer than necessary.

The demi-masters at the water's edge chopped the air with ungainly hands, attempted gibberish incantations. They were nervous, of being seen to be foolish, of a million rules unknown, and so they stuttered and stumbled over the unpronounceable. *Pathetic*, Miranda thought. How could they expect to bend magic to their will when they couldn't even control their own mouths and bodies?

Somney watched from a distance. The scowl on his face confirmed her assessment. These young adults had been thrown into a world where the route to success had to be found, not followed. Cosseted upbringings had left them ill-suited to the task. Miranda closed her eyes. The constructs she had memorised whirled inside her mind. Crisp cubes and cuboids, pyramids, cones, prisms, cylinders and spheres jostled for attention.

Three young masters practised amongst the neophytes. They were an altogether different matter. Watching them at work was a lesson in itself. They moved gracefully, muttering numinous incantations, movements aligned to the magic. She could see that too, dimly, or at least sense it in some way. Its presence ebbed and flowed from one area to another, evading the wills of the masters like an unwilling partner at a dance. Anticipating its next move seemed to be the art of the game.

The masters' dress was as outlandish as their exercise. The first, a brooding type, seemed to have made a fetish of nature. He wore a robe of leaves and a crown of mistletoe and ivy, and stank like the countryside. *Organic.* She thought his approach a cliché, like something from a child's story, boring and obvious.

The second was the most beautiful man she had ever seen. He wore only a loincloth and every one of his gestures ended in a display of perfectly aligned muscle. Watching him was a guilty pleasure. She tried not to stare.

The final master had put out his eyes, or else had persuaded someone else to do it, and recently. His face was wrapped in gauze, its edges steeped with blood. A week ago, she would have been disgusted; now her revulsion was tinged with an admiration for the dedication of the act, his total commitment to the craft.

Master Somney called a rotation, and Miranda nervously took a place at the water's edge. She stood between two posts, waist high and weathered, between Nathan and the master who looked like a shrub. This close to the water she could see a sparkling cold light, not on its surface but just above it.

Wild magic — and she could see it with bare eyes.

She glimpsed two newts. They seemed to fly in the limpid water, like courting dragons.

It begins.

She started with a prism, a shape simpler than a cube, but somehow more impressive. For her ritual, she had devised something between a dance and a signalman's code, pieced together from the esoterica of her studies. To every pronation of the palm and extension of the elbow, beckoning and sway of the waist, she had assigned a tone and theme; major or minor, flat or sharp. Together they formed a dance that was also a song. It was a secret language; a complete work that bordered on genius. She knew it instinctively and revelled in the confidence that it gave her.

She began to weave a pattern with her hands, singing and stamping out the rhythms that she sensed around her, held the image of the prism in her mind and believed it to appear before her. It was hard to distinguish the exact moment when reality succumbed to her imagination, because it happened with so little effort, but it did — and the faintest outline of her perfect shape hung in the air before her, persisted without effort.

Miranda shrieked with delight.

She threw more shapes into the air, each simple but assured. Before long, a collection the pride of any geometer hung before her. She looked around. Master Somney was watching her intently. As she caught his eye, he signalled that she had done enough, and that her practice time would soon end.

It was a surprise. It seemed to Miranda that she had been working for only a few minutes. Yet the sun hung lower in the sky. With a wave, she disassembled what she had made, watched the sharp-edged forms collapse and dissipate like gossamer in a storm.

The demi-masters around her were struggling to construct anything coherent. The sun warmed her face, and the salty taste of the sea brought to her mind the summer days in the duchess's garden at Baembra.

All was well in the world.

It was time to try her experiment.

She imagined a rose, or rather the idea of a rose. She supposed that idea to be a single point and to that idea she began to attach associations: colour and shape, scent, romantic fancies, each described with mathematical precision. The phantom of a shape began to form in front of her. It didn't look anything like a rose, more like a dandelion, or a sea urchin, but its form was strong. She sensed a melodious whispering from the magic, like a choir just out of earshot.

"Stop messing with my work," Nathan said angrily. Miranda's rose-map was absorbing the magic around itself, suffocating his feeble efforts.

"I'm sorry, I'm doing it all wrong," she lied, and dismissed her experiment with a motion. She had gone too far in the structuring of it, and didn't want the others to understand what she was doing or to copy her. They couldn't anyway. They weren't smart enough. She looked around. Lavety was staring at her in a certain way. Wickedly. Thin-lipped. So were the rest of his clique.

Of course. Dinner is awaiting.

Somney announced that the training was over and called Miranda to him as she was leaving the garden.

"Fine work, even if you got a little muddled towards the end. Don't stop practising. It'll be the real thing before you know it." Over his shoulder, Miranda saw Big Albert applauding discreetly.

●

"Do you enjoy sleeping with men?" Miranda asked with a twinkle in her eye. Lavety cleaned his teeth with his tongue, took another swig of wine and tossed his monogrammed napkin over his barely touched meal.

"You refer to my accommodation, I suppose. I paid my roommate to take an empty bunk in another room. I sleep alone."

"That must have been expensive." Lavety shrugged and waved at their surroundings.

The hall in which they dined had been prepared beautifully. Perched high above the kitchens, its arched windows, delicate by the standards of the Convergence, had been dressed in flowing drapes. A small orchestra played somewhere out of sight — or maybe it was a device. That was an interesting idea. Wreaths of fresh autumn flowers covered the twenty-foot expanse of table that separated Miranda from her host. Whatever message Lavety was trying to send, he had spared no expense. At least he hadn't paid for dancing dogs or jesters, Miranda thought. She hated both.

"You chose beautiful flowers," she said.

"Forgive me for speaking plainly, Miranda, but I am a busy man."

"Hurry all you like. A book deserving of my attention awaits in my chamber."

"That is the heart of the matter."

"My chamber?"

He chuckled and pointed at that which she carried beneath her head. "If I sought the favours of your body, I would have approached Her Grace directly."

"How romantic."

"It is your work here that concerns me."

"You want me to help you with your studies?"

"No, I want you to cease yours."

Lavety stared at his bejewelled knuckles disinterestedly. It was quite an act, Miranda thought, to appear bored after a request like that. *Impressive even.*

"Surely you do not fear competition from a lady?"

He scowled. "I am no fool, Miranda; I know how clever you are. I had the university send me your examination papers."

"You did?"

"And your work on the Drowner's Finger. I saw what you were doing. It is time for you to leave."

"And if I will not?"

"I am prepared to make a substantial donation. Pay monies directly to your estate."

"I belong to the duchess. Anything that you give to me belongs to her."

"And the support of my family is of utmost importance to her cause."

There was no clever parry or riposte to thwart that sharp truth. "She is grateful for it," Miranda replied, eyes downcast.

"I have a younger brother who prefers the company of men in all ways. He is gentle and discreet. He could be made available to you for marriage. Thereafter you could both live as you wanted."

"I am here by Her Grace's command."

"Nobody can command you to master the cunning, and the Convocation of Masters will never elect a woman to their ranks."

"If that is true, you have nothing to fear," she said miserably.

"I have no fear. But if and when a promotion to master becomes available, it must be mine."

"By what right?"

"Miranda, the orphanage is a worthy institution. The wards also. The existence of your kind protects the North from falling into unworthy hands and salves Her Grace's soul. Nonetheless, an orphan cannot take the place of a Lavety. That is impossible."

Miranda arranged her silverware neatly on her plate and folded her spotless napkin into a triangle. "Lord Lavety. Thank you for inviting me to dinner, it was delightful, but I am feeling a little unwell and must return to my chambers."

It wasn't entirely untrue. She rapped on the table and her chaperon pulled back her chair.

"Miranda, you are not welcome here, amongst these men. Why put up with the indignity of it?"

"For the sport of it," she replied, with as much gaiety as she could muster.

He looked at her queerly. "Whatever happens after this, do not say that I did not warn you."

●

A grotesque number of stairs lay between Miranda and her room, good exercise and more than enough time to worry. What if the Lavetys did petition Her Grace, ask for Miranda to stand aside for the sake of their son's advancement? What would Mother decide? It would be a tough choice.

She bit her lip.

Miranda had done good work at the pool, and it had been noticed. The idea that rewards and recognition would come in due course was comforting and, like most comforting thoughts, a falsehood. Childish. Lavety had unwittingly alerted her to what needed to be done. A part of her mind was already set to the aggrandisement of her progress. To being noticed.

Something else bothered her. Not just the burning in her thighs. What had Lavety meant when he said that he had seen what she was doing? It was easy to understand why he felt threatened by her presence, but why had he looked at her so oddly when she had left him.

She entered her room and it was as if she had fallen backwards into a well. Her stomach plunged, and her surroundings became as dark as the deepest dungeon, despite the candles that burnt brightly on the walls.

The duchess and her governess dangled before her, hanged from the ceiling side by side. Thick ropes stretched their bent and broken necks. Wet hair curtained their faces. The skin of their hands and feet was grey. Miranda turned to flee but the door through which she had just entered was gone, replaced by a swirling maw of blackness, an oily wall of writhing limbs. The ropes creaked. Miranda turned. In unison, the corpses lifted bowed heads. Their eyes were the colour of rancid milk.

The duchess cried out. Her tongue lolled green between her yellow, bloodstained teeth. Miranda screamed. The governess smiled benevolently.

"Stupid bitch," she said, with the voice of a man. Miranda screamed again. Every insult or hurt she had ever endured, real or dreamed, was repeated in a diabolical chorus. Screams raced to tear themselves from her throat. She could not think.

"Bitch. Orphan. Dirt." As they railed against her, the corpses hitched their legs like marionettes and thick streams of blood poured from between them. Miranda retched. The thick blood soaked her bed, splashed her desk, poured onto the floor. The crimson torrent rose to her ankles.

For some reason that brought her to her senses.

She became calm. *This is sick*, she thought, *awful and stupid, wanton, juvenile and sadistic, but it isn't real*. She closed her eyes, put her hands over her ears and waited. After a few minutes, the chaos in her mind ended.

She dared to look. Her room was pristine. Without hesitation, she went to the whistle-tube by her writing desk and called for a messenger.

●

There was a knocking at her door, which meant Edmund had come quickly. Miranda opened it, relieved to see him.

He dropped to one knee.

Miranda gawped at the embarrassing genuflection and checked that nobody in the corridor was watching. *Mister Sutton truly knows nothing of manners*, she thought. It might have been amusing on a different day.

"Arise and enter, please," she said.

"I came as quickly as I could." He prostrated himself, pressed a cheek flat against the floor. That was beyond embarrassing, and she began to wonder if he was party to Lavety's cruel joke.

"What are you doing?" she asked icily.

"Looking for a trigger." He got to his feet. "Nothing mechanical. It was probably heat, or light. Can I see the device?"

Miranda pointed vaguely at the tiny contraption on her writing table and returned to her favourite place, the windowsill, draped herself in a woollen throw and tucked her knees under her chin.

Daniel inspected it closely. "Four triangular plates, and in the centre . . . some kind of clockwork. A vial. And a little gold horn like a trumpet flower."

"I imagine it folds up into a pyramid," she said.

Edmund leaned over it, sniffed cautiously and wailed. The shock of his cry cost Miranda her balance and she feared a plummet into the atrium. Edmund stood stock still, his shoulders bunched, eyes squeezed tight and fists clenched into white balls.

"Dogs' cocks," he shouted, trembling as tears rolled down his cheeks. After a few seconds, he relaxed a little, blew hard through pursed lips. "By the gods. That was awful."

He pinched the bridge of his nose and blew a shot of snot onto the floor. It was ungentlemanly in the extreme.

"What happened?" Miranda asked.

"Hallucinations." He dug his fingers into his brow as if to gouge the memory of them out of his head. "I guessed that some alchemical vapour was involved in the trap. There must have been a little left in the device. The last of the evidence is up my nose. That was stupid of me."

That was when she regretted having called for him.

Edmund was the only half-friend she had in the Verge, or at least the only one she was willing to share this incident with, and she wanted comforting, a friendly voice, not to play a game of censors. *I will ask him to leave, politely.* She twisted from her perch and found herself in his arms.

The surprise of it paralysed her. He tucked her head gently under his chin, and embraced her like a brother. She allowed herself to accept the warmth of his comfort and then realised, to her surprise, she wanted to hold him too. But by the time she had decided to put her arms around him, he had already stepped away.

"I can't imagine how terrible a full dose must have been." His face clouded with anger. "Do you know who did this?"

"Lavety," she said.

Edmund stood, ruminating. *Not again*, she thought, *I can practically hear the cogs whirring.*

"No, it wasn't. At least not without help. I can't enter the Masters' Quarters without an invitation, and neither can he, and there's no way Lavety built that trap on his own. A master did this, or at least one was involved."

It was hard to dispute his logic, even if he was wrong. "Lavety, Talon or some other bastard I've never heard of. What difference does it make, really? None of them cares about what I can do. They all want me gone."

"I don't want you gone," Edmund said, "and neither does Somney. I think he likes you." She glared at him in silence. "Anyway you can't go. You're the best by far. Everyone knows it, even if they won't admit it. Cunning's your calling."

"My calling?" she snapped. "What could someone like you possibly know about that?"

He looked at her as if she were a child having a tantrum. "It's obvious," he said calmly.

"I'm sorry."

"Don't worry, it's normal. You've had a fright. It's better this way. If you're angry at me."

"Thank you."

"I'll deal with Mr Lavety." There was something odd about the way he said it, flat and cold and with a look in his eyes, dangerous, like a razor left unattended. For an instant, she felt a little afraid, for Lavety, and for herself.

"No," she said, "don't even think about it. The Lavetys are powerful and I have no proof. That little horror was meant to provoke me, so I shall do nothing, tell no one. If anyone mentions it, I shall tell them that I laughed, that their prank bothered me not at all." He looked disappointed.

Her chin jutted proudly.

Edmund raised an eyebrow. "Fair enough," he said, "but keep your door locked, and your window. Who knows how far they'll go."

He still seemed to be brooding on what had happened to her as he left. His words stayed with her.

'Cunning is your calling. It's obvious.'

She wondered what her governess would think about that.

THE STRAIN OF THE YOKE

A shove of Kareem's pole sent the punt gliding towards a floating dock of planks and barrels. Overhead a man stood in a crow's nest lashed to one of the wide stone pillars that supported the cistern's roof. Jon supposed he was a guard; he was armed with a pike fourteen foot long and steel-tipped, but his eyes were closed and he leaned against his weapon as languorously as a drunkard propped up by a lamp-pole.

"Soldier!" Kareem shouted.

The man's lobster-pot helmet clanked against the shaft of his weapon as he convulsed to attention. He saluted Kareem with the enthusiasm of a treadmill donkey and offered Jon the haft of his weapon. Jon grabbed it and pulled the punt to dockside.

"Report to me at the end of your watch." Kareem cast a stern glance upwards, tethered the boat and set off into the ramshackle encampment that hung in the darkness. Jon shared a look with the watchman and followed after.

The route took them from platform to platform, float to float, across precariously balanced planks and untrustworthy rope bridges. Jon moved slowly, nervously watched his steps and the swirl of water below.

The shantytown was a hive of activity. Men worked iron, faces glowing red in the light of a makeshift forge. In another place, women carved printing blocks by candlelight. A line of derelicts waited to be served from a foul-smelling cauldron of stew. They passed a veteran with a sea-lion moustache who demonstrated the manufacture of firebombs. He looked old enough to have fought in the War of Edicts. The fellow made a joke and his students guffawed.

If the business of the encampment was deadly, its atmosphere was that of a festival. Everywhere they went Jon heard talk of rebellion and Barehill's name.

He was at the centre of it all, sat at a ring of benches set around a brazier, lecturing a small group of earnest-looking fellows, puffing at his pipe and asserting his finer arguments with its stem. He still looked young and untested, but down in this place Jon noticed an edge to his manner that he had somehow missed before. The idea that the boy was an imposter seemed fanciful now.

The censors will be pleased, Jon thought, and felt his stomach tighten.

Here, the sweet smoke of rose charcoal scented the air.

"Take a pew, big man. You'll get your chance when the boss is done," Kareem said, and whispered something to Barehill. He smiled and, without a break in the rhythm of his speech, signalled his audience to make a space for the newcomer.

Jon squeezed between a young maid, whose dirty scarf failed to hide a cleft lip, and the traitorous godsworn who had let him into the temple of the Devourer.

"I weep at the perilousness of our situation," Barehill continued, "how close our country stands to ruination. Some claim that all men will benefit from magic eventually — the rich first of course." There were chuckles from the audience. "They say that one day there will be machines for everyone. I fear no greater prospect."

The crowd eagerly awaited Barehill's explanation.

"Don't listen to me, listen to one another." Barehill singled out an elderly wastrel with lank hair. "Herryk — that's your name, isn't it?"

"Aye," the man replied, proud to have been remembered.

"Tell us how you came to be in this place."

"I was a lightsman on the canals for twenty years, sir. I attended the tunnel under Needwood Forest."

"Hard work — and dangerous, I imagine."

"I was attacked a few times, by smugglers and the like."

"How did the canal owners repay you for your bravery?"

Herryk's eyes glinted angrily. "They fitted the tunnels with glow-stones, said flames was unreliable, though none had ever gone out on my watch. Damn liars. They just didn't want to pay my wages. I told them that straight. They paid me my last and sent me on my way."

Barehill's pipe stem compassed the audience. "Imagine a future with no need for honest labour, where no skills are passed on from father to son. Where the elite decide what we learn and how we learn it. They say we should work with machines. The truth is they plot to replace us with them. What they offer is slavery in disguise."

Barehill pointed to the girl sat next to Jon.

"What about you, young maid? Tell us your story."

She spoke slowly and her voice slurred.

"My uncle told my pa that there was work for girls in the city, said the manufactory men would provide lodgings and pay twenty shillings for a year's labour."

"Was that true?"

"No sir. Uncle brought me to a manufactory, but they would not keep me. They said I was too slow with my hands. Uncle said I would have to earn my keep another way. He was the very worst of men. Every night he tried to ruin me." She began to sob silently.

Barehill dropped his head in shame. "Modern living brings out the worst in men."

Jon patted his hand awkwardly on the girl's shoulder. It was a sad story, he thought, and he pitied her, but Barehill was wrong to think that modern living was to blame. The worst in men needed no excuse to make itself known.

Barehill drew deeply on his pipe, concentrated on its bowl as if he communed with some hidden devil hiding in the flames of the pipe-weed.

"And why does the Wise Council allow these things?" he said. "I swear to you it is the rottenest, wickedest and most tyrannical government that ever existed. They want to turn us into little things, creatures of fear controlled by the few, more like ants than people."

"What must be done?" the girl called out. Barehill stood.

"The roguish ministers of the Wise Council play into our hands. Their fortunes stand upon our misery. Their detestable policies forge a bond of necessity between the people. We see it every day; feel the mood on the streets turn in our direction. The citizenry begin to feel the strain of their yoke. We are the Freeborn. We have been chosen by history. It falls to us to lift it from their shoulders."

"Yes," some cried.

He speaks better amongst his friends, thought Jon, *and hidden in the dark.*

It was still a load of old bollocks.

Barehill turned to him, as if a reader of minds.

"Not all are convinced. The middling folk, the bakers, the farriers, do not know on which side they stand. Whether to follow greed or conscience. What say you? Jon, the miller, a man neither rich nor poor." Jon bit his cheek. He didn't like it that his name had been mentioned, but if this was a test, he had no choice but to pass it.

"I've been honest all my life, law-abiding, yet my business has been ruined by magic. That cannot be right." That was something they could all agree on, and the ragged listeners nodded in appreciation of his brevity. With a creeping sense of dread, Jon realised that they wanted more from him.

"You should heed your master's words," Jon said and pointed at Barehill.

"I am no master, only a spokesman," Barehill pronounced. "We are the Freeborn, answerable only to ourselves."

Barehill signalled that his lecture had finished and his gaggle of wastrels dissipated into the camp, talking excitedly amongst themselves. He came to Jon while Kareem loitered in the background. The bowl of his pipe flared bright in the subterranean gloom.

"What do you want from me, Miller?"

"I begin to see the sense of your words," Jon said slowly. Barehill eyed him cynically.

"Been reading our pamphlets, have you?"

"Yes."

"You are a terrible liar, Jonathan Miller. I know why you're here."

Behind Barehill, Kareem slid his sword from its scabbard. Jon looked about, deciding which way to run, if he got the chance. There were armed men everywhere.

"It's for the same reason that all men come to me," Barehill continued, "because you begin to see that you have no other choice."

Kareem clicked his sword back into its sheath. He looked disappointed.

"So what do you want from me?"

"Money."

Barehill waved his pipe across the tents and shacks of the Holt. "Does this look like a bank to you?"

"I passed the soup kitchen — you live off scraps, your men are starving."

"Precisely my point."

Jon had the words planned, his explanation for coming. He took a breath first, but still he rushed the words. "I have a mill, I make flour. I could supply your army. If you tell me where to deliver it, we could make an arrangement."

"A dangerous business. Why would you take such a risk?"

"I told you already, I need the money."

Barehill searched his eyes. "There's a price on my head. I have good reason to distrust men who need money — especially those who come so rapidly to my cause." He raised a finger and Jon looked up to see an archer in another crow's nest, notching an arrow to his bow. "You were not a rebel last week. Not even a prisoner of the Evangelicy would convert so quickly. There's something you're not telling me."

"If I cannot pay him by the end of the week, Peacock Matthew will take my mill."

"The truth! Hail Abjemo!" Barehill clasped his palms excitedly together in parody of an Evangelist.

Jon warded himself from evil with the sign of the eye. Barehill laughed.

"Just a turn of phrase. I am no believer in the 'One God', though I'm sure some would love to add heresy to the list of my offences. It's fortunate for me that you really do need the money, because I really do need to feed my men." He made a signal to Kareem, who began to stoke something in the fire beneath the brazier.

"Before we do business two things must happen."

"Yes?"

"First you must swear to keep my secrets."

"On my life."

"No, not your life; I have that already. On what matters most to you. On the Mother and the Father. On all of the gods. On the lives of your family. On your mill. On your honour. You must swear these things before the All-seeing."

Kareem rolled his eyes at all the god-talk, but it made Jon's blood run cold. What Barehill demanded — that would be a terrible oath to break.

"Ready?" Barehill asked.

The day was turning into a nightmare. *If the gods have brought me to this moment*, Jon thought, *it must be for a purpose.*

He made his promises.

Kareem approached with a taper.

"Now you must take our mark. Become one of us."

Jon realised it wasn't a taper that Kareem carried. It was a brand.

"Bare your chest."

The symbol that glowed in the metal was a shovel clasped in a fist. Jon beheld it with horror.

The eyes of watching Freeborn glinted around him in the darkness. The archer drew his string tight. *The censors will understand*, Jon told himself, *when I explain.*

He untied his shirt, held Kareem's eye, grunted through his teeth as his skin was scorched. The air filled with the stench of burnt meat. Barehill handed him a bottle of clear spirit. Jon drank deep, splashed the wound and cried out.

❂

Barehill's tent was small and dark, no grander than the rest. Maybe that was the point. He took a puff from his pipe and tilted his head in the direction of Kareem, who waited outside.

"Some of my men warn me not to deal with you. They think you're trouble, a stranger, maybe a spy. The brother of a censor."

"Daniel fled the seminary. He isn't even an aspirant any more."

"Maybe. Or maybe that is what Magistrate Lang would like me to believe. Lang is a devious man."

"My brother isn't devious. He lives life like the bolt from a crossbow."

"Well then, it's a good job that the decision falls to me. Our numbers swell and a poor army marches on soup alone. A good general knows when he must take risks and I know a desperate man when I see one. I will buy as much flour as you can make. A tunnel runs to Turbulence, with an exit near to your mill. I will have my men dig a supply shaft so that we can take your deliveries unseen. Shall we talk terms?"

Jon wondered why he hadn't thought about bargaining with Barehill before. *Maybe I never expected to get this far.* But he slipped easily into the comfortable rhythm of commerce.

"I'll need payment in advance, every month, to buy the grain. Quality strains that will keep in this damp."

"How much money?"

"Eight pounds each week, for a ton. You'll get four hundred good loaves from that. Feed a hundred men."

"Thirty pounds a month. No more."

"Agreed." Barehill shook Jon's hand vigorously, and Jon was pleased with the terms for all of the second it took him to remember that he did not intend to honour them. *The moment I'm out of this hole, straight to Bromwich Seminary.*

Barehill whistled for Kareem.

"Take Jon to the treasury and fetch thirty pounds. Help him carry it back to the mill, and assemble a gang to start on the new tunnel."

Kareem spat on the floor. "You're the general."

Jon followed Kareem to the edge of the shantytown. Huddled Freeborn regarded him with curiosity and suspicion. He pulled up his collar, stooped his head and hoped not to be recognised. After the censors had dispersed these miscreants, some might seek revenge. He needed to be careful.

They came to a crossing made of two ropes, one underfoot and one overhead, that extended into the pillared darkness. Kareem trod the tightrope with ease, passing the other rope from hand to hand in a fluent rhythm. Jon wobbled his way across. It took them to a haphazard breach in the cistern's wall, a small room, rough-hewn from the clay and supported by wooden posts and cross-braces. Inside, buckets full of copper halfpennies and farthings sat amongst open-topped barrels full of swords. Freshly oiled guns were racked on the walls. That was something else to warn the censors of, when the time came.

"Make sure you count it right," Kareem said.

On her knees, Laila was busy scooping coins from the buckets onto a set of scales with a trowel. She was dressed all manly in breeches and a corseted shirt. Kareem rested against a wall, his eyes planted firmly on her arse. Jon watched the money pile up. There was a lot of it.

"Laila," Jon said. Her auburn hair flicked across her face as she turned to him and his heart beat disobediently.

"Barehill doesn't need a guard for his treasure," Kareem said. "It's common coin, well handled. Fun to imagine what you could do with it though." He winked at Jon as he picked his teeth with his thumbnail.

"Whoreson," Laila returned casually. Jon chuckled, watched as she filled the strongbox to the brim with the coins she had weighed. It was a handsome thing with a complicated lock, the iron plates painted with red flowers.

"Thirty pounds in coppers." Laila wiped the sweat from her brow. "More than most families see in a year."

Kareem handed Jon his walking stick, loaded a wheel-lock pistol, keyed back its hammer and stuffed the gun into the back of his trousers. Laila grabbed a dagger belt from the wall and strapped it around her thin waist. Weapons made Jon nervous, but what had he expected in the company of villains?

The men lifted the strongbox together; Kareem strained at its front, holding its handle behind his back with both hands, while Jon held the rear with one. A rowing boat waited for them outside. They carefully lowered the treasure into its hull, and set off for the tunnels that led back to Turbulence.

THE MYSTERY OF THE GODS

The pillar of white light, captured by the temple's glass steeple and projected through the oculus embedded in the apex of its dome, blazed so bright it seemed solid. It was a wonder — the glory of the gods made manifest. Daniel raised his arms above his head, made the broad circle of He-who-lights-the-way, and reminded himself that he had not come to pray.

The Verge's temple was unlike any he had seen before, a single chamber without a transept, its inner sanctum hidden behind the central pillar of a double arch. The entire width of back wall was a crude carving of a fish — or whatever creatures had filled the sea before them. Daniel frowned in incomprehension. The place seemed ancient beyond measure. He called out and his voice reverberated emptily around the room. He went to the altar and knelt in front of the sun idol that rested on its rainbow cloth.

A godsworn entered the room, his footsteps loud and clumsy. He was an old man, clean shaved and olive skinned. A raven-black ponytail braided with gold rings lay across his shoulder and a gold disc dangled from the menat that circled his neck. He brandished an ivory wand with a taper wound over its end and swept around the room lighting thick wax candles that lined the walls in small iron baskets.

"What is that carving?" Daniel asked.

The godsworn stiffened at the sound of his voice.

"A pagan relic," he replied in a whine, "a depiction of the Dreamer, carved hundreds of years before the truth of the Rational Pantheon reached our isles."

"He-who-sleeps-in the-ocean?"

The godsworn pursed his lips. "The primitives called him by a different name. This island has always been a magnet to the ignorant."

Daniel raised an eyebrow at the boldness of the claim.

"You cannot mean the masters of cunning? Surely they are the opposite of ignorant."

"If the world is a dream of the gods and all of our experiences illusion, how is it within man's gift to meddle with those dreams?" Daniel disapproved of the oblique response. Maybe the godsworn was an idealist, the kind of man naturally inclined to radicalism and mischief.

More candles flickered into light as the godsworn continued his task. When he realised that Daniel was not about to leave, he spoke again.

"Have you come to make an offering?"

"Will you aid me?"

"You wish to barter with the divine, do you? Is the scent of a promotion in your nostrils? Have you caught the pox from a serving girl?"

Daniel laughed. If there was a god of rudeness, then this man served it.

"I was hoping that you could lead me in prayer. I seek guidance from the Father." He wanted the man's attention, and no godsworn could refuse such a request.

"Why?"

Daniel disguised his surprise as deliberate hesitation, as if choosing his words carefully.

"I'm not sure that I belong here."

"I could say the same myself."

"I've a difficult decision to make."

"Go on."

"My family insist on my presence — they see it as the route to a greater fortune — but I find the Convergence a cruel and godless place." Daniel thought of the prank played on Miranda.

The godsworn focused his attention on Daniel fully, for the first time, appraised him with a searching stare.

"Forgive me, son-in-dream. It's usually only the jealous and the greedy who trouble this place."

"Then my concerns are justified?"

The godsworn joined him at the altar, placed his wand in its holder. "Do you have a prayer in mind? Maybe something from *The Enigmatic Book of the Netherworld?*"

"The First Catechism," Daniel said.

"Of *The Book of Gates?* Every child in the Unity knows the words." Daniel tried to look hurt, gave the man a plaintive look. "*The Book of Going Forth* is its proper name. Surely you don't need me to lead you through the first prayer?"

"My brother used to read it to me; I find it comforting," Daniel said truthfully.

"Very well then, a prayer against schismatic thinking. Let us submit to the Mystery of the Gods."

The godsworn knelt beside Daniel and took the disc from his neck. He struck it with his flaming wand and it chimed like a gong. Soft sparks showered the altar.

"What are their names?"

"None shall be given," Daniel attested.

"What is their scripture?"

"It shall not be written."

"Who are their prophets?"

"We shall suffer none to live."

"Let your deeds match your words." The godsworn set down his wand and returned the disc to his neck. "It is done. What's your name, son-in-dream?"

"Edmund Sutton."

"Think upon on this, Edmund. When your soul is weighed in judgement, will a greater fortune avail you then?"

"Do you think I should abandon my position then? Is the Convergence such a bad place?"

"The cunning arts were forbidden for a thousand years. Do you imagine that was for no reason?" The godsworn spoke slyly, Daniel thought, like an animal circling a baited trap.

"What reason could there be?"

The godsworn sighed. "What is it all for? These luxuries and strange devices. How will they help men to unburden their souls?"

Daniel nodded piously, considered his position. The godsworn was no friend of the Verge, but seemed too open in his opposition of it to be a true enemy — unless that was his trick. Daniel wasn't sure what it all meant, but at least he felt like a censor. He was *investigating*. It was a start.

"I would like to reflect on your wisdom and to discuss the matter with you further, once I have examined my conscience."

A deranged rattling filled the air as a monumentally wide man waddled into the temple. His robes glittered like fish scales and rattled like a chorus of bells or tambourines. *Obviously a master.* The godsworn directed the obese man towards a pew and turned distractedly back to Daniel. Both winced as the master sat down with a crash of cymbals. He pointed a chubby finger at Daniel.

"Leave us," the master said. "I have a private matter to discuss with this fellow."

"Of course," Daniel said. As he reached the temple's exit, he used a trick that Hernandez had taught him, threw the door open and ducked behind a pillar. As the slamming drew the god-sworn's eye, he dropped to his belly and crawled under a pew.

The godsworn's feet approached. Daniel silenced his breathing and watched the man stroll straight past and bolt the doors to the temple.

There was a monstrous rattling as the master stood.

"Bolb."

"I've come to make another offering."

The godsworn sighed. "It's the third time this week. You cannot expect the gods to be so hasty in answering, especially one absent from prayer for so long."

Bolb barked like a seal. It took Daniel a moment to realise that he was sobbing.

"I could help you better if you would share your burden, tell me what grieves you."

Bolb shook his head as if he were a child refusing dinner.

"Fear, guilt and sorrow; these are the burdens of all men. We have all done things of which we are ashamed." Bolb remained silent. "Then let us pray together, to the gods above and below."

Bolb tossed a handful of jewels onto the altar and knelt beside the godsworn.

"Father. Mother. All-seeing. Dreamer. Devourer. Judge. Help this poor soul recover what has been lost to him." Bolb flapped his arms above his head and around his body, praying for all he was worth.

Daniel watched the master's pleading. It was pathetic, desperate. He had seen it before, in men praying before their execution. It stank of guilt.

After a while, they stood. The godsworn released the temple door. Bolb exited, his face cast down with sorrow. The sombre clashing of his robe was like a dirge. Daniel waited until the path was clear, and hurried out after him.

The master had disappeared into the busy atrium but Daniel could still hear the chiming of bells above the ruckus. He ran into the throng of vendors and craftsmen in pursuit. The crowd made him wary, but he suppressed his instincts and pushed on. The rattling grew closer; Daniel guessed no more than thirty paces ahead. He slowed down and established the correct distance for shadow-work. A gap opened in the crowd and he saw a goatherd guiding his flock with a crook. Daniel heard the bells jangle at the necks of his beasts and cursed in frustration.

At a florist's stall, a plain maid was arranging lilies in a coppered flute.

"The master with the bells, the fat one, which way did he pass?"

She pointed towards the seaward side of the tower. "That way. You'd best hurry though; Bolb's not a patient type." Dan scoured the atrium, hunted with urgent determination, and though he was sure he could hear the master, just out of sight, he found no trace of him.

•

At the eighth hour of the night on the landward side, the Verge was inhabited only by wind and shadows.

The lock of the door clicked open. Daniel slipped his pick into his pocket and stepped into the solarium that exhibited the Verge's innovations. The hall was built into the outer walls of the tower and enclosed in a bubble of diamond-shaped panels of glass. In the dark of night, its scant illumination came from the blinking lights of strange devices that balanced on mahogany display stands within cabinets and vitrines.

He found the hekamaphone at the far end of the hall. Its horn was silver rather than bronze and the small glass phials within it were empty and unlabelled, but otherwise it was identical to the one he had seen in Lang's office. As he prepared the blood-water, Daniel wondered if it was possible to eavesdrop on a conversation between the devices.

He waited until the appointed hour and then tipped the drop into the open top of the glass. It seemed to fall in slow motion. The tiny ruby waves it sent racing to the side of the alembic slowed and then stopped dead, leaving perfect concentric circles vibrating in the water. The winds of oblivion began to snarl.

"Reporting," Daniel said in a low voice.

"Are we certain of privacy?" Lang replied, calm and alert.

"Alone, but not certain of it."

"Interesting. Make your report."

"I have delivered the package."

"How was it received?"

"Grudgingly."

"What duties have you been assigned?"

"Observation of the demi-masters."

"What else?"

"Nothing."

In the pause that followed, Daniel heard nothing but ghost noises.

"Tell me what you can."

"Corbin is concerned with the circumstances of the crime. He suspects that the deceased was somehow . . ." He struggled for the right word. ". . . involved?"

"What else?"

"I have discovered no signs of dissent or subterfuge amongst the demi-masters."

"Of course not, they arrived after the murder."

"A ward of the duchess is amongst them."

"Ward Miranda."

"She has enemies. I have gained her confidence."

"That is unexpected. Keep a respectful eye on her."

Daniel grinned. "Yes sir."

"Is that all?" Lang said. Daniel counted to three, under his breath.

"I have begun to investigate, on my own initiative."

"Without Corbin's consent?" Lang's displeasure was obvious.

Daniel's throat tightened. "A reconnaissance of the temple. The godsworn who serves there seems no friend of the Convergence."

"I did not ask you to investigate the godsworn."

"A master has been visiting him recently. He's made several visits since the murder, few or none before."

"What is your intuition?"

"It seems odd, too much of a coincidence. Maybe the gods guided him to me."

"The gods? Men's affairs are no more than cobwebs in their eyes. It takes a brave one to place his trust in them."

"Yes, sir."

"I ordered you to report on Corbin, not disobey him. What were you thinking?" Daniel had no answer. The hekamaphone crackled awhile.

"It's bad enough having one untamed censor in the Convergence. Make one more mistake like that and your mission is over. Do you understand?"

"Yes sir."

"Good. Now what is the name of this suspicious master?"

"Pendolous Bolb. I have learned that he's highly regarded as an artificer. He once constructed an automaton that could play the complete works of Sinistaru on a harpsichord and cornet."

"I know who he is; he built the mechanical owls that watch the border with Erdin. Not an obvious suspect, nor a man to be trifled with, but I will look over his file. Now tell me, what progress has Corbin made?"

"I have no idea. He hasn't spoken to me once since the day of my arrival."

"What? This whole situation is completely unacceptable. I will send a message to Corbin. He should learn to obey his superiors better."

"Yes, sir."

"Will you be able to access this instrument again?"

"I believe so."

"Next time you'd better have something useful to tell me."

The hekamaphone shuddered and fell silent.

THE HIDDEN MAKER

"You are about to witness the source of our power. I hope you are well prepared."

Prepared for everything except the waiting, Miranda though, as Master Somney's silver skullcap dipped out of view and the convoy of demi-masters shuffled to another ungainly halt. They had been descending for almost an hour now, through tunnels that led deep into the bowels of the island. The excitement of what was to come was greater than any Miranda could remember, but the journey of half steps was infuriating.

The party began to move again. To call it a convoy would be an exaggeration; only ten of the demi-masters who had crossed the causeway with her remained, mostly those who had achieved some success at the Drowner's Finger. *Including the one who set that trap in my room, the bastard Lavety.*

There were a few others, *too proud or stupid to leave of their own accord*, including Edmund, irrepressibly tenacious Edmund. She felt a little sorry for him. He had tried hard, when they had finally allowed him to train at the Drowner's Finger. The way he bit on his tongue while he concentrated was hilarious, but his efforts ranged from feeble to hopeless.

This is not the right time to be thinking about boys.

Miranda ran her hand along the wall beside her and closed her eyes. She felt the damp stone sliding under her gloved fingertips, recalled the construct she had spent a week fabricating.

It floated serenely above in her mind's eye, like a giant snow-flake or spider's web. She drifted around it, inspecting every angle with the anxious pride of a sculptor preparing a masterpiece for a public unveiling.

A triangular arch with the henge icon of the Convergence emblazoned on its keystone marked the end of the passage. The symbol was bold and abstract, a deliberate offence to tradition, nothing like the intricate heraldry of the nobles with its shields quadrant and beasts rampant.

The demi-masters emerged onto a paved ledge that jutted precipitously into the peak of a vast domed cavern. Spherical glow-stones on delicate silver pillars cast pools of light onto the jagged roof that curved only a few feet above. The strange illumination drained the colour from Miranda's tawny skin, turning it an unhealthy ashen grey. She felt the rock throb underfoot.

Master Somney stood at the edge and puffed out his chest, motioned to the crowd to face him and began to speak too loudly, as if he were trying to make himself heard over a commotion.

"Today will be the first practical test of your cunning. Your first opportunity to demonstrate the extent of your talent."

The more boisterous of the demi-masters whooped or cheered in agreement.

"That which lies below drives our profits and the prosperity of our land. It is my firm belief that those two fortunes, the Honourable Company's and the Unity's, are linked inextricably. I am old enough to remember the days when the Cunning operated alone and in secrecy. Back then the cliché of the magician in his fortified tower, or indeed the witch in her cabin, hidden in the woods, was true." He looked at Miranda.

"A cottage industry," Lavety quipped smugly.

"The old ways were restrictive and dangerous, the accumulation of magic a slow and tedious affair. We eked out small deposits with our cauldrons and grimoires, invested what we could in runes, enchantments and curses. Our own bodies were the conduits through which these transactions passed and the risks were terrible. If our cunning failed, magic would whiplash our souls as it turned wild and returned to its source. We ran the risk of becoming monsters, or worse! Disappearing. Spontaneously combusting."

Somney seemed for a moment to lose himself in the memory of friends lost to those perils.

"What are the risks today?" a demi-master asked worriedly.

"Inconsequential, if procedure is followed correctly," Somney said. "The Convergence is a new paradigm. The use of constructs removes our bodies and souls from the equation. We derive magic from a single shared resource. We have made its collection efficient. We can profit without taking personal risk. That is an unparalleled achievement in the history of man's endeavours."

The demi-masters nodded appreciatively. Miranda reserved judgement, and wondered where all the risk had gone.

"Before we progress I would like you to take a moment to appreciate the beauty of what we have created. Gaze into the abyss, but only for a moment, then continue onwards." Somney pointed towards a stairwell leading down. "And be careful at the edge; the fall is not survivable."

Miranda moved slowly, waited to peer down into the darkness.

Far below, at the base of the cavern, a circle of grey-blue standing stones topped with heavy lintels surrounded a dark lake. Huge lanthorns at the periphery of the cavern's gloomy expanse directed beams of light onto the henge, which in turn cast long shadows across the water. The arrangement resembled a giant eye, its iris black beyond black.

Miranda stared at the eye, and it stared back at her. An obscure radiance, like the sun behind a cloud, forced her to squint.

She felt the ledge trembling beneath her feet and steadied herself. A tumble over the precipice would deposit her directly into the centre of the lake and the idea of landing in that dark water was more terrifying than a certain death on the rocks to either side.

Her cheeks began to sting as if scorched by desert winds.

A train of yellow-robed figures, as small as ants, spiralled the lake, widdershins, like a clock running backwards. They seemed to be casting or placing within it objects whose nature was impossible to discern from so high above. Other men in extravagant costumes stood at the base of a few of the stones, at the water's edge, waved their hands in mysterious patterns. Her teeth began to rattle and she tasted metal and acid in her mouth. She counted the stones. There were twenty-three of them.

I am watching the masters at work, she realised.

Her hair began to singe.

"Enough!" Somebody pulled Miranda away from the edge. It took her a moment to recognise Somney. He searched her eyes. "You were compelled. I did not expect that."

"Compelled?" Miranda asked, startled by the slow realisation that she had momentarily lost control of her mind.

"Wild magic is devious. It can make a person lose track of time, one of the more subtle ways in which it evades capture. I'm sure you've read tales of sages who spent their lives obsessing over an apparently meaningless text. That's a related phenomenon." Somney checked her over as he spoke, as if looking for dangerous insects, stepped back seemingly satisfied with what he had not seen. "Your gums will bleed tonight, and your skin will darken and peel. Let your pain be your lesson. Now join the others."

Miranda realised that she was alone on the platform, and hurried on her way.

She rejoined them in a room that looked like a mortuary, buried deep within the cavern's walls and lined with deep shelves. A technician wearing a yellow gown, like the ones she had seen around the lake, stood on a box at the far end of the room, addressing the crowd.

". . . stop the magic messing with your soul. The size can be adjusted at the back."

Where is Edmund? Miranda found him pulling one of the lurid robes over his head.

"What did I miss?"

"You look like you've been chewing on bees. What happened?" She touched her lips. They were swollen. "The pout suits you. We're to put these on, and goggles, then line up by the door." He waved at the yellow robe laid out on the shelf before her.

It was identical to the one Edmund wore. Hooded and broad sleeved. As tailored as a sleeping bag. *Utterly hideous.* The scarf sewn into its collar was an intricate interlacing of alchemical symbols. *To protect the face*, she guessed. Wearing it, she would be indistinguishable from any of the other demi-masters.

She loosened her bodice for comfort. Dorian, the red-headed demi-master from Caistor, whistled at her wolfishly.

"Never seen a woman before?" Edmund shouted back. Miranda frowned; his chivalry was unnecessary and unhelpful. Dorian was a joke. How the foul-mouthed idiot of a demi-master had managed to structure a competent sphere in the Drowner's garden she could not imagine, but he wouldn't be leaving the Convergence any time soon.

She ignored them both and slipped the stiff garment over her ordinary clothes. The goggles were brass with amethyst lenses and a buckled leather strap. She tightened them to a fit impenetrably dark, then let them drop around her neck and joined the expectant queue of demi-masters at the armoured door.

"Clear," Somney shouted.

"Clear," the technician confirmed. He covered his face with his scarf and spun the door's hand-wheel.

The demi-masters emerged through another tunnel onto the floor of the cavern. The henge at its centre seemed distant from where Miranda stood, obscured as it was by wooden cranes, lanthorn stands and crowds of technicians who directed, monitored and recorded. Waggon-loads of ritual items emerged on a railed trackway to be collected by an endlessly circling troop of yellow uniforms. The men and machines operated quietly and efficiently, a perfectly coordinated whole.

"Welcome to the floor." Somney was almost shouting now. "The efficient division of labour means that the Convergence can accumulate more magic in one day than the druids and witches of our history did in their collective lifetimes."

Like a child pretending to be an owl, Somney made circles with his fingers and placed them over his eyes. "Please . . . behold, our Hidden Maker!"

Miranda pulled on her goggles.

There was an explosion in the centre of the cavern. The air around Miranda seemed to solidify and then splinter into shards at the speed of breaking glass. She flung her arms before her face and braced for the impact.

None came.

An impossibly loud roaring filled her ears and mind, yet she felt herself unharmed. It seemed impossible that she could have survived the rending. She slowly withdrew her face from the crook of her elbow, daring to hope that her colleagues had not suffered. It took a moment for her mind to adjust to the violence of what she saw.

A fountain of crackling energy erupted continuously from the dark lake at the centre of the cavern, looping back upon itself in a torus and being absorbed by the lintels of the standing stones. The energy was invisible except for where it touched the world, and at those points, nothing was as it should be. Time and space were broken.

She began to notice the shadows of men swaying against the ethereal flame and the strangeness of it all overwhelmed her. Against all reason, she ripped her goggles from her face and saw the world renewed. The chamber was undamaged. Technicians continued to work undisturbed. The demi-masters stood uninjured at her side. Some were cowering. Others seemed unaffected by the vision. She wondered if they could not discern it. She flipped the goggles back over her eyes and the maelstrom returned to view as shocking as before.

No explosion then, she thought, *just an irresistible revelation*. Miranda looked more closely, began to see details in the chaos: flares, coronas and delicate tendrils that escaped the tumult and wended into the walls of the chamber.

Master Somney led the shaken demi-masters closer towards the lake.

"Observe the exchange of offerings."

Miranda tracked the silhouette of a technician against the dazzling spectacle. He knelt at the water's edge, held aloft a sword bent double and set it to sink into the murk. It reminded her of the offerings that the ancient people of the Unity had made in groves and swamps in the days when they had worshipped the trees and the sky.

A shower of icy sparks flurried from the water's surface, as if a fire had been stoked. They whirled overhead and were absorbed into the spinning torus.

"An enormous amount of magic passes through this space. The liquidity is immense and we add to it continuously."

As they entered the ring of standing stones, the eye of the storm, the glare of the magic seemed to diminish. Miranda followed the others down a shallow flight of steps to the very lip of the basin. Chairman Gleame, Riven Gahst, Talon Turon and the birdman awaited, and they chatted as casually as if they were having tea.

Not one of them was wearing a protective outfit. Gleame was dressed in his white robes. Miranda was amazed by Gahst's corset; no lady at court had achieved so severe a constriction of the waist. Talon hung suspended from a web of cables strung across a steel frame. Cocooned in his rags he looked like the unfortunate victim of a giant spider. Geoffrey the birdman stood by his side, balanced on one leg and arms spread.

As awful as they were, Miranda thought, there was something magnificent about these men in their element. She had seen more than her fair share of barons and kings. The power that these men wielded was different: not ephemeral or dependent on the acquiescence of others, but a simple fact indivisible from their being.

Somney spoke again. "At this point you may be wondering why we do not require protection from the magic. The answer is simple — we have no need of it. As a master grows in cunning, magic becomes increasingly visible to him, and is held in check by his power-presence."

"The magic becomes afraid," Gahst said.

"That is a spurious conjecture, and not a view shared by our more profitable masters," Gleame said. "A better analogy would be the repulsion of iron by a magnet."

Gahst turned away with a bitter look.

"We are the shadow of the fisherman falling across a river. Swim into my net, little fishes," Talon clucked. Geoffrey jabbed his head forwards like a heron.

"Master Somney, please continue," Gleame said.

"Cunning will profit you greatly, but it requires aptitude and comes at a price. In the end, it is up to you to prove whether your presence at the Convergence is worthwhile. We will begin with a demonstration by Master Talon."

The demi-masters turned to face the suspended master as he began to recite a mantra of numinous vowels. He wobbled in his web as he chanted and its twisted cables seemed to amplify his voice. His breath became visible, addling the air like a heatwave, and stretched out across the water.

A square of faint, bright lines appeared as if being drawn by an invisible mathematician. New angles branched and turned and soon the ghostly outline of a ziggurat hovered before them. Talon's intonation shifted and the shape began to drift towards the geyser of magical energy. It dipped into the vortex and quickly filled with crackling motes. Talon fell silent and the shape, now alive with energy, drifted back towards them.

Miranda led the demi-masters in applause. The process had not seemed effortless, maybe the opposite, but Talon's artistry had been flawless. Tears of wonder softened her eyes. Then she remembered what Talon had said to her, about the incapable minds of women, and she blinked them away, ashamed.

A pair of technicians rushed to the side of the lake clutching a taxidermic marvel, a stuffed ape-child with cartoonishly wide eyes. Talon's construct twisted and shrank as he guided it through the air into a small opening in the curiosity's back. The technicians screwed tight a panel in its head and depressed the creature's eyes. It waggled its feet and they stood the creature upright, walked it away, head bowed, dull eyes fixed unseeing upon the ground.

"An excellent display, Master Turon," Gleame said.

"That device might just be a toy, but it was commissioned for no less than fifty pounds," Somney noted.

"Now that you have seen what we're cooking, who wishes to place his hands inside the cauldron?" Talon cackled and the web-frame buzzed with his excitement.

"Find out if you like the taste?" Gahst added sullenly.

Miranda held back. She knew that Talon's display had made the process look deceptively easy, and while he would not recognise her in the yellow uniform, she did not want to give him the satisfaction if she made the first attempt and failed.

A demi-master stepped forward.

"What should I do?" a muffled voice asked.

"Go home," Talon said.

"Maybe you could say something a little more helpful," Somney retorted.

Talon rolled his eyes. "There is no correct method; what matters is your intent. I use my voice — others wave their arms or dance like idiots. You must do whatever best suits the occasion and your mood."

"Observe the magic. Focus on how it reacts to your will," Somney added.

"Some see the act as sub-creation — akin to a god imagining a world," Gleame said.

"An idea attractive to the ego, but dangerous," Gahst said.

The brave demi-master faced the lake, motionless and silent. Miranda stared at the back of his yellow hood. For a minute, precious little happened and she began to shuffle her feet impatiently. Then a line appeared in mid-air, like water freezing slowly to ice. A box began to form, though its edges grew unevenly and the angles were incorrect, *like a drawing made in the dark*, Miranda thought. A corona blazed out from the torus to lash the incomplete shape and the novice jumped back, startled, yelped in frustration as his clumsy lines faded out of sight. Miranda thought she heard something like laughter, the distant mirth of a thousand invisible children.

"Not bad for a first attempt," Talon said, an eyelid drooping oddly.

Emboldened by the conspicuous failure, other demi-masters volunteered. The masters worked through the queue of yellow uniforms. As always, Miranda waited to be last. She wanted to see what she was up against.

The first formed a small cube. Although it only captured a few specks, he punched the air as if he had won a tourney, and was applauded roundly. Somney instructed him to dismiss the construct and its delicate lines scattered on the winds of magic.

The next tried a complicated structure that faded into nothingness as it collapsed under its own ambition, half completed. The next two failed to produce any effect at all. Miranda tried to discern which one was Edmund by the way they retreated from their failure. Oddly, those who had held to the back of queue had more success. They conjured simple shapes. One created a construct shaped like a bottle whose neck folded back into itself. It was confusing to look at, and it didn't capture any magic, but it made the masters laugh and Gleame patted the demi-master on the back as he stepped aside.

Then there were two.

The demi-master ahead of Miranda stepped forward and created a pyramid. Its lines appeared immediately and with the certainty of a fact. The masters glanced at each other in approval. It was impressive, in a traditional kind of way.

"What is your name?" Gleam asked.

"Lavety," the uniform replied, and the pyramid blinked out of sight. *Of course, it would be him*, Miranda thought, and prepared to do better. She stepped to the edge of the lake, closed her eyes and put her palms together as if praying.

"Work at your own pace," Somney advised.

Miranda reached for the creation in her mind. Her eyes flashed open and she faced the swirling storm, grabbed a fleck of magic with her will. She felt it tug against her, and was filled with a sense that she had chosen wrongly, that of all the thousands of tiny specks swirling before her she had chosen exactly the one that did not belong to her, that it would not work, that she was being irresponsible, meddling with something beyond her comprehension.

It was an obvious ruse on the part of the magic and she ignored the emotions.

She began to turn and sway, dancing with her hands. She drew the speck of magic into the centre of her vision and wrapped it in a tiny sphere, from which several lines grew, like the spines of a sea urchin. Another speck was drawn to each of these and encircled in turn, and so the structure grew. She began to see patterns in the swirling clouds of magic, to be able to predict where it would move next, and how it would try to evade her.

Her construct took on layers of complexity, grew ceaselessly. She became aware of a noise in the background, a voice urging her to stop. *Another ruse of the magic*, she thought, and ignored it. The work overcame her, absorbed her, obsessed her, and then suddenly it was done. Complete. A magnificent, lucent shape like a natural crystal filled the centre of the henge. It was exactly as she had imagined it.

". . . stop, stop," Gahst was shouting.

"It's done," Miranda said quietly. The cavern was silent. The eyes of every technician and master were fixed on her construct, or on her.

"Dismantle it immediately," Gahst ordered.

"Under no circumstances," Somney countermanded. "That construct could power a warship. It is worth at least ten thousand pounds."

Gleame addressed the cavern confidently. "Everyone back to work. Technicians, fetch a suitable container." He stepped to the edge of the lake to examine Miranda's creation more closely. "Fascinating. What is it?"

"My relationship with my governess."

"Explain," Talon said.

"A diagrammatic abstraction. Like an alchemical formula, or a family tree."

"The girl made it," Somney said to Talon, laughing.

"I can hear that from here," Talon replied. "I knew it was dangerous, allowing a woman into the Convergence."

"Then maybe you'll agree to forgo your share of the profit that this construct will bring?"

"Gentlemen, please," Gleame said. "Miranda, from which tome did you copy this idea? I am not familiar with it."

"It is based on Master Talon's theory of ritual, of creating complexity in the abstract. Human relationships are the most unnecessarily complicated things that I can imagine."

"You claim this idea as your own?" Talon scoffed.

A squad of technicians arrived carrying a large copper box on their shoulders. It was covered in levers, dials and strange symbols. They set it down and flipped open a lid in its top.

"We have not trained you for this. To transport the construct, you must reimagine its location," Somney said nervously. Miranda understood, gently willed her construct towards the aperture.

"What do I do now?"

"Release the construct," Somney said.

"How?"

"To invest a construct into a device you must forget it, forever."

Miranda's whole body trembled with the effort of concentration. The construct began to flicker. A few motes of magic escaped from it, and the torus sucked them back in. She tried to focus, to keep her creation stable. "What do you mean 'forget'? I can't just forget her."

"Yes, you can. Your ideas are entwined with the magic now. It will happen if you let it. All you need to do is let the construct go." Somney gestured at the device. He was telling the truth. Miranda could feel the magic tugging at her memories.

"I don't know."

"This is just one conception of her; you can have others, make a new one."

Tears wetted Miranda's face.

She had so many happy memories of her governess, shared fantasies and hopes. She had used all of them in her construct, turned soft sentiments to hard angles. Calculated her love. If only she had been given more warning, more time to prepare.

The needles on the dials on the side of the copper box began to edge into the red. It started to hum violently.

"It's falling apart," Somney shouted. "The construct cannot hold. If you mean to continue, do it now."

"I can't," she sighed.

Talon was right, she realised. She was weak. Soft. The metal of the copper box began to squeal. The technicians around it turned to run.

Then Miranda saw that Talon was grinning absurdly in the middle of his metal spider's web, saw the eyes of Lavety standing beside him. All of them were laughing at her, on the inside. She knew it.

Damn you all.

She let a lifetime of affection fly free from her mind like doves uncaged. An ecstatic rush of power filled her veins. For an instant, she felt that she was a giant, the size of the moon, saw the masters and demi-masters as little things, toy people, to be crushed in her palm or stomped underfoot.

Then she heard a noise like cannon shot and the sound of men screaming.

Her world turned to blackness and she knew no more.

COMPLICITY

Laila led the way through the tunnels, her box lanthorn held low so that Jon and Kareem could see their feet. The way was branching, featureless, earthen and too low for upright walking. Jon strained to control the strongbox that swung between them. His back and fingers hurt. He wondered how he would explain the route to the censors, once he was free.

"How do you remember the way?"

"I wander the tunnels, when I want to be alone," Laila muttered.

"Who made them?"

Kareem chuckled with derision. "They are the workings of the Devourer, according to that idiot godsworn. He calls these tunnels the belly of the beast. I guess that makes us its shits."

Jon would have made a sign if his hands were free. Instead, he said a little prayer and wondered what kind of folk might have trod the depths in the time before Bromwich existed.

They came to a ladder that accessed the basement of a derelict house, wrestled the strongbox up it and crept to the frontage, wary of absent floorboards and the rodents that scurried about. They crouched by a glassless window. It was the dead of night and no souls troubled the street. *Colemore Street!* Jon could see the silhouette of his mill tower less than two hundred yards away. He breathed deeply. Laila vaulted the sill, dashed across the road and signalled for the men to follow.

"Let's go, and make it pistol quick," Kareem said.

Jon needed no encouragement. The open air of the city had never tasted fresher to him. They jogged towards the mill, the cumbersome trunk swinging awkwardly between them. Only within sight of the loading-bay door did they slow to rest.

"Seems to me I spend my life carrying things for you," Kareem puffed jovially. Laila hushed him and crouched, her eyes alert. They set the trunk down beside her. Jon squeezed blood into his sore fingers and imagined being safely back in his home.

"Wait here," he said. "It opens from the inside."

He was halfway to his front door when it banged open and the street briefly flooded with a soft light. The face of the man who emerged from his mill was shadowed by a hooded cape, but his bronze badge was clear to see against the midnight blue of his uniform.

"I thought I heard something." The censor spoke with a hard, calm voice that Jon immediately recognised from the canals. He approached in a way that warned against sudden movement, but he didn't look vexed.

"I wasn't expecting a visit — is there a problem?" Jon raised a hand in greeting and stepped forwards to hold the censor back, to keep him away from Kareem and Laila.

"No problem. I brought Daniel's possessions from the seminary. There wasn't much: some clothes, an old leather ball, a book. I thought he might want them when he returns."

"That was good of you."

Jon heard movement behind the corner of the mill, and imagined Kareem and Laila readying their weapons. His small hairs stood on end and his legs stiffened.

The censor continued, seemingly oblivious, "Daniel was a good boy, a magnificent warrior. He wanted to join the Brotherhood so badly. He should have trained for another year."

"That's what Anna thought," Jon said. A bead of sweat ran down the side of his face. *Why couldn't the censor tell that something was wrong?* For some reason Jon felt like giggling.

"Your wife seems a fine woman. Loyal." The censor lowered his voice. "She asked me to talk with you, said you might need help with a private matter."

"Let's talk inside." Jon moved to guide the censor towards the door, but as his foot crunched on the cobbles, he heard the scrabbling again. This time the censor moved his hand to the hilt his cutlass.

"Wait!" Jon warned as the man bounded past to the corner of the mill and then stopped sharply. Jon couldn't see what had made him halt, but even in profile, he noticed how the man's eyes steeled.

"I recognise you — from the docks," the censor said. "The stevedore."

Jon fought the wobble in his legs, the urge to run for his door.

"That's right," Jon heard Kareem reply. "I carry." There was a hollow thud. *Kareem's hand slapping the side of the strongbox,* Jon guessed, and wondered what Laila was doing.

"What's in the strongbox?"

"Payment for the miller."

"At night? In that thing? What kind of payment?"

"He's made a deal with my master," Kareem said.

He's trying to drag me down with him, Jon thought and remembered his pledge that Kareem was to be the first Freeborn whose identity he revealed to the Brotherhood. There was no way that Kareem could talk his way out of this one.

"I'm having a look inside."

The money would take some explaining, though.

"Be my guest," Kareem said, "the miller has the key."

"Bastard," Jon blurted.

The censor turned to face him. "You two need to get your story straight."

The censor's gaze snapped sideways and, in an action Jon could barely follow, his cutlass sprung from its scabbard and twirled in a whistling arc.

Kareem's forearm, with his pistol still gripped in his hand, came spinning through the air. Before they thumped and clattered onto the street, or Kareem even had a chance to scream, the censor's blade reversed its course and sliced upwards.

There was a dull thud, and then Kareem's hapless head came rolling around the corner to halt at Jon's feet. The eyes remained alight for a moment, focused but uncomprehending. The lips twitched.

The censor turned his bloodied blade on Jon.

"Don't kill me," Jon yelped.

A black shadow crashed onto the censor's back and smashed him to the ground. For a moment, Jon didn't understand what had happened. Then he saw a bulging sack on the road beside him, grain spilling from its split seams. He looked up. Laila's face peered over the railing of the reefing stage, eyes fierce with concentration.

Instinct lifted the censor to his hands and knees. He regarded Jon drunkenly.

Laila caught him two-footed between the shoulders, lashing his face into the cobbles. His teeth scattered like pearls from a broken necklace. Metal skittered on stone as the cutlass spun from his grasp. Laila bounced painfully off his back and lay on the road, gasping for breath.

I must help him, Jon thought desperately.

The censor's blurred eyes fixed on his cutlass. He crawled towards it, through the slop and litter that edged the street. Laila drew a short dagger from her belt and gouged it deep into his calf. The man grimaced, belly-dragged towards his weapon an arm's length away.

Jon stared at Kareem's pistol, the censor's blade lying in the dirt, and prayed for help or witnesses.

"Do something," Laila hissed, and stabbed the censor in the thigh, who kicked back at her with his good leg and caught her cheekbone with a crack. The censor's hand was inches from the cutlass.

Jon felt warm and light, as if he was floating in a bath.

In a flailing effort, Laila leapt frog-like onto the censor's back and straddled him like a lover. She pulled back his head, her fingers slipping on his bloodied chin.

"No!" the censor burbled.

Laila sliced deep, opened his throat like a second mouth. Air hissed out of it. She left her blade quivering in the side of his neck, and rolled off his twitching body. For a moment, all was silent. Jon felt the night air cold on his face. Suddenly he was very tired.

"They're both dead," he said, and wondered at the idiocy of the observation.

"Useless bastard."

Laila looked up at him with hard eyes, her clothes slick with blood so freshly red it matched her hair. Her gaze turned to the censor's steaming corpse. She took Kareem's pistol and shoved it into her dagger belt, kicked his head into the gutter. It was only then that Jon realised the insult wasn't aimed at him.

"We have to get this mess indoors before anyone sees it."

Jon prayed for the panicked bell of a watchman ringing for the town guard.

"What are you waiting for?" Laila said.

"I'm not helping you. Run if you must."

"Don't be stupid, Jon. You did your best with the censor. Kareem was too slow, but we can't leave the bodies. If there's an inquisition they'll see everything."

The words came like a slow slap to the face. Jon replayed the day's events in his mind. He pictured himself tying the red scarf to the railing overhead, travelling to Barehill's base, shaking hands with him. Taking his brand. Taking his money. Standing and watching while his people murdered a censor. That was what the censors would see if they took confession. He realised what he had done. The pieces fell into place, a mosaic made of shit.

He walked dumbly to the door of his mill, closed it behind him. The hall glowed orange with the light of a dying fire. He could hear Anna shuffling about upstairs, in the bedroom. He imagined going to her and holding her.

Anna, I've ruined everything, forever.

For the first time, he understood why Daniel had fled his failure.

He crept on tiptoes up to the minstrel gallery, into the mill tower and locked the door behind him, went down to the loading bay and slid open the folding door. The street was silent. There was no town guard. No candles burned in the windows of the buildings opposite. There was just Laila, the murderess, covered in blood.

He grabbed the censor by the boots and dragged his body into the loading bay while Laila gathered Kareem's remains. It was abattoir work and it made him retch. The strongbox came last. After everything was inside, he collapsed onto a pile of empty sacks. Laila looked down on him.

"I can't blame you for losing your nerve; I've seen it too many times before. But there's no way back now. The sooner you accept it, the easier it will be for you."

Jon ignored her. He just wanted her out of his house.

"When I tell Barehill what you did, he'll trust you a little more. He'll be sad to see the end of Kareem. Gods know why."

"Anna," Jon said, his mind elsewhere.

"Does she know?"

"What?"

"Does your wife know? That you're one of us?"

Jon shook his head. Laila fetched a bucket of water from the back of the bay, grabbed a dusty overall from a hook.

"Good. It's better that way. After I'm gone, you clean up outside. Now hold this."

She passed him one of the bloodstained sacks on which he had been lying, peeled the clothes from her body and dropped them into the bag. He tried to ignore her body, striped with trails of blood, her chest and loins inches from his face. She ripped strips from the bottom of the smock.

"Turn around."

Jon faced the wall while she wiped herself clean.

Laila threw the bloody sack against the wall. "When you've finished, put your clothes in this — anything with blood on it. Burn it all. Make sure there's nothing left they can take confession from."

He knew she hadn't finished, yet he turned back anyway and caught a flash of red hair between her legs as she pulled up the overalls.

"Will you be alright? To get back?" he said, ashamed of his lechery. She nodded and ran soft-footed to the door, glanced in both directions and then was gone.

Jon emptied the bucket of bloody water over the blood in the street, scattered sand and sawdust to cover the stains as best he could. He bolted the folding doors, wrestled the bodies of Kareem and the censor into sacks and laid a canvas on top of them. Buried that under heaped sacks of flour.

Exhausted, he clawed at his own bloody garments as feebly as a toddling child, and stuffed them clumsily into the bag. Naked and soaked with sweat, he went back to the mill's hall and dressed himself in a moth-eaten suit of Father's, retrieved from the rag box.

The only sound in the mill was Mother's snoring.

Jon tried to imagine how his family would survive after the censors had done business with him. Cheeks wet with tears, he added two handfuls of kindling to the hearth and when the flames had risen high enough, tossed the bloody bag into the fire. Visions of death flooded his mind and, try as he might, he could not force them out.

I know why the gods are punishing me, he thought. *I know why I deserve this.*

He remembered standing in the minstrel gallery looking down at Father sitting in the same chair by the fire, staring into the flames, feverish and immobile. He looked feeble, old before his time. Jon had been sent up to work on the sails. The bastard had just sent Dahlia and Daniel to fetch his wine from the vintner. That was the moment that had cursed him — that had cursed them all. Why send Dahlia? Jon had known that something was wrong straight away.

So why didn't I say anything? Why didn't I go after them? Why didn't I stop it from happening?

CRUITHIN'S FINEST

The porter saw Daniel approaching and stepped out of the lodge.

"Bright and early, Mister Sutton. Do you intend to walk the bay?"

"My ambition takes me further afield. I plan to spend a night camping in the Lakes."

The porter frowned. "You'll be lucky if the weather holds. If the masters let the tide in, you'll have to sleep in the stable yard." Daniel nodded to show that he had understood and opened the wicket door in the Convergence's immense gates. "I could summon you a chaperon? It would only take a minute." Daniel patted his scabbard, winked and stepped outside.

Seaweed popped under his feet as he crossed the shingled causeway. Grey waves slapped against the invisible barriers to either side of him and he realised that he thought nothing of it, that he had begun to see the miraculous as commonplace. The idea troubled him a little, so he stopped to gaze into the murky water and startled a fish whose lashing tail left a stream of bubbles in the water.

Daniel requisitioned a fine white gelding from the stables and galloped up the highway to the sky burial.

Brother Adelmus's corpse was gone, the name engraved into the head of the cross the only reminder of his murder. The message Corbin had scratched on his door had been deliberately cryptic, just a cross and an arrow pointing downwards, but

Daniel knew what to do. He unearthed the bottle buried under the tall grass at the base of the cross and tipped out a small map. It showed a location half a day's ride to the south. Bandit country. He checked that he was alone before readying his wheel lock, keying back its clockwork firing mechanism and loading it with powder and ball. He tucked the weapon into the bedroll behind his saddle, its grip out of sight but easily reached.

The lands to the east of Seascale possessed a bleak kind of beauty, all sharp hills, deep lakes and barren meadows, the shrubs and grasses grazed short by sheep that were nowhere to be seen. A few lonely trees twisted by the wind stood sentry on the edge of rocky escarpments.

Daniel made his way along narrow tracks and across boulder-strewn slopes that plunged into cerulean lakes. It was a bright day, but the sharp-edged shadows of the hills and clouds brought a chill to his fingers.

South of the hills, he rode a muddy half-track through woodland for several miles. He saw a trio of burial urns made of stacked slate, and a water mill, long abandoned, that somehow reminded him of home.

It was dusk when he reached a peaceful valley, lined with beeches, oaks and hazels whose leaves were already turning hues of yellow, red, purple and brown. Wind whistled in the trees and a watercourse gurgled nearby.

The place that Corbin had chosen for meeting could not be mistaken; the sprawling red sandstone walls of a ruined monastery filled the vale. Daniel marvelled at its size; it was at least the equal of Bromwich Seminary. He could not imagine how such a magnificent building had come to be built in such a lonely place. Fifty years past, it would have been a monument to the wealth and power of the godsworn. Now ivy clasped its walls and their stones were vivid with white moss.

Daniel dismounted his horse and led it beside him, a hand wrapped firmly around the grip of his pistol. They moved down the sacred procession, roofless and carpeted with moss and grass, into the shell of the mighty tower that once held a sanctum. A canvas tent had been pitched inside its soaring walls, and a ring of pebbles had been placed on the ground. A chestnut warhorse stood untethered, chewing on some grass. Daniel whistled the three-toned censor's call and it bent a leg and bowed its head. Daniel tied his own horse alongside. It flared its nostrils and snorted, but soon the horses were nuzzling.

"You've a better disposition than your master," Daniel whispered, and patted the chestnut's flank. He was unstrapping his saddle gear when he heard Corbin's voice behind him.

"Evening, Mister Sutton." The prosecutor was carrying a jumble of twigs and branches. He dropped the sticks onto the circle of stones. "Get to work on a fire."

Daniel obeyed without comment and Corbin headed back into the trees. By the time he had returned with some more branches, Daniel had the kindling sparked and was warming his hands.

Corbin fetched a rabbit from his saddlebag.

"You hunt beasts as well as men," Daniel said.

"I bought this in the Verge's market," Corbin said, and stripped its skin off with one hard pull.

Night descended. The campsite filled with the nutty smell of cooking game.

"Well?" Daniel said.

"Lang's instruction was to meet you. I promised nothing more."

Daniel chewed for a while, choosing his words carefully.

"This investigation falls within Magistrate Lang's jurisdiction. He's keen to understand how our investigation progresses, as is his right."

Corbin spat a bone into the surrounding darkness. "Our investigation? What great secrets have you uncovered?"

"Do you wish me to make a report?"

Corbin didn't answer, so Daniel shrugged and held his tongue.

"If you must," the prosecutor said wearily.

"There is no reason to suspect any of the demi-masters."

"Do they suspect you?"

Daniel ignored the sarcasm. "I've been discreet. Most seem oblivious to the censor's death."

"That it?"

"I have spied upon the godsworn, as you instructed."

"What!" Corbin's face clouded

"He's no friend of the Verge."

"Godsworn were ordering the Cunning burnt alive less than thirty years ago and the Brotherhood of Censors were doing the burning. Why would he be a friend?"

Daniel shrugged again.

"So you've uncovered the sweet sum of nothing."

"One thing." Daniel slowly finished his rabbit, savouring every sinew. He noisily sucked the juice from the bones, gazed into the fire as if considering. He wanted Corbin to be in no doubt that he was doing him a favour. "I noticed a master acting suspiciously."

"Everything they do is suspicious."

"Lang is looking into his files."

Corbin's eyes narrowed and he spat into the fire. "Is he? And what would this master's name be?"

Daniel gnawed on scraps as Corbin studied him.

"It seems to me that I've made more progress than you have," Daniel said, and settled back on his elbows.

"Insolent pup." Corbin stared at him dagger-hard and for a good while. It was supposed to be intimidating. Corbin was a scary man, no doubt, but Daniel had seen worse. Eventually Corbin settled back himself, and let out a deep sigh. "At least you've got some balls on you." He rested his head on a log, closed his eyes. "These are the facts of the matter. The censor left the Verge in the middle of the night. I think by sea, because his coracle is missing. He left a fire burning in his room, which means he intended to return or he didn't want it to be known he was gone. He was lured to the stables and ambushed, or else was caught by surprise during an investigation."

"If his killers were waiting for him, then somebody inside the Verge knew of his plans."

"Maybe. I've checked the porters' register. Everyone who left the Verge in the week before the killing has returned since. I've been to Ravenglass as well, where those roughs came from. It's a pissant fishing village. Nobody knows anything."

"Were there any clues in his room?"

"Adelmus lived a lonely life. There was nothing of interest in his chambers. I've taken confession from the main gate and his room for hours and seen nothing. I'm still hurting from it. I'd take confessions until my brains ran out my nose if I thought it'd help, but I don't know where to look. Or when." Corbin jabbed at the fire with a stick and embers spiralled into the night air.

"Then we're stuck — apart from the master."

"Are you going to tell me his name?"

"On one condition."

Corbin scowled, but Daniel knew he had no choice. "State your terms."

"You let me help you."

Corbin drummed his fingers on the mossy ground.

Daniel spread his empty hands. "Agreed?"

Corbin nodded, defeated. "Very well. Now what does this master call himself?"

"Pendolous Bolb."

"Sounds ridiculous."

"That's the point of it."

"And what have you got on him?"

"He's found religion."

"That's hardly a crime, even in the Verge. What's got Lang so interested?"

"Since the day Adelmus died he's been bothering the Verge's godsworn, praying for aid and forgiveness."

"That's all?"

"Yes."

"That's thin. Thinner than a leaf."

"But I feel something," Daniel said.

"Me too," Corbin said, "though I hate to admit it. And my intuition's let me down many times before. Let me think."

Daniel grinned broadly and got to his feet, sauntered over to his horse and returned with a bottle. Its contents glowed amber in the firelight. He threw it to Corbin who caught it overhead, one-handed. "I knew you'd see reason. Eventually."

"What's this?" Corbin knocked the wax stopper from the neck of the bottle with the ringed pommel of his sword and savoured its aroma. His eyebrows leapt. "Cruithin's finest. Ten years old, and from a maple barrel to boot. Where'd you find this beauty?"

"The Verge has many secrets; its wine cellars are not one of them. I find myself well paid as a demi-master, a man of means."

Corbin took a swig and let out a hearty sigh. It was time to make peace.

"That's a gallows sword, isn't it? Good choice for a prosecutor."

Corbin laughed. "In Dalriadan 'gallo' means foreign. My ancestors were mercenaries, from Erdin. The people of the

Six Kingdoms called us galloglashes, foreign warriors. It's got nothing to do with hangings."

"How did you become a censor?"

"The Brotherhood had eyes on my da for years. They tried to recruit him even before he was a hero. There was good money in fighting back then, so he said no — died on the end of a lance in the War of Covenanter."

Daniel thought of his own father, red-eyed, drunk and despondent.

"I'm sorry."

"No need to be. He wasn't a good man, but I learnt the art of the sword from him, as he was taught before me."

"And the Brotherhood?"

"I didn't hesitate when they asked. Battle's changed. It's all pikes, culverins and grenadoes now. In a fusillade, a poet of the blade gets slaughtered as quickly as a farmhand." Corbin stood, unsheathed his sword. The sound of singing steel sent a shiver of pleasure up Daniel's spine. "Have a look."

Daniel took the weapon, balanced it on the crook of his arm, careful not to let his oily fingers stain the blade. It was a marvel, perfectly balanced and lighter than it looked.

"What's it like in the Six Kingdoms?"

"Always raining. The food's a horror. It's famous for its songs and banter only because there's nothing else to do, aside from fight and fuck."

Daniel suppressed a laugh. The men from the Kingdoms whom Daniel had met in Turbulence were touchy about their homeland — touchy and belligerent. He decided to be conciliatory. "The Kingdoms have a troubled past."

"Bollocks," Corbin said, still smiling. "It's a miserable little island about as far from the centre of things as you can get. Too poor to be worth conquering. How many times has the

Unity been invaded? Eight? Nine? It's happened to us once, but we talk as if we're the great oppressed. When we can't find an oppressor, we fight each other. All our legends are dust-ups — cattle raids and shagging the neighbour's wife. That's why we take our religion so seriously; it's a good excuse to kill each other. How can an island that small have six kings? Its fecking ridiculous." He took a swig from the bottle. "Still, the violence keeps me busy, and at least it's not Erdin. This investigation is almost a holiday for me." Corbin passed him the bottle. Daniel rubbed a tear of mirth from his eye. "Enough about me. Tell me about the demi-masters."

"They're strange. They seem to think they live in a world beyond harm. They're full of confidence and certainty, but for no reason that I can fathom. They've never been tested."

"It's a common failing. They confuse their success at school with being clever."

Daniel shrugged. "I don't see what harm it does them. If they fail at the Verge they'll go home to rich families, live easy lives."

"Don't envy them. Most will end their days angry and bitter."

"You must be joking," Daniel said, imagining life in a palace.

"The world will never recognise the greatness they see in themselves, and because they aren't clever, they'll never understand why. It drives them mad." Daniel laughed again. Corbin shook his head. "Well-educated fools are no laughing matter; they're the most dangerous people in the world."

"Why's that?"

"Because they rule it."

"You're a good sport, Corbin," Daniel said, looking for another piece of rabbit to eat. It was all gone. He sucked the scraps from a gnawed leg. "What have you got against Lang?"

"That man is a chameleon; he shows all colours but white."

"You're wrong, he's midnight blue all the way through."

Corbin grunted. "What do you make of the duchess's ward? I've seen her about with you; all long legs and copper skin."

"Miranda — she believes me her friend." Daniel thought about the accident and frowned.

"Believes, is it? I heard about what happened. How does she fare?"

"I don't know. Something struck her in the cavern. It looked bad, but they made us leave before I could get a good look. I tried to visit her in the infirmary, but they won't let me see her."

"Don't worry, lad; if she was badly injured there would have been repercussions. We'd all know by now."

"She's that important?"

"Don't be doltish; she's prize property of the duchess."

Daniel nodded. "She's better than the others. I mean she has the most talent."

"So how do you find her?"

Corbin was a persistent bastard, Daniel thought. "She's not like the girls from Bromwich."

"Got all her teeth, has she?"

Daniel grinned. The banter reminded him of long drinks with his brother.

"It's not just the clipped accent. She talks too quickly. I can't understand half of what she says. When she's concentrating, she carries her body like an afterthought. When she knows she's being watched, you could balance a cup of tea on her head without spilling it."

"You still haven't answered my question."

Daniel thought about her properly for the first time. "She's funny."

"And easy on the eye. Perfect mouth. She probably wants to know what's in your pants, even if she doesn't realise it yet.

Keep it tucked away, that's my advice. It'd be a shame to disappoint her."

Daniel took a greedy gulp and threw the bottle back to Corbin overarm. "What about you? Got a wife back home?"

"Careful, son. Spilling this would be a crime." Corbin said, waving the question away with his hand. "So what do you hope to get out of all of this?"

"To become a censor," he replied without hesitation.

"For sure? It's a lonely life. Makes you think differently. You start to see guilt in everyone. Even when you don't, people act as if you can. You see some horrible things. Moreover, there's the sight. After a while, it begins to leak into your dreams. You lose track of what you've seen with your own eyes."

Daniel wondered why Corbin tried to dissuade him. "The place I come from, it's a mess. You can't live a good life. People are killed — go missing for no reason. Nobody notices or cares, not even the Brotherhood. I want to protect my family. Do you know what will happen to me if I don't get ordained? I won't join a gang and they'll bleed me for refusing. They'll bleed me anyway for trying to join the Brotherhood. I go home with a badge on my chest or not at all."

Corbin nodded respectfully and they watched the fire burn out together.

"I guess I could give you a chance to prove yourself. First off, it's pleasant enough meeting under the stars, all these souls smiling down on us, but we need an easier way to talk."

"Let's stick to bottles," Daniel said, sloshing the dregs of the whisky. "I'll put this in a private locker in the wine cellar, give you a key, and leave my reports inside."

Corbin thought awhile. "You reckon yourself a censor. Then prepare to receive your instruction."

Daniel leaned forward in anticipation. "Yes, sir."

"I'm going to start calling in the masters for questioning. They're a devious bunch, won't trust me one jot. I'll send a summons to Bolb, but he won't be the first. I want him nervous, not running. Your job is to watch him, close as you can."

It was a familiar gambit. Daniel had seen how the prospect of a meeting with a censor could make guilty men do foolish things.

"Sounds solid. But I won't be able to follow him into the Masters' Quarters; it's not allowed."

"Do what you can."

Corbin went over to his horse and pulled a mandolin from the saddlebag.

Daniel looked on in horror. "You're joking me. The gods wept." Corbin tuned the instrument and strummed a few chords to test it. Then he broke into a battle-camp song, his voice rich and warm.

> *"In the ground, there lives a king,*
> *   Who sits upon an iron throne.*
> *Wears a cloak of bended wing,*
> *   Waits in the double-dark alone.*
> *Cold and rot don't bother him,*
> *   He wears a crown of coffin nails.*
> *When you leave this rotten life,*
> *   He'll listen to all of your tales.*
> *Stack your deeds upon the scales,*
> *   Grand or small, he'll make no pause . . .*
> *Just measure how the balance tips,*
> *   And cast your soul into his jaws."*

"That was a little less painful than I expected," Daniel said. Corbin's pupils glowed red in the firelight.

"Being a censor is a serious business. You put your life at risk to serve justice, even when no man wants it. Our mission is divine. The bastards in the Convergence think they live beyond our power. This is our chance to prove them wrong."

The undertaking was the sort of adventure Daniel had dreamed of as a child.

"What if I get caught?"

"That's easy. Don't get caught."

"Lang said something about pretending to be a spy, an execution."

"Sounds severe. It's the politics, probably."

"Does the Brotherhood really expect me to sacrifice everything? To die just to keep a secret?"

"Maybe it's unnecessary," Corbin said, grinning mightily, "but don't let my gentle manner and good humour deceive you. I'm the coldest bastard you'll ever meet. I would take your head from your shoulders in an instant, and gladly, if it pleased justice."

"Cheers," Daniel said, raising the bottle. The sweat on his brow had turned cold. He took another swig. "And thank you for trusting me."

"I'll leave at dawn," Corbin said. "You tidy up the campsite."

THAT WHICH REMAINS

Miranda is a goddess. She floats resplendent in the void with a star cupped in every palm of her countless hands.

The world revolves beneath her feet.

Gripped by a terrible vertigo, she dwindles to a mortal form and plummets earthwards to land heavily on hands and knees. Fetid swamp air permeates her body and she retches. Men dance around her to the rhythm of drums and the bestial wailing of women and children. The quaggy soil swallows her whole and she is drowned in cold mud.

Reborn, she gazes from the bottom of the sea through unblinking eyes, waits aeons in the lightless depths. Gradually she becomes aware that she is dreaming other lives, and in that revelation, her dream becomes lucid.

Swirling clouds of magic surround her, guide her forwards to a distant future.

They bring her to a woman, much like herself, sitting in a cubicle amongst hundreds, crouched over an ugly glowing screen that displays a game of cards.

The woman casts nervous glances over her shoulder, afraid that she might be spotted by her foreman. She has been playing the same game all day, convinced that if she wins in exactly the right way, the man who has said he no longer loves her will change his mind and return home.

It is a mad thought and the woman is talented, the last of her kind — though she does not know it, so her ritual has some power. A small tear appears in the fabric of reality, and from that tear, a single speck of magic emerges.

It is beautiful.

A sad resignation overtakes the woman and she closes the game, returns to her work. Miranda watches the magic, cast adrift and half formed, hovering in the air, restrained by the possibility that the woman may return to the game that is also a spell.

Finally, starved of control, it fades into otherness.

Miranda feels an infinite sense of melancholy. The last spark of true magic has left that grey world. From that moment onwards, its every outcome will be subject to the unbending, tyrannical laws of nature.

She follows the speck through place and time, feels streams of magic join the race, twist and spiral alongside her, like dolphins chasing a wake. Her heart is filled with joy. The shadows of figures tower above her, looming beyond scale.

They are watching her.

The tides of magic draw her ever faster towards a finite point that she can sense but cannot see. Her stomach lurches with the acceleration.

She sees it at last, a fractured disc of inestimable scale, sucking the magic from a billion realities. She hurtles towards it, covers her face in anticipation of the collision. There is a whip-crack noise and she is spat, soaked in brine, into the empty cavern of the Convergence.

The air fills with the sound of screaming.

●

Miranda sat bolt upright with a gasp. Pain lanced from her foot to her thigh. She howled and howled, then yelled for help. There was no reply. She screamed again and damned the world a whore, tried to open her eyes, failed, apologised to the blackness, sobbed, fell backwards and passed out.

The second waking was easier.

First, she caught the scent of the sea, and felt a warm light upon her eyes that resolved into sight as her lashes slowly unglued. She saw a plain, bright room. White linen curtains billowed in tall windows, and gulls circled in the cloudy sky beyond. A nurse sat silently at the foot of her bed, and when she saw that Miranda had woken she dashed from the room, leaving her unattended.

The pain returned, this time as a dull ache in her legs.

I was wounded, in the explosion.

The calico bedding smelled fresh. There was no deathly hint of infection. Miranda sighed. It took a while to gather enough courage to draw aside the bedsheets, to raise the simple gown in which some stranger had dressed her. Her thighs were mottled blue. She gingerly tensed her right thigh, and was relieved to see it rise a fraction, though the pain of the movement brought tears to her eyes. She tried the other side and tipped, rolled sideways in agony and then realised. Her left leg. The knee and below. It was gone.

"My leg! Someone has stolen my leg!"

She screamed and screamed again.

The nurse returned. "For the pain," she said, and pressed a vial against Miranda's lips. The liquid smelled of ginger. Miranda downed it frantically. It had the consistency of gruel. Her terror faded and the room slowly took on a sparkling hue. The concoction was powerful. It wasn't that the pain and horror had passed; simply that she had stopped caring about them. Miranda noticed that the gown she was wearing was embroidered with lilies and giggled inanely.

●

Gleame entered the room accompanied by two guards who waited patiently at the door. He shooed away the nurse and took her place at the foot of the bed. He had brought flowers and a long walnut box like a gun case.

Miranda could see crystalline tendrils of magic trailing from him in all directions.

His eyes flicked over her. "My poor, dear girl. How do you fare?"

"I feel fantastic," she burbled merrily.

Gleame inspected the empty vial by her side. "That potion is a powerful one, but its effects are short-lived."

"I had strange dreams. Wonderful dreams. I danced with magic."

"The apothecaries of the Verge specialise in concoctions that alter perception. Some are used for research . . . Miranda, it's your well-being that matters to me."

Because of your precious licences, Miranda thought, *your monopoly*.

"What day is it?"

"Ayrday."

"Ayrday was yesterday."

"You've been asleep for a week, recuperating. Her Grace has been informed of your injury." Gleame seemed to be talking to the flowers. "I don't know what to say. Nothing like this has ever happened before."

"Lucky me."

"I promised Her Grace that I would keep you safe. She insists on speaking with you as soon as you are capable."

Miranda marvelled at the jewels on Gleame's walking stick. Their glister seemed to fill the room. "Where does magic come from?"

Gleame frowned. "Many places. You have worked the henge. There are institutions in other lands with similar facilities and,

I imagine, many smaller ventures unknown to me. What do you remember of the accident?"

"No, before then, before people." Miranda tried to focus on Gleame's face. She noticed how smooth his skin was.

"Miranda, please! The accident?" Miranda felt the clammy grasp of fear. She remembered the explosion and her chest tightened.

"Stop the screaming!" she yelled.

"Screaming?" Gleame looked around, confused, waved for the nurse.

"The men around the box."

"Ah. The technicians." Gleame nodded gravely. "That was unfortunate. We lost one when the container sundered. He was struck by one panel, you by the other." Another vial of medicine was poured down Miranda's throat, and her chin stopped trembling, the remorse washed away. "A most regrettable incident. Do not worry, Miranda, the Convergence looks after its own. His family has been well compensated."

"I'm so sorry."

He pulled his chair alongside her bed. "Dear Miranda, the fault was not yours. There is nothing wrong with your construct. It is magnificent. The holding device was simply not strong enough to contain it. The technicians underestimated its power, and one of them paid the price."

Miranda wiped a tear from her eye. "I'm tired."

Gleame stood. "I have spoken for too long. I should let you rest."

He couldn't wait to be gone, Miranda realised. "What's in the wooden box?" she asked.

Gleame lifted its lid. Inside, nestled in a cushion of silk, lay a leg, life-sized and sleek, obsidian black, crafted from metal, wood and leather. Its surface was as smooth as lacquer, but cold to the touch. A vein of silver marquetry ran down its side.

They mean for me to wear it, Miranda thought, and knew that she ought to be horrified. She tried to be, but she couldn't. The leg was perfect, beautiful.

"It is the least I can do." Gleame put the half limb clumsily back inside the box. He looked genuinely upset.

Miranda rested her head on her pillow and retreated into darkness.

●

The next time, Miranda was better prepared.

"How many days?" she asked sleepily, to put him off his guard.

"Two," Gleame said. "The nurse says you slept like the Dreamer."

"I should return to my studies," she said, so that he would know that she did not intend to leave.

"Miranda!"

"And I wish to discuss the accident," so that he knew he was not forgiven.

By now, he could tell that she was trying to manipulate him, he just didn't know why.

"It seems your faculties are intact, and let us thank the gods for that, but you should be resting, not worrying yourself."

"I made a construct."

"An understatement," Gleame said.

"And it holds?"

Gleame nodded. "Why do you ask?"

"How?"

"Master Somney foresaw the danger of its power. He had the presence of mind to shield your construct within a simpler one of his own. It was a temporary solution, but it bought us enough time to save the magic you captured. Somney hates to leave money on the table."

"You sold it?"

"The device commanded an enormous sum. The bidding was a marvel."

"To whom?"

"An overseas buyer."

"Go on."

"The Northmen seek to establish a forge at Giron. There is iron in the hills there, but precious little forest. In winter the sun barely crests the horizon, and then only for a few hours. Your construct is to power the bellows of the forge and the glow-stones of the town and mine. It is a fascinating project. I negotiated a share of the profits in addition to the price."

"We sell devices to Northmen now?" Miranda said, imagining a raiding ship powered by magic.

"The Wise Council believes that if their minds can be turned to industry it might curtail their enthusiasm for war."

"Really?"

"Let us focus on the most important matter — your health."

Miranda swung her legs, the real and the artificial, over the side of the bed and tried to stand. She balanced on her real foot, grasped the mattress with both hands.

"That which remains of me is in rude health."

"The duchess wishes to hear it from you, directly."

Miranda let the contraption attached to her left thigh slowly take her weight, nervous that the inexplicable suction that held it in place would not be strong enough. It was, and the pressure on her wound did not hurt as much as she had expected. She gasped in surprise at the coldness of the floor, felt through toes that were not of her body.

"I will inform her that I have grown rich from Northmen's gold."

Gleame coughed uncomfortably.

"What?"

"It's not so simple. All of the work you do here is the property of the Convergence."

"What!"

"The Honourable Company is a partnership. The masters alone share in its profits."

"I get nothing?" It was barely a question; the answer was so predictable.

"Most demi-masters struggle to cover the cost of their wages and lodging. The matter never arose before."

"I'm not sure which will offend Her Grace more, the carelessness of this establishment in allowing my injury, or this further insult."

Gleame flinched. Miranda's reproachful gaze invited a better offer.

"I cannot change the rules of the Convergence, only a Convocation of Masters could do that, and then not retrospectively."

"What do they think of this state of affairs?"

"We have an interesting debate on our hands. It appears you have broken the system. Master Somney thinks you are genius, on the brink of developing a completely new type of cunning. I am sure he would be willing to give you his share of the profits."

"What about Talon?"

"Talon thinks you are a threat to our traditions, a liability. So does Gahst."

"The others?"

"Most want to know more about you, to see your work firsthand. Many do not believe what happened, or suspect luck rather than skill."

"And what about you, Chairman?"

His eyes lit up. "Our approach has always been to become more like magic, unworldly. Your approach is very experimental, not at all what I expected. I always assumed that female magic would be homely, but it works magnificently. That is all that matters. I established the Convergence to allow magic to develop unfettered, free of rules and regulations. You are a vindication of my approach."

"A vindication?" Miranda winced as she manoeuvred back onto the bed.

"I would see you overcome this mishap. I would see you set on the fastest possible path to greatness. I would move you upstairs. Assign you a master's chamber. Afford you dedicated staff. Unrestricted access to the library."

"All of the trappings of a master but not the position," Miranda clarified, *as if those things could make up for an amputation.*

"Miranda, achieving the position of a master takes years. Decades. Not a few weeks."

"I accept your offer."

"Excellent," Gleame warbled, unbalanced by the speed of her response.

"On one condition."

"A condition?"

"Adrian Lavety." From the look on Gleame's face, she realised that she must have said his name with a little too much spite.

"His father is a dear friend of mine," Gleame said defensively.

"Of course, yet the Convergence is far from his father's demesne."

"The Lavetys are an important family," Gleame said warily.

"Almost royalty, but not quite. Not like the duchess." *Though I cannot be sure that she would support what I am about to say.*

"What do you expect of me?"

"I simply want to be sure that the rules of the game are fair."

"What game?"

"You have seen that I am the most capable of the demi-masters."

"You are very talented."

"And have made the greatest sacrifice of us all. When the time comes, when a seat comes free on the Convocation, it should be the most talented whom you propose for the vacancy. We can both agree on that, surely." Gleame stared at her and then his face cleared and she knew a veil had been lifted, and that he saw her clearly for the first time. You could almost say that he looked proud of her. "The idea that I have been gravely injured, chasing only an illusion, would distress my mother deeply," Miranda added, and then worried that she had overcooked it.

"What if the duchess insists on your return to Ebarokon?"

"We cannot allow her to hold this unfortunate incident against the Company, to use it as an excuse to revise the terms of *our* licences. I will not let that happen. I will set her mind at ease on all matters."

Gleame pursed his lips.

"I cannot guarantee your election. That is a matter for the Convocation of Masters. I can only make the proposal."

"Of course."

Gleame's cane tip-tapped on the ground as he thought. Then he smiled a narrow smile and bowed sharply, from the neck, as befitted a powerful man.

"Good," Miranda said. "I will let the duchess know how well I am treated, as soon as I am well enough."

Gleame signalled to the nurse that Miranda was free to be discharged and left with his guards. The pain in Miranda's thigh returned as the steady click of his cane receded, but it could not prise the smile from her lips.

MAKING AMENDS

A fist hammered on the mill's door.

Jon stared deep into the fire dancing in the hearth. His fingers clawed around the arms of the chair in which he'd sat all night, praying and thinking of what to say to Anna. The words still hadn't come.

The fist hammered again, authoritative and implacable. *It isn't Peacock's men, or the door would already be off its hinges.* Anna sighed and wandered over from the pantry, dressed for temple and cradling the baby. She opened the door to a pair of censors. It was all that Jon could do to turn his head.

The taller was fair and wiry, chisel-faced with a scar that travelled from brow to jaw. His companion was dark and stout, in a hard way, with a chest like a brandy barrel. They were sweltering in their heavy uniforms and iron hats, and looked like they hadn't slept in days.

"Mistress Miller," the stout one said, "I am Brother Norbury. Will you have us in?" Before Anna had a chance to answer, his companion pushed past her and made a quick reconnaissance of the hall.

"Brother Josephus," he said, and with equal certainty. "You know why we're here." Anna shook her head a little too quickly.

Norbury said, "Brother Nielsen left the seminary last night. Came here to drop off some effects. The property of a Daniel Miller."

Josephus bent to look under a piece of furniture. "He left a note in the logbook. Immaculate handwriting has Brother Nielsen."

"He didn't return." Norbury removed his helmet and ran his hand across his shaved head. He stared at Anna until she turned her face away in fear, then searched Jon's for an answer. "We are investigating."

"Tell me what happened between yourself and Brother Nielsen."

Anna started to babble incoherently. Norbury raised his hand to slow her. She gulped and calmed herself. "It was like you said. He came by, dropped off Daniel's things, then left."

"That all?"

"We talked awhile. I asked for his advice on a private matter."

"Private, eh? What about you, Mister Miller? According to our reports, Brother Nielsen had a run-in with you a few days back."

Jon had nothing to say.

"He was out all night — drinking," Anna said.

The lanky censor stood over Jon with crossed arms. "Look at you, all covered in sweat. You must be the only man in Bromwich with a fire lit."

Anna mimed the draining of several flagons.

"Big night, was it? Care to tell me where you were?"

Before Jon had a chance to answer, the beanpole chortled and returned to his companion's side. "I'll take confession, you be beholder."

"Is there to be an inquisition?" Shock and fear fought for control of Anna's face.

"We haven't the time, nor the men to spare," Norbury said. "A convoy was ambushed on the road to Baembra this morning. Men were shot and gunpowder stolen. We'd best be out looking for it. Nevertheless, there are rules to be followed when a brother disappears. A quick confession will be enough. Where was it that you spoke to Brother Nielsen?"

Anna pointed and the censor drew a symbol on the floor with a chalk from his pouch.

Jon had never seen a confession taken before. He decided that he needed to leave the room, and quickly.

Jon called after Josephus in a cracked voice. "You'll need keys, for the padlocks, and help moving the equipment in the mill tower." The censor summoned him with a wave and he followed up the stairs.

The censor searched the bedrooms first, made his apologies to Mother Miller, though she made no reaction when he came into her room.

Jon's fists were locked and his mind raced. As they got closer to the mill tower, the smell of blood flooded his nostrils and he wondered why the censor could not smell it also. He fought to keep his breathing steady and his heart still. Daniel had said the censors were trained to notice these things.

Censor Josephus ducked under a low beam and slid down the steps to the loading bay. Jon sucked in air noisily as the censor began to work his way around the room, peering inside bags and under canvases. Soon he stood over the pile of sacks in the loading bay.

"Give me a hand with these." The censor grinned mercilessly. Jon started to lift them slowly to the side.

"Not very fit for a miller, are you?" The beanpole tossed them as casually as street urchins into the back of a prison carriage. To Jon the empty bags seemed to weigh two hundred pounds. The censor shifted aside the last of the sacks and saw lumps under the canvas. "She seems a little nervous, your wife." He grasped the double sheet by the corners.

"She doesn't know anything about anything," Jon blurted, and inwardly cursed at the implication that he did.

"Is that right?" Norbury flung the sheets aside and the phantom stench of slaughter returned to Jon's mind. The censor dug his boots into the piles of straw which lay beneath. He looked disappointed. "Why don't we have a peek upstairs?"

Jon looked up at the trapdoor in the ceiling through which he had hoisted the bodies and prayed to the Father for the courage to continue.

They went up to the stone floor. The censor talked as he searched.

"I knew a man once, lived off Slainey Street. His wife was a wash maid, none too bright, but loyal as a dog."

"Right," Jon said, unsure where the story was going.

"He had a limp, or feigned one. Liked to wear a half mask. I'd see him hanging round the square in front of All-Saints, late at night and looking shifty. When things went missing from the great bazaar or a lady's purse was snatched, more than often the man they described was the same. Thing was, I could never prove it was him — make the connection. No matter how many times I forced him to empty his pockets, I never found anything on him. His wife complained to my superior about 'harassment'. Claimed he was an honest man."

The beanpole stood tall, levelled eyes with Jon.

"Now I don't like that kind of thing — people wasting my time and making me look stupid, so I made an effort. One day, I saw him pass his wife in the street; she was bringing some dirty linen from High Town to the laundry. He gave her a hug. The next day, same thing happened. That time I followed her, searched the basket after she dropped it off. Know what I found?"

"I can't imagine." Jon was getting a migraine.

"Coins. A diamond earring. A cufflink made of gold."

"Justice Advances," Jon said.

"Exactly. She swore blind she didn't know a thing about it and so did he, but I can't say I didn't smile when I hanged the both of them."

The censor stood by the misshapen, canvas-wrapped lump that rested against the millstone, the only object on the stone floor whose purpose wasn't obvious. Jon wondered if the censor was biding his time on purpose, to compound his misery.

"What have we got here?" Josephus drew a knife from his belt and lifted the edge of the canvas.

"Anna doesn't know."

The carousel horse seemed to glow with delight at being discovered. The censor turned on Jon triumphantly.

"I don't suppose you've got a licence for this? Paid the taxes, have you? Didn't think so. I could smell it on you, the guilt. I have a nose for it."

Norbury shouted up from downstairs, "I've taken confession, seen all. It's as she said. Brother Nielsen spoke with the wife and then left."

"You wouldn't believe what I've found up here, Brother. It reminds me of that time we found the missing racehorse at the knacker's yard."

Josephus gesticulated at Jon with his knife. "I can't imagine what the fine for this will be. Substantial, I warrant. Let's hope it's not stolen. I'll be back soon, for further investigation. Don't even think about absconding — I would consider that a prevention of justice."

The censor hopped backwards and slid like a sailor down the stair rail.

Jon lifted his chin and stared at the trapdoor to the cap room, behind which the strongbox of coins lay next to the bodies of Kareem and the censor, entwined in a rotting embrace.

The gods had been merciful. He had been spared.

He patted the carousel horse on the forelock, and it seemed, as he lowered himself down the ladder, that in some indefinable way it was smiling at him.

●

Anna was in Mother's bedroom, stripping bedclothes and giving her a bed bath.

Jon embraced her. For a while they just stood, brow on brow, his hand cupped behind her head, the baby between them. Then she pulled away gently.

"That was terrifying," she said.

"Yes."

"The tall one said they'd be back. What did he mean? Did you tell them about the Peacock?"

Jon wiped the sweat from his brow. "You did well, Anna. You're my rock."

"Where were you last night?"

He shook his head.

"I can't help if you won't talk to me. You scared me this morning, in that chair. You looked like a corpse."

He saw himself as she had seen him, useless and despairing and his mouth filled with the black taste of self-disgust. He wanted to tell her everything, about the dead bodies in the cap, the cache of Freeborn's money, to show her the mark that Barehill burnt into his chest. His conscience dared him to. He saw Kareem dying. The censor dying. Laila's advice came back to him: *It's better if she doesn't know.* The murderess was right.

"Go to temple, keep praying for us."

"What if it isn't helping? What if it doesn't work?"

"Don't lose faith. Dance for the gods. Listen with your heart. You know it helps."

She ducked her chin to hide her face. "I know."

"Never give up, Anna. Never let them beat us."

"My Lion." Her soft embrace took his breath.

Anna went downstairs. Jon sat on the edge of Mother's bed. "What am I to do?" he asked her.

Mother had nothing to offer but wheezing.

Protect Anna and the baby. That was the most important thing. Jon finished cleaning Mother's face. Then he stuffed some soapy rags into his nostrils, went up to the cap room and tried not to look at the sacks that held the bodies as he counted out coins from Barehill's chest.

●

The heat of day was fading fast when Jon reached the Bell Jar. He eyed the changed tavern mistrustfully. There was a queue outside. Dishevelled men of all ages held weapons, makeshift and antique, and a new sign hung above the door — an orange-painted board, marked in the upper quadrant with a peacock feather trailed by three diamonds. It was the flag of a militia, newly formed.

"Wait your turn," shouted a dirty-bearded peddler. Jon ignored him, and pushed his way inside.

The Bell Jar was the busiest he had ever seen it. Harriet dashed madly from table to table. She winked at Jon without pausing in her work. Raymond the innkeeper scowled from behind the bar as he dried a flagon with a grey-stained cloth. The tables had been rearranged like a royal court, and Peacock Matthew was its prince.

The bright feather of his hat bobbed excitedly as he conferred with a pair of censors. *Norbury and Josephus!* Jon made to exit but Big Shark jabbed a tattooed finger in his direction that fixed him to the spot. The censors turned and stared.

"Wait your turn, Miller," the Peacock shouted imperiously. Whatever was happening, it looked suspiciously friendly for a meeting between censors and a gangster. Jon slouched over to the bar and ordered a half pint that he couldn't afford.

The end of the bar had been requisitioned by a dour-faced man who wore the ribboned cap of a recruitment clerk. Jon watched as he took the names of ragged men, inspected their armaments and handed them a wedge of cheese and a pint in return for a signature. He wasn't turning anyone away.

When the censors had finished with Matthew they shook his hand, which was the unlikeliest thing that Jon had ever seen, and then they came over to him. They pressed their knees into the back of his own, pinned him painfully to the bar.

"We're watching you, Miller," Josephus said and shoved him in the back.

The tavern door banged closed behind them.

"You can't be everybody's friend," said Raymond the landlord.

"If you'd be so kind as to join us," Peacock shouted, and ordered a round of gin petards. Jon picked up a stool, sat opposite Matthew and the Sharks.

"I'm sorry to hear about your lack of customers," Matthew said, "but I'm afraid the week is up. I assume you've brought the keys to the mill. Hand them over and we can be friends again. I might even have a job for you now that you're out of business. I'm in need of big men." He grinned mischievously.

Jon swung his arm and the coin sack crunched onto the table.

"Are you taking the piss?" Big Shark said in a voice of gravel and broken glass.

"Five pounds."

"In pennies and tuppences?" Matthew asked.

"Yes, as it happens."

"Bugger me." Matthew gazed at the bulging sack in wonder. "Been prising up floorboards? Mugging beggars?"

"Count it," Jon demanded.

Even the Sharks shrivelled at the prospect. Peacock spun his hand in the air dismissively.

"Why bother. You're an honest man. That's your thing, isn't it? Like my hat." Matthew rocked back on his stool and flicked one of the cap feathers up so that it balanced above his head like an exclamation mark. "So where did you get it, then? All this lucre?" He searched Jon's face for an answer. Jon could not tell if the villain was more amused or disappointed.

"I'll be going now." Jon rose to his feet, as Harriet set down the tray of gins with a wry smile.

"Sit down, Jon. A deal is a deal. I've no complaints. I'll buy myself something nice with these coppers. A timepiece maybe."

"A couple of censors?"

Peacock smirked. "Have some faith. You can't buy justice in this land. Funnily enough, though, it turns out justice can buy me."

"What did you tell them about the horse?"

Peacock feigned indignation. "You mistake me for a snitch. No sir, I have become a gentleman."

Jon laughed aloud and took up his drink.

"I jest ye not. I have taken a commission from the Brotherhood of Censors to raise a company of double-armed men. I am now the colonel of the Trained Band of Turbulence."

Jon almost sprayed his liquor. He choked on it instead.

"These excellent fellows by my side are my captains." Big Shark pointed at the orange ribbons newly looped around his tattooed biceps. Littleshark waggled an orange cravat.

"The world's becoming ridiculous," Jon said, still coughing gin. "I expect it'll be raining frogs by the end of the week."

Matthew's eyes twinkled. "We are living in dangerous times. The streets are plagued by gangs. Dissenters prowl at night, working mischief. There has been rioting in Lambourne, a manufactory damaged in Brightstowe." He leaned forwards confidentially. "In Turbulence itself, a censor has gone missing. This is a time for patriotism, not jokes."

Jon jabbed his thumb over his shoulder at the wastrel recruits. They reminded him of Barehill's men. "These men don't care about the Dowager Duchess or the Unity any more than you do. They fight for bread and their families. What do the censors think you're going to do with your infirm army anyway? Keep the peace?"

"I'll admit I've a few scores to settle. Wylde's gang has been encroaching. I've been meaning to make an example of him for a while. If there is trouble, it will only go to show how badly the Brotherhood need me." For a moment, Matthew's eyes took on a faraway look.

"Get too big for your boots and Gordon might get upset." Jon had set that barb to rile, but Matthew just shook his head.

"Gordon's a money man. We have an understanding." He shot back his drink, reclined in satisfaction. "Let's have another to celebrate your first payment and my promotion."

Jon downed his shot and wiped his beard dry. "I'll be going."

"Don't fancy the company? Don't tell me our friendship is about nothing but money. I thought we had so much in common."

Jon stared at him balefully. "You have my money, Matthew. I hope you enjoy the spending of it."

The Peacock shrugged. "Money, luck, love. It all runs out, eventually."

THE MOTHER OF INVENTION

Whispers and stares followed Miranda from the infirmary to Chairman Gleame's chambers. The black shift she wore over her hospital gown could not hide her limp or the orderly who walked beside her, holding her elbow discreetly. Miranda hated being helped, but it would be worse to be seen to stumble or fall. She cursed the stiff, weak flesh of her uninjured leg that burned with every step, while its obsidian twin supported her weight with an effortless assurance.

Gleame's guards, the same fellows as before, saluted her smartly as she entered his magnificent office. Fluted pillars, spiralled with quotations from important texts, supported its roof. Gilded sculptures of lions and goddesses were positioned tastefully around the room, deadlocked in a perpetual game of hide-and-seek. The seaward side, once a colonnade, had been sealed with a broad expanse of latticed glass. Playful waves tapered towards a distant horizon.

Set before the panoramic window were two high-backed chairs, black and gold, and between them a drinks table. Gleame sat in one of them, contemplating the horizon and swirling a cerise wine in gold-lipped crystal.

"Miranda, Ward of the Grand Duchess of the Wrekin and the North," the orderly intoned with calculated deference. Miranda signalled for him to leave and approached the grandmaster gingerly. The pain in her thigh flamed.

"Quite a spectacle," she said.

"On a clear day you can make out the peaks of Ellan Vannin." Gleame set down his glass and pointed seaward. Either his eyes were sharper than Miranda's or she was looking in the wrong direction.

"I've heard the island is beautiful."

"I considered it as an alternative for the Convergence, many years ago. How are you feeling, my dear? Is the device comfortable?"

"I'm getting used to it."

He rose from his seat and took Miranda's arm, led her between his antiquities to one of the many small alcoves that lined the walls, and drew aside the fur-lined curtain that screened it.

A full-length portrait of Her Grace hung inside. The duchess smiled gamely from a bucolic garden paradise where white harts frolicked with unicorns and scarlet birds with trailing tails sailed across a cloudless sky.

Miranda leaned closer, tilted her head from side to side. "Such a likeness is impossible. It's as if I look upon her reflection. Is this a painting?" She reached to touch it.

Gleame stayed her hand. "Please. It's a tapestry, woven from your mother's hair and extremely fragile."

Miranda looked more closely. It was true. The sheen of the weave shifted like water.

"What is it for?"

"Communion."

"Like a hekamaphone?"

"The hekamaphone is designed for the modern world. This is ancient cunning. Unique. In many ways totally impractical."

"It's beautiful," Miranda said.

"That too," Gleame said with a hint of nostalgia.

He took a candle and small pair of scissors, plucked a wispy white hair from his brow and without asking snipped a raven one from hers. Fascinated, she did not think to complain. He twisted them together into a tiny braid which he burnt in candle flame, captured the smoke in a douter and sucked it into his cheeks. The room filled with a sickly sweet aroma as he puffed his cheeks and blew onto the tapestry with pursed lips.

A moment of hanging stillness, then the surface of the tapestry writhed and whispered, made an itchy, rustling sound as the countryside image of her mother was lost in a confusion of colour. Miranda gasped in wonder as it resolved into an image so lifelike it seemed more like a portal than a vision.

Miranda had never been invited inside it, but she immediately knew from the golden hue of the masonry and the beautiful objects all around that what she saw was Her Grace's private office.

In its centre stood Her Grace, dressed in her full finery. The ribbons in her hair, rosette at her bust and abundance of pearls that edged her collar battled ambitiously for attention. She also wielded a sizable fan. Her demeanour seemed that of a potentate being kept from an important negotiation, but she always had that look about her. The sounds of a party could be heard in the background, gay laughter and the chinking of glasses, but Miranda could tell she had the duchess's full attention.

Miranda's governess, dressed in simple black and white, stood in the background, anxiously twisting a handkerchief.

Miranda curtsied formally, though the movement brought tears to her eyes. "Your Grace."

"My dearest Miranda, thank the gods. It is such a joy to see you with my own eyes." The hairs of the tapestry made a dry sound as the duchess's lips moved, adding a breathless quality to her voice.

"I am honoured," Miranda said.

"Tell me the truth of what happened. Leave out not the slightest detail."

"I caused an accident. The injury that I sustained will serve as a reminder to be more careful in the future."

"Injury! What happened to you is a disgrace! Show me the wound."

Miranda coughed pointedly and Gleame turned away as she raised the hem of her gown to her knees. Her governess blanched. *What a squeamish woman*, Miranda thought.

"Gustaf Gleame, what have you done?" the duchess thundered. "You promised me that Miranda would be safe."

Gleame's face writhed as if every feature was trying to avoid the duchess's gaze.

"Your Grace," Miranda said, "if anyone other than myself was at fault they have already paid in full. A man was lost to the Convergence as a result of my error."

The duchess's pearls twitched irritatedly on her chest. "Lost or killed? What kind of a man? Assure me that you were never in such danger." She fluttered her fan furiously.

"Never. The grandmaster holds my safety amongst his highest concerns."

"I am profoundly distraught by the whole affair," Gleame said.

"So you should be. This whole incident strikes me as very peculiar. And Miranda — it is so unlike you to be involved in trouble."

Miranda caught her governess's eye and the woman winked at her. Miranda turned back to her mother, confused by the familiarity. The duchess's eyes narrowed.

"We must get you home at once."

"If it pleases Your Grace, I would prefer to serve you here," Miranda said, and was shocked by how miserable the mere suggestion of leaving the Convergence made her feel.

The duchess nodded approvingly then turned to Miranda's governess. "You have seen that she is safe. Unless Miranda has something she wishes to say to you now, return to your duties." Miranda stared at the duchess, nonplussed and shrugged. The governess bowed deeply and, as she departed, blew Miranda a kiss. Astonished, Miranda wondered what the woman was thinking.

"Gleame tells me that you are very talented, says that you may become a master in time."

Miranda dragged her attention back to her mother. "That is certainly my ambition. If it serves to please."

"Then focus on your work. I expect great things." The duchess turned to the chairman. "Gleame — do not disappoint me again."

"Never," he declared.

"Now, if you will excuse us, I require a moment alone with my ward." The chairman nodded sagely and patted Miranda on the shoulder as he left the antechamber. The duchess beckoned. "Daughter, come nearer."

Miranda leaned close to the tapestry, squeamishly afraid that its wriggling hairs would tickle her face. "Mother," she whispered.

"Finally we can talk like human beings."

"Thank the gods."

"How are you truly? Is it all as you described?"

"I look like a plum under this gown. I suppose I was lucky to avoid worse."

"And yet you protect Gleame's reputation. I wager you've made an arrangement with him, you clever girl. Tell me more of your work."

"It's exciting, interesting. They ask a lot of me, but I am capable." *More than capable*, she thought. "I am developing a new form of cunning."

"Is that necessary?"

"It's changing the way I conceive of the world."

"Are you lonely? Should I send your handmaiden?"

"Gods, no." They both laughed.

"How about your governess? You have always been so close." That was true, as far as Miranda could remember, but the intimacy seemed inappropriate now, childish.

"I have grown out of her, I suppose." Miranda knew why, and felt a sudden need to change the subject. "Mother, how does our cause proceed?"

"The Wise Council does nothing but bicker and delay. The ministers know that they need a leader but the southern barons begrudge the power of the North. My spies are hard at work, changing minds. I will be appointed before the year is out. The endless politicking bores me."

Miranda smirked; her mother loved politics more than any other vice.

"Tell me about your liaisons. I understand the eldest of the younger Lavetys is at the Convergence also. Have you spent much time with him?"

The word 'Lavety' provoked a cold unease. The events of the past week had pushed Adrian's vendetta from Miranda's mind completely, but now the images of blood and gore rushed back. She needed to be cautious. Mother had asked the question for a reason.

"We have little in common," she said hesitantly.

"Nonsense. You went to Alchester together, and you are both from important families. What matters more than that? One day a Lavety could be your husband."

Miranda swallowed the vile response that had leaped into the base of her throat. "I have dined with him, Your Grace."

"Good. The Lavetys are important allies. Keep in his favour. Anyone else?"

"There's a boy I like, but I think he just wants to be friends."

The duchess snorted in amusement. "An armiger? Of good blood?"

"New money, but I find value in his company."

"He's handsome, then?"

"Practically burnished."

Her Grace bellowed. That was her true laugh, rarely heard. "I trust you're being careful." Miranda thought of her leg and laughed as well, raising one of Her Grace's finely plucked brows. Miranda grinned broadly.

"How about you?"

"Young lady! Your impudence is astounding. You know I have no time for the petty nobles of the Unity. Now pay attention, what I said to Gleame was true. If you were to gain a seat on the Convocation — that would be of great value to me."

"I know. I will do my best, as I love Your Grace."

The duchess smiled. "Of all my girls, you have always been my favourite, Miranda. We should speak again, soon."

The tapestry of her mother rustled one last time and the image of Her Grace's office dissolved into verdant green and brown. The delicate hairs still smelled faintly of her. Miranda reached out to stroke them, glowing with pride. As her hand brushed its surface, she saw a few motes of magic slip between her fingers and drift into nothingness.

HUNTING THE DARK

Daniel compared the hand mirrors like a desperate suitor, as if choosing the right one was the most important decision of his life.

"Silver from the Western Isles or Anatole. Which is more fashionable?"

The jeweller smoothed his moustache to hide his frustration. "The ladies are fond of both kinds, sir."

It was an absurd question, but the crease of worry in Daniel's brow was no act.

Where is Bolb? The master had entered the Verge's temple almost an hour before. That was too long. *Did I somehow miss him leaving? Does the temple have a hidden exit?* He put down one of the mirrors he was feigning interest in, picked up a perfume jar and flipped it over in his hand.

"Begging your pardon, sir, but you've looked at that three times already."

Daniel knew, and secretly admired the stall-keeper's patience.

"Tell you what, buy that mirror and the jar and I'll throw in this comb for free. Walrus tusk and ebony. You won't find better in the North." The man ran a fingernail musically down the comb's teeth. Daniel ignored him and kept the mirror angled at the temple's entrance.

A flash of iridescent light caught in the glass. Bolb had finally emerged from his prayers. Daniel hissed in relief and scattered an uncounted handful of gold onto the stall.

"I'll take this one — keep the change."

The jeweller clapped his hands in delight. "You forgot your comb," he called after Dan's disappearing back.

Bolb had jangled his way into the bustle of the atrium and Daniel was determined not to lose track of him a second time. He moved expeditiously, keeping the master close, using the crowd for cover, disguising his movement and intentions, dropping to his knees to retrieve an imaginary coin or pull up a stocking whenever he thought the master might turn, and using the hand mirror to keep him in sight.

Bolb traipsed mournfully through the market, oblivious to it all. Tears had smeared the greasepaint on his calf-like face and streaks of black kohl stained his puffy cheeks. *Grief?* Daniel wondered. *Or fear?*

The hunt led towards the fastness of the southern wall where the natural rock of the isle rose a little higher than the stalls, stood jagged and exposed. Bolb slipped out of sight into a short passageway. Daniel ducked behind a row of plucked geese that swung from a poulter's awning, counted to three and followed after him.

The passageway was a blind alley lined with rough stone, yet Bolb had disappeared.

Impossible. Daniel ran to the statue at the end of its short length. The comely maiden from some obscure legend proffered a verdigris-stained dish with both hands. A lever jutted incongruously from her thigh. Daniel suspected a secret passage and worked the pump. A slug of water plopped disappointingly into the rough-hewn water trough below. *There must be something.* He desperately searched the rocks for some telltale crevice or hole.

It could only be seen from a certain angle. Perpendicular to the side of the trough and well hidden in the rocks was an iron hatch stamped with the Verge's henge icon. The portal spoke of dark and forbidden places, but its lock was broken and it was a fraction ajar.

Dan looked over his shoulder. The atrium was busy but nobody was watching him. He discarded the mirror, pulled at the door, made himself thin so as to let in as little light as possible, and squeezed through.

It was some kind of drain or pipe. A metal stairway, suspended by chains of rod, descended into absolute darkness. The scent of sea spray blew from somewhere far below. He could hear the faint jangle of Bolb's receding footsteps above the sound of dripping water. Daniel cursed inwardly. There was no time to fetch a lanthorn; he would have to chance the dark.

He scampered along what he supposed was some kind of gantry, fingers looped around its crooked handrails. He used the light-stepping technique, sweeping his feet on the iron in smooth semicircles, like a skater on ice, his passage rapid and silent.

Far ahead, and slightly below, bobbed a pinprick of light. *Bolb.*

The roar of running water became louder, echoed all around. Within it, Daniel heard something else. A living, squeaking presence in the darkness. The flapping of leathery wings. *Bats*, Daniel reassured himself. *It can only be bats.*

Bolb's tiny light was closer now, a weak beam like the mirrored flame of a lighthouse radiating from the peak of his silhouette. Without warning, it stilled. Daniel heard the rattle of keys, the turn of a lock. For a brief moment, the master stood framed in a rectangle of light. Daniel crouched low and pressed himself against the rails, half closed his eyes to preserve his vision.

Bolb had gone through a door; Daniel could now see the faint trace of light through its frame and keyhole. He stalked silently to its threshold and peered through the keyhole. All he could see was the silver and gold of Bolb's back. He pressed his ear against the cold iron of the lock and strained to hear the muffled conversation that had begun inside.

"What are you talking about? Give me that."

A man's voice, old and rasping. *Who are you?* Daniel wondered, and shuffled tight against the door.

"A summons from Corbin? We all received one."

Dan stole another look through the keyhole, grit his teeth in frustration.

"What can we do?" Bolb sounded desperate, *and a little angry*.

"Nothing," the other man replied. "Corbin is a thorough man . . . business of an ordinary investigation."

"You've ruined me . . . a pointless risk."

Bolb's voice raised to a porcine squeal. "How dare you! This insane enterprise was your idea."

Daniel clenched his fist in triumph. Lang was right! There was conspiracy at the heart of the Convergence. Now he was uncovering it. He would be a hero.

Something leathery and squeaking brushed against his neck and tangled in his hair. Daniel thrashed it away and yelped. The men in the room fell silent.

Daniel felt a shift in the air; the undeniable animal sensation of a hunter scented by his quarry and suddenly turned prey. He backed away from the door and stumbled with a clatter, froze, pressed himself low to the iron. His ankle burned in the darkness. He listened to the mocking echo of his fall and the hard beating of his heart.

The mechanism of the lock turned.

The door swung open and Bolb stood silhouetted, his bulk pyramidal and immovable. A malign radiance crackled in the air around him. A beam of crimson arrowed from his brow, swept the darkness.

Daniel was bathed in light. He covered his face and prayed that it had not been seen. Bolb spread his arms and from each of his wide sleeves snaked a machine of crawling metal. Ruby lenses shone bright in their tubular heads. One wound itself around a railing and scented the air with its needle nose, the other dropped to the gantry floor with a heavy clang and edged forwards, sniffing at the ground.

Daniel forced the panic back and tried to remember Brother Hernandez's instruction for snakes. He edged backwards without making a sound, but the machines' eyes sensed his movement and twitched in his direction. He grasped a rail, pulled himself up and ran for his life, pursued by the mad clatter of pin-prick legs.

He realised immediately that he had set off in the wrong direction — the way back towards the atrium was behind him. He was sprinting into the unknown, running blindly through the deep workings of the Convergence and an unforeseen turning would send him tumbling over a rail into abyssal darkness.

A notch on the railing ripped the skin from the webbing of his thumb but he was running too hard to care. His lungs burned and his legs burned but still the clattering metal drew closer. Dim bands of brown light appeared all around him; the gantry had entered an encirclement of iron pipes made visible by a faint light ahead. The rat-a-tat of metal on metal grew frantic.

In the distance, above the hammering of his boots, he heard the sound of men working. He burst into a long room where men tended a knotted maze of pipes and tank work, ran past them with no thought other than putting some distance between himself and the hunting machines.

The workers stared at him bemused as he barged between them. Was he the only one who could hear the furious tapping of pointed legs over the hiss and clank of the plumbing?

THE CENSOR'S HAND

He burst through doors, ascended stairs, kicked up clouds of coal dust as he raced through a gallery of furnaces where sweating stokers were laying fires. The ovens poured heat onto his skin and into his lungs. The acid of his lungs burnt his mouth.

The running in him was over. Breathless, he skidded to a halt, grabbed a shovel from a coal pile and turned to face his hidden enemy. The fire-gates cast red stripes of light across the gallery. The only sound was the roar of hot air and flames.

It dropped from the ceiling, a flash of silver death. Dan slapped the thing aside with the blade of the shovel, but it twisted in the air and its beak lightly grazed his forearm before it clattered undamaged to the floor. As the segments of its body rotated to upright, Daniel raised the shovel overhead and plunged its edge into the contraption with all of his might. *Not even a scratch.* He set his weight onto the blade and pinned the thing to the ground. His arm felt weak, stung like a burst blister, and he saw the surface of his scratched skin had erupted into a frothy stew.

Poison. The metal worm wriggled against the shovel. At any moment, its twin could be upon him. Daniel looked to the nearest furnace, smashed his boot into the latch that held its fire-gate shut and howled in pain as it swung open. Released, the automaton lunged. He stepped back and batted it deep into the furnace with one deft scoop. There was a dull clang and a spray of embers as it hit the back wall. The flesh of his palms sizzled as he slammed the latch home. The metal beast, glowing dully with heat, thrashed inside its new prison. Biting his lip to mask the pain, Daniel fled again.

He lost track of the myriad chambers through which he sped. There were breweries and smelteries, tanning pools and granaries. A pantry filled with rounds of cheese the size of cartwheels. A vivarium full of beasts terrestrial and aquatic. Never in his life had Daniel expected to see a mythic creature, but in that place, he saw narwhals and giant jumping rats, awaiting a journey to the cooking pot.

He entered a hall, lined with colossal shelves and rotating columns ringed with brass stairs, that containing nothing but books. Floating trays collected them and deposited them in a tiny portal set high in a far wall. The feeling of that place was ominous and confusing and he left as quickly as he could. As he travelled further upwards, he saw more people. He slowed his pace and tried to appear casual, despite the dirt, sweat and wounds that covered his body.

The pain eventually caught up with him but the machines did not. Soon the corridors and halls he passed became familiar. He made his way back into the crowded atrium, somehow surprised by how little attention he was paid. He crossed towards his chambers convinced that every window or crevice he passed concealed a watcher, human or mechanical.

For the first time in his life, someone had wanted him dead, not in boast, jest or the wild fury of an altercation, but just killed, plain and simple. The realisation of it strained his pulse and made his body cold. He shivered, hugged his shoulders to hide his fear, as much from himself as any other. The reality of adventure was not what he had expected. Nothing like it at all. All at once, he felt a little older.

3

FLAMES OF REBELLION

"Bastards. Bastards. Bastards." Sweat glossed the knotted muscles of Jon's back. He mumbled into his unkempt beard as his pitchfork bit deep into the straw. He dug ferociously, flinging clumps across the loading-bay floor to drive away the fears that circled and pecked at his mind like vultures. Heedless, his thoughts returned to the corpses rotting in the cap room overhead. He imagined Norbury and Josephus at his door, come to take him away.

When the work was done, he rested on the pitchfork, panting like a dog, and stared at the crude trapdoor he had uncovered, three planks of cheap pine laid over bare earth. He lay on the ground and put his mouth to a knothole.

"Anyone there?" he called quietly and hoped for no reply.

A voice echoed back, muffled by the timbers, but very close. Jon could feel breath on his face, caught the warm vinegar stench of another man's sweat. He glared angrily into the darkness. The voice came again, louder this time.

"I said open up. It's hotter than a monkey's armpit down here."

Jon lifted the planks and sullenly stacked them against a wall, exposing a pit as rough as an army latrine that gaped in the floor of his loading bay. The top of a ladder appeared at its maw and Barehill hoisted himself out, his clothes spattered with dirt and clay.

"This is taking too long," Jon said, dry-mouthed.

"We're working as fast as we can." Barehill laid a patronising hand on Jon's shoulder. "Be calm. Where's your good lady?"

"Anna's taken the baby to temple. Gods know we need the help."

Barehill grunted. "Man is alone in this world, which is why we must help each other. Have you told her yet?"

Jon nearly threw a punch, but a small band of men wielding picks and shovels were already clambering out of the tunnel behind their leader.

"Evening Bertrand, Dyer, Will," Jon said through gritted teeth. He had been leaving the digging crew flasks of water for days. They nodded their respects.

"We'll have it fixed up proper by nightfall, Mister Miller," Will promised.

"Men have been digging through the night since they heard about your battle with the censor," Barehill said. "I've had more volunteers than I know what to do with."

The workmen grinned in unison and Jon's stomach wrenched. The news of the crime was seeping through the city like pestilential water. Barehill pulled his pipe from his pocket, set to lighting it.

"Beat a censor with a knife," Dyer exclaimed. "Fucking lethal, you are."

"It seems you've become a bit of a hero," Barehill said.

"Too right." Bert was flushed with excitement.

Jon shook his head in dismay. He was being fitted up. Once enough men started to believe a story like that, it became true.

"Laila was there, she saw . . ." At the mention of her name, she appeared from the tunnel shaft, as if a phantom summoned from a grave. She was dressed mannishly, in a shirt and breeches, caked with dust. Her neck was streaked with sweat, and it had pooled in her collarbone. She stood, arms crossed, faced him with a look he could not read.

"Ask her," he said.

"I've never seen a big man move so fast."

The bitch. Jon flushed with anger. He wanted to smash her face in, though the thought of hitting a woman turned his gaze to the floor in shame.

Dyer tried to catch his attention. "Mister Miller? You alright?"

Barehill stared at him quizzically.

"I have to go," Jon said.

Barehill looked concerned. "Where?"

"My rent is due. If I don't pay the Peacock this afternoon he'll have my mill and your army will have to find its rations elsewhere."

"The gangs are wicked — tyrants by another name. Matthew's time will come soon enough, and Wylde's. All of the gangs and their collaborators."

"Good luck with that. I still have to pay."

Barehill blew a smoke ring and the loading bay filled with the smell of fresh tobacco. "Do what you need to do. We'll finish up here. I'll place a tail on you, for your safety, and set a lookout for your wife."

❋

Jon walked the twisting route to the Bell Jar pursued by bad thoughts. Anna still didn't know about the bodies, that was the main thing, and he had enough money from Barehill to keep the Peacock off his back for the time being. But then what? He might have tried his luck with the censors, despite everything, but that was before he had seen how they operated. Now he suspected they might hang him, just to be on the safe side. Running away was out of the question. If Mother was well, it might have been possible, but Norbury and Josephus would be after them faster than a fox on a rabbit.

He continued towards the Bell Jar. A few feral dogs and cats crossed his path. The dogs fled at the sight of him, which made sense — they didn't fancy ending the evening roasting on a spit. The cats, being godlike and sacred, knew that they were safe, even if they didn't understand why.

He looked at the clouds, fixed his gaze on one that loomed ominously overhead like the tall-eared shadow of He-who-sits-upon-the-mountain.

"What?" he shouted at the sky. "What am I supposed to do?"

His voice echoed in a peculiar silence. The streets of Turbulence were so curiously empty that he felt he might be in some kind of nightmare. Even the gangs' lookouts were gone from their usual positions. He reached Swan Alley.

"Jon." The whisperer was Bill, hiding in a doorway.

"Dog's breath! You're supposed to be a tail, not an escort. Get away from me."

"Can you smell it?"

Bill was right. Turbulence air was always full of dirty smells, but today there was an unmistakable foulness, the acrid scent of black smoke. Fires were bad news in Turbulence's tightly packed streets; they could take two dozen houses before a break was made and the ruins left to burn themselves out. Jon picked out the tallest of the derelict buildings that surrounded them.

"Hold onto this and wait." He tossed his coin sack underarm into Bill's midriff sending him skidding backwards. "That's Barehill's money. So you'd better not lose it."

He kicked the door of the abandoned townhouse, sending it sliding across splintery joists to tumble into a half-exposed basement, and capered across a treacherous framework of rotting floorboards to the remains of the manor's staircase. He climbed cautiously, grasping at newels, wedging his wide feet between the balusters.

Storey by storey the smell of smoke grew stronger. He clambered onto the roof through a gaping hole and shuffled across loose red tiles to gain a vantage point beside an unsteady chimney.

One of Bromwich's gigantic manufactories was ablaze. Gouts of flame jetted from its tall windows. Its sails made great wheels of fire in the sky and around them scraps of blackened cloth, peeled from the rigging, swirled in the air like a flock of monstrous starlings.

Jon stood slack-jawed, paralysed by wonder and terror.

A crowd of hapless men, ant small and silent in the distance, threw buckets of water at the inferno. *Futile*, Jon thought. Taming such a blaze was impossible. The manufactory crested a ridge, and the magical breeze that had once powered its sails now acted as a bellows, making an oven of the building.

He heard a distant crack, like a rifle shot, as a top-floor window exploded and sent a cascade of glass showering onto the crowd below. *The heat of the fire*, Jon thought, but then a man leapt from the aperture, his arms flailing as he plummeted. Another followed. Then a couple appeared at the precipice and joined hands. Jon shouted at them to stop, that the fall was certain death. They leapt before his words had finished and the pair disappeared from view.

Nobody deserved to die like that. Jon's anger reached for someone to blame. He raged at the unknown fool who had caused the fire. The manufactory owners might have ruined him, but he had nothing against the men and women who worked for them. Then he remembered the firebombs he had seen in Barehill's secret base, and vomited over the roof tiles.

A ragtag gang of ruffians awaited Jon on the street. They were armed with picks and staves, wore the orange ribbons of the Trained Band of Turbulence. Bill was their prisoner. He glanced nervously at Jon from their midst. A muscle-bound militiaman held Jon's sack of coin.

"What do you lot want?" Jon shouted as he picked his way out of the crumbling townhouse.

The patrol's portly captain waved his antique crossbow in Jon's direction.

"That sack of coin belongs to the Peacock," Jon said.

"Damn right it does, and you can help us deliver it. You're coming with us, to Temple Place."

"For what reason?"

"Partly because Colonel Peacock requires your audience. Mostly because huntress here says so." The captain slapped the stock of his crossbow carelessly, and Jon flinched, half expecting the quarrel to shoot into his guts.

CHAINS OF COMMAND

The creak of floorboards overhead informed Daniel that he was no longer alone. He kept his breathing shallow and silent, watched from inside the timber framework as a man descended the long stairs to the rough earthen floor of the wine cellar, and hoped that his long wait was over.

Shadows danced on the walls as a lanthorn swayed in the visitor's hand. Its light receded into the rows of casks and stills, was raised to head height to the locker whose brass plaque was engraved with the name 'Edmund Sutton'. A shadow unlocked its cross-hatched door and took out a bottle, squeaked free the cork, tipped out the tightly rolled scroll hidden inside.

It has to be Corbin. Daniel clicked his tongue in mimicry of a drip. The flame was extinguished with a sharp puff and, in its dying light, Daniel saw the shadow duck and roll aside. He grinned in the darkness. It felt good to have caught the devil unawares. He clicked his tongue once again, louder, to let Corbin know exactly where he hid. The bastard tapped him on the back of the shoulder.

"What are you doing, boy?" Corbin whispered.

"Master Bolb — he tried to kill me."

"Has your cover slipped?" Daniel thought he heard a blade being drawn. He shook his head and then realised that the gesture was invisible in the dark.

"He didn't see my face."

"So why are we meeting?"

"We have to change the plan. It's too dangerous."

Corbin chuckled gently. "I warned you it would be like this. You're afraid, that's all."

"No I'm not," Daniel lied.

"One day you'll recognise this sort of fear as your best friend. It keeps the mind sharp. More importantly, it means we're on the right track. Now tell me what you've learned."

"Bolb's working with someone else."

"How do you know?"

"He met with another man. Someone old."

"Old? For fuck's sake, boy!"

"They talked about your summons. He's guilty, Corbin."

"What if he is? I still don't know of what, or why."

"I'd bet my life on it."

"You did that already."

"I can't follow Bolb again; he'll be looking. We have to try something else."

Daniel waited, heel to haunch, while Corbin considered his options. "Alright then, change of plan. Here's what we're going to do. I'll interview him late at night. Be polite and boring. Kill him with detail. Take hours. I won't learn a thing, of course, not from the likes of him. Not without knowing what I'm looking for."

"I don't understand."

"While I'm questioning him I want you to burgle his room."

"Burgle?" Daniel squeaked.

"Search it. And no one can know, not even Gleame."

"What about Lang?"

"Fuck Lang."

"You want me to burgle the master who constructed the mechanical owls that watch the border with Erdin?"

"That was him, was it?" Corbin sounded impressed.

"Why don't you just perform an inquisition?"

"Of a master's room, on your hearsay? Bolb would make it political. Insist on a warrant. By the time I had one, he would have removed the evidence and I would be left looking an eejit. My plan is better. It's a good plan. Don't allow fear to cloud your mind. Focus."

Daniel twitched as Corbin patted him on the shoulder. *Patronising bastard. You aren't the one risking your life*, he thought, and felt his scorched and torn hand throbbing in the dark. "I'm not afraid, but Bolb has machines that move and kill. Anything could be waiting for me in his chamber. He knows that he's watched. The risks are too high."

"You asked for my trust, Edmund, now earn it."

Daniel felt nothing more than a fleeting breeze as Corbin's presence dissolved into the darkness.

●

"What should I do?" Daniel said.

The magistrate's words susurrated in the hekamaphone's horn. "You have done well to gain Corbin's confidence. He seems keen to take risks. Reckless even. This investigation is more than sensitive. One might almost imagine that he puts our good relationship with the Honourable Company at risk deliberately."

"Corbin seems determined to expose the guilty at any cost," Daniel said.

"That is his way," Lang said, as if in agreement. "I cannot overrule him in this investigation without good reason, especially on a matter I am supposed to know nothing about. Be careful. Do not underestimate Bolb's power, temporal or arcane. He is a very clever man, one of the Convergence's founders. I wish I had more helpful advice to offer."

Daniel remembered the eyes of Bolb's creations searching for him in the underworld. "Have your investigations uncovered anything?"

"There's nothing in our files on Bolb, but I do not have a file on everything," Lang said. "From what you say it seems more and more likely that there are traitors within the Verge, but, as I have said, Bolb is a powerful man. We cannot move against him without evidence that is . . . puissant." Lang emphasised the foreign-sounding word. Daniel guessed that it meant the good stuff.

"Then maybe Corbin is right; it would be best to search Bolb's room before we make an accusation."

"Only if you don't get caught. Only if there is something to find." Lang's hesitation betrayed his deliberation. "Your bravery is not in question, Daniel, but this is a task that would challenge the most skilled of brothers."

"I will not fail," Daniel said, and immediately regretted it.

"It is a grave thing you will attempt."

"I know."

"If you find anything of importance then I must learn of it first."

"Yes sir."

"I should have equipped you with poison. It was a foolish oversight."

"Poison?"

"You told me that Corbin refused the pistol I sent him with the dispensations. I want you to take it with you."

"Surely you don't want me to take up arms against a master?"

"Don't be absurd — it is for your own sake. I would not like to see you suffer unnecessarily. I'm sure it won't happen, but if capture becomes unavoidable, a shot to the head would be best. Do not fire the gun inside your mouth — that cripples as often as it kills. Aim for your temple or the bridge of your nose. Escape will be painless that way."

UP THE BEACH

Miranda wandered between the piles of books and randomly placed furniture that filled her new room. She was fully absorbed by a soapstone covered in small triangular scratches almost invisible to the naked eye, but clear and crisp through the long-handled magnifying eyeglass that she wielded in her rune-decorated glove. The script was well preserved and mostly legible, simple and beautiful.

She cast the stone onto the glowing coals of her altar and watched the offering blacken as it surrendered to the flames.

She considered the unfinished luxury of her new chambers while her experiment unfolded. The air was thick with the smell of varnish and lavender. Mirrored tiles glittered on the walls like seams of jewels. A voluminous bookshelf, an alchemist's brewery, a draughtsman's easel and a sacrificial altar, the prices still chalked on their sides, waited for arrangement according to her instruction.

Her attention snapped back to the stone on the altar as a geyser of wild magic burst from the flames. Miranda selected one of the sparkling motes, studied it as it drifted aimlessly across the room like a dandelion seed. She adopted a mystic pose and compelled the magic to submit to her will, holding it motionless in the air. She made it dance awhile and then released it with a finger-shake and a word, watched it fade into some other realm.

She grinned like a fool.

Edmund was right. Cunning was her calling. A cackle of delight burst unbidden from her throat — the laugh of a mad old lady. She covered her mouth in horror and hoped that nobody had heard.

A polite cough informed her otherwise. Her factotum and maidservant had returned. She ignored them and tried to remember in which of the Verge's tomes she had seen a similar phenomenon described. Was it *Ghayat Picatrix? Sefer Raziel?*

She retrieved the stone from the fire with a pair of tongs. Just as she had expected, another script had appeared upon its surface; the letters glowed a dull red.

She waved her magnifying lorgnette in the air absentmindedly. "It is an amulet — for protection and good fortune, dedicated by a wealthy lady to a soldier. Probably her son." Her staff smiled pleasantly. Vacantly. *I might as well be talking about the weather*, she thought, and set the tablet aside with a sigh. "It is so very wonderful, you see."

"Milady, if I may . . ." her factotum began.

She shushed him. It was the first time she had seen them wearing the uniforms she had designed, sharp-cut, grey-black and lined with red brocade. He was very handsome, the equal of any courtier in Ebarokon, stood with a bandmaster's poise. Her ward-sisters would be terribly jealous. The maidservant was a head-turner as well. Tender. She blushed demurely as Miranda smoothed down her lapel. They made a startlingly pretty pair, exactly as Miranda had hoped. Beautiful twins would have been even better, but none were available.

"The Verge's tailors deserve their reputation. Is my robe ready?" she asked as if she didn't care, though frankly she couldn't wait to see it. The factotum presented a ribbon-tied box and awaited her instruction. "Leave it on the settle by the door. I'll try it on later." He clicked his heels together. Miranda flapped at his feet with irritation. "Less of that."

She hobbled quickly to her easel, more from habit than the slight pain in her leg, and signed a scroll that hung from it. "This is a list of books I require from the library." The young girl took the paper and curtsied with a grace that testified to endless years of practice, swollen ankles and sore knees. Miranda remembered it well. "And the room is still a little bare; it needs more flowers. I want roses."

The maid chasséd from the room. Miranda thought that she would like to watch her dance. She would ask her to sometime.

"Milady . . ." the factotum started again.

"What is the rarest drink in the buttery?"

"Merret." Miranda didn't recognise the appellation, and raised an eyebrow for more information.

"It is a recent invention, milady — a scientific beverage, popular at parties."

"Why so?"

"It's terribly expensive."

"Is that all?"

"The bottles make a report when opened, and it has bubbles."

"How delightful. Buy all of it, and the next shipment in advance. Induce a drought of Merret." The factotum nodded his approval. "One other thing — no visitors without appointments."

"Milady . . ." The man would not be denied.

"What is it?"

"Does that include Master Sutton?"

She surprised herself with a blush. "Why do you ask?"

"He awaits downstairs."

"Why didn't you tell me? Tell the guards to permit him to the Masters' Quarters . . . No!" She scampered for the dress box by the door. "Make him wait ten more minutes — fifteen."

She dashed to her bedroom, injury forgotten.

•

"How do I look?" Miranda pirouetted as best she could, and her robe spun charcoal, silver and red.

"Beautiful." Edmund Sutton spoke flatly, his hat in one hand, an unremarkable bouquet of flowers in the other. His blond hair was a mess. The bottom button of his high-waisted doublet was undone. For some reason he was wearing gloves.

"Pathetic," Miranda snapped, and stormed over to him, a flapping fury of new silks. "I don't care how much you drank last night. Pay me proper attention and try again. And avoid clichés."

His brow furrowed in concentration. "Magisterial?"

That was better than she had expected.

"And how do you like it?"

"It's slightly terrifying. It makes you look like a master."

"Precisely. This is a statement of intent." She beamed with joy and ran her hands down her sides. He looked confused. "Attire so magnificent that my promotion becomes inevitable. Creating the right impression is half the battle won." She stood coquettishly, hands on hips, inviting him to inspect her. There was no doubt in her mind that he was impressed.

"I won't ask what it cost."

"Nothing compared to this." She went to her new altar, taking her weight on her enchanted leg and kicking back her heels to show off a pair of new crocodile boots. "A stele from the Tophet of Qart-Hadath." She drummed on the dark-stained rock with her hands.

"I have no idea what you are talking about," Edmund said. He was adorable sometimes. *If only he were a little smarter*. "I see you're limping a little. I feared worse."

Annoyed that he had noticed, Miranda waved the comment away.

"Would you like some Merret? I have some coming."

"Are we celebrating something? Your recovery?"

"I made a breakthrough this morning. In translation."

"Is that what this is all about?" Edmund inspected the broad parchment that hung on her draughtsman's easel. He read from it. "Ambergail of Thurwell. Charlotte Mouser. The rain it doth rain." He half sang the song's title. "I know that one. Louise Smith. It's all gibberish."

Miranda wondered how frequently he embarrassed himself with foolish comments and shook her head in an attempt to forestall another. It didn't work.

"I know! You attempt to describe a dream. But then why are some of the phrases crossed out?" That wasn't quite so dim-witted a guess, she supposed, but still utterly wrong. Miranda ushered Edmund aside and covered her writings with a linen sheet.

"They are ideas to base constructs on. For my demonstrations." He didn't seem to understand. "It's a list of memories that I can live without."

"I hope I'm not on there," Edmund said.

"Not yet," she said gaily. "The tally includes friends who do nothing but criticise. Melodies that I loathe but cannot forget. Heartbreaks. Dead pets. New Year's presents. You would be in poor company."

"You dislike getting presents at New Year?" Edmund said, his mouth upturned in wry amusement.

"Always. I never know what I want, and I'm terribly disappointed when I don't get it."

He laughed at that, and it was a lovely laugh, deep and honest. "You're using memories to trap magic. Instead of shapes."

"Emotions are powerful and complex. Described accurately, even more so. Imagine the mathematics of love. The map of a friendship."

He mulled the concept over and turned serious, quizzical. "When you turn these memories into constructs, do you forget them? I mean the moments and people, entirely?"

"Oh no. They just become disassociated."

"What do you mean?"

"Indistinct. Matters of no importance."

"Eventually you might run out of memories you don't care about."

That was almost astute, Miranda thought, and felt a tug of melancholy. There was a sadness about forgetting, even forgetting the worst of things. Some of the older entries in her diaries were beginning to read like a stranger's fiction. On the other hand, maybe that was something else, just the natural consequence of growing up.

"I'm sorry," Edmund said, seeing her frown. "I didn't visit to turn your mind to work." He twisted his hat in his hands. "I plan to walk the bay later this afternoon."

Miranda thought it a most peculiar thing to bring to her attention. "What of it?"

"I was hoping that you might accompany me, if you're feeling strong enough."

Miranda clapped in delight. "I shall bring a bottle of Merret."

❋

Wet shingle crunched under their heels and the taste of salt hung in the air. Edmund had dressed gallantly in doublet and breeches. A russet cloak patterned with tiny slashes hung rakishly from his shoulder and a dress sword swung at his hip, an affectation Miranda usually disliked, but today somehow made her feel safer. Miranda wore a bodice and stomacher over a green gown, superficially rural but heavily embroidered with the most fashionable patterns. A small picnic hamper swayed by her side. They walked arm in arm.

"You won't be able to enjoy this for much longer," Edmund said. "There will be no escape from the misery when winter sets in."

Miranda looked up at the turbulent sky. He had said it archly, but it was true; the North would be grim in winter and Hardknott impassable once it snowed.

"It's getting easier," she said, "now that I have staff to keep me company."

"I cannot believe you reside here happily."

"I have my books," she said sharply. "I didn't travel all the way from Lundenwic to make friends." *Gods' breath*, she thought, *must I criticise everything he says? He's trying to be kind, even if he's wrong.*

She looked out to sea. The Convergence glowered on the horizon. Truth was, its strange presence was a comfort to her. It was becoming *home*. She thought of her new rooms and decided to invest in a chaise longue, deep quilted and embroidered with roses.

"You don't understand. You have land and responsibilities. My alternative to this place is a dull husband."

"You're a ward of the duchess."

"Exactly. If I were her son, it would be a different matter entirely. Anyway, it's more complicated than that. I don't hate it here. Sometimes I love it. Even the worst of them. Take Talon, for example — he's a pig, but he has a prodigious mind. His contribution to the efficiency of cunning has been immense." She bit the inside of her cheek. *Must I always bring the conversation back to the serious?* In compensation, she gave him a honeyed smile. "Besides, the Verge is not so different to the Royal Orphanage. Here at least my enemies are open in their hatred. Girls can be much crueller."

"The pillow fights must have been dreadful."

"That's all we ever did. Day and night, in our small clothes — or naked. The feathers got everywhere."

He laughed, a little embarrassed, which served him right. "Tell me truly, what was it like?"

"They wanted us to be perfect. There were rules for everything: how to walk, how to talk, and when and where and to whom. We were taught to think in straight lines, like dogs or small children."

"Rules aren't childish; most exist for good reason."

Now Sutton was being too serious. "Sometimes I imagine what it would be like to be completely free," she said.

"That is the prerogative of the dead," he replied.

They walked awhile in silence.

"Is there anyone you miss? From home?" he asked.

"Nobody special."

"What about the duchess?"

"I love her with all of my heart, but I see far less of her than I would like, excepting the portraits and statues. There are many ward-sisters and she is a busy woman." Edmund picked up a pebble and threw it skipping across the water, absurdly far into the bay. "Enough about me, Mister Mystery. What about you?"

"What about me?"

"Do you miss someone?"

"My family."

"You have a family!"

"Not like that. I miss my brother, and his wife. My niece-to-be."

"All of them? That's unusual." He smiled, but from the look on his face, she knew it was true. "You know I just realised, I know next to nothing about you. What about your parents?"

"My father passed to judgement a long time ago. You won't find him amongst the stars. My mother, I haven't spoken to in years. There was a sister once." A spasm of distress crossed his face, and he fell silent. She took his hand.

"Enough of the past. Talking with you is easy Edmund — I'm glad you're here." *By the gods, now I sound like a besotted maid*, she thought, but she did not release him. "I mean, most of the men here treat me like a curiosity, or an imposter. Even the ones who tell me I am a prodigy."

"You're different to the others. They can all see your skill."

"Men rarely see women as equals. What did Merbal say? 'The glory of the Father burns the eye. The Mother reflects his light in greater beauty. But when the moon obscures the sun all becomes darkness and men are fearful.'"

"Poisonous crocodile bile," Edmund said. "That's the only Merbal I can remember. The murder of the twelve godsworn or something."

"Merbal is delightful."

"I had a bad teacher, the kind of man who calls a window an embrasure. He seemed to revel in being not understood."

"Sweet."

"What?"

"Poisonous crocodile bile is sweet," she said. Then she decided to be brave. "I meant talking with you sweetens the time."

He smirked. "I don't know how much longer I'll be at the Verge."

Of course, why didn't I think? He has yet to structure a simple cube, and his parents are passed away. If his brother's older, he'll inherit next to nothing. If he's the elder, he will need to return to his estate before winter. It's a wonder that he's here at all. Miranda's heart sank. "Maybe I could help you with your studies," she offered anxiously.

Edmund guffawed. *My offer has insulted him*, Miranda thought, and tried to read his face.

"Then I suppose we should make good use of what time we have," she said.

Without warning, Edmund scooped her from the ground and sprinted towards the tall grasses in the dunes. Too surprised to feign shock, Miranda squealed in delight as the sand flew.

"What do you think you're doing, Mister Sutton?" she giggled in his arms. She had never imagined that he would be so bold or impetuous. When they reached the waving marram grass, he spun her by the waist and lowered her gently to the ground. She turned to face him, prepared for a kiss.

Edmund lay beside her, flat on his chest, and peered out through the stems.

"I don't think he saw us."

"What?"

"Bolb," he hissed, as if that were a reason for concern. Miranda rolled flat and parted grass to make an opening. The fat master was wading, out on the shingle. She slid back onto the sand and began to loosen her frock. "Are we breaking a rule? I wasn't aware the Convergence had any restrictions on romance."

Edmund was transfixed, and not by her.

"What's he doing?" he whispered.

She crawled back up the sandbank, wondering what could possibly be so intriguing. Some sand slipped inside her bodice, which was exceedingly annoying. Master Bolb stood in the grey waters, dowsing the surf and sand with a device that looked like a horned lanthorn chained to a pole. Waves lapped around his ankles and each splash sent a faint chiming across the shoreline. She had never seen a man look so forlorn.

"Cockle picking?" Miranda jested. "What's so interesting about Bolb anyway?"

"He's looking for something."

"That's funny. I never imagined him as the out-of-doors kind."

She wondered if Edmund's fascination with Bolb was an evasion. Maybe, under all of that bravado, in the final moment, Edmund Sutton was shy of girls.

She was not as innocent as society demanded that she pretend. She rolled onto her back and tried to pull him down into the dunes. He was too strong for her, held himself above her like a plank, hands pressed hard into the earth, neck arched. *He's paying more attention to Bolb than to me*, she thought. It was vaguely insulting. Before she came to the Convergence, she would have feigned outrage and stormed off, terrified of rejection. Not any more.

She wrapped her hands behind his back and felt the power in his body, leaned forward and kissed him. His resistance crumbled. He kissed her in return. She closed her eyes and gently bit his lip, stroked his thick hair, breathing him in. He ran his lips down her neck, butterfly light. Then it stopped.

"What is it?" she asked dreamily.

"Miranda. Will you do something for me?"

"Maybe," she said, and held her mouth a little open.

"Use your cunning." She opened her eyes. Sutton's back was arched again. He was staring intently into the distance. "Use it to see what he's doing? Please."

By the gods! She moved reluctantly back to her peephole. Bolb had moved to the shore and was using the pole of his lanthorn to sift through the sand and shingle. Occasionally he drew an arrow or a stranger symbol in the ground.

She became intrigued, despite the annoyance and the steam in her body.

"Your whims are harder to follow than Riven Gahst's theories," she said, but the pleading look in Daniel's eyes was almost as hard to resist as the opportunity to show off. Miranda settled down into the sand and concentrated, prepared a ritual. She spread her palms and focused on the rune-laced fingers of her sable-trimmed gloves, crossed her wrists in front of her eyes, then cast her arms aside as if throwing away the world. The air around her became tense, and Bolb's magic crisped into view. Gouts of it burst from his lanthorn in short tentacles, twisted and probed the ground around him.

One of the tendrils sensed Miranda. It reared like a spitting cobra and raced across the sand towards her presence. Bolb's device sought magic, she realised, and broke her spell with a double click of her fingers. The magic retreated as quickly as it had come, but Bolb's head snapped in her direction.

Sutton buried his face in her neck and covered it in kisses, and she hooted in surprise. Then he was looking at Bolb again.

"He thinks us lovers," Edmund said.

"He's more convinced than I am."

"He's leaving. What did you see? What was he doing?"

"Edmund Sutton, this is disgraceful. I did not come here to assist you in some strange adventure." She stared at him defiantly. "You have not earned the right to use me so." She moved her knees apart, let the silk of her gown slide down the insides of her legs. "Show me."

Lust flared in his eyes. He placed her arms above her head and took her mouth with his. His lips seared hot and his heart beat hard. She took in the smell of him and the sea air, made a feast of his mouth. He caressed her breasts through her bodice, then lifted one of her black boots by the heel and rolled her skirt carefully down her leg. His hand travelled slowly along the inside of her thigh, touched metal. He paused, eyes wide with surprise.

"Does it bother you?" He shook his head, kissed her deeper. She took him by the hair, grabbing his head roughly with both hands. She felt his tongue between her lips. The sun broke through the clouds as a tingling warmth filled her body. He reached down and her belly tightened like a board. *Too soon.*

"Lie back, Mister Sutton." He did as she commanded and she straddled his waist, felt the hardness between his legs. She rocked gently back and forth then settled on him, letting him take her full weight.

There was a fearful crunch. He howled in pain and rolled aside, pitching her into the sand.

"What did I do?" she cried as the floaty lightness fled from her body. Edmund clutched at his back, tears in his eyes. She looked at the ground where he had lain. Something protruded, man-made. She brushed away sand. "A shovel. My poor gallant." She laughed hysterically, wrapped her arms around him, pressed herself against his back.

"Let me see." Edmund clutched his side with one hand and brushed away sand with the other. Curiosity replaced the pain in his voice. "It's not a shovel. It's a paddle." He began to dig faster. She watched him work, strong, tireless and completely preoccupied.

"Have we found buried treasure?"

He clawed furiously at the soil, and then used the paddle to dig faster.

"Now this is becoming strange," Miranda said. She perched on the slope of the dune and straightened her skirt. There was something about watching him work that she liked.

He stopped and wiped the sweat from his brow. "It's a coracle."

"What's so exciting about an abandoned boat?" she asked, slightly disappointed. Then she remembered the bottle of Merret, sealed with its peculiar plug of wood and wax. *Twist or pull?*

"It's not been abandoned. Look at the position of the rocks — under the sand. How the oar is laid. It was hidden. Buried."

He seemed certain. She looked at him curiously. "Playing censor again? I don't think that's your strongest suit."

Edmund flashed her a scowl, hauled the small craft from its hole and emptied the last of the sand from it. He ran his thumb along its thin gunwale, discovered something and stopped. With immaculate timing, Miranda popped the stopper of the bottle sending it flying overhead. A fountain of fizz flowed from the bottle and she mouthed the foam. It was delicious.

"You're right. It's just a boat," Edmund said, but Miranda saw the fire of revelation in his eyes.

"I was hoping for something a little more exciting. Let's celebrate anyway." He collapsed beside her. He looked so happy it was impossible to be angry with him. She held out the bottle to him. "Are we going to row back to the Convergence in that thing?"

He took a deep swig from the heavy bottle and kissed her fiercely. "You are my lucky charm, Miranda."

His mouth tasted sweet. *You are an enigma, Mister Sutton*, Miranda thought. She laid back and didn't care at all.

FROTH AND SPLINTERS

The dusty patch of disputed territory in front of All-Gods was normally a place where duels were fought, where lover's wine and temerarious oil were trafficked openly, and stolen valuables found new owners. It also happened to be the temple where Jon and Anna had got married.

The captain of the patrol jabbed the tip of his crossbow into the small of Jon's back, pushing him towards it.

A few hundred of Turbulence's grumbling denizens had been corralled into that dusty space, surrounded by a thin ring of shabby enforcers who wore salvaged breastplates and archaic helmets, scarred by the damage of old wars and adorned with the orange scarves, caps, ribbons and bands of the newly formed Turbulence militia.

The ring of men parted at the captain's command and the patrol and Jon and Bill were shoved deep into the rabble.

"My coins," Jon shouted at the backs of the patrol, but they paid him no attention. The ring of enforcers hefted weapons and dared him to try to follow.

Jon looked around. He hated crowds at the best of times, and the shoulders that pressed around him here were tense and hostile, the babble of the strangers angry. No one seemed to know why they were there. Some brawlers from Gordon's gang watched from the periphery, and there were curious lookouts from across town, from Wylde's gang, the Blinders, the Sloggers and the Damned Crew.

More of Peacock's men stood on a platform freshly erected in the square's centre. The ensign of the militia — an orange flag, six foot square — flapped proudly above their heads. Whatever was about to happen, the Peacock wanted attention.

For now, there was nothing to do but wait.

Jon looked up at the peeling gilt and broken crenulations of the temple and wondered why the gods had allowed such a magnificent building to fall so far from grace. He remembered Anna making her wedding oaths. The single bronze coin that had been her dowry. Dan pelting them with cinnamon and flour afterwards. The Old Faithful, the wrinkled old women who had been temple girls before the Great Cleansing, sweeping clean the steps and offering blessings for pennies. Today the crones were nowhere to be seen, and the temple's ochre doors were barred. Jon thanked the gods for his great height and looked for Anna's shawl in the throng.

Gilbert Gordon, the black heart of all Turbulence business, appeared on stage. He was a small man with a shaved head and hard-to-recall features. Inconsequential-looking. He preferred it that way. He got what he wanted through leverage and deceit. Some of the audience didn't know who he was. Those who did feared and hated him in equal measure. Gilbert took a place at the rear of the stage and observed.

The Peacock's men cheered as their louche leader mounted the platform. He was wearing an orange doublet, decorated with second-hand medals and as gaudy as a baboon's arse. A freshly minted medallion of office lay on the oily skin of his hairless chest. He carried a blunderbuss.

So that's how he decided to spend my money, Jon thought. *He bought himself a toy.*

Littleshark trailed behind Peacock, dragging a youth by a chain. The young man was shackled by the neck, gagged with canal rope, his wrists bound behind his back. He stared at the crowd with wild eyes. Big Shark followed. He rolled a barrel of the Bell Jar's finest onto the platform and tipped it upright. Peacock levelled his blunderbuss and blew its lid off, showering the crowd with froth and splinters.

An execution looked likely. The audience roared its approval and faced the platform expectantly.

"Lords and ladies," Matthew proclaimed in an impresario's drawl. He was unconvincing as a military man, Jon thought, but his manner got a laugh from the crowd. He made them quiet with a careless wave of his gun, and became serious. "You all know about the fire. Today it was a factory; tomorrow it could be your home. There's an evil at work here in Turbulence — malcontents who would see our city burn. My troop has been entrusted with the power to keep you lot safe and I will keep you safe by any means." Jon and Bill exchanged glances.

"You doing censor's work now?" a man in the crowd shouted angrily. Matthew ignored him. Gilbert mouthed the heckler's name into the ear of a militiaman.

"We caught this villain nailing bills to a wall." Matthew hoicked the boy's chain. The crowd booed. "He'd a pocket full of sedition. Rhetoric against the duchess, treason against the Wise Council, blasphemies against the gods. Just bits of paper, some might say, but I call it kindling — to start fires in the minds of fools."

"Recognise the boy?" Jon whispered. Bill shook his head discreetly.

"We cannot let the fire of dissent spread. We must crush out the spark with our heels." Peacock stomped on the stage dramatically and it boomed like a drum.

"Get on with it," an Old Faithful yelled from the crowd. Peacock raised his arms to quell the laughter.

"I will now demonstrate how to put out a fire."

Matthew delivered a sharp kick to the prisoner's stomach. As the boy doubled up the Sharks grabbed the seat of his pants and plunged him headfirst into the barrel. Some men cheered, others booed. Jon thought he saw a fight breaking out on the far side of the square. The boy's legs thrashed so hard in the air that the Sharks had to hold his ankles to stop the barrel from tumbling. Ale sloshed across the platform. Gilbert Gordon stepped back to save his shoes. Peacock's men began to count out the time. "Thirteen, fourteen . . ."

A voice like tar called out from Court Lane.

"Let him go."

The crowd turned as one. *Wylde had come.* A posse of his men, bearing arms and firebrands, had gathered at the entrance to the square and Wylde towered over them, his powdered face an ugly sneer. He was wearing his fighting trousers and a battle wig whose barbarous spikes hung down about his knees. Its raven locks had been waxed for the occasion and glistened in the sun.

"Let him go? Why would I do that, you ridiculous noodle?" Matthew replied, his blunderbuss slung casually across his shoulders.

"You've no right to be thief-taking in my territory. That boy's one of mine." The prisoner's upturned legs were starting to move a little less energetically and Wylde's men looked twitchy. Jon started to push his way towards the edge of the crowd.

"I don't think so," the Peacock replied sardonically. At his signal, the Sharks pulled the boy upright. Ale poured from his mouth and he spluttered weakly. Peacock grabbed his chin, turned the sodden face towards Wylde. "For starters, I don't see any make-up. Also, his trousers aren't around his ankles."

Peacock let go of the boy and the Sharks plunged him back into the ale.

"I don't care if you take him for a ranter, that boy's street candy and he's on my roll." Wylde hefted a spiked mallet. Matthew shrugged. The crowd was beginning to grow nervous. The upturned legs had stopped moving and a miasma of animal fear had begun to spread. A few, seeking exit from the square, pushed against Matthew's line of orange troopers, who locked arms to contain them. Jon figured that he was standing directly between Wylde's men and the stage, which had to be the worst position he could imagine.

"You're a bit of a gamester," Matthew taunted. "How about we play jackals for him? Maybe a hand of tarot?"

"I draw first," Wylde yelled, and raised his mallet. His men roared, presented a collection of rusty sabres, woodsman's axes and spiked bats.

"There's going to be a riot," Bill said, mastering the obvious. Jon looked at the stage. Gilbert Gordon was making an inconspicuous exit, surrounded by a small bodyguard of terrifying men.

"If you want him, come and get him," Peacock taunted.

The Sharks tipped the barrel over and the body of the prisoner spilt limply onto the edge of the stage. His eyes were rolled back and his tongue hung loose.

The horror of the corpse panicked the crowd. Men and women bolted in all directions like startled deer. The Trained Band beat them back, trying to form a wall around the stage. Wylde's men charged, raining rusty blows onto the heads of all who obstructed them.

"Run!" Bill shouted and disappeared into the frenzy.

Madness had taken a hold. Men were fleeing. Men were fighting. Old women and young children were being trampled. Where passage was blocked, ordinary denizens punched, kicked and threw cobbles at each other for no reason that Jon could discern.

The crowd pulled him like a riptide, drawing him towards the fighting. He recognised a shawl as Anna's and grasped for it, pulled it from her shoulders. *Grey hair, not Anna.* The stranger wheeled away, her face swamped with terror, and was sucked into the crowd.

A boy crashed into Jon's stomach and drove the wind from him, knocking him half to the ground. A torrent of scrambling knees battered at his head and sides and then a man tripped and fell across Jon's back, pinning him down. He tried to breathe and sucked in a thin harvest of dust. A flailing fear took hold of him. He grabbed at the legs that passed in front of his face, trying to pull himself free, and succeeded only in dragging another man down. Their desperate gazes met through the copse of legs that divided them, then a hobnailed boot collided with the man's head and he slumped, out cold. The little air left in Jon's lungs was failing him. The world slowly darkened.

I'm dying, Jon realised. Memories came unbidden and disconnected. He saw his wedding. Anna holding his newborn. Himself as a young man, too old to be playing in the mill tower with Dahlia and Dan, but doing it anyway, the three of them smiling and laughing together. He looked down from the minstrel gallery as Father sent Dahlia and Dan to get the wine. He made one final prayer to the gods for forgiveness.

I'm sorry, I tried so hard.

"No."

The voice inside his head was impossibly strange and loud.

"*Open your eyes.*"

He obeyed and saw a blurred world. The figures that encircled him were no longer human. One had talons, great and golden, the next crocodilian claws. He saw a tentacle that was fog and flesh made one. Pillars of flame and ice. *Revelation*. He threw back his arm to shield himself from the radiance and the weight shifted from his back.

Cold air shocked Jon's lungs, brought his vision into focus. The feet around him were mortal. Dirty. Trying to trample him into the ground. An incredible anger exploded within him. With a screaming effort, he rolled himself free and pushed himself to his feet, roared at the heavens. Even in the pandemonium, the mob recoiled from him. He barged through the riot thinking only of reaching Anna. He guarded his head like a boxer and lashed wildly. An onrush of confused faces was beaten aside by fists like hammers, felling anyone who did not clear his way.

Open space. He clambered over a stack of benches into a side road, and ran until his lungs could not sustain him. Then sanity returned. He retched. Hot saliva drooled from his nose. He put his hands to his knees and laughed in mad exultation.

He looked back at the square. Peacock's stage was on fire. The body of the young boy hung from its side, a blackened statue. The crowd was dispersing, but there was still some fighting and Jon could hear screaming in the distance. A few escapees ran past him, eyes cattle-dumb with fear. From the safety of the passageway, he watched a little longer. His hands hurt. He inspected them. His knuckles were ragged and his fingers flecked with other people's blood. The sun flashed wearily from the Temple of All-Gods. He nodded grimly and set off for the mill.

●

Jon could hear the baby screaming from half a street away. The relief of it brought a bounce to his stride; Anna was home safe. He jogged the last of the rise in a curious calm.

I was spared for a reason. What reason?

He paused before he entered the mill, wiped his torn knuckles painfully on his breeches and beat his doublet against a post to get the worst of the dust from it. The baby's tantrum still hadn't subsided, which troubled him a little. She was normally so calm. Something must have terrified the pickle. Anna had done well to get her home unharmed — she would need some calming too, no doubt. He touched the crescent moon above the door and went inside.

All eyes turned to him.

Anna was gagged, bound to one of the dining chairs. She briefly paused in her fight against the ropes to scream a warning with her eyes. Laila stood behind her holding the wailing baby. She rocked it desperately and without tenderness. Barehill and his men flanked Anna, hands clamped on the back of her chair to stop it from toppling. In the middle of the hall lay two sacks, black and sticky with old blood. The stink of spoilt meat hung in the air.

Anna's chair leapt forward a banging inch as she threw herself towards Jon. The baby's wailing grew louder.

Anna cried out to him. A small froth accompanied the sound and she began to gnaw on the strap that invaded her mouth.

"What's this?" Jon's bellow blasted the room like a bomb.

"We was interrupted," Dyer said, pleading against Jon's fury with raised palms, "bringing the bags down." He looked accusingly at Bertrand. Anna's struggle became a frenzy. *She's going to hurt herself*, Jon fretted. Barehill produced a tooth-edged knife and held it to the back of Anna's head. He looked as calm as a butcher at the block.

"Don't you dare touch her," Jon said.

"I tried to explain, but she wouldn't listen," Dyer said. "She made a dash for the observation deck — started calling for the town watch."

"It's called a reefing stage."

"She hasn't been harmed," Barehill said, and cut away Anna's gag. She gasped twice, wiped her mouth on her shoulder and began to shake. Jon knelt at her feet and dabbed ineffectually at the tears that streaked her face. Her chest racked. He had never before seen a person cry that hard. He stood and held her head tight to his chest, glaring at Barehill. She whimpered.

"It's alright, love. You're safe now."

She squeaked, "Who are these people? I thought we were being robbed. I thought they were going to hurt the baby."

"For mercy's sake, give her back the child." Something in the way he said it made people rush to obey. Barehill cut Anna's hands free and Laila pushed the baby into her red-raw arms. It was the first sensible thing anyone had done. For a second the whole of Anna's attention was on her daughter, and then her faculties returned. She looked at Jon.

"Who are these men? Did Peacock send them?"

"No," Jon said.

"I don't understand. Make them go away." Anna shut her eyes and waited, as if it was that easy, as if Jon could set things straight with a click of his fingers.

"It's not as simple as that," he said. Anna opened her eyes in dismay.

"It's time to tell her, Jon," Laila said.

Barehill's men looked at him with an air of solemn witness, as if presiding over a harsh but necessary ordeal. Jon wished them all dead. *Freeborn indeed. These false comrades.* A guilty fear took him then, which quickly turned to anger. He pulled back his shoulders, rose to his full height.

"This is my house — my mill," he boomed. "Nobody tells me what to say or do."

Anna didn't agree.

"Jonathan Miller," she wailed, "what have you done?" His spirit sunk at her cold tone. Then she became shrill. "What's in those sacks? They stink like death." A look of horror shrouded her face.

Yes, *they do*, Jon thought.

The room's eyes fell on him again, waited for his move. His eyes were only for Anna. He began to burble, to tell her all at once about the things he had done for her and the family. The excuses and explanations chased each other out of his mouth, tripped each other up.

She held up a hand. "I don't understand."

"I think it's time that someone else explained," Barehill said and went over to a sack. His fingers turned red with old blood that flaked and dusted from the flax as he worked at its knot. His men exchanged nervous glances. Too slowly, Jon moved to cover Anna's eyes.

Barehill cast the ropes aside, pulled down the sackcloth and lifted Brother Nielsen's putrescent head by its hair. "Your husband has taken our mark. He's one of us now, whether he likes it or not."

Anna wailed again. So did the baby. It was hungry.

RABBIT HOLE

I ought to be celebrating, not moping about the place.

Miranda tugged her rune-gloves off and slapped them onto the marble worktop. Her vexatious mood was all the more irritating for its lack of a solid explanation. It wasn't Lavety. His first glimpse of her magnificent robes had provoked a pleasing scowl, but she hadn't heard a word from him since his dreadful trick, though her campaign to win the support of the masters was now well known. It wasn't the politics either; her demonstrations were going better than planned. In the last two days, she had won the support of three more with barely a hitch. Essossilam, Nirmeen and after this morning, Baldwin.

Miranda picked out the masters' names on her copy of the Convocation's roster and put her mark against them, tallied the totals. Promises outnumbered refusals now, though both were too few for certainty, and some of the commitments tended towards vagueness. Convincing masters to support her promotion was a slow and intricate business that required research and guile. Arranging audiences was a trifle though. Anyone could see that from the pile of invitations waiting on her settle. They all wanted to see if the rumours were true, to see her new form of cunning in action. To meet its mistress.

What is it that bothers me? Maybe it was that bloody pig.

Miranda recalled a morning mired in the business of killing. She knew now that she did not enjoy creating engines of war; death and destruction were not arenas in which her creativity dwelt easily, but impressing Master Baldwin required it. He was famous for his application of cunning to military matters, which he saw as magic's most proper use, and he held those he considered squeamish in particular contempt.

In retrospect, her first demonstration had been a bit silly. She had animated the ossified remains of an ancient reptile, unearthed on a nearby beach, making them snap and claw. The monster would terrify the native savages of the Far West, she had argued. It could not walk though, and she doubted many would be foolish enough to put their head in its mouth. Baldwin had said he liked it anyway, though Miranda did wonder exactly where he was looking as she demonstrated it halfway up a ladder.

Her second invention had been the winner. She had imbued a silver bullet with an irresistible longing for the beating of hearts. It had no greater accuracy than ordinary shot, but once lodged in flesh would burrow its way, slowly and inexorably, towards the vital organ. Before making it, she had persuaded herself that the deadly intimacy was poetic. The pig that had noisily succumbed to its malice in the testing range had put an end to that fallacy.

Why did I insist on firing the rifle myself?

Miranda relived the moment she had struck the creature in the leg. Watching the bulge of her bullet worm its way under the poor creature's skin had been an exercise in visceral, squealing horror. Yet the pig's misery had turned out to be a blessing in disguise; it had made her invention seem cruel. Baldwin had enjoyed the animal's suffering almost as much as he had been amused by her poor marksmanship.

Her last exhibit, the pillow knife, had been almost an afterthought. An attempt to appeal to Baldwin's idiotic sense of male superiority. She had embellished the long dagger that her governess had provided: strapped its hilt with love charms, retempered its blade with sensual oils, and invested in it a particularly spiky construct based on a painfully unresolved love of her youth. The sum of these enchantments meant that any man or woman stabbed with the weapon would fall irresistibly and profoundly in love with its wielder. She thought the effect hilariously melodramatic, like a device from a bad opera, and described it to Baldwin in romantic terms. He had barely cast a glance at the delicate, brass-hilted blade.

"A suitably womanish device," he had declared, and made a vulgar joke.

He was a revolting man, which didn't matter at all because she had won his support. Baldwin wanted to be chairman one day. That was obvious. He wanted voices in the Convocation who valued the military arts, but none threatening enough to be considered a rival. Miranda had played the part beautifully.

She had made him a gift of the bullet and the skeletal beast, kept the pillow knife for herself. She doubted that any of her inventions would be used in combat, and even if they were, feeling guilty would make no difference. If the memory of their creation continued to bother her, she could always put her disquiet to use. Invest it in some device and rid herself of the unwanted emotion for a modest profit.

But it wasn't the pig that vexed her.

Her thoughts returned to Edmund and that day on the beach. She closed her eyes and imagined sand between her fingers, listened to wind in the sea grass. He had said he was going to leave soon. Was that the problem? Did she really like him that much?

She needed to tidy her mind.

●

It was early afternoon when Miranda returned to the beach. The sky was as iron-grey as her robes. A flock of sandpipers was her only company. Small dark waves washed the shingle. The wind whipped her hair about her face. Without Edmund, the shoreline felt changed — lonely and desolate.

Miranda sighed. There was no point in lying to herself. The whole business on the beach was what troubled her. Not only what she felt about Edmund, but everything else that had happened. Mister Sutton had been far too excited about Bolb and that boat he had unearthed. Master Bolb's behaviour had been beyond bizarre. She imagined what might have happened if she had allowed his magic to attack her and shuddered. Bolb had been doing something important. Determining exactly what, might win his support. Moreover, she hated not being in on a secret.

She picked out the grass-covered dune of their tryst from the hundreds that huddled together like the backs of beasts, and touched the sand where they had lain. It was cold where she remembered it warm. She dropped to her belly and tried to place where Bolb had been wading.

With the Convergence so near, it was easy to draw on its power. She weaved her hands in a pattern based on an ancient liturgy of Baphomet to which she had ascribed new meanings and felt the fire and spice of magic in her blood. Her pupils widened and the world was bathed in a shattered light.

She turned towards the Verge. It blazed in her mind like a roughly rented tear, through which a white sun dazzled. The black rocks of the island glowed like diamonds. Gossamer trails of magic drifted from its core and arced overhead to disappear into the distance.

Where Bolb had stood there was nothing. She rose and strolled towards the waves, casting her gaze all around. Nothing in the surf, nothing in the sea, apart from the faint glow of the magic invested in the Verge's causeway. If there was anything to find, Bolb had been looking for it in the wrong place.

Inland then, to a higher place with a clear view.

Long grass gave way to clumps of gorse and dusty soil as she made her way up the hillock towards the funeral cross of the murdered censor. It glowered, as forbidding as a gallows. Her good ankle twisted twice on the ascent. The first time she merely winced, and was saved by the surety of her metal leg. The second time she swore like a drunken highwayman.

As she stood, something caught her eye and was gone as quickly. She lowered herself carefully and saw it again, this time clearly. Something magical was buried in the ground. She moved towards it, stooped low like a poacher stalking a grouse.

A rabbit hole? The dirt at its entrance was blackened. She rubbed some between her fingers and watched it turn red. Dried blood. The burrow's mouth was cobwebbed, but the living power of the thing buried inside flickered in her mind. The magic was contained, shielded in some way, designed for stealth, but obviously powerful. It lay only an arm's length inside.

Miranda flattened her dress and pressed against the ground. Her hand hesitated at the warren's mouth as she fought against the notion that some adder, fox or vicious brock might lurk within, waiting to snap off her fingers. Loose earth crumbled between her groping fingers and then she found an edge of material, thick and strong. She pulled at it and was astonished as it pulled back. It was as if some small creature tugged against her, had grasped the other end of whatever she held between its teeth.

With all her strength and a determined twist of her body, she yanked her prize free in a shower of dirt.

A damp leather glove, with a hand still inside. It was horrible. Then she noticed the details. It was midnight blue, left-handed. The curving eye of He-who-sits-upon-the-mountain and his Thrice~Crossed Swords were stitched subtly into its back.

The gauntlet of a censor.

She looked over her shoulder at the funeral cross. Cold sweat prickled her brow.

Put it back, she thought and looked around for witnesses. A few distant fishing boats bobbed like seeds in the grey soup bowl of the bay. Some men, little more than dots from where she knelt, were tending horses in the stable yard. As far as she could tell, she was alone. She stared at the soiled blue leather. The glove was heavy, unyielding and unnatural, and there was something inside it. She brought it close to her nose and sniffed, expecting the distinctive odour of desiccated flesh.

Alive!

Blue fingers flailed at her face. Miranda flung the gauntlet away with a yelp and fell painfully on her backside. The five-fingered beast thudded to the ground, righted itself with a leap. For a second she thought it would crawl at her and she kicked herself backwards, but it turned and made a scuttling dash back towards the safety of the burrow.

"No you don't!" Miranda dived for the hand, grabbed it by the wrist. It splayed and thrashed like a furious crab. She used her vision on it and saw the power of the thing. No longer subterranean, it shone like a star — its construct contained enough magic to power a battering ram. She inspected the silent fire coursing within its metal framework for the trigger that activated it and tapped its abdomen three times. The hand froze. Panting heavily, expecting a trick, she eyed it with suspicion.

What now?

For a moment, Miranda wondered whether the hand was what Bolb had sought, allowed herself to imagine that the discovery was a coincidence. That was a ridiculous self-deceit. Nobody would leave something that valuable just lying around. But if it was what Bolb sought, what about Edmund? What was his part in all of this? She looked at the hand more closely.

What was it? The magic in the hand was of the most serious kind.

She shook her head. *I'm being an idiot; it's none of my business.* A sensible girl would walk away — consign the discovery to the wasteland of memory, leave it to someone else to find. Then she remembered watching Corbin read the past at the covered bridge. What would happen if he saw what she had done?

Miranda placed the hand in her picnic basket, covered it with a few handfuls of sea grass and some moribund flowers and started back towards the Convergence. Her mind skittered as she walked along the causeway, the choices still champing at her as she reached the tall teak gates. Her heart began to drum in fear. An inescapable feeling of guilt, that she would be discovered and punished, chilled her. The porters had never searched her before; why would they do so now? They would be loath to offend her, surely. She was practically a master already. Soon they would be answering to her commands.

She decided to take the hand to Corbin immediately. Would she be punished? Her heart froze. Maybe she should ask Gleame for his opinion first — defer the matter to his judgement. Not Gleame, Mother. Mother was a master of difficult situations. She would know exactly what to do.

Miranda realised that she had reached the door to her chambers, and that nobody had paid her a second glance.

It was impossible to know what to do with the hand without understanding what it was. She would examine it, briefly, and then rely on her own judgement. That would be best.

BREAKING AND ENTERING

There was no way Daniel was going to bring a pistol inside the Masters' Quarters. Even if he wanted to, there was no way to hide it in the waiter's outfit he had stolen; the waistcoat was a size too small, maybe two, and the ends of the lock picks hidden in its pocket dug painfully into his stomach.

Daniel wended his way unchallenged and unquestioned through the forbidden corridors. The higher he ventured the older the Verge seemed to become. Panelled corridors furnished with glow-stones gave way to mazy colonnades and wall walks, open to the elements and illuminated only by the stars. He would have been lost after a few turns if not for Corbin's map, which he had memorised to the smallest detail.

The entrance to Bolb's chambers was a simple wooden gate.

Daniel wiped away his sweat. At this moment, if all had gone to plan, Bolb would be sweating too, in an interview room as Prosecutor Corbin bludgeoned him with an unceasing battery of questions. Maybe he would be asking about the coracle, of which Daniel had informed Corbin in a hastily written note.

He knocked and waited. There was no reply. He knocked again to be sure, rolled his shoulders, readied his picks, and prised the latch. It opened easily. Waiting behind was a monster.

Bolb's inner door was a bewildering entanglement of plates and catches, bars and bolts. There were at least a dozen key-holes and the metal portal was dotted with dark lenses and bright eyes carved from rubies, pearls, emeralds and other jewels he could not name. Daniel stared at one and it stared right back. It blinked. He spun away and stood trembling, his back pressed against the corridor's cold wall. The Brotherhood's most devious entry-man would not have known where to start. His lock picks wilted in his hand.

There was no other way in. Daniel looked to the end of the passageway where a staired turret overlooked the sea. It was rounded with oriel windows that were narrow but no more so than his hips. He went to one, strained his neck outside and looked sidelong. The pair of bastion windows that protruded from Bolb's rooms glowed across the dark, their panes of leaded glass invitingly open.

The span to the closest was less than twenty yards. Daniel had spent his youth in a mill-house, riding sails and sliding on ropes; he had no fear of heights. Even so, the idea seemed more than a little crazy. The drop to the boulders that foamed in the waves below was five times that.

If I fall there won't be a body to find, just food for fishes.

He looked across the sheer face of the Convergence and planned his crossing. Reaching out, he ran his hand across one of the cart-sized blocks of grey-green stone that formed the Verge's wall. It was smooth and slick with seagull shit and lichen, treacherous. He shook his head in frustration. There had to be a way. He looked again. The wall was dry set. The gaps between the stones looked wide enough to accommodate a finger or a toe, and were close enough that he ought to be able to make use of both together, at a stretch. It was possible. The greatest danger would be at the start.

This is how you earn the Thrice~Crossed Swords, he told himself.

With a prayer to He-who-sails-the-wind, he slid his body out of the narrow window, grasped its surround with desperate fingers and pulled himself upright on its thin sill. He clung to the side of the Verge like a lizard, stretched tall, belly pressed flat against the stone. A gentle breeze ruffled his hair. Groping for purchase, he reached a leg down into the void, felt the thin gap and gradually let his toes take his weight.

He fixed his gaze intently on his grabbing point, swung free of the safety of the lintel and drove his fingers into the wall.

They held.

He took a moment to get his balance, and then began to ease his way, one hand or foot at a time, across the wall. His shirt grew cold and wet, and his cheek scraped across rock. He heard seagulls circling below, reminding him of the danger. He concentrated on his fingers and suppressed the instinct to hurry as he gained the measure of the movement.

Daniel placed his ear at the edge of Bolb's window and listened for sounds behind the whistle of the sea breeze. He jumped and hooked the lintel with both hands. It shifted, loose in its mortar. His legs kicked in the air as gravel pattered his face, then his feet found the sill and he scrabbled inside, landing behind an ornate workbench littered with clamps, lathes, callipers and hammers.

The room's odour was extraordinarily foul, a heady mix of blacksmith's forge and sweaty stockings. The clicking and whirring of a hundred tiny clocks filled the room, making a sound like an orderly beehive. Daniel lifted his head above the furniture and surveyed the room he trespassed.

No sign of Bolb.

Stacks of devices, technical or wondrous, covered every inch of wall. Armillary spheres and clocks crowded with incomplete automatons. A half-faced fox sniffed the air with its bronze nose. A three-legged unicorn pawed at the ground with an ivory hoof. A knee-high harlequin balanced on one leg and played the flute. Birds made of leather and feathers flapped around a porcelain cloud that transported a troupe of cavorting nubiles. A bejewelled dragon, suspended from the ceiling, sent gouts of copper flame flashing from its mouth. Above them all, hung mobiles of the planets.

Problem is, Daniel thought, *I'm not looking for marvels.*

He spotted a corner shelf devoted to scrolls and books and scanned through them. Insanely complicated technical tracings, sketches of erotic frescoes, anatomies and bestiaries were all annotated in the same illegible handwriting. Daniel faced the dull realisation that he had absolutely no idea what he was looking for. He squeezed the bridge of his nose. If Bolb had something to hide, something that Daniel could take, where would he put it?

He hunted for containers.

Several ornate boxes with latched tops, each the size of a shoebox, lay on a small round table. He opened one and its contents sprang to life — a tiny theatre in which wooden figures performed the plays of the ever-living poet in endless repertoire. He wondered how much it was worth. The others were the same: dioramas of famous battles waged to the command of tiny trumpets, miniature orgies depicted with frightening accuracy.

A crystal carafe attempted to follow him into Bolb's other room. It rocked back and forth on gilded chicken legs, searching for a glass in which to pour its long-evaporated contents. Daniel shooed it back into the workshop and closed the gate behind him.

The austerity of Bolb's bedchamber was startling. It contained an iron candlestick, a single bed, a plain mannequin and a mirrored vanity. A garnet casket sat on the vanity, open and empty.

Bolb's metal door looked just as imposing from the inside, and no more openable. Daniel realised that he was going to have to retrace his path across the Verge's wall and cursed under his breath. Determined not to cross to that gulf empty-handed, he lifted Bolb's mattress, the only hiding place he could imagine, and found nothing but dust.

Come on, Daniel. You fancy yourself a censor. Act like one.

He grabbed a stick of white greasepaint from the vanity and etched the Sigil of the Gods onto the base of the garnet casket that rested upon it. Kneeling, he held the casket high and closed his eyes.

He quelled his fear of being discovered and his impatience, forced the buzzing of Bolb's devices from his mind and focused on the sound of his breathing and his heartbeat, steered himself into the gentle rocking rhythm of the meditation ritual. He felt the air about him become completely still and opened his eyes to a blurred world. The shock of his success nearly cost him the vision.

He supressed the emotion as his instructors had taught him and slowly untangled himself from the illusion of time, watched patiently as an indistinct spectre of Bolb ate, worked, sat and wrote all around him. Daniel's ability was slight, so the after-images were very recent. Daniel watched Bolb pace, observed the master's nervousness, his dread of meeting Corbin.

He felt a pain in his forehead, in the present. The effort was already taking its toll. Daniel reached further back in time, watched as Bolb's movements became a haze that filled the room, looked for a pattern or exceptions to one. There were moments of stillness in the routine. With an effort that burnt his mind, Daniel concentrated on the hours of inaction and glimpsed Bolb sitting at his desk, scrawling into some kind of journal or ledger, almost motionless. When he had finished writing, he disappeared into a wall.

The vision broke, too hard to maintain, dumping Daniel back into the present. He grinned and tasted the blood dripping from his mouth; saw the small black puddle that had formed between his knees. The blood had already dried at the edges.

He had no idea how long his confession had taken. That was normal for the inexperienced, but it meant Bolb might return at any moment. He had to find the master's book. He stood dizzily and searched the suspect wall for a lever or button, found a crevice just wide enough to admit his little finger. He did so and a section of wall slid smoothly aside to reveal a short staircase leading up to a chamber.

The smell of sex lay heavy in the windowless room. At its centre, a petite lady slouched in a low-sided velvet armchair. She wore a mother-of-pearl mask cast in a sluttish leer. Her long white gloves matched her stockings and an immodestly short gown. A soft lace garter stretched around one of her varnished thighs. The thing was a puppet, a life-sized doll made of wood and bone. A mockery of a real woman. Daniel glimpsed white porcelain between her legs.

With a clank and whir, the automaton's head flopped vaguely in Daniel's direction. It beckoned him forward with the curl of a finger.

Daniel ignored the invitation and circled the room looking for a niche or alcove where Bolb's mysterious tome might be hidden. A collection of masks and wigs hung on hooks on the back of the chair to which the mechanical madam was attached. There was a race and temper to suit every occasion. Nothing else. He tousled his hair and sat on his haunches, then circled the chair, his hands stroking its fabric for pockets and pouches. Still nothing. The puppet's corset was fastened with whalebone buttons; the buttonholes were loose and worn.

Something hidden within the doll?

He knelt before the mechanical madam, stifled a laugh as it clasped an ankle in each hand and ratcheted its legs up and apart. *Bolb's a proper old pervert*, Daniel thought, as he worked at the buttons.

The automaton whirred, crossed its legs behind his back in a love embrace and stroked its heels down the base of his spine. The clanking of the metal was ridiculous, but the movement was disturbingly real. Daniel marvelled at the perverted genius of it. The corset came undone, and Daniel peeled back the lace. A brass-edged book nestled neatly inside the doll's iron frame. He grabbed it excitedly, failed to hear the faint click as it came free.

It was a diary like any other — page after page of braggado-cio, misery and self-deceit. He flicked towards its end, caught glimpses of text.

> ... *the death of the censor* ...
> ... *Corbin arrives* ...
> ... *evidence of my hand* ...

The fragments read like a litany of guilt. Daniel was thrilled. He tried to stand up and realised that he was trapped.

The womanly machine dropped one of its legs behind his rear, hooked and pulled. Daniel lurched forwards, his back arched in panic. He pushed against the doll's perfect chest with all his might. Its gloved arms enfolded him; one slid across the curve of his back, the other pressed its thimble fingertips hard into the back of his head.

The doll held him immobile, face-to-face, its fixed ivory smile promising a kiss.

Tiny holes opened in the pupils of its eyes, and its lips part-ed into a straight slit. A curved blade like a bird's tongue began to slide from its mouth. Needles as thick as boil lances extruded from its eyes.

Terrified, Daniel jabbed a knuckle into the crook of the doll's elbow. The Brotherhood's knowledge of pressure points and grips was useless against metal. He grabbed the doll's throat with both hands and twisted. The automaton was immeasurably stronger than any man was. Daniel's resistance turned its whirring to a whine, but did nothing to slow the pull of its embrace. The muscles in his arms burnt. The points of the needles blurred in closeness.

His flailing hand grasped for anything with which to block the blades, found a mouth and a nose — a spare mask hanging from the back of the chair. He grabbed it and jammed it between his face and the extruding metal. The lacquer pressed into his face, the relentless pressure of the blades scratching its surface. He heard it crack.

He stood with a yell, lifting himself, the doll and the chair in one piece and flung himself backwards, twisting his body as he fell. They tumbled together down the stairs to Bolb's bedroom in a bewildering jumble of limbs. Wigs, masks, gears and bolts scattered as they went.

The doll took most of the impact, crashing into the side of Bolb's bed and splitting from the chair. Daniel heard a rib crack as he slid across the floor, bounced into one of Bolb's bedsteads and came to rest against a wall. He saw the room sideways and in great pain. The doll lay frozen like a dead insect, its limbs curled inwards.

There was a muffled cry from the corridor. Someone had heard. The bolts and plates of the armoured door, only a few feet away, began to spin. Daniel shook metal fragments from his body. He grabbed Bolb's diary and ran for the workshop window, swung himself into the cold air outside. A tearing pain seared through his chest. His vision darkened and he clutched at the surround, teetering on the edge of consciousness.

"My love!" A roar of outrage filled Bolb's chambers. Daniel could not afford to wait for the pain to pass. He swung onto the slippery surface of the Verge's exterior and edged away with frantic, nauseous movements. In his haste he missed his footing and his vision blurred again as he took the whole of his weight in his arms.

Pendolous Bolb's head emerged into the night air only yards away from where Daniel hung. He shone a light out to sea, then down towards the shore. Daniel held his breath but it did not help. Bolb turned towards him, saw him.

This time there was no way to hide his face.

"You!" Bolb shouted, and ducked back inside his room. Daniel, half blinded by the light and the pain, scrabbled recklessly towards the turret. If Bolb summoned help, there would be a guard at every window before he could make it back inside, or maybe the master would simply prise him from the wall with a broomstick.

A long metal finger reached out of Bolb's window, then four more, as if the skeletal hand of a giant were reaching around its sill. The bulbous black body of a spider emerged, its abdomen throbbing with gas, its glass eyes and fangs swirling with a yellow liquid that could only be poison. It scuttled towards him, unhindered by fear or gravity.

Why didn't I bring that bloody pistol?

The spider paused, refocused it lenses, adjusted its footing and leapt a yard horizontally across the sheer wall. Daniel tried to do the same with a swing of his arms. His fingers slipped. He dangled from the wall by one hand. The spider jumped again, landed with a clatter of springs and regarded him without mercy.

He saw the reflection of his terrified face repeated a thousand times in its senseless eyes. There was no point in trying to run; the turret window was too far. Daniel listened to the clicking of the spider's metal brain as it calculated his demise. He cleared his mind as Brother Hernandez had taught him.

Bolb hissed in triumph from his window.

The monster made a murderous leap, fangs bared. With perfect timing, Daniel flung Bolb's bronze-bound diary hard into its face. The two creations collided, mid-air. Daniel and Bolb watched them plummet, legs flailing, pages flapping. They shattered upon the rocks three hundred feet below and disappeared into the surf.

Bolb's moon-like face gnarled with rage and disgust and disappeared from view. Daniel scaled the last few feet to the turret window, and slipped through to the safety of the corridor inside. Bolb emerged from his chambers and waddled towards him, bells jangling furiously.

"Who are you? What do you want?" the master screamed, and then stopped, as if suddenly afraid. "You cannot escape. I will call for the guards. Seal off the Masters' Quarters."

Not if you're as guilty as I know you are, Daniel thought.

"Guards!" Bolb shouted.

Shit, Daniel thought, and ran.

"I know your face," Bolb screamed after him. "I know your face."

THE WEIGHT OF A TEAR

Bertrand and Dyer stood outside the bedroom door holding Mother in a stretcher. Anna grabbed armfuls of neatly folded clothes from the wardrobe and rammed them into a laundry bag. The baby hung contentedly from its hook on the wall. It blinked and smiled at Jon. Anna would not look in his direction.

"They made me take their mark," he said.

Does she think I'm a rebel? A criminal? No better than Peacock Matthew? A storm of excuses gathered in his mind, but he stayed his tongue. Anna and the baby were in danger if they stayed in Turbulence. She was shaking. Seeing her this upset made his skin prickle with guilt, but if her disappointment in him would carry her safely out of town, then he would bear it.

"Barehill promised safe passage. There are tunnels to the countryside," he said.

Anna shook her head in disbelief and started to cry again, sobbed while she packed.

Does she think I'm a murderer?

"I didn't kill the censor. I don't know why they keep saying that. It was Laila. I tried to stop her."

Anna coughed tears from her throat. "Then why didn't you turn her in?"

"An inquisition would look bad. The facts would seem against me."

"I'm sure they would," she said bitterly.

"If they looked inside my heart they'd know different — but they won't. You saw what those censors were like, Norbury and Josephus. Real censors aren't like the ones in Daniel's story-books. Their idea of justice is a man on the end of a rope."

When the packing was done, Anna called for Bert and Dyer and they came for the sacks. She took the baby from the wall. Jon prepared himself for insults and fury. With Anna, it was always best to let her have the last word.

"Come with me," she said. "We could go to the colonies, to the Far West, start over again. No one would find us there, not even the censors."

He saw that she meant it and pictured it for a moment, a life without position or property, scraping a living from the mountains alongside convicts, deserters and escaped slaves. There was no need to reply, she had known his answer before she asked. It was sweet of her to talk soft like that though, to give him the chance to walk away.

"I can't. The gods have a plan for me."

"You're not making any sense. The gods don't care about people like us."

He shook his head. "They're going to give me a sign — I just don't know what it is yet. When matters are settled, you'll return to Turbulence and see that I was right."

Anna hugged him and whined her heartbreak.

"Someone's going to come for you, Jon, and then they're going to kill you."

•

Jon waited for the mill to clear. The occasional rattle of the winch chain in the tower told him that Barehill's men were still lowering flour sacks into barrels to be rolled back to the Holt. That was all right, they wouldn't bother him. He surveyed his unmade bed, draped with a few duds that Anna had left behind. It had been a long time since he had slept alone. He picked up a pair of her ripped stockings, held them to his face and breathed her in.

Imagine how awful it would be if Anna was right, he thought, if the heavens were empty or indifferent. Then it would just be him alone and against the world.

There was still a bottle of potato wine in the pantry, only a few years old. He could mix in some herbs to ease the pain of his bruised knuckles and bring sleep. He went down into the hall and found the bottle in the place he remembered, wedged behind the pantry, dusty and unopened.

The liquor was a quarter gone by the time Barehill's men had departed, and Jon's head had already begun to swim, but it was too soon to call an end to the night's merry misery.

Some fresh air was called for.

He took a candle and went up to the bagging floor. He tripped on the threshold of the reefing deck and was saved by its hard iron railing. Winded but still alive, he clutched his belly and laughed.

Across town the ruin of the manufactory still smoked. *A wreck that big will smoulder for days.* All trace of its once mighty sails had gone; not even the poll-heads remained. A sooty breeze stroked Jon's face. It was strong, unnaturally so. With the manufactory gone, the cunning that had ruined him was now working to his advantage. His own mill's sails, locked and furled, creaked overhead yearning to be set free.

Buoyed by the night air he soaked in the city. A curfew had been imposed, and when nobody was allowed on the streets, the traffic travelled above ground. A few roof-runners were plying their shadowy trade. Jon drank some more, listened to the nightingale chatter of their young voices, watched as gossip and small packages were exchanged across the narrow gaps between the tenement houses. In Turbulence there was always a way around a rule.

A patrol came marching up Peek Lane, turned into the street called The Froggary and headed towards the mill. They were a mixed bunch — a few of the duchess's guard and a censor thrown in for good measure. Jon's first instinct was to duck back inside the mill tower. He changed his mind. *Blast them all to stars. If they come for me, I'll know that Anna was right.* He stood as tall as he could, stretched his arms out wide in the shape of a cross and dared the armoured men to see him.

The patrol marched straight past the mill, headed for the safety of the barracks in the Dowager Duchess's residence. It was another sign, for sure.

"The gods don't care about people like us." What Anna had said made no sense. If the entire world was a dream of the gods, then how could they imagine something about which they did not care? Every brick in every building was part of their conception. Every branch in every tree. Soon enough they would send him a sign, show him what needed to be done.

Jon rubbed his forehead and smelled the liquor in his sweat. All men might be equal in the eyes of the gods, but the Peacock still needed paying, and soon. It was time to count out coins again. He climbed to the bin floor, mounted the ladder to the cap and poked his candle through the trapdoor.

The strongbox was gone, stolen, and he knew who had taken it. He roared with rage and blundered down rungs, intending to run the tunnels all the way to Barehill's base.

The chest lay unhidden on the stone floor, next to the carousel. *Barehill's men moved it when they brought down the bodies*, he realised, and felt foolish. The room still stank of corpse meat. It reminded him of Father, before the funeral, lying in state in borrowed velvet. He had spent three days at his side, stifling in the summer heat, waiting for mourners who never came.

He opened the chest and let a handful of coins slide through his fingers. *I'm too drunk for counting work*, he thought, *too drunk to be useful to anyone*. He wedged his half-empty bottle into a gap between the beams of the walls and lay uncomfortably on a grain sack.

Soft footsteps below. It had to be Laila. He peered obliquely through the trapdoor. She was looking for him on the reefing deck, still dressed like a man.

"Been sent to cheer me up?" he called down with an embarrassing belch. She looked him over, judgemental and disapproving.

"We need to talk," she said.

"Let's talk then."

"It's cold down here." She rubbed her shoulders. Jon hadn't noticed until she said it because the drink had hidden it from him, but she was right. Winter was nearly upon them.

"Come up then." It was proper that they talked where the stink of death was strongest. *Let it settle on her skin*, he thought, *remind her of what she's done*. He poured some liquor on his fingers and sniffed the drops up his nose to keep the death smell at bay.

Laila climbed the ladder sinuously and looked around the room. The carnival horse brought a child's wonder to her hard face.

"The colours. They move." She played peek-a-boo with her hands. Jon had forgotten that particular illusion. It didn't bear confirming, half-cut as he was. Just the idea of it made his head spin.

"I thought the Freeborn were against magic," he said.

"Can I?" She pointed at the horse. Jon shrugged. She sat astride it and rocked a little. The act was transparent, Jon thought. What kind of a fool did Barehill take him for, to send his girlish temptress on the very night that his wife had departed?

Jon threw himself into a routine of axle-checking and cog-oiling. It was hard to concentrate. Wine-addled, it seemed the parts themselves repelled his inspection. He thought about loading some grain into the hoppers. That was heavy work and he was still sober enough to know he was too drunk for it.

"George has given me orders," Laila said. "There's a mission. It's very dangerous." She pretended to sound nervous, uncertain. *A good actress*, Jon thought, and wondered into what she was trying to lure him.

"Seems like a waste of a young woman," he said.

"I'd volunteer anyway," she said defiantly.

Jon pulled at a gear strap looped around a rafter, hung from it one-armed, like a mountain ape.

"Then you're as crazy as he is." He suppressed another belch, souring the inside of his mouth.

"I don't agree with everything he does. He can be very cold sometimes."

Jon continued his aimless tinkering. In the weak yellow glow of the lanthorn Laila's hair shone more burgundy than orange.

She watched him working. "Don't be like him."

"Your man's a right bastard, that's for sure."

She looked away. "He's not my man. We are the Freeborn."

Jon snorted. "For a start he could stop telling people that I killed the censor. What if one of his men gets captured and sells me out?"

"That's not his fault, Jon. I told him that you did it. I told everybody."

Jon's face tightened. He balled his fists. "You lying bitch."

"I did it to protect you."

"What?"

"You saved my life from that censor, or at least you tried to. I owe you, Jon, and my lie keeps you safe. George doesn't always play fair. The men respect you now. Bill, Dyer and the others — some of them call you the Lion."

The flattery made him angry. The woman was trying to manipulate him, pull his levers. He glared at her in silent fury, or at least tried to against the spinning of the room.

"Why are you here?"

"George needs you for the mission as well. He's coming tomorrow morning, to explain." She could barely look at him. Finally, the truth was revealed. Barehill needed him, for something serious. Was Laila his offer? The reward? He watched her chest rise and fall as she breathed, traced the shadow of her boyish jaw on the valley of her neck.

"I don't agree with what he's doing — with how he's going about it," she said.

"Say no then. What's so special about George anyway? Do you do everything he asks?"

"Jon, you're not listening to me. I'm trying to help you, save your family."

"It's not me that needs saving, it's you."

Laila caught the look in his eyes and slid backwards off the horse, stood ready on her toes. Jon slammed the trapdoor closed with a kick and tied the latch closed with the leather belt, kept her in his sight the whole time.

"What are you doing?"

"Making sure we won't be disturbed." He rubbed the spit from his mouth with his sleeve and staggered towards her, steaming with drink and intent.

"Stop. No," she said.

He watched the bulge in her throat rise and fall as she swallowed. She slipped sideways, tried to circle away from him, tried to keep pillars and stacked boxes of parts between them.

"This isn't you, Jon. Something's gone wrong in your head."

He stalked her clumsily, kicking tools across the floor with his leaden feet. He had her trapped now, blocked into a corner by a half-sail too heavy to lift. He loomed over her; her eyes grew rabbit wide.

"I came up here to help you."

"I know — get down on your knees."

"What?"

"I want you on your knees."

"No."

"Kneel and pray. Pray for forgiveness. Look into your conscience and you'll see. You're not beyond saving. The gods brought you here tonight, not Barehill. Listen to them and you'll see that you're on the wrong path."

The side of her hand slammed into his neck and then she hit him across the face with a thick wooden dowel. He fell to his knees, clutching his head, and collapsed sideways onto the floor. She jumped onto his chest. Faster than he could draw a breath, she snatched a dagger from behind her back and pressed its edge against his throat.

"You're an idiot, Miller. I could kill you without blinking."

Her brown eyes flared with anger, but he met them without fear and held his voice firm.

"But you won't, will you? Your conscience sent you to me for a reason."

Laila searched his eyes and could not hold his gaze. She got off him, slit the leather and opened the trapdoor, lowered herself down.

"You need my help," Jon mumbled, rubbing his chin. There was no one to hear him, but that didn't matter; the gods had revealed a part of their plan.

NOT THE WISEST

Miranda's gaze travelled the length of the man lying naked beside her. The tiny blond hairs on his arms seemed to glow in the dawn light. She savoured the ridges of muscle that laddered his chest and came together in the hard triangle of his belly. He smelled like cinnamon. She wanted to live inside that scent, for a while at least.

Edmund Sutton — who are you? she wondered dreamily.

His arrival had been as melodramatic as a virgin's dream. It had begun with a frantic banging on her door, pleading to be let into her chambers, his whispers nearly a shout. She had been half asleep and quarter of the way through a bottle of Merret, trying to forget about the metal hand suspended in a vice on her workbench, and about to light her remembrance candle.

She had greeted him with a laugh. Edmund had sneaked into the Masters' Quarters dressed as a waiter. He looked like he'd climbed the walls to reach her. Ragged and wild-eyed, he had sworn she ruled his mind; that he had needed to be with her since that moment on the beach. It was so absurd. So romantic. She had pretended to believe him and invited him inside.

Miranda stretched and yawned. What an excellent decision that had been. Her heart had been in her mouth when she had remembered the metal hand, but to her relief his eyes had glided over it without a trace of recognition or surprise. He had trembled as if an innocent when she let her dress fall, seemed almost afraid of touching her. Not for long though.

He was as proficient between the sheets as he was mediocre in his studies, which he proved more than once. That was a worry. What if he was one of those men who shagged anything in a petticoat, from a milkmaid to a washstand?

She ran a finger across the waves of his ribs and he woke with a start. His face creased with worry. Did he think he had made a mistake? She slid her ebony leg over his bevelled thighs and kissed his shoulder playfully. *Don't worry, Mr Sutton, it was no mistake.*

"Thank you for last night," he said.

"I am amazing," she replied, and batted her lashes.

A blond lock fell across his forehead as he turned to her with a forced smile.

"I have to get out of here."

Furious at that, she hit him over the head with a pillow. The pillow knife lay exposed in the headboard. Embarrassed, she reached for it, to move it somewhere less dangerous. With a speed that she could not fathom, Edmund's hand snaked out and clamped around her wrist, twisted it painfully. His fingers were like vice irons. She was scared until she saw the mortified look on his face.

"I'm sorry, Miranda. I wasn't . . ." He trailed off and let her go gently, smoothed back his hair with a look of self-disappointment, flipped the pillow knife in his hand and caught it by the blade. Miranda gasped. "It's a beautiful thing." He offered its haft. Heart in mouth, she checked the blade for blood. It was clean. *Thank the gods.*

"I'm not allowed to be here," he said.

He wanted a sharp exit, it seemed. That wasn't a problem; Miranda desired to return to her study of the hand, but that was no excuse for making it so *obvious*.

"Let's order breakfast for two," she teased.

"In the Masters' Quarters? Miranda, I wasn't invited. I have to escape." He looked nervously out of the window, as if the birds themselves might be spies.

He was correct, technically, though Miranda couldn't imagine that the punishment would be severe.

"You have been a very naughty boy, Mister Sutton. Maybe they will set a censor on your tail." She winked at him. Edmund looked at her as if she were mad. He could be very literal sometimes.

●

The subterfuge was delightful, like something from a comic opera, even if Edmund took it a little too seriously. They emptied out her tapestry chest and she lined it with a white fur, so that he would be comfortable. He was not a contortionist, nor comfortable in the end, but they got him inside eventually. She carved a subtle rune into its heavy oak lid that would discourage attention and invested it with a little shimmy of power, a construct based on the memory of a tedious work of abstract art. A pair of hastily summoned porters cursed and groaned at the weight of the load, groaned again when told to deliver it to Mr Sutton's chambers. She blew the box a kiss as they manoeuvred it out of her door and her face flickered with suppressed laughter as it clattered against the granite frame.

She would ask Mother to find out more about his family, but before that, there was serious work to be done. A decision to be made.

Miranda inspected the hand. It hung suspended in a heavy clamp she normally reserved for alchemical experiments, stood alone on her cleared marble workbench. With the dirty leather peeled away, and its metal fingers cleaned with turpentine, it looked marvellous. A work of unparalleled craftsmanship. A masterpiece of metal and wire. At first her mind filled with wonder at its complexity and then it buzzed with curiosity. She reactivated its construct with three sharp taps yet it remained motionless, like an artist's model. She began to take notes.

The machine was one of Bolb's creations, of that she had no doubt. No other master had such a command of artifice. It was the magic invested within it that intrigued her. That was not Bolb's forte — if anything he was considered a bit of a dullard when it came to structuring, yet the power of the construct was immense. It was also strangely passive and contained. She could imagine no use for such a thing. Maybe the hand was simply a vessel to smuggle tamed magic out of the Verge.

The implications were frightening and she was at a loss, but the problem was not hers to solve. She put down her papers and turned her mind back to the conundrum of to whom to deliver the wretched thing. Gleame? Corbin? Mother? It was such a relief to know that Edmund hadn't recognised it. Imagine if he had, that he was some kind of nobleman thief. *A foreign agent.* Now that the fantasy was impossible, it was delicious.

She whistled for her factotum and he came scurrying.

"Inform Chairman Gleame that I seek an audience with him. Tell him that the matter is sensitive. Assure him that I will provide an explanation once we are together. Tell him to expect me within the hour."

The factotum opened his mouth as if to contradict her, then bowed less deeply than she would have liked and left the room with a dismayed look on his face. *That man does not respect me enough*, she thought.

She stared at the hand once more. An enigma from within an enigma. The sooner it was out of her life the better, but she hated not knowing what it was, or why it was important. She caught herself picking at her teeth with the nib of her pencil, a bad habit from her childhood, and drew an enormous question mark over her drawing of the contraption. Suddenly she stood bolt upright, as if stuck by lightning.

She opened her notepad to a new page and placed her pencil in the palm of Bolb's creation. Its fingers grasped it delicately, and immediately began to write. A stream of words and numbers flowed so quickly that Miranda knew at once that she would need more paper.

●

"Chairman Gleame will see you immediately, milady. He was a little surprised . . ." Miranda waved her servant silent. The ridiculous man looked like he was going to faint. He was not up to the job, and that was no good. She would have him replaced in a couple of days, she decided, and for the remainder, she would ignore him.

She fed another sheet of paper to the hand.

"My gown," she called out.

Her maid glided into the room from the bedchamber, crossed her legs and dropped into a curtsy worthy of the ballet. That was much better.

"Which would milady prefer?" she asked. It was a fair question; there were several.

"Red and black, with pearls sewn into the bodice."

The script the hand was producing was small and perfectly accurate, a scribe's dream. Miranda's eyes flitted back and forth across rows of numbers, letters and symbols. They meant nothing to her but had a pattern, and a pattern meant meaning. Was that what the hand was made for? To carry a message? If it were incriminating, that would explain why Bolb wanted it back so badly. She passed papers from hand to scribbling hand, as her maidservant undressed her, applied lotions, meticulously styled her hair and tied the new gown tight around her waist. Finally, she presented the rosewood jewellery box. Miranda decided to do without ornamentation on this occasion and dismissed her, then called her back as she tipped the rubies and diamonds onto her workbench in a rude pile.

The hand was still writing. There was no way to know for how long it would continue. Forever maybe? Far longer than she could afford to keep Gleame waiting. She turned it off, prised the pencil from its fingers and placed it inside the jewellery box.

●

Big Albert was waiting outside Gleame's office with two guards, both stern-faced and armed to the teeth. Miranda doubted their presence was meant to reassure her. She became uncertain as she approached, noticed how the natural humour had disappeared from Albert's face. She was about to turn back to her room when he spotted her and the guards stepped aside without having to be told. Albert followed her into the chairman's panoramic office. The sun was at its zenith and light reflected from the ocean and rippled on the walls.

"She's here," Albert said to Gleame, with more familiarity than befitted his station. Gleam dawdled by one of his statues. His white robes hung slackly by his sides, and his eyes were watery. It seemed he expected bad news.

"I had to cancel an important meeting for this. What is the matter, child?"

Miranda held out the rosewood box.

"I found something," she said.

"Albertus," Chairman Gleame commanded. The big man took the box and brought it over to his expansive desk, withdrew the bright metal hand, held it up to the light.

"Recognise it?" Gleame said.

Albert shook his head. "I'll check the records," he said, and selected a tome from one of the bookshelves.

Gleame turned, looked at Miranda quizzically. "When did you find it? Today? This morning?"

Miranda cleared her throat. "No, yesterday — at Seascale Bay. In a rabbit hole."

"That's not everything." She pointed at the box.

"I thought this was padding." Albertus slowly unfolded the censor's gauntlet and dangled it before Gleame. It took a moment for them to understand what they were looking at. A curious look, between horror and sadness, took hold of Gleame's face. Albertus just looked angry.

"It was hiding. The hand, I mean. I believe it is the work of Master Bolb."

"It is," Gleame said and turned to Albert. "Anything?"

"It appears to be ex-inventory — unauthorised."

"This makes no sense. Bolb has no need for gold. Why break his oaths?"

"Should I have him summoned?" Albertus asked.

The grandmaster sighed deeply and slumped back behind his desk. Miranda realised that Gleame cared for the man. "No. Close the causeway and fetch Corbin."

Albertus hurried from the room, his amiable gait gone. He moved like a guardsman preparing to repel an assault. Miranda stood alone with Gleame. His eyes flicked back and forth between her and the glove.

"How did you find it, Miranda? Why?"

"I saw Master Bolb searching the beach. My curiosity got the better of me. I thought I could do better."

Gleame looked at her dubiously. "Does anybody else know?"

"I haven't shown it to anyone."

Gleame looked at the hand closely, examined its details with a professional's eye. When he had finished, he leaned on this desk, fingers in his hair, shoulders hunched, and stared at the soiled glove.

"He was my first apprentice, Miranda, my greatest."

"I understand."

"No, you don't. I assume that I can count on your discretion in this matter. You have already proved yourself one of the Verge's greatest students. If your actions today have saved us from peril, the Convocation will be more than grateful."

"Maybe there's an innocent explanation?"

"No. There was a disturbance last night in the Masters' Quarters. A thief escaped. Matters are getting out of hand."

Miranda knew better than to ask, but whatever Gleame suspected had happened, one thing was clear — it was very bad. She thought about her night and felt sick to her stomach. *There is something else. A man hid in my room last night. He is built like a warrior and he has been my lover.* Her mind said the words but her lips stayed sealed.

Gleame caught the whiff of unease, raised a brow. "You shouldn't worry, Miranda; you did the right thing, bringing me the hand. Your mother would be proud of you."

THE SECRET AGENT

I lost Bolb's diary.
He's seen my face.
I've failed.

Daniel sat in his narrow bunk with his back pressed against the headboard and considered the possibility of death. His sword lay ready on the sheets by his side, his pistol nestled in his lap. Lang's instructions had been clear. If he could not escape, one way or another, he should die.

He looked down at the pistol in his hand, stared down the tunnel of its barrel and imagined placing it inside his mouth, the acrid smell of powder and the taste of cold steel pressed hard against his palate. Lang had said he should put the gun to his temple. Maybe that was supposed to make the act easier. He was well aware of his duty to the Brotherhood. He also knew than not one atom of his person was ready for death.

His death could not serve justice, nor his soul. Wasn't suicide supposed to be a sin?

Maybe not, if suicide served justice.

He lowered the pistol. The whole idea was ridiculous. Who could possibly be expected to shoot themselves in the head? Fuck that. A dead man could not become a censor. He knew what Jon would tell him — *"Trust in the gods."* He was never going to kill himself.

So why am I still holding the gun?

His bedpan was full of piss and he could smell the fear in it. He cursed himself for not having attempted an escape in the morning, before the tide of masters had flooded the causeway. A notice shoved under his door had informed him that nobody could leave the island. It was a temporary inconvenience, it had said, as if anybody would believe that.

He was trapped, couldn't even crawl back to Lang to beg forgiveness and a second chance. Now there was no chance. The only question now was who would get to him first: Bolb, Corbin or the Verge's guards.

Miranda might help him, with her magic and her brain. She liked him, or at least his smile and his body. What excuse or story would persuade a ward of the duchess to assist a wanted fugitive? Even the truth was bad. He had used her in the service of justice. He pictured her bewildered expression in the afterglow of their loving. He had loved that look. Making love to her hadn't felt wrong, but he couldn't see her agreeing.

He slapped his thigh. Why did his mind turn to the carnal at this time? His duty was clear. If he could not avoid capture, he was to keep his mission a secret at all costs. He examined the gun once more.

Torture was a fearful prospect.

●

The crashing on the door echoed in Daniel's heart.

Corbin's voice boomed from the corridor. "Open up — in the name of justice."

Daniel made a quick prayer for courage to He-who-lights-the-way, raised his pistol and went to the door. The wood bulged obscenely at the next impact; its hinges came loose from the wall. Daniel levelled his gun. One more crack and the door burst open.

Corbin punched Daniel backwards into the room with an open palm, and raised his longsword beside his head in an ox guard, the tip pointing at Daniel's face. "Hold," he commanded.

Daniel stumbled backwards, arms raised. Albertus ducked into the room, a hanger with a blade as wide as a butcher's knife clasped in his meaty hand, and kicked the door shut behind him, blocking escape with his massive body. His face froze.

"A pistol!" he warned.

Daniel felt the weight of the wheel lock in his hand, waved its muzzle at both men.

Corbin lowered his stance. "Drop that weapon. You're under arrest."

Daniel raised the pistol slowly towards his own head, but kept his finger from the trigger, held it loosely in anticipation of what would come next.

"Stop him," Albertus yelped.

Corbin hooked the gun from Daniel's hand with a twisting jab of his blade, and then swept it flat at the back of Daniel's knees. The move was not perfect, and Daniel nearly dodged the blow from habit. He let the blade connect with his calves and the slap of the metal seared like a scalding. He collapsed to his knees, lights flashing before his eyes.

Before his senses could right themselves, a boot came down hard on his ankle, sending a shooting pain up his leg. Albertus forced a bag over his head and Daniel choked as its cord tightened around his neck.

Someone pulled his hands behind his back. The bag smelled of dread and dried sweat.

"You're coming with me, son," Albertus growled in his ear, lifting him roughly by the shoulders.

"And not a word until I say so," Corbin added, from further away. "Or I break your legs."

Yes sir, Daniel thought as he was hauled to his feet. Albertus twisted his arms behind his back, held them high in a simple lock that Daniel could have escaped with a flip, had there been any point. He rode the pain and wondered where he was being taken as he was bundled down corridors and up flights of stairs.

His captors stopped several times, ducking behind corners, whispering that the coast was clear. They moved in the manner of kidnappers rather than constables. Wherever his destination, Corbin and Albertus did not want him to be seen. At last, he felt a soft carpet under his feet, and his captors seemed to relax a little. He heard the sound of blade scraping on blade, and his back stiffened in fear.

A chopping block? He had expected a dungeon. Headless would be one way to keep him quiet. Then he was in a warm place that smelled of rosewood.

Light blinded him as the bag was pulled off, then the blur of the room slowly resolved itself. He was standing in an office, one that made Magistrate Lang's look tawdry by comparison. Light flooded in from a latticed window that overlooked the sea. In the far distance, he could see mountaintops. Standing around him were Chairman Gleame, Albertus and Prosecutor Corbin.

"Is this the wretch who invaded the Masters' Quarters?" Albertus asked.

"I'm certain of it," Corbin replied with smiling eyes, though his face was as expressive as an anvil.

"What do you have to say for yourself, boy?" Albertus asked. Daniel feigned sullen defiance. The chairman would not look at him.

"What were you doing in Bolb's room?" Albertus demanded.

Daniel wondered how much he knew. He looked at Gleame and then at Corbin for a clue. Gleame was trying to pretend he didn't recognise him, and the effort of it seemed to be making him ill. Corbin revealed nothing.

"I've no idea what you are talking about."

"Master Bolb called for guards last night. Commanded that the Masters' Quarters be sealed."

"Why would he do a thing like that?" Corbin piped in cheerfully.

"His room was ruined," Albertus said.

"What's that got to do with me?" Daniel asked. Albert kicked him hard in the ribs, connected with the broken one. Daniel wailed and dropped to his side in agony. Corbin pursed his lips in a parody of concern.

Albert stared at Daniel menacingly. "We know you weren't in your room last night. Speak up, boy, or I'll have my friend here find the truth for me, and he is cold." He pointed over his shoulder at Corbin.

"I will tell you nothing," Daniel said in an accent he hoped sounded vaguely foreign. Corbin snorted in amusement. Gleame looked embarrassed and confused. Albertus spun around furiously.

"I see nothing amusing about this matter," Albertus said.

"Quite right," Corbin said. "Take him to the desk."

Albertus punched Daniel in the rib again, and Daniel screamed. Half dazed, he was lifted up onto the desk. Albertus lay across his back, pinning him down. The weight of the man alone was agony.

Face pressed against the walnut, Daniel saw Corbin approach. The prosecutor forced Daniel's left hand flat against Gleame's desk, dug a finger into the pressure point on the back of his hand, causing his fingers to splay. He drew his serrated hunting knife from his belt.

"Must we?" Gleame pleaded, his voice reedy.

"Who knows how much time we have," Corbin said. "Look at me, boy."

Daniel turned his head and spat at the prosecutor, searched for a sign in his eyes that what was happening was not real.

"I've seen you poking around, boy, searching and listening. Tell me what you've been up to."

"Never," Daniel said.

"Your loyalty is about to be tested."

From the desk, Corbin took a rosewood box that Daniel recognised as Miranda's, and he wondered if she had betrayed him as Corbin grasped Daniel's left hand tighter and forced Daniel's little finger across the top of it.

"Albertus," he said, and handed the big man his knife, "the tip."

You fucking maniac, Daniel thought, his mind whirling towards panic.

"Gladly," Albertus said and sliced it off.

For a second there was no pain and then Daniel howled.

"Cunts," he screamed, accent slipping, and then whined through his teeth like a wounded puppy.

"One last chance," Corbin said. "I know who you're working for — and you know that I know. Now tell these fine gentlemen who you really are, and I'll let you keep the rest of that finger. Go on — I give you permission."

Daniel stared at him disbelievingly. What was his intent? Was it some kind of crazy test? "Never," he hissed spitefully between gritted teeth. Corbin nodded to Albertus. Daniel couldn't watch. The bone of what was left of his little finger cracked loudly as the knife cut through.

Daniel wasn't sure if he screamed that time.

Albertus pressed Daniel's head into the tabletop with a broad hand, and placed the top half of Daniel's severed finger in front of his nose.

"I will never talk," Daniel whispered, his accent now pure Bromwich.

Corbin roared with laughter and patted Daniel on the back. "Not bad," he said. "Not bad at all."

"I apologise," Corbin said to the others, drying his eyes. "My young assistant plays a passable nobleman, but his range is limited."

Albertus looked at him nonplussed. Gleame had turned a little green.

"Your assistant? You told me he was a foreign agent, you lunatic!" Albertus roared, his cheeks purple with rage, veins bulging on the side of his head.

"This young brave isn't a spy or a thief. He's an aspirant, working for me."

You bastard, Daniel thought, through the agony of his hand, and glared at Corbin. The decision to end his secrecy was Lang's to make, not the prosecutor's.

Albertus furious was a terrifying sight, like a malign haystack come to life. His eyes demanded an explanation that would make sense of it all. "Who allowed this? Why wasn't I informed? Why doesn't the Convocation know?"

"The sensitivities of the Convocation are not my concern," Corbin snapped. "One of my brothers was killed here, and I am beginning to understand why."

"The Convergence does not operate under the Brotherhood's sufferance," Albertus shouted.

"This is not helping," Gleame said. Corbin and Albertus drew apart like scolded dogs. Gleame pulled aside a handkerchief to reveal the metal hand on his desk. "Edmund, can you explain what this is?"

Daniel recalled seeing something very much like it on the workbench in Miranda's laboratory. "I have absolutely no idea."

"What happened in the Masters' Quarters?" Albertus demanded.

"That is not a conversation for all ears," Daniel said.

Gleame cleared his throat. "Albertus is in charge of the Verge's security. He has been kept in the dark for too long already — and only because it was absolutely necessary. Please continue."

Daniel crossed his arms. Corbin's smile faded fast.

"It is allowed," Corbin said.

"No, it isn't," Daniel said.

"I'm giving you an order!"

"You do not have the authority." For a moment, Corbin looked like the Devourer himself and Daniel believed himself a dead man. Then the prosecutor sighed and calmed himself.

"Chairman, I trust you have a hekamaphone somewhere in this office. May I suggest we make use of it?" Gleame nodded.

"This is impossible," Albertus said with a scowl.

•

The four men crowded around the crackling device, Daniel with his left hand wrapped in one of Gleame's fine silk handkerchiefs. It throbbed maliciously. Daniel wondered if Gleame had a bottle of Carthusian hidden somewhere.

"You say the ward Miranda found the device, and that Bolb constructed it, without permission," Lang's voice hissed out.

"Yes," Gleame said.

"Has anyone discovered what the device does?"

"It contains an enormous amount of power, according to the girl. She has a talent for these matters, is most perceptive."

"Then my worst suspicions have been confirmed," Lang said.

"What suspicions?" Albertus's angry face twisted in the brass of the hekamaphone's horn.

"A few weeks ago a foreign spy was intercepted by my men in a coaching inn north of Bromwich. He was killed in the struggle, but a substantial amount of coin and jewellery was discovered about his person. Moreover he carried a dagger whose hilt concealed forbidden writings."

"What writings?" Corbin asked.

"Scriptures of Abjemo. I believe he was an agent of the Evangelicy on his way to the Convergence. That he was sent there to exchange the riches for something."

"That is an outrageous claim," Albertus said.

"Yes it is," Lang sighed. "Daniel, tell us what happened last night."

"Daniel?" the three men said in unison.

"Daniel Miller," he confirmed.

"It would be better if this was kept within the Brother-hood," Corbin said.

"Things have gone too far," Lang said, "and we are not the enemy of the Honourable Company of Cunning. Please proceed."

If Corbin could have throttled the hekamaphone, Daniel reckoned he would have done so. Daniel told them all of his adventure in Bolb's room and said nothing of Miranda.

Albertus became more and more outraged as he elaborated. "You sneaked into the Masters' Quarters without permission, in disguise, burgled a master's room, almost destroyed it . . . and your only achievement was the discovery of a diary which conveniently no longer exists?"

"Was there anything of use in the diary?" Lang asked.

"It was mostly miserable. I saw Adelmus's name, and Corbin's. Some talk of a hand. I thought he meant his own, but he must have meant the one you've shown me."

"No other names?"

"No."

"You've got nothing," Albertus said, "that's the truth of it. This is a disaster. When the other masters find out about this — censors spying in the Convergence, breaking into their quarters. This will cost me my job." He turned to Gleame. "I can't believe you sanctioned this."

Gleame said nothing.

Albertus began to pace the room. "How did you escape, Miller? I sealed the Masters' Quarters and we searched everywhere."

The room went silent.

"I cannot say until I've discussed the matter with Magistrate Lang."

Before Corbin could react, Lang said, "The Brotherhood does not reveal its methods. We have the hand, and for now, that is enough. I understand the sensitivities. What has been done was necessary for the defence of the Unity. Did anyone see Mr Miller taken prisoner?"

"No," Corbin said. "I made sure of that."

"He cannot continue spying," Albertus said. "I will not allow it."

"There is no need, I have a plan. But we must act as quickly as we can."

As they regathered around the hekamaphone, Daniel waved his bleeding hand reproachfully at Corbin.

"You were supposed to shoot yourself," Corbin whispered. "You got off lightly."

A NEST OF VIPERS

Trails of cloud scudded overhead like ghost fingers reaching for the horizon. They looked close enough to touch. The cawing of the seagulls that circled below sounded worryingly distant. Far away, Miranda could see the rounded peaks of Ellan Vannin. The island hunched in the frigid ocean like a leviathan in slumber.

Miranda gripped the edges of her chair and reminded herself that the parapet was a good ten feet away and that the Convergence had stood for many years and not once collapsed. *Vertigo is a bit like love*, she thought, fighting the fluttering in her chest. *If I ever needed to describe the sensation to a person with no feeling for the seductive power of edges, or the pull of great heights, the peak of the Convergence would be the place.*

The freeze-dried air made her cheeks prickle but she was warm, wrapped deep in the coat of an ice bear, a fur so white it seemed to glow. Its long hairs tickled her nose. As Miranda waited, a solitary waiter, his face a riverbed of wrinkles, ceaselessly rolled a silver drinks trolley between the empty tables around her.

Miranda's hand moved carelessly to her sternum, where the slip of paper was tucked into the top of her corset. On it was transcribed a single line of the codex produced by Bolb's mechanical hand. It lay hot against her skin, like a love letter from a wicked and dangerous man.

Master Somney appeared from the pavilion door and grimaced at the bitter wind. She waved to him as gaily as if he were freshly arrived at a summer picnic. He took a black fur wrap from the waiter, ordered a drink, and strode towards her, businesslike, the sharp tap of his staff accompanying his every other step.

"Hot rum. I recommend it." He set his copper mug down on the small, mosaicked table, sat at an angle to Miranda, facing out to sea, and wrapped himself tightly. Miranda watched the clouds passing inverted on the silvered crown of his head.

"Mother's favourite."

He shot her a sideways glance with his bloodshot eyes. "I was introduced to the duchess a few years back, at Dowdeswell. I was taking the waters."

"No doubt she was there for the horses." Miranda finished the story for him and smiled knowingly. It was a little crass of Somney to try to impress her with his status. It was not such a great thing, to have met her mother. She made a point of meeting people.

"We discussed matters of trade and a point of theology. She is a formidable woman, with strong convictions and a sharp mind. You remind me of her, in some ways."

Miranda stirred the pink tea that chimneyed steam from her delicate glass, tested the heat of it with puckered lips, and sipped noisily. "Some people say she's obstinate."

"Men mostly, I presume. Men who have failed to persuade her to do what they want. Why have you brought me up here, Miranda? It's freezing. I've already pledged you my support, if the opportunity for promotion to master ever arises."

"You were one of the first to do so."

Somney nestled back into the warm comfort of his fur and clasped his steaming drink in his bare hands. "You should be careful what you wish for, Miranda, this place is not what it once was. In the dark times, when we were hunted by censors, the Cunning learned to help one another to survive, to learn. We shared our knowledge, revelled in each other's achievements. We had to. Now all I see is ambition and petty rivalries. Men drunk on gold and pride. The Convergence has become a nest of vipers."

Poor Somney, Miranda thought, *maybe he's getting old. Tiring of the game.*

"I am indebted to you," she said. "I came to the Convergence upon your allowance and I will never forget that — no matter how far I rise." She gave an ambassadorial smile which he acknowledged with a grunt.

"I am pleased that you remember it that way. A memory for favours is a rarity in any place. So why have you summoned me? Do you wish to discuss tactics?" Somney took a swig of his hot rum and leaned back in his chair, feeling more relaxed.

"I feel that I can trust you," Miranda said. Somney flinched at that, checked over his shoulder. The waiter was trundling on the other side of the platform; she had made sure to wait for that.

"Trust me to do what? In what way?" Somney said nervously. Miranda leaned forward, slid the tiny scroll out from between her breasts and offered it to him. Miranda smiled as his eyes alighted briefly on her chest. He took the paper and unfurled it as if it might be poisoned, scanned it through narrow eyes.

"Where did you find this?"

"Inside a tome." His owlish eyes grew hard and incredulous. "Chapman's *Chaotic Thesis* . . . chapter five," she added unconvincingly.

He stared at her directly and the pattern of his irises began to curl and spike like sea flowers. Miranda suddenly felt naked.

She cursed herself. He was a master of the Verge, not to be taken lightly. She had no idea what powers he had. She summoned all of her effort to hold off his gaze. He saw her resistance and chose to relent. For a while, he did nothing but savour his drink and admire the blue sky.

"It's not really my speciality, that sort of thing."

"What isn't?"

"Structural notation. Advanced magimatics." He returned the slip of paper. "I have a good nose for trouble, Miranda — I've seen my fair share. If I were you, I would lose this scrap."

"Of course. But what does it say?"

He rocked back in his chair and looked to the clouds for a decision.

"It's always the same problem with the Cunning — their insatiable and idiotic desire for knowledge."

"Knowledge is power," Miranda said.

"Don't bandy clichés. Knowledge is like money, it only grants power to those who have more than they need. Most become its servant." He set down his mug, rotated it a quarter turn, grabbed his staff with a look of resignation and stood. "Come with me."

Miranda took his arm and they walked together towards the low wall on the landward side of the platform. Miranda faltered before they reached the edge, released his arm.

Somney stepped onto the parapet. Miranda gasped, felt her knees weaken. The precipice at Somney's feet was unimaginable.

"Trust me, Miranda," he said, and held out his hand. It was a test. Heart hammering, she scraped the soles of her shoes on the paving, and joined him.

It was impossible not to look down. From the great height, the giant boulders that lined the base of the island seemed as small as coals and the birds that circled above them nothing more than specks of dust. She screamed inwardly as her fear sought to betray the strength of her legs. She clutched at Somney's elbow and focused on the wobbling horizon.

"You are brave, Miranda. Brave and determined, but it is easy to be brave when you do not understand the danger."

Miranda's stomach churned. *He must be joking*, she thought, and felt the void pulling her forward. She clutched at Somney's arm and willed him to step back onto the platform.

"Look down," he said. "Tell me, what frightens you most?"

She forced herself.

"The rocks." They looked like countless jagged teeth, the greedy jumble of a shark's black maw, sucking her down.

"That which frightens you distracts you from the real danger. Do you want to know what frightens me?" She nodded stiffly, as if the movement of her chin might cause her to lose control and fall. "The causeway. It has been flooded and no explanation has been given as to why. Not even to the Convocation. There are rumours. Last night there was some kind of commotion in the Masters' Quarters. Do you see what I'm driving at?"

She didn't. All she could think about was the drop, but she nodded anyway, eyes clamped shut.

"And today, out of the blue, you show me that little scroll. The danger is not down there, you see. It is in here." He tapped his staff gently against the back of her head.

"I understand," Miranda said, praying for the ordeal to end. Somney led her back from the brink and guided her to her seat. She sipped at her tea, hands shaking.

"Do you still want to know what the fragment is?"

"I feel that I must." It was hard to tell if the look on Somney's face was disappointment or admiration.

"The text is an excerpt from an inventory. I saw fragments of dates, quanta, partial descriptions of devices. Beyond that I cannot help."

That was interesting, but gave little to work on. Miranda put down her glass and placed her hands around Somney's, warmed them with gentle strokes. He blushed a little.

"You said it wasn't your speciality. Whose speciality is it? Please."

"Riven Gahst is the most advanced theoretician in the Verge, but his ideas have become more and more unconventional."

"In what way?"

"He does little profitable magic any more. Many of the masters see him as a troublesome burden."

"Riven Gahst."

"Miranda, please do not pursue this matter any further. I fear it may be greater than either of us."

Miranda stood and pecked Somney on the cheek. He blushed fully this time. He was a decent man, and not half as world-weary as he pretended. He must have known that his plea was pointless.

4

THE HOROLOGICAL BOMBARD

Two of Barehill's men stood guard inside the mill's door. Another two knelt on the gallery, arquebuses primed.

If Norbury and Josephus show their faces today, we're all fucked, Jon thought, as his attention drifted back to Barehill and the plan he had laid out on the dining table.

"A horological bombard," Barehill repeated.

It was hard to focus. Jon's head pounded and his gut was raw from the booze. There was something else as well, a certain nagging feeling that he had or hadn't done something he was supposed to. He tried to remember what it was.

He had woken in the bin room, lying on the floor. That much he knew. His mouth had tasted like a war — still did, and there was a pain in his head that exploded his view with stars whenever he coughed. A big bruise as well.

I must have fallen over in my stupor, he thought. *Hit my head on a beam.*

"Go on," Laila said. He knew she was involved somehow. Every time he looked at her, she wrung her hands or stared at the table. *I must have said something when I was drunk, fought with her.* She was talking to Barehill as if he wasn't there. He prayed to She-who-reflects-his-glory that he hadn't done something worse.

"I've been working on this idea for a long time." Barehill produced a stub of a white wax candle and wedged it into a bejewelled hoop of brass and oak that looked like a sorcerer's napkin ring. He tapped an opal on its side with the stem of his pipe. "The placement of this gemstone determines the hour at which the candle ignites."

"Cunning, and stolen, no doubt," Jon half belched, his mouth sour and dry. Barehill ignored him and rotated the marker a fraction. The wick snapped alight. It was a clever trick.

"Place this in a container loaded with black powder, and at the appointed hour." Barehill drew apart his hands as if to describe the bursting of a balloon. "Boom."

"You've invented a cannon for cowards," Jon said.

"We did not start this war."

"How many people have you killed this week?"

"Do you know what was made in that manufactory?" Truth be told, Jon didn't. He resisted the temptation to shake his head. "Weapons. Everybody who worked there knew that. Guns and pikes and cannon."

"People have a right to defend themselves."

"To be loaded with grapeshot and used against women and children. Have you heard what happened at Lambourne? The so-called 'riot'. It was a massacre of innocents! Last night the patrols rounded up three of my men for posting bills. They will never be seen alive again. We must strike back."

Jon shook his head. "The duchess hopes to be made the head of the Wise Council. She must be seen to be strong. If you start a rebellion in Bromwich she will put it down, hard and fast." He cast his voice around the room. Barehill's men shifted uncomfortably. "You can't fight her like this. You don't stand a chance."

Barehill's fist slammed down on the table. "I am not here to politick. The Bell Jar is going to burn tonight. It needs to be done."

"The Bell Jar?" Jon was incredulous.

"It is the centre of oppression in Turbulence. Their symbol of power amongst the poor. The people of Bromwich need to see a demonstration of our power. Just imagine it. Peacock the usurer shredded by the very coins he has tried to extort from you."

"It's not extortion," Jon said. "I agreed to his terms."

"No more Bell Jar. No more militia. No more Peacock. All of our problems solved in one swift blow."

"Murder and madness."

"You're the only one of us who can get into the Bell Jar without a fight," Laila said.

"I'm not one of you."

"There's not another soul in Bromwich who believes that," Barehill said.

"There are no greater sins than murder."

"Yes there are," Laila said sharply.

"I will not kill innocents," Jon shouted.

Barehill's face went taut with anger. "There are no innocents. There are the Freeborn, there are the enemy, and there are collaborators." He dragged his fingers across his forehead in exasperation. "Laila, leave the room. Report back in an hour." She did not shift from her seat. Barehill roared in anger. "That is an order, Captain. And take your men with you."

Laila stood, cast a pained look at Jon and hurried to the loading bay.

Barehill glared across the table. A vein pulsed on his temple and he drummed the table with his fingers. Jon regarded him with contempt. He considered vaulting the table and strangling the man. If only he had a gun or a knife.

"Do you understand what has begun, Jon? What a civil war is compared to your little problems."

"I won't do it."

"You must think of your family."

"I am. Anna was right. I'll join her in Aldergrove, leave this afternoon. The mill is practically yours already. Let me take Laila with me. She won't survive this."

Barehill's eyes widened in amazement. "I can't decide which you are most: brave, insane or stupid. I took you for a weakling the first time I met you. Gods know where you get your confidence from, but you misunderstand the situation. Your family is not in Aldergrove — Anna has seen too much for that. I have had her taken to a safe place. She's under my protection."

Horror bubbled in Jon's stomach. Suddenly he was sweating again. There was no point in telling George Barehill what kind of a man he was; they both already knew.

"Mother preserve them."

"They will not come to harm if this thing is done. But I will not guarantee their safety unless I know that you are with me."

"You're holding them hostage."

Barehill said nothing.

"Haven't I done enough already?" Jon asked pointlessly.

"We must all make sacrifices."

"And what if I say no?"

Barehill dismissed the question with a shrug.

"Too many have died in this struggle for one more family to make any difference."

ENTRAPMENT

Gleame and Corbin ducked into an alcove; Daniel continued alone. Albertus had taken a different route and was already standing at the far end of the corridor, sword drawn. Torchlight glinted in his eyes and played on his broad blade. He waited until Daniel had seen him, and then moved to a position concealed in shadow.

You want me to be afraid, don't you? Daniel thought, and checked the dagger strapped behind his back.

The entrance to Bolb's chambers was exactly as he remembered. A tangle of iron machinery, impenetrable and forbidding. The glass and gemstone orbs that studded the door's surface seemed to bear a greater malice than before. The bell pull beside it dangled like a hangman's noose.

Remember to breathe.

Daniel was afraid, of course, but not only of the danger. This was his final chance, his moment. Lang was watching from afar, expecting greatness. Corbin really was watching. Gods knew what he expected. Daniel signalled to the prosecutor that he was ready and felt his throat tighten.

He rang the bell, half expecting a fusillade of poisoned darts to bury themselves in his flesh. Nothing happened, which was better than a death by frothing convulsions. The pressure in his blood made his wounded hand throb. He squeezed the bandages and waited for a response.

The grotesque magnification of an eye blossomed within one of the precious stones.

A shrill facsimile of Bolb's voice piped from some hidden place. "You! I will have you flayed, you wretched piece of . . ."

Daniel jutted out his chin, flexed his chest. "I have the hand," he said.

The eyeball blinked a few times and then disappeared. Silence. *Does he prepare a defence?* Daniel wondered. *Does he set his machines to kill?* There was solitary click, then another, then a cavalcade. The multitude of cogs, gears and latches that formed the surface of the door whirled and jerked. There was a thin whistle of sucking air, and then the door cracked down the middle and swung open.

Bolb stood before Daniel, moon-faced, nostrils flaring. His robes rattled in fury. *Is the fat man going to strike me?* Daniel widened his stance in preparation but Bolb stepped aside. Daniel breathed deep and re-entered his lair.

The room seemed smaller than before and less cluttered. It had an oily, freshly cleaned smell to it. Daniel was amused to see that Bolb had already fitted makeshift bars to his windows. Bolb withdrew an ornate key from the now closed door. Daniel tried to note which keyhole had been used, and realised that he could not recall, though he was sure that he had seen it as clear as day. The image in his memory was imprecise, corrupted. The trick stank of cunning.

No escape for either of us then, until this matter is settled.

"The hand. Show me it," Bolb said.

"Do I look like a fool?" Dan held out his empty palms. Bolb ignored the bandages.

"Where is it?"

"In a safe place."

"No place on earth is safe for that device."

"Then you should have been more careful with your invention."

Daniel took a bauble that was half compass, half timepiece from Bolb's worktop and rolled it between his fingers.

"Why should I believe you?" It was pathetic, how Bolb's mind sought an escape from the obvious truth, or maybe Bolb was just fishing, attempting to discern how much he knew. Daniel bluffed.

"I have it, and the censor's glove. That is all you need to know."

"How much do you want? Five thousand?"

He mistakes me for a blackmailer. Daniel held the silence, to see how far he'd go.

"More?" Bolb wrinkled his nose in disgust or confusion. "Ten thousand?"

"Your money isn't enough," Dan said, trying not to be distracted by the idea of ten thousand pounds.

Bolb stared at him, appalled. "What else then?"

Daniel's self-assurance grew. He knew from his training that a suspect who asked questions was trying to convince himself that he still had the power to escape his fate. Such confidence betrayed a deeper weakness.

"Plans, designs, the secrets of its making."

"Why?"

Daniel let Bolb's bauble roll from his fingers. It shattered on the floor, leaving a wet stain. "A man in your position does not ask the questions."

"What you ask is impossible. The plans are in my head. Even if I had written my part down . . ." Bolb gulped himself into silence.

"Your part?" Daniel said pointedly.

"Who are you? What are you?" The fat master was sweating profusely. Another good sign.

"Who I am is none of your concern. I want the plans and the money. Then I'll leave you in peace. I promise."

"How do I know you haven't already copied the message? That you won't betray me anyway?"

A message! Daniel thought triumphantly. "Don't you trust me?" he said, and borrowed Corbin's evil wink.

"No, and you will not leave this room alive unless I allow it." That was a surprise. Cornered Bolb suddenly seemed braver.

Daniel shrugged. "I got in without your say-so. If I die, the censors will get involved. We don't want that, do we? Me dead and you swinging from a yardarm."

"I will pay for the hand, but drawing up plans will take time."

"And I want the name of your accomplice."

"You change your terms already!"

"His name."

"Murderous leech."

Daniel laughed, dry and hollow. "I don't recall a master of that name."

Bolb stuttered in disbelief at the joke.

"You have already betrayed your position, the Honourable Company, the Unity; why stop there?" Daniel asked.

"I have betrayed nothing. You are the villain here. That is plain to see if you look at the facts of the matter." Bolb seemed to be talking mostly to himself now, lost in a fantasy of forgiveness and redemption.

Dan stepped right up to his face, barked at him, showering him with spittle. "Lose your position. After a censor's death. After delivering your machine into the hands of the Evangelicy."

Bolb staggered as if Daniel had caught him with a left hook.

"The Evangelicy?" Something in Bolb's face changed. A righteous fire burned in his eyes and Daniel had the withering sense that he had lost control of the conversation. "Foul servant of Abjemo — now you shall know me better — as a master of the cunning arts."

Bolb cast his arms wide and a cruel curved dagger appeared from his sleeve, jewelled and jagged-edged. Bewildered by Bolb's declaration, Daniel stepped back into a fighting stance and snatched his dagger from behind his back, ready to defend himself.

The master did not advance, but turned slowly, in a dancer's whirl. The bells of his robe began to shiver and chime in discord, like a band tuning its instruments before a symphony.

Daniel leapt forwards to tackle the master as his back was turned, but mid-stride a noise like a million hornets swarming knocked Daniel to his knees. He felt light-headed, as if he had risen too quickly and the blood had rushed from his head.

The edges of Bolb's robe became indistinct and the sound of his bells grew to a whine. The whine became shrill and the room became a blur. Daniel's eyes trembled in their sockets. He dropped his dagger and clutched at his head trying to hold it steady, covered his ears. It made no difference. Cold vomit reared in his stomach. The pitch went higher still. Noise became indistinguishable from pain.

Through his tears, Daniel could see Bolb's mouth gurning, a black triumph welling in his eyes. He was saying something. Whispering? Shouting? It was impossible to tell.

Against all sanity, the vibrations grew stronger. Bolb seemed edged by darkness, as if the room were fading around him. The muscles of Daniel's torso could no longer hold him upright. He fell onto all fours, clutched at the ground just to stay upright. The bones of his body shook like the levers of a broken machine. His teeth chattered hard enough to break. He opened his mouth to save them and watched a thin stream of bile pour onto the floor.

Bolb drew closer. Daniel could see the sickle edge of his blade dangling low. The cacophony was unbearable. He tried to retreat to the calm place in his mind, to escape the squealing pain that racked his body. Some feeling returned to his left arm — enough that he could lift it. He held it outstretched, tried to keep Bolb at bay, as hopelessly as a drunken vagrant.

Bolb hopped from foot to foot twirling in a mad spiral. Daniel felt the bones in his head cracking.

The door sundered in a spray of metal and precious stones.

Daniel could not hear the explosion, but he felt the gearwheel that slashed across the top of his cheek. Bent scrap scattered across the floor. From where he was curled, he saw legs rush into the room, two pairs of boots, brown and midnight blue.

Bolb's bells chimed in unison, and every glass object in the room turned to sand. Corbin slumped sideways to the floor, his eyes rolled back into his skull, his hands rigid on the haft of his longsword. Albertus fared worse, landed badly on his face. His hanger skated away from his open palm, spinning across the floor.

Gleame strode into the room. His robes and body blazed with a cold, white light that bleached all colour from the room. Daniel closed his stinging eyes and whimpered.

A new noise emerged over Bolb's deafening buzz — words spoken in a voice so low and terrible that the foundations of the Convergence itself seemed to tremble. Gleame became so bright that Daniel could see his outline in blurred blood red through his closed eyelids.

"N'gnog, Ulnzhro."

Some freedom of movement returned to Daniel's body. He rose to his knees and turned his head. Gleame stood in the doorway, holding his jewelled cane in an obscure alignment. Its head shone like a constellation of dying stars. Unfathomable vowels and consonants issued from his mouth, though his lips did not move.

"Ph'ep, Ooboshu."

Bolb screamed in rage. Tools and artefacts flew at Gleame from the walls, were deflected by an invisible force. Blood oozed from Bolb's nose.

"Ebunma, N'gotha."

Daniel's body stopped trembling. It felt bruised and weak, as if stretched on a rack. He shivered some energy into his muscles. Albertus's hanger was only an arm's length away. He saw his chance, dived for the blade and plunged it through the hem of Bolb's skirt.

Bolb collapsed with a wail and the room crashed into silence.

Daniel rolled onto his back and listened to the shocked complaints of his body.

Corbin clambered back to his feet, his longsword in his hand, a frightful look in his eye. He raised the blade overhead and slashed the point of it down through Bolb's pitiful body. The master's ornate robe split apart, and slumped around him. Bolb cowered in his undergarments clutching at his bleeding calf.

"Master Pendolous Bolb," Corbin said, "in the name of the Brotherhood and all that is just, you are under arrest."

Gleame winced at the words as he checked Albertus's pulse. He turned to Bolb, his face torn between anger and incomprehension. "This is an outrage," he said.

His guards appeared at the door.

Bolb's reply was sullen. "The Convergence would not exist were it not for me."

"This is no longer a matter for the Convergence," Corbin said as he hoisted Bolb to his feet by the scruff of his neck, practically lifting the fat man off the ground. "Are you alright?" he asked Daniel.

By way of illustration, Daniel put his finger in his mouth and pulled out a few tiny fragments of tooth.

"Good work, son. Very good. Now come with me, we've secrets to learn."

"First I must make my report to Lang," Daniel said.

For an instant, Corbin was angry, and then his shoulders slumped.

"You're right, I suppose. Meet me in the cells when you're done."

Daniel saluted from the floor, hand to neck. "Justice Advances."

The words never tasted sweeter.

Corbin marched Bolb from the room. Albertus made a groaning noise, and sat upright. He groggily rubbed the darkening bruise on his forehead, and clicked his nose back into place. Gleame ordered one of his guards to follow Corbin, the other to carry Albertus to the infirmary. He turned his attention to Daniel.

"Lang certainly knows how to pick his men."

Daniel looked at the wreckage around him. He had destroyed the master's room two nights in a row. That had to be some kind of achievement. Young aspirants would be reading about the case in years to come. He would make a point of describing the damage in his report.

RIVEN GAHST

Miranda peered through the narrow window at a featureless sky. What had Edmund called it? *An embrasure.* Riven Gahst's room was not much bigger than a prison cell. The shells of several hundred sea urchins hung from its ceiling suspended in silver nets. His bed was little more than a plank. Actually, it was a plank. That Gahst had let her in himself had surprised her most of all. For a master not to have a coterie of servants seemed the greatest of his eccentricities.

"This isn't what I expected," she said.

Gahst was wearing his peculiar garb — a skirted corset, strapped leather, and of course the metal that pierced his head and hands.

"This cell is close to the library, which has always been my greatest passion," he said, his tongue spike clattering disconcertingly. "Miranda, you waste your time in visiting me. I will not support your promotion to the Convocation, no matter how hard you plead."

It was reasonable of him to assume that was why she had come. "Do you think it is an unsuitable role for a woman?" she asked.

His laugh sounded like the cough of a dying man.

"I have no doubt of your powers, Miranda. I oppose you because I am certain of them. You have a wealth of talent, unusual gifts, but you must understand that I have not voted in favour of a promotion for more than a decade. Two, perhaps. There are too many masters as it is. Far too many." He looked sad, as if he were retelling a joke that nobody ever understood.

"I did not come here to ask for your support; I came here to ask for an explanation."

"I do not need to justify myself to the likes of you."

"Maybe I am being unclear. I am interested in your theories."

The metalwork around his face rattled angrily. "Because they are inconvenient to the creation of wealth. I have no time for demi-masters who hope to win favour with Gleame by disproving my work."

"No," Miranda said sharply, and Gleame recoiled. It was funny, she thought, how confused some men got when a woman took command. She sat down on his plank. It was as uncomfortable as it looked, but at least it wasn't covered in nails. "My mother taught me that the least comfortable thoughts are the ones that deserve the most attention. I come of my own accord and with an open mind, seeking knowledge." She crossed her hands upon her knees to make sure he understood she wasn't leaving without an answer. Gahst pulled nervously at the wires between his brow and his lips, causing him to grin and frown at the same time.

"Mother, you call her, but you are not of the duchess's flesh." He paced the room. His thorn-wood skirt scratched on the floor like kindling being dragged to a funeral pyre.

"I am a ward of the duchess. We are her sorrow and her joy."

Gahst didn't seem to hear. Miranda could see his mind racing. She watched impassively as his expression cycled, like a wheel of fortune, through suspicion, fear and hope. When it settled, his eyes seemed almost feverish.

"Yes. Your genius. Maybe you will understand, can make her see. Maybe you are the one." He knelt at her feet and she winced at the crunching of the thorns against the bare flagstones.

"Show me your secrets," she whispered, like a trusted confidant. He was putty in her hands now, and Miranda had absorbed too much incoherent lunacy in the last month to fear any more.

"I have not invested magic in a decade. The trappings I wear are the only remnant of my craft. I have devoted all of my time to hekalogy — the study of what magic is and where it comes from."

"Your 'Theory of Hidden Makers'?"

"More than that. Its true nature."

"Magic is like fire or wind, so says Master Turon."

"A metaphor is not an explanation. It would be better to say that magic is like light, taken for granted by all, but with no understanding of what it really is. Nobody knows, and nobody seems to care. That is the problem. I have devoted my life to that question. Does magic have a cost? Do we borrow from our Hidden Maker without truly understanding the terms? What if the terms are not in our favour?"

"But surely the Hidden Makers are also a metaphor? It is we, the Cunning, who do the real making."

"Oh no. Not at all."

"So what are they?"

"I have seen them revealed — in numbers and in dreams." Gahst dragged a writing chest from under Miranda's seat and withdrew a ragged map, which he rolled open across the length of the chamber's floor. The chart was impossible to follow, a labyrinth of equations, symbols and orbits. He jabbed at signs and numbers like a child squashing ants. "See here, and here, and here."

As Miranda looked closer, she saw that the document was a collage — cuttings from ancient tomes sewn to fresh vellum and marked by Gahst's spindly hand. It seemed a portrait of madness.

"My calculations show that there must be other convergences, in other universes. They are the Hidden Makers. Not people, not at all. The magic we invest is not only that which we create, it is part of an ocean. One that we drain to irrigate our land. We take our magic from other worlds. I will show you."

Miranda let Gahst speak for an hour or more. He did so rapidly, without pause for breath or punctuation, explaining synchronicities she could barely see, and reciting magimatical formulae that she did not understand. Then without warning, he wheezed like a donkey and fell silent.

"Do you see? Not yet. I go too far, too quickly. You must come again. Learn more while we still have time." He rocked back and forth on his haunches. Dots of blood welled on his thigh where the thorns had freshly pierced.

"Are you feeling unwell?" Miranda asked.

He could not hear. He was speaking only to himself now, lost in his mind. "When you understand, you will persuade Gleame. You will persuade your mother. Yes. They will listen to you."

Gahst grabbed the hem of her dress, began to pull at it. Miranda raised her hand to slap him and remembered the fishhooks that protruded from his eyebrows.

"Master Gahst." Her outraged shout brought him back to his senses. His whole body shook as he carefully replaced the scroll in its case. Miranda was beginning to feel a little scared. She waited until he appeared calmer. "Persuade them to do what?"

"To bring an end to this madness. Miranda, my theories prove that the Convergence is a house of cards, that for years we have been taking far more magic from it than we could possibly hope to replace. All of that magic, that power has been spread across the world. Imagine what could happen if, all at once, it were taken back. Or worse yet, cut loose."

Alarmist. Paranoid. Gahst's rantings were the worst kind of outlandish speculation. They reminded Miranda of those scurrilous pamphlets that claimed every shocking event in history to be the result of some vast conspiracy.

"So what are you suggesting? That we diminish our efforts? What about those who depend upon us? The colonies in the Far West? The threat of the Evangelicy?"

What about the power of the North? she thought.

"It is too late for that. The Convergence must be abandoned — completely."

Gahst was insane. No wonder Gleame wished to discredit him.

"On the basis of your speculation? Even if your theory of other worlds is correct, there are no reasons for concern, no signs of danger. That hardly seems like a crisis to me."

"That is the whole point, Miranda. Don't you understand? No crisis is shocking in the making. That is precisely why they happen. The apocalypse does not carry a calling card or send a herald in advance. If there were signs of danger, people would be forced to act, the disaster would be prevented. The end of the world does not come expected; it sneaks and it prowls."

Miranda stood and brushed down her skirt.

"I have taken too much of your time, Master Gahst," she said. *In addition, wasted too much of my own.* He saw that he had lost her.

"I have not convinced you. You must come again. I beg of you, Miranda. I will present my thoughts more clearly." Something in his desperation delighted her.

"On two conditions."

"Anything."

"First, you must support my election to the Convocation." She held up her hand to pre-empt his objection. "If I am to speak on your behalf, that is where my voice will be heard most loudly and all the more so for the rarity of your blessing." Gahst would see the sense in that proposal, whether or not there was any. "Secondly, you will explain to me what this is."

She handed him the tiny scroll from her bodice, warm and a little damp from her skin.

He held it at arm's length, pinched between his split nails. As he read, he seemed to both shrink and become light, as if an unpopular king forced to abdicate from a throne that he hated.

"I have no time left," he said. "The hand has been found."

Miranda was gripped by the inescapable feeling that she had made a terrible mistake.

"Yes, it has."

"Where is it now?"

"With Chairman Gleame."

"I see." She seemed to fade from Gahst's sight then, become a ghost to him. Gahst undid his skirt and let it fall to the floor with a clatter. He slowly began to untie his corset, revealing the taut, grey flesh of his back.

"What is the hand?"

"A complete audit of the Convergence and its entire works. Every one of its secrets."

"You planned to betray its secrets. That censor discovered your plot — and you killed him." Miranda stepped away from him, suddenly afraid.

"Maybe I did." Gahst slipped the corset from his shoulders and began to unhook his piercings. "But I betrayed no one. I was betrayed. I cannot understand how. The censors have inflicted countless harm on our kind, but Adelmus and I understood each other. It's hard to like censors, they are hard men — but I liked him. I trusted him. I thought he was honourable."

"What are you going to do?"

"Whoever killed Adelmus won't have any trouble dealing with me. I'm just an old man."

That was true. Standing unadorned, he looked commonplace, like one of the gardeners at the orphanage. He stood before her stark naked, handed her his huge scroll, and a palm book from his desk. "These contain everything you need to know. Do with them as you will. Now leave me alone."

She took the documents, tucked them under her arm and left.

On the way back to her chambers, she stopped by Sutton's room. When she knocked on the door there was no answer. She scribbled a note to him quickly, telling him to call her urgently. Then she noticed there was a man in the corridor outside. He looked like an ordinary porter, but there was something strange in the way he watched her. Somney had been right to warn her. She could feel danger in the air — true danger, drawing close around her like a net.

THE BELL STREET MASSACRE

The strongbox seemed to get heavier with every crunching step towards the Bell Jar. Jon tried to keep the rhythm of his pace steady, but he could not stop the damned thing from swinging. Its engraved handles were coming loose in their brackets and bit deep into his fingers. He resisted the urge to pause for breath. If he stopped, then he would start to think about the killing, and he might not be able to continue.

You have no choice. Think of your family.

Barehill had set the candle to ignite in less than an hour. Jon imagined the bombard in the base of the strongbox shifting, the timer slipping, the candlewick sparking into life and igniting the powder, blasting him into fiery oblivion. Scattering him and Laila across the street in a shower of coins and broken limbs. He wanted to vomit.

Keep moving, one foot at a time. Anna. The baby. Anna. The baby.

It didn't help that it hurt to breathe. His chest was bruised and swollen, the pain of the previous night made real by his sobriety, and multiplied by his hangover. At least he could remember now. What had he been thinking, to imagine that he could salvage the soul of the murderous wench who traipsed behind him? What kind of an idiot confused the urgings of wine with the will of the gods?

Laila carried the other end of the strongbox. She was disguised in a cloak and breeches, her breasts strapped down tight.

You'd still have to be blind to mistake her for a man. Why Laila? She was half his size, barely able to hold up her end. Jon could hear her puffing with the effort. Because she would see the job done, *no matter what.* That was why. Before they'd left the mill, she had loaded a pistol in front of him, no bigger than her fist, two barrels, over and under. She'd never said it, but he knew that it was meant for him, in case he tried to run.

Peacock's curfew had yet to be lifted and the streets were empty, eerily devoid of the night urchins and bandits who normally sought the pennies of the sympathetic and the easily intimidated.

They reached the unnamed stretch between Urikon Street and Swan Alley and turned into the top end of Badly Street, sticking to the shadows. Jon halted suddenly. Laila slipped and he felt the chest crash painfully into the back of his knees. For a moment, the whole of its weight was on his sore knuckles, and his wrists twisted backwards, close to breaking. Then Laila had the other end again, and he was left with a numbing pain and a heart thudding so loudly he imagined she could hear it.

The orange flag of the Turbulence militia hung limply over the entrance to the Bell Jar, illuminated by the dim light of a brazier. Three guards stood on lookout, a ramshackle arquebusier, a crossbowman who looked more like a peasant on a hunt than a soldier, and closest, a bill man. Wisps of conversation drifted over to him, talk of women and war.

He needed to call ahead, to make sure that the militiamen were not surprised into action by his unexpected appearance, but his throat would not obey. His head went light and a throbbing sigh ebbed and swelled in his ears. He foresaw the calamity of what he was being told to do, imagined the mangled bodies and ruined lives.

These people are all insane. The Freeborn, the gangs, the militia, even the censors. All they care about is killing each other.

He looked over his shoulder. Laila had sensed his uncertainty, was watching him like a viper. The pistol was already in her hand.

"I'm going to count down from five," she said.

He couldn't do it. He hated Peacock, thought him evil, maybe even wanted him dead, but that wasn't the same thing as blowing him and his friends to pieces.

There had to be a reason for all of this, for fate to have led him to a place so strange. Jon looked up as Laila whispered down the numbers. She-who-reflects-his-glory was nothing more than a waning crescent in the sky, slim to almost gone. He had always prayed to her for wisdom. It had rarely come.

"Zero," Laila said. "Don't force me to kill you."

Jon's bowels loosened.

"Barehill will kill me anyway."

"I won't let him. I know where he has taken your family. I'll take you there after this is done, let you all go free. I swear it."

"Why should I believe you?"

"I've been thinking about what you said last night."

"Yet you're still making me do this?"

"Yes," she said, and raised her gun.

Jon stood rooted, unsure what to do. He closed his eyes. A dog howled. For a moment, he was confused, and then the omen became as clear as the road in front of him. This was not a moment to lose faith; it was time to place his trust in justice, in He-who-sits-upon-the-mountain. Daniel would laugh if he knew.

"Keep quiet," he whispered. Then, to his surprise, his feet began to move of their own accord. Against all reason, he approached the guards and called out his name. The bill man levelled his polearm in Jon's direction while the others hurried to load weapons. The arquebusier fumbled his ramrod, cursed as it spun from his fingers and clattered out of sight.

"Idiot," his mate yelled and raised his crossbow.

"I've come to make a payment," Jon shouted. His throat was as dry as a grain chute, but his legs carried him forwards with a confidence that belonged to a stranger. The bill man was Rollo. Recognition flashed in the tattooed foreman's eyes and he leaned easy on his oversized weapon.

"Gods, you've got some balls on you. Don't you know there's a curfew on?"

"Which means I don't have to worry about street pirates."

Rollo laughed at the gall of it. "Who's the lad?" Jon shrugged.

"Never mind." Rollo grasped a large key from his belt. "Head on in, then. And fetch me out a pint of warm ale when you've done your business."

The Bell Jar had a new door, thick oak and ironclad, painted with a feather.

"I think you ought to have a look up the street," Jon said. "I saw someone sneaking about up there."

"Can't, mate. Strictest orders." Rollo opened the door with a proud flourish.

The Bell Jar was shockingly crowded inside, brimming with soldiery and hangers-on. The air was thick with talk and candle smoke. A piper and a drummer were hammering out a rendition of 'Over the Hills' rough enough to scorch the ears of the deaf. Rollo's tough young workmates were arm-wrestling at the bar. They wore breastplates, fastened around their waists with leather belts. The helmets that hung from the hooks between their shoulder blades made them look like hunchbacks. He saw the old drunks too. Maybe they hadn't noticed that the Bell Jar was a military affair now. Maybe nobody could be bothered to turn them away.

Harriet the barmaid was spying on a game of cards. She didn't see Jon through the crowd, for which he was grateful.

The Bell Jar's not a tavern any more, Jon told himself, more a barracks. *The idea co*mforted him little as he took the strongbox from Laila. Her hood was pulled down and she had raised her scarf to cover her face.

"Leave out back, by the privy," Jon said. Laila shook her head. The steely look she gave him was tinged with fear. He realised that she would not leave until she was certain that the job was done. "Wait for me here then."

He pushed his way through the room, sweating like a pig. The men around him exchanged salvos of chatter and abuse, paid no attention as he dragged the chest between them. He listened to the little things said in the conversations going on all around him, though he normally paid no mind to other men's business.

The censors were at Peacock's table. Brother Josephus was plotting with Matthew over a map, discussing some stratagem. Brother Norbury stood a little aside, his left arm splinted and thick with bandages. The Sharks lounged behind them all, faces as flat as irons.

The men in blue turned to face Jon together, as if they could smell gunpowder and guilt from across a room.

"What have you got there, Miller? More stolen magic?" Norbury pointed at the strongbox accusingly with his capable hand.

Mathew turned, appraised the situation and gave Jon a broad wink. "Be at ease, Brothers, I am this man's rentier, he comes to make payment. You'll have to wait your turn, Jon. I am discussing matters of great importance with these gentlemen." He ran his sleeve across his lips. "Harriet! Bring us over a round, love — and a pint for Jon. He must be parched."

The strongbox was attracting a fair amount of attention now that Matthew had mentioned payment. Lumpishly

commanding the centre of the floor, every poor man in the Bell
Jar seemed to be dreaming of what was inside it.

I'm going to tell them, and soon. I just need to pick the moment,
Jon thought. Laila was still watching him like He-who-sails-
the-wind. He sat on top of the strongbox, imagined he could
feel the candle in the bombard creeping towards ignition.

Harriet pressed an unwanted ale into his hands with a
knowing smile. The censors folded the maps.

"Well, don't stand there all shilly-shally, bring it over," the
Peacock said.

There were no clocks in the Bell Jar. *It must be ten minutes
to the hour at most*, Jon thought, *maybe less*. Jon heaved the chest
onto the table.

"Pretty box. Open it up," Matthew said. Jon swung back
the heavy lid. Peacock whistled. "So this is where you've been
hiding all those coppers."

"Do I recognise that chest?" Josephus said, eyeing it suspiciously.

"Hands off, lads," Peacock said a little too sharply, then
added, "begging your pardon, of course." He dug out a handful
of coins, let them rain back inside.

"Last week's rent," Jon said. "Next month's too."

Peacock looked confused. "You've paid last week's already.
My fourth captain brought it to me in a bag. That was a stroke
of luck, mind; it nearly got lost in the riot." He dug his hands
deep into the pile. "This all of it? Everything you've got?"

"All of it."

"And you're giving it to me now? In advance?"

"Yes."

"Where's the sense in that?"

"Making the trip every week, with the curfew on. It's dangerous. Hard." Jon could feel sweat pouring down his face. *Is

Laila still watching me? He looked over his shoulder. She was. Everyone else's attention was on the band, who had launched into a raucous but enthusiastic finale.

"You getting tired on me, Jon? Giving up?"

"Maybe I should take the money back?"

"Maybe you should. You know what they say, old son. Stay in the game." Jon saw something in Peacock's face then, and felt a fool. The villain didn't care for his money, not especially, nor the mill. He just enjoyed seeing him stretched thin, on tenterhooks. Failing in front of Anna.

Norbury spoke.

"Sorry to interrupt your merriment, gents, but there's a rebellion in Turbulence if you hadn't noticed. We've business to attend to."

"Don't think we've forgotten about you, Miller," Josephus said. "We'll visit soon enough. Lundy evening by the latest."

The Sharks put the strongbox under the table and Jon was dismissed. He looked for Laila and saw her signalling to him from the back of the tavern, pointing frantically at the exit. Time was up. Maybe he had left it too late, but he'd never be further from her than he was now. He looked at the Sharks, the censors. He looked into Peacock's eyes. By the gods, the man was a prick, but that wasn't enough.

He leaned forward and spoke clearly. "There's a bomb," he said.

Josephus' head snapped around. "What?"

"A bomb. Get everyone out, now."

"What are you talking about?" The censor jumped onto the table, scanned the room for barrels of gunpowder.

"It's in the strongbox." Jon turned to the tavern, shouted at the top his voice, "Everybody — get out now!" Josephus' eyes dropped, and Jon leapt into the crowd, towards the bar.

"Everyone out!" Matthew shouted, but only a few heard him over the music, and they weren't sure what to make of it. At the bar, Jon grabbed Harriet by the elbow. She yelped.

"Outside. *Now!*" Jon dragged her by the arm.

"Oi, Miller! What are you doing?" complained Raymond the landlord.

"Jonathan Miller, can't you see that I'm serving? Are you drunk, you randy old goat?" Harriet grinned and tried to wriggle free.

Nobody's leaving, Jon realised with horror. *They should be running*. He pulled her so hard she nearly fell over.

"Out," he shouted.

"You're hurting me," she complained, but stopped resisting. "I always took you for a family man."

"Freeborn! Freeborn!" Jon looked over his shoulder. A young soldier was pointing, not at him, but towards Laila. She had her pistol in her hand, at full stretch above her head. Somebody had pulled down her cloak to reveal her shock of red hair and another soldier gripped her arm, was holding it upright. Laila clawed at him, scratching his eyes. Confusion reigned as the militiamen tried to work out who was being accused, and what was to be done about the matter.

Laila grabbed a helmet from a soldier's back and planted it square in the face of the man who held her. He reeled back, his nose spraying blood, and she sprinted past Jon and Harriet for the exit.

The crowd erupted.

Peacock and the Sharks were already halfway across the room. The censors were stooped over the strongbox, frantically emptying out coins. Jon scooped Harriet from her feet, and charged for the street.

How many seconds?

"Run for your lives!" Jon screamed, and shoulder-barged a man out of the way, made it four yards into the street, tearing past Rollo and his men.

"You! Stop!" Rollo protested.

Night turned into day. Light flashed across Laila's fleeing back, freezing her image in mid-stride. Then came the crack of a giant's whip and the vulgar sound of a thousand bottles breaking. An invisible pair of hands knocked Jon topsy-turvy. A ripped tankard flew past his face and embedded itself in a wall on the other side of the street.

He dived to the ground, rolled twice. Harriet slipped from his arms. All sound ended then, apart from a shrill ringing in his ears. It was like when Father had slapped his head with a fixing mallet, but on both sides. He staggered to his feet. The air was hot and sharp, his back felt wet. He put a hand to it and cut his fingertip on a piece of glass lodged next to his spine.

Jon surveyed the wreckage. Harriet had rolled only a few feet away. She was lying, face up, coughing up a storm, surrounded by blackened coins. There was a fierce graze across her shoulder.

He looked back to the Bell Jar, expecting to see ruination. The iron door of the inn was open, the orange flag of the militia hung above it. For a moment, Jon wondered if the tavern had somehow withstood the bomb, that the gods had revoked its power in some mysterious way. Then he saw that the windows were blown, their leads reaching outwards like desperate hands, and that around the door Rollo and his men lay motionless on the ground. Jon could not comprehend what he had done. It was too big for him.

Laila faced him across the sulphur haze, tears streaming from her eyes. She levelled her stub-nosed pistol at his head.

"Just do it," Jon said.

Laila's finger quivered over the trigger as she fought against the evil in her mind. Then she lowered her hand and ran.

From inside the tavern screams and moans built into a hideous chant. A fire was starting. Someone shouted for water. The survivors grew louder. It was terrible. Jon began to cry. He ran across the road, ducked behind some shattered brickwork, and cowered in the dark.

Why aren't I dead? There has to be a reason.

The men who had listened to him, those who had made it closest to the door, began to stumble out, smoke venting from their tattered clothes. Peacock and his Sharks were the last of them. Big Shark bent double and coughed his stomach into the gutter. Littleshark spat furiously. Jon thanked the gods for saving every soul he saw, even them.

Harriet was sitting upright now, eyes struggling to focus. He could see her thoughts gathering in the haze. She knew what he'd done, of course, figured it out straight off. She'd always been smart.

"That girl what done it. She went that way!" Harriet screamed hoarsely, and pointed down Bell Street. Peacock and the Sharks turned to Harriet, saw where she meant, and set off at a run. Harriet staggered back towards the Bell Jar to see what good could be done.

Bless you, Jon thought, and set off after them.

Laila made a good chase of it. She was fast, but the Sharks were quicker still. Peacock followed as best he could, limping from a new wound and shouting blasphemy and bloody revenge. Tenement windows opened up above, and the streets were haunted with cheering at the sport. Jon followed them as best he could, but his boots had started to fill with the blood that was running down his hams. Soon he was a hundred yards behind. It ended somewhere near the top of Lea Lane. Laila turned and fired her pistol. Littleshark launched himself forwards, grabbed at Laila's heels. She tripped and fell, scrambled free, but then Big Shark speared into her waist, drove her into the ground. She screamed in pain as she twisted over on a knee and they tumbled down together. Peacock arrived at the sprawled trio and kicked Laila hard in the stomach to keep her down.

"That was fun." He heaved great breaths that sent clouds of fog into the night air, walked in a circle to recover himself. His face contorted. "You fucking bitch, what did you do?" He kicked her again.

The Sharks grabbed Laila and hauled her upright. She screamed for help and looked desperately in Jon's direction. Jon pulled himself deeper into the shadows of a derelict doorway and watched Littleshark punch her in the jaw.

"Don't mess up her face," Peacock said. "Use some common sense."

Laila cried out once more and Jon's stomach turned spastic. "Look, love, no one wants to help you so why don't you just keep your fucking mouth shut."

She kicked out at him, caught him above the knee and yelled again. Big Shark clamped a meaty hand over her mouth and she bit into it. He cursed but did not flinch. Peacock laughed through the pain. "Gag her."

"With your hat?" Big Shark said, apparently oblivious to the teeth in his fingers. Peacock shed his left boot, rolled a dirty stocking down his shin, bunched it and shoved it into Laila's mouth.

A window frame squeaked from the tenements above. Peacock shouted skywards, "Censor business. Pass us down a light or I come back tomorrow, angry."

There was muttering, then some scrabbling, and a rusty old lanthorn was passed down on a pole hook.

"Much appreciated," Peacock said and raised the light to Laila's face. "Just look at the fire in those eyes."

The power of his slap turned her head. He stepped back to see the whole of her.

"Very nice. So why are you dressed all mannish then?"

Muffled defiance was the whole of her response. He held up a hand.

"You're right. This is not the place for explanations, and it doesn't look like they'll come easy either. Two censors dead and my headquarters ruined. Come on, lads; the Bell Jar's out of the question. It's a shithole anyway. Let's get her to The Kennels. Find out what the fuck is going on around here."

Littleshark pulled Laila's breeches down and bound her legs with them. Big Shark hoisted her over his shoulder and they headed back down Lea Lane.

Jon pressed himself hard into the corner of the doorframe as the trio trooped past with their wriggling bundle. Laila saw him in the shadows, and their eyes locked. She flailed her body and tried to scream, but the Sharks paid no attention.

When the posse's footsteps were no more than faint echoes he allowed himself to breathe again. He could not imagine what the Peacock would do to Laila at his mansion. Actually, he could. She was so young. Not quite enough to be his daughter, but something else maybe — a sister. A little younger than Dahlia would be, if the evil men who had taken her had let her live.

A black rage against Peacock, Barehill and all the murderous bastards of the world who had fouled him with schemes and ambitions boiled inside him. Why couldn't men be good? Why did they always put their own lives first? What had he done to the Bell Jar? How many people had he killed?

Everything was such a mess.

He bit his raw knuckles, started at the pain. There had to be a reason for it all, if only he could see it.

Then he saw it, clear as day. Laila had been captured and she was the only one he could trust to tell him where Anna was. Laila had said she would let Anna go free and then, against reason, Laila had let him live. That meant she could be saved, and if she could be saved, maybe everyone could be saved. Even himself. A long time ago, he had let his sister be taken and the gods had cursed him. Now he'd have to risk everything to rescue Laila. The symmetry was obvious. Divine. What the gods wanted.

Jon brushed himself down and turned in the direction of Peacock's mansion.

HOME TRUTHS

Miranda had made a fortress of her papers. To her left, arranged in stacks as deep as an Evangelist's Bible, were the pristine writings of the mechanical hand. To her right, on an ornate wooden easel, rested the key to their secrets: Gahst's codex.

She looked again at her notes; the information she had decoded through the night. Much of it was mundane, by the standard to which she had become accustomed. The lists of amulets, potions and scrolls that the Convergence had produced were interesting only in respect of their huge volumes. There were other things though, rare and secret: flying warships. Wheeled automata armed with fire lances. Intelligent poisons. The names of the customers who had ordered them.

The demons were not in the detail, they were in the totality.

The hand offered a complete and true audit of the tower. A record of every construct structured and invested, every device created, every sacrifice made and offering deposited.

Miranda dangled her quill loosely and stared at the numbers in disbelief. It was the third time she had completed the calculations and she was beginning to worry. Understanding Gahst's antilogisms and at the same time performing complicated magimatical calculations was a challenge, but she was getting better at it and could see no mistakes. She palmed her eyes.

She had worked the numbers three times and the result had been the same. The amount of magic that the Cunning had drawn from the Convergence was far greater than the amount that had been created within it. Not just a little greater, many times more. It didn't make sense. It was madness even to try to calculate such a thing. How could you begin to estimate the amount of magic created by the breaking of a mirror or the hanging of a horseshoe? It was like trying to quantify love.

Gahst had done it anyway.

Her mind groped towards a conception of magic as Gahst had described it in their brief meeting; a sea of power that encircled the universe, born from the minds of all thinking beings. Dreams borrowed and shared. The sum of the difference between what was real and what was not. Gahst seemed to believe that this pool contained a life, or lives, of its own, if 'lives' was the right word for such things — celestial consciousnesses with a beautiful, terrible power.

Why did I look for that hand? she thought. Why did I take it? *So stupid.*

If his numbers made sense, it had to be his assumptions that were wrong. Maybe they were based on old cunning and wild magic, not the modern ways. She started over, reworking the numbers.

●

Miranda's maidservant pinched out the dwindling candles on her desk, scooped the spent wax out of their flowery holders and replaced them with fresh ones.

"You should sleep, mistress. At least let me fetch your nightwear."

The girl was right. Miranda was exhausted and her attempts to refute Gahst's work were getting increasingly desperate. His theories were far-fetched but not impossible, and his calculations were starting to feel elegant. Elegant was bad. Elegant meant they might be correct.

"Have I received any messages? A reply from Mister Sutton?"

"No, milady."

Miranda let her mind drift as the young woman undressed her and gently brushed her hair. *What does it mean, if Gahst is right?* she wondered. *If there is some imbalance or deficit in the magic of the Verge?*

Gahst was an eccentric even by the standards of the Convergence. If anything, his obsessions had discredited the study of magical theory, lessened the analysis of its risks. That was not sensible. The Convergence should be seen to be taking every precaution. As a member of the Convocation, she would have the resources to make a proper investigation, and the power to act on its findings.

"Have you been working all day, milady?" It was unusual for the maid to speak out of turn, but Miranda needed the distraction and so she let it pass.

"I haven't stepped outside my room."

"Then you haven't heard about the arrest."

The skin on Miranda's face prickled with fear. "A demi-master?"

"It's supposed to be a secret. When I went to fetch fresh candles, I tried to take the shortcut through the old bakery, but it was guarded, and they wouldn't let me pass. They weren't rude though. I got one of the old porters to tell my why."

"What?" Miranda snapped, annoyed by the tease.

"They're using it as a prison, for Master Bolb." The maid let his name roll in her mouth like a sweetened truffle.

"Why?"

"Why not? They make all the bread in the kitchens now."

"Why was Bolb arrested?"

"I bet that censor Corbin was behind it. I don't trust him. His eyes are always smiling but he has a cruel walk."

Why the silly woman supposed that she might care for her opinion of the prosecutor Miranda could not imagine.

Bolb had been arrested. It was because of the hand, of course. Because of what she had done. Her fears ran riot. She imagined Corbin questioning her in a dark cell. *How did you come to know of the hand? How did you come to find it? What were you doing on the night of the disturbance?* She tried to remember exactly what she had said to Gleame, what she had omitted, what could be considered a falsehood. *I must get my story straight*, she thought. *I must talk to Edmund. Confront him.* The possibilities of that conversation filled her with dread.

She would talk to Mother first. Mother always knew what to do.

●

Miranda blew the acrid smoke over the tapestry of her mother with a kiss. She understood the magic now, could see it curling from her mouth to mingle with the woven tresses. The tapestry was old; Mother's hair had not been that colour for many years, but it was still connected to her by strands infinitely stronger than those which had once graced her head.

The surface of the tapestry tightened at the touch of the smoke, contracted like skin under a needle. The perfect image of a countryside idyll blurred and reformed into the duchess's Office of State. The duchess looked serious. To most people she looked serious all of the time, but Miranda could see the smile in the corners of her eyes. She was dressed in a purple and white robe, her wig glamoured with diamonds and onyx studs. *Seeing a man later this evening*, Miranda reckoned.

"Your Grace," she said.

"You're dressed like a master," the duchess observed. Miranda twirled, sending the crimson hem of her dress spinning to her knees.

"But I am not a master yet."

"Gleame tells me that the day draws close."

"There are many left to persuade."

"You leave nothing to chance."

"As you taught me." Miranda showed her happiest smile.

"He tells me that no student has achieved mastery in so short a time."

"Yes."

"The Lavety boy also covets promotion. We need to discuss that."

"We do?" Miranda hadn't thought of Lavety since he had made his threats. Certainly not since finding the hand.

"Yes. There are things I would like to discuss with you once your promotion is assured. What value it might have if used in the right way, to influence the Lavetys. I have a list . . ."

"Mother, there is something I need to ask you."

The duchess started at the interruption, but did not bark. "About the Lavetys?"

"A more important matter."

"Really?" she replied sardonically and adjusted her wig. "Well, don't be shy. There should never be secrets between us."

"It is important, complicated. I discovered something terrible."

"Oh. That." The duchess seemed so unconcerned that Miranda would have assumed she had been misheard, if it were not for the fact that the duchess never missed a thing.

"You know?"

"That you found the hand of the censor — you of all people. Gleame told me. Truly the gods were at work when you were delivered to my door."

Miranda laughed with surprise, but it was a cold laugh.

"My discovery pleases Your Grace?"

"It does not please me at all. If I had imagined for one moment that you would be caught up in such a dreadful businesses, I would never have permitted you to travel to the Convergence in the first place. Thank goodness the matter has been resolved."

Miranda gave her that look.

"Am I wrong?" the duchess asked. "Am I missing something?"

"The hand had a message in it."

"Gleame told me that you delivered the hand directly to him," the duchess said.

"I did."

"Then the matter is resolved."

"I understand a great deal about magic now, Mother, the theory and the practice."

"Of course you do." Mother had put on her expression that signalled the end of a conversation. Miranda shuffled her feet uncomfortably.

"I think the hand was meant as a warning, about the Convergence."

"A warning to whom?" Mother looked deadly serious.

"I don't know, but if there is some merit to the warning, shouldn't I be investigating it for you?"

"Do you think you know better than Gleame?"

"Maybe I do," Miranda said under her breath.

The duchess's cheeks reddened, which was her version of rage. "What did you say?"

"Gleame is a great man, Mother, but I have a different perspective, that of an outsider." *Moreover, I am smarter*, she thought, *even than him*. She looked at her feet to hide her thoughts. It didn't help.

"What have you done?"

"I decoded the message of the hand."

"What do you mean?"

"I . . . before I gave the hand to Gleame, I made a copy of the message it carried."

"You stupid girl. By the gods, what were you thinking?" The duchess's face was drawn tight with anger, her voice a hiss. Miranda had never seen Mother like this. It felt like being stabbed. Miranda began to tremble, could not meet the duchess's gaze. She bit her lip, tried to blink back her unbidden tears.

"Destroy the papers immediately."

"But Mother, I think maybe there might be some truth in them."

"I did not ask you what you thought."

"I . . ."

"I did not bid you to speak. *Know your place.*" Mother's fists were clenched, her pearlescent nails digging deep into her palms. "Destroy your scribblings, and do not tell a soul. That is my command."

Miranda's chest bucked and she coughed uncontrollably as she tried to swallow her tears.

"Hush — be quiet girl," the duchess said soothingly, her mood changed in an instant. "This is for your own good. You have nothing to fear."

Miranda nodded mutely.

"The censors that Lang sent to the Convergence have caught the traitor behind the plot. They are on the trail of his accomplice. The matter has been resolved. Promise me that you will never mention it again." Miranda sobbed, ashamed of her weakness, and fought to bring her face back under her control. "Promise me."

"I promise."

The duchess put on her best impression of a motherly smile, and Miranda returned the gesture in spite of herself. "Then all is well. You are still my favourite. I will wait for the news of your offer of promotion. When it has been confirmed I would like you to return to Ebarokon, to stay with me for a while. We shall hold a ball to celebrate. You will dazzle my useless court-iers with your cunning and your beauty. Then we will decide what to do next."

"Yes, Your Grace." Miranda curtsied, turned to leave. Then suddenly she felt dizzy. "Mother. You said there are censors at the Verge."

"What of it?"

"There is only one censor here. Prosecutor Corbin."

The duchess laughed, birdlike.

"A secret for a secret then. There is another: a young man from Bromwich who operates in disguise. Even I don't know his name. A commoner, but very resourceful, from what I have heard."

●

Miranda hurried back to her room in a daze, the clattering of her heels distant and dim, lost behind the buzzing in her ears. A dark bubble of self-contempt swelled inside her. *Her Grace was right*, she thought, *I am stupid. Stupid to allow these men of the Verge to humiliate me. To manipulate me. To fuck me. Stupid to talk to her as if we are equals. Why do I insist on calling her Mother? Why does she even allow it?*

Miranda recalled the many times she had called Her Grace 'Mother' in front of strangers, and every recollection made her wince with embarrassment. She imagined how they must have laughed behind her back. It was shameful. Miranda was an orphan, street litter. It was not the duchess's benevolence that had been her salvation, rather her guilty conscience. Miranda's borrowed life was a penance, not an act of love.

Then the bubble burst open, flooding every corner of her mind with its black ooze. Miranda became angry. *The duchess knows nothing of magic, and I did not choose to be low-born.* Why had Her Grace not told Miranda about Edmund? Did she already know that he had fucked her? Had she kept that a secret too? If there were to be an inquisition, how long would it be before the dalliance was known to everyone? How low would her bride price sink then?

Her humiliation was complete. Did she even want to become a master now? What was the point? She did not need to wait to be summoned back to Ebarokon to be married off to a Lavety, or worse. She would have her servants pack her backs and then hand in her resignation.

She rocked back her head and screamed at the walls. Ten steps and she had changed her mind about everything. Use your brain, woman. You are the smartest *person you have ever met. This pain is just a feeling, a transient thing. It does not matter. You can use it to make something. Think about the now.*

Mother was right about the papers, the writings of the hand. If there was to be an inquisition, she might be investigated. They had to be destroyed. That would be no loss. Miranda already understood what they said; nothing she didn't know already. That people took power from where they could find it and worried little about the consequences. Magic and money. Politics and families. It was all the same.

Her whole body lurched and her vision exploded like a golden firework. She fell to one knee and her hand touched the ground. The glow-stones that lit the corridor flared abruptly and a palpitation in the rhythm of the Verge coursed through the stonework into her fingers. She ran to a window and focused her mind, searched the sky for magic. The tendrils that trailed in every direction from the Verge quivered, like fishing lines in fight. She looked at her hands. Tiny motes of magic swarmed around them, like clouds of mist.

Wild magic.

What is happening?

She racked her mind for an explanation, every thought of her life's problems gone. She ran to the other side of the corridor and looked upon the Verge's atrium, waited for the sounds of action and panic.

She heard nothing but wave song and the lonely sound of distant footsteps. She could not be the only one. Others must have noticed. She looked at her hands, and saw that they were shaking violently. *What is wrong with me?*

THE KENNELS

If any of the old mansions on the outskirts of Turbulence re-
tained their original grandeur, The Kennels was not one of
them. From Peacock's boastful descriptions, Jon had imagined
the place to be a palace, but the tall black palings that defended
its grounds like a row of pikemen had long surrendered their
oily sheen to peel and rust. The yellowing walls beyond were
thick with ivy.

Jon crept to the impenetrable ironwork and peeked over
its mossy brick base. The narrow space between the fence and
Peacock's bawdy house was patrolled by beardogs and blood-
hounds, the grass tinged bloody by the crimson light from its
half-shuttered windows. These things were not intended to
appear forbidding. The Kennels admitted any man with the
means to enjoy a few hours of immoral entertainment. The security was to stop the merchandise from absconding.

A pair of doormen, dressed in black — smart for Turbulence — and sporting short truncheons, saluted Peacock's small
party as it passed through The Kennels' gate. They didn't even
glance at Laila, her tied legs bucking over Big Shark's shoulder. Jon thought how terrified she must be, and wondered how
many other girls had passed through the gates in that way. He
sat on his haunches and gathered his courage.

A pair of dogs approached, sniffing the air and straining at
their handlers' leashes. One scented something, faced in Jon's

direction, growled through bared teeth. Then a moan came from an upstairs window, an obvious fakery of pleasure or pain, and the guard dogs turned and howled in response. *The gods are watching closely*, he thought. *Aiding me.* The omen was clear. The omens were everywhere, if you looked for them hard enough.

He stood tall and approached the doormen. They leaned nonchalantly against the gateposts like town criers on a slow news day. Statues of winged beauties smiled benevolently down upon them from the gateposts. *There's some irony in that*, Jon thought. The doormen nodded at him hospitably, but their eyes were like pools of mud.

"A customer approaches," one said.

"How may we be of service?" said the other, looking him up and down.

"I'm here for a lady."

"Right you are, sir. It's a shilling for admission."

"Price of entry," his colleague drawled.

"That's rich." Jon reached into his purse for the coins. The doorman inspected them quickly, slipped them into his pocket.

"There are no threepenny uprights at The Kennels, only beauties, all of them fresh."

Jon crossed the short gravel path to the mansion's double door. It was newly painted and hung with the brass face of a winking satyr, a laurel-wreath knocker looped between its teeth. Before he had a chance to use it, the doors swung open. A robust madam, all powder, wig and thrusting bosom, greeted him with a smile as thick and false as her make-up, and ushered him in with a shameless compliment.

"By what name should I know you?" she asked.

"Take me to the boss," he said.

The smile vanished. She told him to wait and then stepped behind a heavy velvet drape. A young lad in a loose-fitting toga offered Jon a glass of greenish wine to pass the time and he drained it without a thought.

The interior of The Kennels was a little tidier than its façade. Old wallpaper hung loosely from the walls. Anywhere else in Turbulence, it would have been cut away and sold. The gaudy chandelier that illuminated the expansive lobby was ringed with expensive wax, though the candles at its core were tallow. The few men who dotted the sparse interior were seriously outnumbered by the ladies who were meant to serve them. A gaggle of youngish women in chemises and corsets gossiped in a huddle near the fire. *No wonder*, Jon thought, *they must be cold, dressed only in their small clothes.* He made a quick prayer to the Mother for their souls.

In the centre of the room, a blonde and a brunette had draped themselves over a young courier, a man handsome enough that Jon wondered at his need to pay for favours. The girls cooed at him and coaxed him, exchanged rancorous looks above his head. An older lady, raven-haired and silk-stockinged, caught sight of Jon and began to apply a gloss to her lips in a way that invited trespass. The lurid attention disgusted him, and he scowled at her. He thought of Anna and where she might be, and felt helpless. Suddenly the madam was at his shoulder again.

"Come with me," she insisted.

Jon followed her up a curving flight of stairs. As they climbed, Jon's blood flowed colder. He began to sweat. She left him at a door, guarded by men like those who had greeted him outside. They searched him efficiently and finding him unarmed, let him into a chamber no larger than a watchman's booth, where another guard searched him again. Then a door was swung open and he was ushered through.

The walnut panels of the study he entered glowed softly with the light of an open fire. A suite of green leather faced the hearth. The air was warm and languid. *Empty*, Jon thought, relieved, and wondered how long he would have to wait.

A voice with the faintest hint of an Erdin accent, too soft to startle, bade him sit down. Jon obeyed.

"Jonathan Miller. Let us review your affairs."

Gilbert Gordon held a green binder spread wide across his lap. He read from it as if Jon were not there, every so often pursing his lips or taking a sip of water from his glass. Jon kept his counsel. If it were possible to know how a soul feels as its sins are weighed on the scales, Jon thought this was that moment. He was startled by the crack of a burning log and jumped in his seat.

"I see you are ahead on your payments to the Peacock," Gilbert said without a trace of emotion. "That is unusual."

"Thank you," Jon said, with absolute sincerity. Jon had heard that Gilbert Gordon had bad debtors' balls cut off and fed to his dogs. That he sometimes took repayment in blood, and watched hope fade as life drained.

Gordon spoke again, nose deep in the documents. "It seems you are a reliable man, Mister Miller, or at least you were, until tonight. I did not anticipate dealing with you directly. Why are you here?"

"I came for a woman."

"Most do. Yet you enquired after me."

Jon swallowed hard. "I was after the Peacock. He has the woman I want."

Gilbert's face twisted into an approximation of a smile. "I was led to believe the opposite was true."

"The woman I want has been taken captive by him."

"Captive?" The threat of impatience crept into Gilbert's tone.

"Tonight."

"Ah — that woman." Gordon closed the binder softly, laid it on the arm of his chair. He looked at Jon directly for the first time. Jon dropped his gaze.

"Her name is Laila," Jon said, staring at his fingers.

"I believe we are keeping her in the cellar." Gordon rang a handbell. One of his black-garbed men came into the room. "Matthew is required. Immediately." Then they were alone again. As he watched the fire, Jon could tell that Gilbert was observing him.

"I knew your father well," Gilbert said. "He was not a reliable man."

"True," Jon replied. *There's no arguing with that.*

"At one stage he owed me a considerable sum of money."

"That doesn't surprise me."

"We came to an arrangement." Gordon raised an eyebrow in invitation. Jon simply nodded, to show that he understood.

Peacock Matthew bounded into the room, buzzing with sweaty excitement. He was wearing a butcher's apron. "By the gods, this one's hard work. The Sharks haven't been able to get a thing out of her, not even a shit."

"Her name is Laila." Gordon offered the information with an upturned palm, as a gift.

"Well, that's something to start on. Still they've . . ." Peacock noticed Jon and stopped dead. "What the fuck is that cunt doing here?" He produced a knife from out of nowhere, raised it like a pick, advanced on Jon, eyes wide and fixed. "I'm going to gut you like a fish, you fucking traitor."

Jon stood and balled his fists like coconuts. "You'll need more than a knife, Matthew."

"Stop," Gordon commanded with an icy hiss, and slapped the arm of his chair.

"I'm going to fucking fillet him," Matthew said, temples bulging.

"No, you are not," Gilbert said, as cold and hard as a dagger between the ribs.

Matthew stayed himself, lowered his hand jerkily. Jon brought his fists down to his sides but they stayed clenched.

Gordon sighed. "Please mind your language, Matthew."

"Sorry, Mister Gordon."

"Turned torturer, have you?" Jon asked. The Peacock just glared.

"The miller asked you a question," Gordon said. Matthew looked at him for further direction. None came, so he shrugged and told the truth.

"Well, I wouldn't exactly call it torture. Not the bit I do, anyway." He bundled his crotch in his hand and shook it vigorously.

"I want you to give her to me," Jon said.

"You'll be joining her soon enough."

Gordon observed the two men like a jaded critic. "I don't think that is the miller's intention, Matthew."

"What? No, sorry. Don't get it." The Peacock searched Gordon's face.

"I owe her a debt," Jon said.

The room exploded with Matthew's laughter. "Like your meat red, do you? Have you fallen in love again, you bellend? You sure know how to pick 'em." Matthew opened his mouth to speak again, and then stopped to think. His eyes flicked back and forth. "Wait a tick. How did you know she was here? Followed me, did you? After what you did? You've lost your wits."

"An excellent point, Matthew," Gordon said. "Mister Miller is a reliable man. A reliable man in his position would not come here expecting to leave alive. Not unless he had something to offer in exchange for his life."

Peacock's fingers fidgeted on his knife. Gordon spread his hands.

"Please explain, Mister Miller. What have you brought for us?"

"What's he got that I want?" Peacock ranted. "I'll tell you that for free. Fuck all. I have his money. I'm taking his mill. I've even had his fucking wife."

"Pig! Liar!" Jon roared and raised his fists again.

"Sorry, mate, I thought you knew." The Peacock grinned evilly, bounced from foot to foot in readiness for a sudden move.

"This is not helping," Gilbert said wearily. "Mister Miller, what do you propose?"

Jon glared at Matthew.

"Mr Miller!"

"I offer revenge. The Freeborn. I know where they're hidden."

"And how would a respectable man of Turbulence come to know a thing like that?" Gordon asked.

"I doesn't matter."

The three men stared at each other in silence.

"There's a passageway near the mill," Jon said. "Another in the Temple District. Both lead to their base. It's called the Holt. I can mark the way. A godsworn serves them, a soft man. I can tell you what he looks like. He'll show you the way if you force him."

"Why shouldn't I just beat the living shit out of you till you tell us what I want to know?" Matthew said.

"Because I'd never tell you."

Gilbert Gordon raised his hand. "Enough, Matthew. Mister Miller, why do you suppose that I care about dissenters? They are the Brotherhood's concern, not mine. We are paid well enough to assist in their suppression. I have no special desire for this conflict to end."

Jon hoped that he had judged correctly. "George Barehill leads the Bromwich rebels. If your militia were to deliver him to the censors, you would never need fear them again."

Gordon's face twitched.

"And there's a reward."

"A substantial one. Let me consider." He placed his hands together in a triangle, as if in prayer to the Devourer, held his fingertips to his lips. Matthew and Jon watched him intently as he deliberated. He came to a decision.

"Very well. If your information proves correct, I will permit you one day of protection. After that, you will be outlawed, fair game for any of my men, and we will inform the censors of your crime against the Bell Jar. In return you will provide us with your sworn testimony regarding these dissenters, and sign over to me the mill and all of your possessions."

"And you will let me leave — with Laila."

"I will have my men escort you back to the mill. Matthew, prepare the militia for action. Ready the Sharks. Bring me Barehill. But before any of that, fetch the woman."

"They have my family. My wife Anna, my baby, held hostage," Jon said. "I don't know where."

"That is not my concern," Gordon said.

Jon turned to the Peacock. "It matters to Matthew. I know you care about her. If she's their prisoner, you must save her."

Matthew said nothing, but the look in his eyes as he left the room told Jon he had been understood. Gilbert drew a blank sheet from his binder.

"He's a liar. He never had my wife."

The small man raised his eyebrows and readied his pen. "In my experience, people will do or say almost anything to protect the ones they love. Now, tell me everything you know. I want to hear it all."

●

An hour later Jon and Laila left The Kennels by a side door. He supported Laila by the waist, with her arm around his neck. It was the tenth hour of the night and dawn was yellowing the sky. It was not cold enough for frost but the vacant streets were slippery with dew. Laila's eyes kept closing, and she was having trouble walking. He saw that they had taken her shoes. Jon asked one of the militiamen who accompanied them to help carry her. The armoured goon spat in his face but did not strike him. He knew, then, that they were safe for the time being. It was odd, he thought, that the gangster Gilbert Gordon kept his promises, while Barehill the idealist did not. Jon hoisted Laila over his shoulders. She weighed less than a wheat sack. She moaned incoherently as he carried her up Swan Alley towards the mill.

As it came into view, Jon thought he saw the momentary movement of a shadow on the rigging deck. He stumbled to his knees deliberately, as if under the strain of the load, to avert the militiamen's attention. One of them laughed and kicked him on the thigh.

"Get up."

He grunted back to his feet.

The mill hall felt abandoned. There was a little smoke, but no warmth, coming from the fire. The militiamen did not wipe their feet when they entered.

"Make yourselves at home," Jon said, and carried Laila towards the stairs. One of the militiamen made a start for the pantry.

A gun bellowed from the gallery, filling the hall with blue smoke. The militiaman pirouetted and crashed down flat on his face. Another boom and the militiaman standing beside Jon dropped to one knee, clutching at his shoulder. The door of the mill slammed shut to reveal a Freeborn hidden behind it who drove a rapier into the kneeling man's back. Jon saw the front of his shirt stretch out and then the sword's sharp tip emerge through the cloth in a spray of blood.

He gripped Laila tightly on his back and ran for the stairs. Swords clashed behind him. He ducked his head at the sound of another gunshot, heard the grunts of punches taken, and a terrible gurgling scream.

"Get him," someone shouted.

Jon didn't know if they meant him. By the time he had reached the top of the stairs, it was over.

Gordon's four militiamen lay dead on the floor with a Freeborn beside them. The rapierist who had waited in ambush had taken a cut to the thigh, deep enough to accommodate a finger. Jon turned to the young arquebusier who stood at the top of the stairs. The boy surveyed the scene, wide-eyed with shock. Jon guessed that he had not killed before. His companion, another arquebusier, had just finished reloading. The man was Jon's age, maybe a little older. His face shone with admiration.

"What's your name?" Jon asked.

"Haythorn, sir."

"Haythorn, where's Barehill?"

"In the cistern, sir. We heard about the wrecking of the Bell Jar. Barehill saw it from the tower, left when you and Laila did not return. He waited some while."

"They captured Laila," Jon said. "Tortured her. The orange militia are headed for the Holt. You must defend Barehill. Take your men, all of them, and go there quickly. Use the tunnel."

An urgent fear replaced the pride on Haythorn's face. He saluted and hurried away.

Jon took Laila to his room and laid her down on the bed. The journey home had taken a lot out of her and she was barely conscious. He wiped the blood and dirt from her feet and gently rubbed some warmth into their calloused soles, tucked her under the sheets. The mill had become quiet again. There was no point in moving the bodies from the hall. He stepped over them as he made his way to the pantry to fill a bowl with cold water from the butt. He returned to Laila, knelt by her side and dabbed at the bruises on her face.

"What are you doing?" she murmured at the touch of his cloth.

"For the pain," he said softly. "Lie still."

"Don't hurt me," Laila begged.

"It's over now," he reassured her. "It's me, Jon. You have to tell me where Anna is."

"Bastard!" she screamed, and her hips twitched as if to kick him in the guts. *Delirious*, Jon thought, and laid the cool rag on her brow to calm her. "Scum," she whispered. She looked as if she would emerge from her stupor; her twisting became faster and more vicious. He put his arm across her body, held her still. It was surprising how delicate her body felt beneath the thin material. Childlike. She went rigid and her eyes deadened as her soul retreated to some safe and distant part of her mind.

"Rest," he said, "we'll be leaving soon."

Laila wasn't going anywhere, but Jon didn't have much time to act. He had made his decision. Gordon wasn't going to take the mill. Neither was Barehill. *No bastard was.*

He scampered up the ladders to the top of the mill, and broke open the pitchers of lamp oil that were stored in the cap. He poured some over the spare rigging and filled a bucket with the rest. As he made his way back down again, he doused everything that looked flammable. He stopped in front of the carousel horse that had brought him so much misfortune and stared into its dull eyes. There was something in them, a look without intelligence or compassion. He wondered whether magic things could burn, and what might happen if they did. He laid a canvas over it and soaked it through. Then he started on the mill-house.

QUESTIONS AND ANSWERS

"It's not exactly a uniform, but it will do for now." Corbin lifted the white stole over Daniel's head and tugged its tasselled ends until it lay evenly across his shoulders. Daniel shivered as the luxurious silk brushed the nape of his neck.

Corbin smiled knowingly as he smoothed down the mantle. "Cold? It will pass. The vestments of a beholder suit you. Ready, son?" He gripped Daniel above the elbow, gave a reassuring squeeze.

Daniel replied with a grunt. He didn't know if Corbin's newfound warmth was real, nor was he sure if the old dog knew that this was his first inquisition, but he saw no reason to say so. He clasped *The Book of Inspection* in his wounded hand. It was bound in fine leather, bright red and unmarked, the first he had seen with a virgin spine. Its thick pages awaited Bolb's confession, which Daniel would transcribe without annotation or abridgement. He would make as true a reckoning as the weighing of a soul. Later, at the trial, his duty would be to read from it and, after Corbin had passed judgement, to enter the verdict and the punishment and then seal it with silver wire using the special knot sacred to the Brotherhood. It would not be reopened until it was in the hands of the copyists at Tiburn.

A decrepit old man who Daniel recognised as one of Gleame's servants led them down dusty corridors that smelled of cinnamon and nutmeg. Corbin looked the very figure of justice, holding his longsword before him like a battle pennant or a shepherd's crook. His boots caught the lanthorn light and Daniel wondered if he had polished them himself. *For hours, probably.*

The guard spoke to break the silence. "This was a dungeon before we made it into a bakery. Now it's a dungeon again. Funny that." Nobody laughed. "We used to keep experiments down here. Vicious ones. Masters as well, if they had an episode."

Corbin ignored the old man.

Daniel thought about the task ahead, about the taking of a confession.

He had witnessed fragments before, had jostled with aspirants at peepholes for a better view of interrogation chambers. Once or twice, he had even assisted, fetching buckets of salt water and cleaning manacles.

The public were given to understand that the censors' orthodoxy did not allow for torture. That was half true. It was disdained, but not forbidden; considered a failing, a sign of incompetence. After all, if the gifts of sight and logic could not determine guilt, then what was the point of the Brotherhood? Anyone could apply a pair of pliers or hot coals.

Daniel had roughed up a petty criminal once or twice, even participated in a punishment beating. Those were street rules. This was a superior matter. He hoped to learn much from Corbin today.

Albertus awaited them by the fireproof door of an oven — a circle of iron the height of a man with a porthole riveted into its centre. His hand cannon rested beside it, a smoking taper knotted around its haft.

"All's been prepared, as you instructed."

Corbin took the lanthorn from Gleame's man. Daniel wiped the dusty glass of the porthole with his sleeve and peered inside the makeshift cell. Bolb slouched on a stool in his yellowed

nightgown, held a small wooden cup in his hands. A pitcher
of water and a cloth rested on the table before him. His lips
moved, silent through the glass. Daniel was familiar with the
mumblings of the guilty. He had witnessed the babble of men
before the gallows at first hand, heard their trembling calls from
the stocks. He wondered if Bolb was preparing a confession or
rehearsing a defence. *Maybe he wrestles with his conscience.* It was
of no consequence. Corbin would find the truth.

The prosecutor motioned for the door to be opened and Albertus pulled the metal levers that released its bars. The hinges
had been freshly oiled, but the rust was old and deep and the
door screamed like a child as its base carved fresh white curves
into the flagstones. Bolb didn't seem to notice. As Corbin
passed within, Albertus made to follow. Corbin barred his way
with his sheathed sword.

"This matter affects us all," Albertus said.

Corbin frowned grimly. "Only the elevated may witness the
proceedings. Come with me, Miller." Daniel hid a grin as he
sidled past the glowering giant.

"I have a right to know what is said," he called after them.

"No, you don't," Corbin murmured as he sealed the oven
door behind them, banishing all distractions except the heavy
sound of Bolb's breathing and the faint smell of burnt bread.
He hung his cape over the porthole, through which Albertus
was attempting to spy. Bolb finally stirred. His eyes passed over
Corbin with indifference and settled on Daniel, full of hatred
and superiority.

Daniel laughed inside. Bolb didn't seem to understand his
own position, that he was just another criminal, a fat old man
in a nightgown. A weaker person might have felt sorry for him.
Daniel countered his stare with a look of stone and opened *The
Book of Inspection.*

Corbin circled the small table, ignoring Bolb, and placed his sword on the baking stone that lay in front of the red-brick firebox. He prised the candle from the lanthorn and used it to light the pile of kindling that someone had laid in the oven. It flared, and the chamber was bathed in a dull, warm light. Next, Corbin took the jug of water and the cloth and set them next to his sword. Bolb stared at the table, heavy-lidded, as if he were about to fall asleep. Corbin shot Daniel a glance to confirm his readiness. Dan nodded and realised that his fingers hurt, he was gripping his pen so tightly.

"State your name for the record," Corbin said.

Bolb mumbled incomprehensibly. Daniel frowned. The noise was hard to put into words and *The Book of Inspection* was supposed to capture *everything*. Corbin sighed and crossed his arms.

"State your name."

"You know my name."

"Enter the confessor's name as Master Pendolous Bolb, born Martin Stead of Thurlowe."

Bolb's startled eyes snapped in his direction.

"How do you know these things?"

"Enter the inquisitor's name as Prosecutor Niall Corbin of Cruithin. The date is Maatday, the 72nd, Malchus III." Daniel's pen scratched to a pause. "Master Pendolous Bolb, I pronounce you subject to an inquisition according . . ."

"You have no right," Bolb said.

". . . to the laws of the Brotherhood . . ."

"I am a master of the Convergence."

". . . which are divine, and like the gods themselves . . ."

"I have privileges."

". . . stand above all normal jurisdiction." Corbin's voice was like thunder now. Daniel's penmanship became ragged and a few ink spots spattered the margin. *The copyists in Tiburn will not be impressed*, he thought.

The master and the prosecutor stared at each other, unyielding, as if both believed they had the upper hand. Something seemed to harden in Bolb. Maybe Corbin was underestimating him, as Daniel had, twice.

"Master Miller is your beholder."

"You mean notary."

"His duties are sacred. He acts as the master of records and as your witness."

Bolb scoffed at that. "How convenient for you both. End this farce. Let me talk to Gleame. I have been foolish. The hand was a terrible mistake but I have committed no crimes."

"In the course of our investigations you twice attempted to murder my aspirant, Brother Miller."

"I thought he was an Evangelist."

Corbin drew a scroll from his law belt and let it roll across the table. Daniel was trained to read from any angle and at speed, but he recognised what it was before it had even opened. The warrant from the Wise Council, permitting the trial of a master. Bolb unfurled the paper carelessly and scanned it as if it were a list of groceries.

"Read it," Corbin said.

"I already have." Bolb dropped it onto the dusty floor.

"Pick that up." Daniel heard something new in the prosecutor's tone, a slow and deathly edge. He wondered if Bolb could hear it too. The master did not obey. Corbin repeated himself.

"That is a decree of the Wise Council. It is law, something to be treated with respect."

Bolb mouthed something insolent to himself. Corbin bowed low and rested his hands on the edge of the table, arched over Bolb like a wolf over a lamb.

"Pick it up."

"No."

Corbin beat the cup from Bolb's hands, splattering water against a wall.

"Thug," Bolb protested and wrung the fingers of his slapped hand. The room was getting warmer now and the splash on the wall dried quickly. Corbin went to the firebox, unsheathed his longsword and buried its blade inside.

"Is that supposed to scare me?" Bolb said.

"Master Bolb. You misunderstand my intentions. I am here to find the man responsible for the death of Brother Adelmus. The murderer of a censor. When a censor dies, the Brotherhood always finds someone responsible."

Bolb shook his head vigorously. "It wasn't me. Look at me. I'm a fat, old man."

"If you are pronounced guilty — no, let me be precise — if I find you guilty of Adelmus's murder and of treason, the sentence will be death. Your soul will weigh heavy and sink far."

Daniel watched Bolb's face for a reaction, and saw a flicker.

"I know nothing of that which you accuse me. Let me talk to Gleame. He will understand."

Bolb was trying to sound reasonable now, and there was a hint of pleading in his tone. Corbin was doing good work.

"Gleame has no part to play in this matter." Corbin pulled up another stool, sat opposite Bolb. He spoke warmly now, as a counsellor or a friend. "We could spend months on this, fish the truth out of you with words and sight. Confess. It will be better that way."

"Confess what?"

"Confess that Brother Adelmus uncovered your plan to sell the secrets of the Convergence. Confess that your scheming led to his death."

"This is insane. I will say no such thing. Adelmus was with us."

"Then explain the gold that the Evangelicy sent here. Gold to be paid in return for the hand. The hand that you made."

At first Bolb was silent. The fire had made the room hot and Daniel used the pause to rub sweat from his forehead. Then Bolb said, "I don't understand."

Corbin sneered. "You offer no defence?"

"He told us it was a warning."

"Who did? Who is your accomplice?"

"This is impossible." Bolb's eyes spun in his head. Whatever excuse he was inventing, it involved some great imagination.

"Master Bolb, save your opinions on what is possible for the trial."

The master's eyes stilled fever bright, as if he had experienced a revelation. His look filled with conviction. "Adelmus," he said. "Maybe Adelmus was the traitor. That would explain everything."

"Stop," Corbin said. Daniel wrote the word, unaware that the order was meant for him, gasped in surprise as Corbin took the pen and book from his hands and laid them by the oven. Bolb squeezed himself backwards into his chair. Somehow, in the sweltering room, Daniel suddenly felt cold again. Corbin lifted Bolb by his ear, twisted him round and dragged him backwards across the table. The master's spine arched obscenely and he squealed. "Hold him down," Corbin instructed. Daniel glanced at the longsword embedded in the oven and hesitated. "Now."

The fat master shrieked. His eyes searched the ceiling as if help could be found there.

Daniel pinned Bolb's wrists to the table. They were slippery with sweat but the master was weak and could move little with his head bent so far backwards over the edge of the table. Daniel could feel the master's pulse pounding through his palms. Corbin reached for the water and the cloth. Hot steam drifted from the jug's neck. Corbin slapped the cloth over Bolb's face and poured.

A half scream escaped the master's lips and he gurgled monstrously. Daniel leaned hard on Bolb's convulsing body to keep him from flapping off the table. Hot water splashed about as the jug was slowly emptied. A few drops landed on Daniel's hand and scalded, but not badly. Bolb would have a red face for a few hours, but nothing worse. What they were doing was not torture; the rules were very clear on that point.

Bolb retched. Corbin pulled away the cloth and turned his head to the side. The master spewed weakly on the floor. Corbin returned *The Book of Inspection* to Daniel, and then leaned over Bolb's twitching body. He wiped his brow.

"Name your accomplice and things will go much easier for you. Do you understand? I do not like this place and I do not want to stay an hour longer than necessary."

He pulled his longsword from the flames and held it above Bolb's face. Its tip glowed the soft orange of a harvest moon. The water on Bolb's face gently steamed.

"Gahst. Riven Gahst," he squealed in terror.

Bolb seemed to have aged five years in a matter of seconds. Corbin eased the fat man back into his chair. "I thought Riven was my friend," Bolb cried. "He told me the hand was a warning. I made it for him. I didn't know what was in it. I didn't know who it was intended for."

Now that he's begun to talk, he will not stop, Daniel thought as he scribbled. He was surprised at how little notice Corbin was paying to Bolb's confession.

"This session is concluded," the prosecutor said. He lowered the tip of his sword into the spilled water and it hissed on the wet flagstones. "Daniel, we must act quickly. If Gahst learns that Bolb is in our custody, he could be gone before we have blinked an eye." He snatched his cape and banged on the oven door. It screamed on the stone again. Corbin pushed his way out before it was a quarter open. "To Riven Gahst's room. Summon your men. I will explain on the way."

Albertus got his gun.

●

Albertus blew a shrill whistle as they dashed through the Verge's corridors. Armed men appeared from doorways and junctions to join them in the chase. There were more guards hidden in the Verge than Daniel had ever imagined. They had a squad of a dozen men by the time they reached Gahst's chamber.

"Strike swiftly, and strike hard," Corbin whispered. "I want no man injured."

"Do as he says," Albertus said. Then the giant man drew back his firearm and readied his taper. Corbin covered his ears and turned away from the door. Daniel and the guards quickly followed suit.

Fragments of wood and iron pelted the corridor and its occupants. A shaft of light beamed through the hole where Gahst's lock had been. Albertus drew back a massive leg and kicked open the remains of the door. Corbin and Daniel were first through.

Gahst's body swung gently above them, silhouetted against a window of grey-blue sky. A plain chair lay on its side a few feet from where he hung. His tongue lay loose across his chin. Smears of inky blue slime darkened his teeth and ran down his neck.

"Poison," Daniel observed.

"Somebody took no chances," Corbin said.

Albertus blocked the doorway with his bulky frame and ordered his men to cordon off the corridor. They reluctantly moved away, some peering around him to gawp at the dead master. Corbin dropped to his knees and quickly drew the Sigil of the Gods on the floor. Albertus stepped inside the room and shut what was left of the door behind him. The room's edges began to blur, took a slight haze, as if seen through a lens knocked half out of focus, then all was still again. Corbin's expression was blank, but his eyes were furious.

"Murdered?" Albertus asked.

Corbin spat on the floor. "No. Master Gahst sought justice faster than I could deliver it."

"What now?" Daniel asked.

"Back to Bolb. We will finish with him today. Albertus, do as you see fit with the body." Albertus looked both sad and relieved. Corbin looked deep into Daniel's eyes. "There is another matter. The girl was here before he died."

Daniel did not need to ask which girl.

"Before?" Albertus repeated.

"Just before — and she took something from him. A book."

⁕

"Gahst is dead! What have you done?" Bolb did not attempt to hide the fear in his face.

"Less than I would have liked." Corbin looked uninterested now, bored. As if the hard work were over. He paced around the small cell as he spoke. "Your conspirator was a braver man than you are, or more cowardly, depending on how you look at it. He took his own life."

"But he was the only one . . . the only man who could confirm my honesty."

"You mean corroborate your lies."

"I will tell you what happened. Everything."

"Are you ready to confess guilt?"

"I confess nothing."

"Then save your nonsense for the trial. I have all the evidence I need. We will begin tomorrow."

Corbin made to leave the room.

Bolb called after them, "Go to the Voyeurs' Gallery, look there. You will see what happened. You will see the truth."

Corbin turned to Daniel. "You are the beholder. Perform an inquisition. Write down what you see. What are we going to do about this matter of the girl?"

The door to the oven thudded shut behind them.

●

Lang's crackling voice sounded further away than ever. "You have performed admirably, but Miranda's involvement could complicate matters greatly."

Yes, it might, Daniel thought, *and not just for her*.

"What is your command?" he asked.

"You claimed that you have befriended the girl. How close have you become?" Daniel coughed, embarrassed. "I see." Lang let the silence hang. "In direct opposition to my orders."

"I am truly sorry. The action was necessary. I took no pleasure in it." There was another pause and then Lang laughed.

"What a terrible lie. No matter, even your mistakes seem to be working to our advantage. Maybe you were right to trust the gods in this affair."

"Yes, sir."

"What do you make of the situation?"

"She would never betray Her Grace, or the Honourable Company. I suppose her curiosity got the better of her."

"I am sure you are correct. I trust you have told her none of the details of this case?"

"Of course not. I used her as cover once, to spy upon Bolb as he searched Seascale Bay. She might have suspicions — nothing more. I swear it upon my life."

"Her possession of this book is a matter of national security, unrelated to the murder. I assign the investigation to you. I will inform Gleame and Corbin of my decision. Talk to Miranda, discover what you can and report it to me. She is innocent, so it won't take long."

Daniel's heart was in his mouth. "My investigation?"

"Congratulations, Brother Miller, you are made censor."

Daniel pumped his fist with some violence. "I don't know what to say, sir."

"There is no need to thank me, you have earned it. I reward loyal men, never forget that. Right now, I need you back in Bromwich. There has been a bombing and a riot. Sedition runs rampant. We have lost several brothers. I require a man who knows Turbulence from garret to gutter to help me sort the mess out."

"Do I need to take the tests again?"

"The test is a trick, Daniel. The items I lay out on the altar do not come from the boxes; they come from my pockets. Anyone with the sight can see that straight away."

"Ah."

"Now let us discuss this matter of the Voyeurs' Gallery. We cannot afford any further complications with this investigation. I have considered the matter deeply. When you take confession, this is what you will see."

SORROW AND JOY

Miranda's stomach bucked like an ungelded stallion. The pain of it stopped her mid-stride and she locked her arms around Gahst's wide tome to ease the cramp in her guts. She was not immune to moon-pains but this was something far worse, a nausea that had been her companion since her conversation with Mother. At first, she had assumed the sensation to be an accumulation of bad humours, the by-product of so much worry and anger. Now she imagined that her fingers had somehow lifted a poison from the pages of Gahst's codex. Maybe even a curse.

Her stomach kicked again and she covered her mouth with the back of her hand to mask a silent belch. Alongside the churning in her guts, a quiet electricity itched through her veins. Tiny motes of wild magic danced like midges across her vision. She swatted them away.

That was the giveaway. This affliction was not of her body's making. It was something bigger, something to do with the Convergence. *Why can nobody else feel this?* A young master strode past her with a curious expression on his face. It took every ounce of her willpower to stand up straight and resume her passage.

Gleame was the only man who could stop this from happening — whatever 'this' was. She played out the conversation she had planned in her head, explained the intricate theories she had unravelled in Gahst's journals in lucid prose. She imagined Gleame, at first dismissive, then won over by her unimpeachable logic. She stopped herself. She was old enough to know that difficult conversations denied all plans. It was foolish to believe Gleame could be persuaded easily. He might not even agree to meet her. Her mouth ran dry.

Then what? If he would not see the danger, could she turn to Mother? What would she make of Miranda's bold assertions? Her stomach rebelled again, and she stifled a groan.

By the time she had reached Gleame's office, she could barely walk in a straight line. Each of her footsteps hovered in the air for a moment too long, as if the floor repelled contact. She wondered what she would say to the guards at the door. They raised their spear-staffs and stood to attention.

It seems that I am expected.

●

As Miranda crossed the threshold of Gleame's office, her vision cleared and her stomach settled. She regathered her poise and took a moment to savour the absence of pain. Gleame sat alone in one of his high-backed chairs, staring through the panoramic window, locked in contemplation.

Beyond, magic swarmed above angry waves in slowly turning tornadoes of sparkling dust and ice. It was as if the whole island were a hive disturbed. The startling vista bathed the room in an uneasy grey light. Seeing the wild power of the magic, Miranda hurried to take the companion chair beside the grandmaster.

Miranda placed Gahst's codex gently on the table between them, and waited for Gleame to notice. He glanced at it sidelong.

"Dear Miranda, what treasure have you brought for me today?"

There was a distance in Gleame's voice, a hardness to his expression. He rested his hand on the cover of the codex and tapped on its thick leather binding with the beat of a funeral drum. For the first time she noticed how the veins bulged blue on his hand, that he had the skin of an old man.

Is he not even curious? she wondered. If he would not open the book then she would have to explain.

"This book . . ."

"Belonged to Master Riven Gahst." Miranda was shocked. She had assumed the advantage of surprise. Now her plans lay confused. He took the book and flipped it open, skimmed its pages. "I am well aware of what it is, and when you visited him. So are the censors."

Miranda thought of Edmund and was enraged by the distraction. Her skin prickled and her head throbbed. She hurried to calm herself.

Gleame snapped the book shut. "You have become their concern."

"What business am I of the censors?"

"Gahst is dead."

Miranda's head began to spin. At that moment, more than anything else, Miranda simply wanted to go home. Her heart yearned for the person to whom she had once turned for comfort, but the memory of who that was had become grey and indistinct.

"How?"

"I am told it was suicide. I can't imagine they suspect you were involved. That would be absurd."

"Do you know why I brought the hand to you?" she said weakly.

He grunted. "I am powerful, but I cannot read minds."

"Bolb's hand. This book decodes its contents. I was investigating."

"Why?"

"I have become interested in Gahst's theories. I think the hand proves them worthy of investigation, at least to an extent. You must have felt the disturbance. Seen what is happening outside."

Gleame sighed deeply.

"The fluctuation. I am aware of it, of course. I share your peculiar sensitivity to magic. That is why I have surrounded my chambers with a construct to shield us from it."

Miranda felt a misplaced sense of relief that the catastrophe she had been feeling was real. *At least I am not going mad.*

"What are you going to do?"

"Do?" Gleame's brow twitched. "Nothing. It will pass, eventually. Or do you mean about yourself? This business with the censors."

Miranda stood up, stepped between Gleame and the window. Her eyes were ablaze. She pointed at the maelstrom behind her.

"How could I think of myself at a time like this? Look at it, all around us. The chaos in the magic. Our hold on it is collapsing. It is becoming wild again."

"You are confused, child. Master Gahst's death has upset you."

Miranda struggled to recall the brilliant arguments she had rehearsed in the hallways. "The balance of the Convergence. Gahst believed that if the Hidden Makers lose confidence in our enterprise, in our ability to repay them, something terrible will happen."

"Is that what Gahst would have had us believe? That his so-called Hidden Makers are calling magic back? You make them sound like the managers of a bank. Miranda, that is stuff and nonsense. The Hidden Makers are just an idea, like the gods. Magic is a power to be used. Nothing more. If this fluctuation is a problem, it should be resolved through calm thinking, not youthful haste."

"We must tell people. Warn them."

"What would they do? Just to suggest the idea that the Convergence is dangerous, that cunning might be dangerous, might bring about the very cataclysm you imagine."

Miranda shook her head in angry disbelief.

"If we explained . . ."

"Then we would burn. Ordinary people are not qualified to understand the dangers of magic. They would use these stories as an excuse to destroy everything I have built. We cannot go back to the old ways, Miranda. You are too young to understand what it was like. The murders, the crucifixions, people like us living like animals, hunted in the night."

"This has to stop."

"No, Miranda," Gleame said sombrely, "we must continue. If there is something wrong with the Convergence then it is our responsibility to find a solution, to work our way through the problem. Our responsibility to each other and to the Unity. To the North. To your mother."

"Yes," Miranda said excitedly, "we should let the Convergence recover. Cease the structuring of constructs for a while. Make more offerings."

"Impossible. The public only abide us because of the wealth that we bring them. We are clever, we are rich and we are powerful — so in their hearts, they despise us, and everything that we do. If we slow our efforts, and allow people to believe that our power is on the wane, support will disappear. We are already engulfed in this scandal of the hand. How could I possibly explain a fall in profits?"

Does he protect the Convergence, or himself? Miranda thought. Whether Gleame was right or wrong, it was clear there would be no convincing him. She had failed. Miranda imagined the magic born of the Convergence returning all at once, sucked out of the world like water down a drain. Unfathomable quantities of power ripped loose from the structures that contained them. A million souls burnt and torn by their dissolution.

She stared despondently at the swarm outside.

Why can't Gleame see that nothing can grow forever?

What now? Should I run away? Go home?

"Come and look at this," Gleame said. Balanced on a quartz plinth was a crystal mask engraved with the shape of a bennu, its outstretched wings reaching the temples, its long beak marking the ridge of the nose. "They say that it took Mestrakus more than fifty years to carve this masterpiece. Half a lifetime of drilling and grinding with fine powder. Imagine what it must have done to his fingers, his eyes. Yet the slightest tap of a hammer in the wrong place and it would shatter into a thousand pieces."

"I understand," Miranda said, defeated.

"I need to find a way to protect what I have built. I want you to help me find that way."

"Help you?"

"I have always known your power. It runs deep. You are exactly what the Honourable Company requires to make up for the loss of Gahst."

"What do you mean?"

"I called a meeting not an hour ago. I have persuaded the Convocation that we need a new master to replace him. They are ready to proclaim you the first woman of the Convocation."

Miranda's mouth became dry. She licked her lips.

"Do they know? About this?" She pointed out of the window. "Have you told them?"

"They know what they need to know."

"This is wrong."

"Restoring the balance of the Verge will be your first responsibility. There will be no limit on your agency. We will do it together, quietly, with every resource at our disposal. You will become my new apprentice. In time, I will teach you everything I know. You will become a colossus amongst men."

"What about the censors?"

"I will inform Corbin that you learnt of Gahst's treason from your analysis of the hand. That you came to me of your own free will to present your findings."

"I don't understand. What treason?"

"That Gahst planned to sell our secrets to our enemies. That his mad theories were simply a disguise. That he was not a rebel, but a traitor."

"I don't believe it. The trial will prove his innocence."

Gleame stood, walked to the window and stared at the horizon. A bitter look creased his face.

"It has been proved. Prosecutor Corbin has uncovered everything. That is what provoked Gahst to take his own his life."

That's not true, Miranda thought. *Gahst decided to die when he realised that the hand had been discovered. My curiosity killed him.* The thought sickened her and she prepared to fight back tears, but was surprised to find she had none.

"You ask me to perjure myself?"

"Not at all."

"All of this is my fault."

"Corbin is a strange man. He cares greatly about the following of rules, and not at all about the consequences of doing so. I fear for Master Bolb. We cannot afford to lose two masters in as many days. Miranda, you are a ward of the duchess."

"Yes," she said through gritted teeth.

He cleared his throat. "Do you know why they call your kind 'her sorrow and her joy'?"

"Of course."

"The duchess will not let the North fall into the hands of another family, yet her body has produced only girls, who cannot inherit."

"The law is unfair in that regard."

"If a man were to marry one of them, his family would stand to inherit the North."

"A living daughter could put her power at great risk."

"And her life. So the little ones are given to the gods. I could not allow that to happen to a daughter of my own. I would find another way."

Gleame made the offerings sound selfish, evil. That was close to sedition.

"It is no sin if it happens before the soul arrives in the body," Miranda said defensively.

"So they say. Yet Her Grace must feel guilt. For every baby that has suffered she has rescued twenty from the streets. Accepted them as her own. Saved them from poverty or ruination." Now the tears came, sluicing Miranda's cheeks with kohl.

"We say a prayer for the lost ones every night — light candles in their memory."

"You owe your entire life to an atonement. You understand the nature of sacrifice, the ambiguity of right and wrong action. Now it is time to master these things for yourself." He turned to face Miranda, reached out his hand across the table. "Work with me, Miranda. Take up your rightful place by my side. We will repair the Convergence together."

Miranda looked out to sea. The dark waters that surrounded the island were in confusion, the waves topped with sharp spikes, as if provoked. Her mind filled with the consequences of Gahst's prediction; images of the cities of the Unity adorned with flame, drowned in blood. What she might have to do to stop it. She smirked humourlessly at herself. Now that the prize she had been dreaming of was finally in her grasp, she didn't really want it.

THE BATTLE

The bullet hole in the Freeborn's buff coat was wider than Jon's thumb. It was no wonder the poor fellow had passed away so quickly. Jon wiped the blood from the inside of the leather, pulled it on tight and hoped that wearing a dead man's armour wasn't back luck. Next, he took a belted backsword from one of Peacock's men and looped it around his waist. *Now I might stand a chance*, he thought, *outlawed in the wilderness*. He felt ridiculous though, dressed as a soldier.

He picked up the last bucket of lamp oil, poured it over the corpses that carpeted his hall and tossed the empty container into his fireless hearth. *That's that then*, he thought.

There was a deep rumble, the sound of crashing bricks and timber and the mill-house rocked on its foundations, pitching Jon to the floor.

What on earth? Jon got up and ran through the mill, checking for damage. A few patches of plaster had fallen from the walls. One of the thick oak columns that supported the tower had a thin split running down it. None of the damage was serious. He patted the solid beams.

The commotion had come from outside, so he went to look. From the rigging deck, he could see that a gable had fallen from the house across The Froggary, scattering bricks and plaster onto the road. That was not all. Newly formed cracks lined its masonry and its haphazard chimney had collapsed inwards, leaving a gaping hole in the roof. The tinker who lived there with his family stumbled into the street in dusty confusion.

An earthquake? Jon had never presumed to feel one in his lifetime. He thanked the Devourer for the mill's deliverance and then remembered that he had set the place to burn.

Barehill's voice, frantic and desperate, called out from within.

"Jon! Where are you? Where is she?" Jon was not used to wearing a sword and it tangled with his legs as he dashed back inside the mill.

Barehill stood in the carnage of the hall, hands on knees, breathing hard and soaking wet. A small band of sodden men stood with him, Haythorn and his young compatriot, others Jon did not recognise. They all carried weapons. Some of them were wounded. Blood-tinged water puddled at their feet.

"What happened?" Jon asked.

"The militia came for us," Barehill said.

A Freeborn wheezed and coughed. "The bastards unblocked the cistern, barricaded the exits."

"When we tried to escape they cut us down, or forced us back into the water to drown," another said.

"If you hadn't sent Haythorn to warn us, we'd all be dead."

"Where's Anna?"

The men avoided his gaze. Haythorn pointed towards the loading bay. "We rescued as many as we could, then fought our way back here. I sealed the tunnel behind us with a barrel of powder. The whole lot nearly came down on our heads."

Laila cried out from Jon's bedroom. Barehill called her name and ran up the stairs.

"My family. Where is my family?" Jon grabbed Haythorn's lapels and shook him wildly. His pleading eyes said that he didn't know. Jon turned to the others. "Where is Anna?" They looked at him with sympathy, but offered no answers. He struggled for breath through his tightening throat.

I have put myself in the hands of the gods. I must trust them to see me right.

He fought to pull himself into shape. To concentrate on the moment. The Freeborn survivors were aimless, bewildered by the shock of their defeat. Barehill was a fool to have left them without orders. Jon picked out the youngest.

"You — head upstairs to the rigging deck. Keep a lookout, but don't step outside."

The two men who looked strongest he ordered to prepare a stretcher for Laila, the remainder he instructed to wait in the loading bay. "We'll be leaving soon, bring the handcart for Laila. Take up positions of defence inside the mill and wait for my command." They obeyed without question.

Jon ran back upstairs to his bedroom. Barehill stood at Laila's side, looked down upon her supine body as if he could not believe what he saw.

"What did they do to you?" he whispered. It was a useless moment to start caring about her safety.

"Where is my family?" Jon demanded.

"I don't know." Barehill wasn't paying him much attention. He took Jon's bowl and rag and used them to mop Laila's brow. She opened her eyes a fraction, as much as she could.

"George," she said, and touched his cheek.

"What did you tell them?" Barehill whispered, his voice stretched thin with disappointment.

"What do you mean you don't know?" Jon bellowed. He drew the sword clumsily, weighed its dull grey blade in his hand. He would give Barehill one more chance to answer.

"George," Laila moaned deliriously.

"She's killed us all," Barehill said bitterly and left her side. "Thank you for saving her. Whatever your reasons, I am grateful."

"I warned you, didn't I?" Jon said. "You had to jab the hornets' nest." Barehill saw the sword. *Kill him,* a part of Jon's mind said, as it twitched in his hand.

There was a cry from the tower and Barehill ran towards it. Jon chased him up the ladder to the bagging floor, roaring, grabbing at his ankles.

"You said you'd protect them."

The young sentry was cowering by the exit to the reefing deck, spilling powder everywhere as he struggled to load his arquebus. Tears moistened his eyes.

"They've arrived," he said.

Jon and Barehill stood abreast in the doorway and looked out. The remnants of the Trained Band of Turbulence were marching up The Froggary, their huge orange ensign flapping proudly overhead, a drummer rat-a-tatting a marching beat. Two of the militia carried a small battering ram. The bastard Peacock swaggered at the vanguard, the Sharks stolidly by his side. There was no doubting the soldiers' mood. They were already drunk on killing.

"I see you've poured oil," Barehill said. "Whoever is the last of us should set the fire. We can't allow Laila to fall back into Peacock's hands." Barehill offered his hand. Jon regarded it like a lump of offal.

"Get that rifle loaded, ready for my mark," Jon said. Barehill nodded and snatched the arquebus from the trembling sentry. Jon stepped out onto the rigging deck. The militia had formed up on the street below.

The Peacock hailed him in his usual good humour. "Jonathan, you terrible cunt. I thought you'd be long gone by now."

Jon smiled. "Bad luck for you then." The Peacock took off his hat to shield his eyes against the bright sky. His greasy hair gleamed in the sunlight. Jon quickly counted the militiamen. There were nineteen of them.

"I've had a busy night," Matthew said. "Been in the sewers, drowning rats with my friends."

"Where you belong then."

"You'll never guess what we found in their nest?"

"Anna?" Jon leaned forward to catch the answer, prayed that Matthew had protected her.

"A shitload of flour. Know anything about that, would you?"

"Did you find her?" Jon said desperately.

"Nah, mate, I was too busy wading in porridge."

"Did you even look for her?"

Peacock shrugged indifferently. "Where are Gordon's men?"

"Where you belong."

"I guessed as much. You know what — you're starting to sound like your old self again. A proper ruffian. I missed that after you got married. Tell you what; throw me down the keys to the mill. I promise I'll look after your wife when you're gone."

"What does that mean?" Jon said, more confused than ever. "Is she alive? What about the baby?"

"I'll tell you if you surrender." Jon considered it. Even if Anna were alive, knowing would make no difference unless he survived. One look at Peacock was enough to know that if he surrendered, he would not.

"You should have brought more men," Jon said.

"Something's crawled up the pipework, has it?"

Jon spat over the railing.

"Mr Miller, an associate of the Freeborn. Well, I never. You've been playing us all for fools. A greater mountebank I never knew. Honestly, I didn't know you had it in you."

"I'm my own man."

"That you are. Do they know who betrayed them yet? Or are you saving that for later?"

"Now," Jon hissed under his breath, and reached back for the arquebus. It didn't come. "The gun," he hissed through the corner of his mouth. Ignoring him, Barehill stepped onto the rigging deck, leaned over the railing and took aim at Peacock below.

"You will pay for your crimes against the people," he proclaimed.

"Fire!" Jon yelled, too late. Littleshark brought up his elongated arquebus and it flashed blue thunder. The shot ricocheted from the railing and thrashed the rifle from Barehill's hands.

"And who might you be?" Peacock asked, puffing out his chest now that the danger was past.

"A freeborn man!" Barehill shouted defiantly.

Peacock twirled his hat to his feet. "Mr Barehill, I presume. Your marksmanship is as impressive as your writings. I mean to have a chat with you, about what you've done to my pub." Matthew stared at Jon with a look of wry amusement.

"You will never take this mill, Peacock," Jon shouted, as Barehill reloaded behind him.

"Let's test that." Peacock fired his blunderbuss into the air to rally his men. "Up and at them!" he bellowed, and they charged the mill.

●

Jon heard the crash of the battering ram against the loading-bay doors. He opened the trapdoor in the floor of the bagging room and looked down. Two of Barehill's men were waiting in ambush below, bodies half hidden behind the thick oak pillars that supported the mill. One wielded a rapier, the other a thick oak quarterstaff. Barehill angled his arquebus and fired blindly through the loading door. A scream of pain and a roar of consternation echoed from the men outside.

It took Peacock's men several swings to buckle the heavy lock. The door broke open and two militiamen rushed inside, to find the way blocked by Jon's upturned cart. The Freeborn with the rapier jumped up and lunged over it, but the point of his blade slid harmlessly off a militiaman's helmet. The other Freeborn had more luck. He plunged his quarterstaff through the gap and it caught a militiaman on his chinstrap, knocking him out cold.

Peacock appeared in the breach for a second and his blunderbuss scorched the room. The staff-man dropped his weapon and staggered backwards, clutching at his face. Blood oozed between his fingers. Pikes were thrust towards him through the slowly spinning spokes of the handcart's wheels. One missed his shoulder, the second pierced his hand and mouth, smashed his teeth and passed clean through the back of his skull. The Freeborn's body did not fall, rather hung transfixed on the shaft, like a roaster's chicken. To Jon's astonishment, Barehill vomited through the trapdoor.

"Quick," Jon said, and slammed the hatch closed, clamping a padlock around the thick iron of its latch. They ran to the minstrel gallery. The main hall was smoggy and acrid with the smell of burning powder. One of Peacock's men lay face down across the threshold. Haythorn waited patiently in the gallery, his rifle resting on the balustrade, trained on the mill's entrance. His young lad was reloading his discharged rifle.

The bulk of Peacock's men huddled just outside the door. They outnumbered the radicals three to one now, but none dared enter the mill and fall prey to Haythorn's sniping or the Freeborn who waited inside; two halberdiers, a swordsman and the wounded youth who sat by the edge of the door, loading a pistol. When he was done, he reached over and fired into the tangle of legs outside. A militiaman yelled and fell, blood spurting from his groin. A mace swung around the doorframe in reply, and tore a chunk out of the wall above the pistolier's head, showering him with plaster and splintered laths. Before the arm could be withdrawn, one of the broad halberds struck it off, and it flopped onto the floor like a pig's trotter.

"Fall back!" Jon heard the Peacock shout, and he felt hope. Then a grenado came spinning into the room, its fuse showering sparks like a firework. The oil-soaked bodies on the floor burst into flames and the halberdiers turned to run towards the stairs. Jon and Barehill threw themselves into the bedroom, the young lad to the floor. Haythorn ducked behind the newel post. The Freeborn who sat by the door didn't bother to shield his face. Maybe he had not seen a grenado before. Maybe he was hypnotised by its fearful beauty. Either way, the blast shredded him like a rotten apple.

The orange militia poured into the smoke-filled room. Haythorn killed the first man with a shot that made a tunnel of his face. The Freeborn halberdiers and swordsman did what they could. For a moment, they kept the militiamen at bay with their blades. The young lad in the gallery passed Haythorn the spare arquebus and he felled another with a crashing roar. Then the Sharks entered the room. Big Shark flicked a silvered dagger into the throat of one of the halberdiers, who collapsed, scrabbling at his gorget. Littleshark shot the young lad on the gallery through the eye, splattering his brains against the wall.

"Save yourselves," Haythorn said, drew his sword and charged down the stairs. Barehill stumbled out of Jon's bedroom, carrying Laila. Jon took her too, and, one under each arm, they rushed her into the mill tower. Jon barred the door.

"Up," Barehill insisted. Men were hammering at the trap-door to the loading bay. It was nearly over, Jon realised. They manhandled Laila up the steep ladder to the bagging floor, sliding her body along its rails. When they were through, they shut that trapdoor too. The room stank of lamp oil. Jon reached for the padlock but it was not in its proper place. A crash below signalled that Peacock's men were upon them.

Barehill took a lanthorn from the wall and handed it to Jon. "It's time to fire the mill," he said. The lanthorn was not lit and Jon had neither a rush nor a fire striker to hand.

"Hand me your gun and your bandolier." Barehill obliged, laid Laila down on a bed of straw, and stepped out onto the reefing stage. Jon emptied one of the little wooden tubes of black powder onto the corner of an oil-drenched sack. The pyr-amid of tiny crystals sparkled darkly in the sunlight. He cocked the firing mechanism of Barehill's gun and laid it against the black grains.

There was a faint whimpering behind him, like the crying of a child. Laila sat up, her arms limp by her sides. She was crying. Jon did not try to understand her pain; it would be over soon. He squeezed the trigger. The gunpowder burnt brightly for a second, and then the whole of the sack began to flame, filling the room with smoke.

There was a crash and Big Shark vaulted acrobatically through the smashed trapdoor. A feathered hat and a blunder-buss followed after. Peacock poked his head above the boards and trained his blunderbuss on Jon.

"Oh no you don't, you bloody arsonist. This is my mill now."

Big Shark grabbed the burning bag. Flames licked at his arm as he carried it nonchalantly to the bagging rail and tossed it over the edge. Peacock saw Laila sitting dumbly on the straw. He lifted her chin so that she could see him clearly.

"Hello pretty," he said.

Littleshark called out from the reefing deck, "Found him."

Peacock waved Jon onto the reefing deck with his blunder-buss. Jon wondered where Barehill had gone, and followed Big Shark's gaze upwards. The leader of the Freeborn was halfway up the curved cap of the mill tower, nearly at the brass finial that crowned its peak.

"Where are you headed?" Peacock called. "There's nothing up there but the gods." Barehill did not reply, just maintained his perilous ascent, his hands and feet scrabbling on the wood-en slats. Littleshark raised his gun. Peacock whispered some-thing in his ear, and he adjusted his aim.

"Don't let's play silly bollocks. You're worth far more to me alive than dead."

Barehill continued to climb. He had nearly reached the top of the dome. Littleshark's long gun roared and punched a hole through the polished brass, an inch to the side of Barehill's head.

"It looks like someone's going to have to fetch him," Pea-cock said. Big Shark grunted and, despite his bulk, began to scale the mill cap as surely and rapidly as a mountain bear.

Barehill reached the apex. He grasped the finial that topped the mill's spire and raised himself uncertainly upright.

"I was born a free man and I will die a free man," he pro-claimed. His voice echoed across Turbulence's empty rooftops. A few distant runners turned and stared.

"Wrong on both counts," Peacock quipped. They all knew what would come next. Barehill hurled himself from the top of the mill. *He'll never clear the deck*, Jon thought. Maybe he didn't mean to. Peacock and Littleshark dived for cover. Jon caught the look in Barehill's eyes as he fell, defiant to the last. Then his head clipped the railing. Jon heard the frightful crack as his neck broke and watched as his body cartwheeled to the street below.

SECOND SIGHT

Daniel admired his reflection in the tall window of the Voyeurs' Gallery. Midnight blue. The tailor in the atrium had used a heavy-duty thread for the coat and gloves, stitched in the ThriceCrossed Swords overnight, and done it well. Impressive work. The bucket boots were made from the waterproof skin of seals caught in Seascale Bay. The brothers of Bromwich would consider the uniform fancy, but he could already picture the looks on the faces of the maids he passed on his patrols. Behind him a handful of Gleame's guards, directed by Corbin, barred doors and ushered the perplexed and curious bystanders away.

The morning sun caught the metal on Daniel's chest. Without thinking, he raised his hand to touch the newly minted badge, the Thrice~Crossed Swords. It was cold to the touch. Corbin had pinned it in place without ceremony or congratulation, just a warning not to lose it.

"Brother Miller," Corbin called.

Daniel adjusted the sheath of his mortuary sword so that it hung more comfortably and let his focus pass through the window, inspected the decrepit instruments of torture in the Flagellant's Garden. *Maybe Corbin was right, maybe they should never have allowed this place to be built*, he thought. It seemed to bring out the worst in people. Especially those who wanted power and cared little about how they got it.

He shrugged. Although his work was not yet done, he already felt a distance from the vagaries of the Convergence. Some part of his soul was already halfway to Bromwich, and glad of it.

Corbin had taken a seat in the pews and was waiting patiently. Daniel admired his new uniform for a final time and then chose a spot that would give him a good vantage of the high-vaulted room. He drew the necessary sigil expansively on a patch of bare wall. Last night he had worried that Corbin watching would make him nervous, but he did not find it to be so. The chalk felt different in his hand this time, his grip stronger, his strokes surer and more deliberate.

Completed, the strange symbol seemed to remain a part of him — an extension of his will rather than a copy of something learnt. He knelt facing the room, raised his hands, closed his eyes and let his mind slide through time. A sense of the room formed around him in smoky translucence. As he groped into the past, the space became crowded with ghostly figures that mingled silently around him, walking and sitting. He even saw his own phantom pass by, living a moment he no longer remembered. He moved time backwards, stretching the presences into flickering trails.

Daniel focused the vision on the evening of Brother Adelmus's death. He found the crucial moment, and watched it play out in shadow. Riven Gahst entered the gallery and hid behind a pillar. Soon after Bolb entered alone, his nervousness clear from his posture. The two masters conspired together. As they spoke, Brother Adelmus strode into the room and confronted the masters. He demanded the hand with a gesture; Bolb surrendered it. Then he exited through a trapdoor and the masters slunk out of the room. Daniel watched the scene play out twice more, just to be sure. He dwelt as best he could on the misty blue figures, sought an expression on a face or some other sign of intent. It was hard; it had been dark and none of them had carried a torch. Bolb seemed afraid. The expression on the censor's face was unreadable. His mind exhausted, the vision faded and Daniel was returned to the present and a blinding headache.

"Did you see what you needed?" Corbin asked.

"Yes," Daniel said, pinching the bridge of his nose.

"Does it change the case?"

"No." Everything was exactly as Lang predicted. Nevertheless, Daniel couldn't escape the feeling of something missed. It pecked at his conscience.

"What's the matter?"

"Adelmus confronted the two masters. He took the hand from them and departed through the trapdoor."

"To the small dock, no doubt."

"They didn't offer much resistance."

"To do so would have been fatal. Adelmus was of the old school. He had no compassion for the Cunning."

"We are missing something. The story is incomplete."

"It's unsatisfactory, for sure. We'll likely never catch the villains who fought and killed Brother Adelmus. They are still at large, or returned to the Evangelicy. Nor have we been afforded the opportunity to punish Gahst. But at least we have determined the men responsible."

"I guess you're right," Daniel said quietly and rubbed his chin. "What if Bolb speaks the truth — that he was misled into being Gahst's accomplice?"

Corbin shrugged his shoulders. "The law is the law. That is a matter for the trial. Write what you have beheld. I need to prepare."

Corbin motioned to Gleame's guards as he left the gallery and they unbarred the doors. The ghosts that had surrounded

Daniel were replaced by the bodies of the living. A few passing demi-masters recognised him and stared at his uniform in astonishment. He ignored their glances. He was no longer one of them.

●

She keeps me waiting on purpose.

Daniel had made it clear to Miranda's smug factotum that he was visiting on a matter of justice, not society, but he appreciated that even the law was weak compared to a lady's temper. It was ironic though. While he had been occupied with bringing Bolb to justice, a small pile of notes had assembled themselves in his chamber, all from Miranda, all requesting his presence. Now she didn't want to see him.

Is she in love with me? he wondered. That would be tricky. If she were not already aware of his elevation, her servant would be explaining it as he waited. She would be impressed, no doubt. Angry that he had kept secrets from her. Even so, the delay grew irritating. He was no longer playing the bumpkin and did not expect to be treated as one. He began to wonder whether her tardiness was simply a rebuke, or whether she had something to hide. He hammered forcefully on her door. The dainty maidservant who opened for him wiped the martial scowl from his face with a flutter of her long lashes.

"My lady will see you now," she said, and led him into Miranda's laboratory.

She waited amongst her papers and alembics, her back turned pointedly towards him. She was dressed in a forbidding dress of black and crimson that clung to her figure everywhere except where it flared around her shoulders. The sight of her bare neck made him smile, an expression he tried to suck back into his face as she turned on him with furious eyes.

"How dare you!"

"Miranda," he beseeched, and gestured at the maidservant who was staring demurely at the floor. Miranda accepted his point and dismissed her with a wave. Disappointment flooded the young girl's face as she shimmied into an antechamber. *I'd bet my badge she'll listen from behind that closed door*, Daniel thought, and hoped he wouldn't be needing to call her as a witness.

"Is that your real voice?" Miranda asked.

"Yes."

"Your name isn't even Edmund, is it?"

"Daniel, milady. Daniel Miller."

"A miller from Bromwich. With an actual mill?"

"Yes."

"Gods help me." Miranda buried her face in her gloved hands. *The best you'll ever have*, Daniel thought, and allowed himself a wry smile while she could not see. She had enjoyed her time with him more than enough when she thought him a nobleman. He saw a certain justice in the discomfort that her snobbery brought upon her now.

"I am made censor, milady, since we last met."

"And I am to be made a master," she retorted.

"Then it seems we have both achieved what we deserved."

"You got far more." She almost spat the words.

"I need to make a brief enquiry of you." She glared at him in silence. "We know — I mean the Brotherhood knows — about your visit to Gahst. The book you took from him. It has become a matter of record."

"I went to him because I suspected him of treason. I needed proof. The moment I had it, I went to Gleame. The grandmaster will attest to this."

She spoke to him now as if he were a functionary, as if he had never known her. That was unnecessary.

"So I have been told. Come here, and stand close to me."

"Not on your life."

"Miranda," he barked, "you must understand your position." The shock of his words had the desired effect, and so he calmed his tone. "You may be unhappy with my methods, but at this moment I represent the law. We can close this matter gracefully. Or would you prefer that I take you into custody?"

Slowly, grudgingly, Miranda came towards him, head bowed, arms folded across her chest.

"Closer." She stood next to him now. He could feel the aura of her body. "Now look me in the eyes. I want to know something." She looked up at him then, and he saw a chaos of emotion in her eyes. Hatred, hope, pride and fear. A curious smile hid in the corners of her mouth. "Were you involved in Brother Adelmus's death?" She stared at him for a second, uncomprehending, then her eyes turned to sadness, and she shook her head. It was never possible to be certain, but she seemed to be telling the truth.

Daniel pulled his book of observations from his belt. "I believe you. Tell me what happened." Miranda shivered as she returned to her desk. She arranged her artefacts as she spoke, looked out of her window, out to sea, anywhere but at him.

"After I found the hand I had an inkling of what it might be. I realised that the information it contained might be Gahst's work. I tricked Gahst into lending me his book by telling him that I believed his theories. When I had my proof, I took it to Gleame. That is all."

"You should have taken the hand to Corbin in the first instance," Daniel said. "But the error is understandable. I see no call for a reprimand." He smiled.

"Is that all?"

"What did the hand contain?"

"An inventory. A catalogue of the workings of the Convergence." Miranda sounded sadder than ever. That made him wonder.

"Not a warning?"

Miranda's head whipped around. "How did you come by such an idea?"

"I cannot discuss the particulars of the case."

Miranda considered Daniel sharply. He imagined her inscrutable mind calculating with fearful intensity. She spoke hesitantly and chose her words with care.

"I know that Bolb crafted the hand. I imagine that he was tricked into doing so. It is possible that Gahst told him it contained a warning of some kind. Of what, I cannot imagine."

"That is conjecture."

"Bolb is innocent, Edmund . . ." Miranda bit her lip in shame at the mistake. "Brother Miller. Daniel. He must be afforded clemency."

"That's not up to me." Daniel could tell that Miranda imagined she had some power over him — hoped he might bend a rule to help her, return a favour for her favour. *You don't understand*, Daniel thought sadly. *Bolb is guilty. I've seen it myself.* He studied her for a while, the beautiful, otherworldly, bookish girl, unsure of what he felt. Then his mind turned suspicious, and he wondered why she sought to protect Bolb.

"Is there anything else I should know? Anything you want to tell me?" he asked.

"What will happen to you now?"

"I will return to Turbulence. I have unfinished business there. A family." Her face flared in anger again, and he stepped back smartly, held up his hands in innocence. "A brother and a niece. No other. I swear it."

"I let you be with me," she said accusingly.

"Yes — in the course of my investigation. That will not be mentioned at the trial. There is no need."

"Is that all you have to say about it?"

"I like you, Miranda. Really I do." He remembered Lang's words. "I did only what was necessary. For justice."

"I am a ward of the duchess!"

"And I am honoured to have known you." It was true, and he hoped that she could hear the truth in his words.

"Honoured?" Miranda let the word hang heavy between them, and stared at him, through hooded eyes. For once, he had no idea what she was thinking. Then she seemed to come to a decision, and smiled curiously. "Do you imagine that I have finished with you, Daniel Miller?" she said, and sashayed over to her library.

"What do you mean?"

"When you are in Turbulence, I may desire to speak with you."

"How could I possibly deny it?"

"Such things can be arranged. My mother could speak to Lang."

"Your mother speaks to Lang?"

She looked at him as she had so many times before, as if he lived in a simple world, where things had to be explained slowly. "I need some of your blood. Just a little. For a hekamaphone. I plan to make one of my own."

Why not? He held out his arm and removed his glove. His left hand had taken so much punishment over the last few weeks he couldn't see the harm in a little more. Miranda walked towards him, as if in slow motion, her pillow knife in one hand, an earthenware bowl in the other. He studied the blade in fascination. It was a beautiful thing, much like her, not a weapon of war but delicate and deadly. A blade that long, up and under the ribcage, would end you rightly. Out of instinct, he prepared himself for a sudden movement. Miranda stared at the stump of his little finger in shock.

"What happened to you?"

"It's a long story."

She hesitated, then laid the blade across his palm and pulled it sharply.

"By the gods, Miranda! You nearly took off another one." Daniel clenched his fist to stop the flow of blood. "Bring me a bandage."

She watched, fascinated, as his essence streamed into the container.

"I took more than I needed," she said, and leaned up close, searching his eyes for something. He noticed the colour of her irises then, a dazzling green he had somehow not paid proper attention to before. His heart fluttered, and despite the pain in his hand, he felt no anger, only a kind of warm contentedness. He squeezed his hand tight.

"If you need that much blood you must mean to speak to me often. Pardon my Omek, but it stings like fuck."

She leaned forward and kissed him full on the lips; let the tip of her tongue touch his.

"Maybe," she said. His mind fizzed like a firework. By the time he had thought to embrace her, she had gently pushed him away. "Hadn't you better get on with your work?" she winked. He left her with a soaring heart, grinning like a dog.

⬤

It was no longer proper for Daniel to work amongst the demi-masters. He prepared for the trial in the same guest room that Miranda had been allocated when she first arrived at the Verge, a detail he thought somehow ironic.

He wrote his final testimony falteringly into *The Book of Inspection*. Every few minutes he stopped, and replayed his conversation with Miranda in his head. Even his throbbing palm reminded him of her. He signed his name and his position as a censor below his testimony. He imagined Miranda sitting in the same seat, working on some arcane theory that he could barely hope to understand, except in the vaguest terms. She had said that she wanted to speak to him again. Did that mean that he had to wait for her to do so, or was it an invitation to write to her? He was not much of an artist with words. Maybe that was a bad idea.

He had laid out the physical evidence for the trial neatly on her bed. There was the hand, in all of its complicated glory, and a pile of parts taken from Bolb's room. Gahst's codex, which was an incomprehensible jumble of alchemical symbols, magical numbers and formulae, and finally Adelmus's few possessions: a miniature portrait of a battle, a few crystal goblets and a decanter that did not match, his spare clothes, and a blood locket, identical to the one from Lang that Daniel wore around his own neck. He swept them aside and buried his nose in the bedsheets, searching for a trace of Miranda's scent. He smelled nothing but soap and the faint odour of the sea salt that got into everything at the Convergence.

He sighed. What had come over him? He had always needled his Turbulence friends who were daft enough to become besotted by some goose-kneed wench, watched in disbelief as cowards assaulted men twice their size in defence of a whore's honour. In the receiving chambers, he had listened to men and women explain how passion had led them to kill. He had always thought love to be lunacy. Until now.

THE TRIAL

The entrance to the lecture theatre was barricaded by a wall of jostling bodies. A scrum of craftsmen and servants, men, women and children, pressed and craned for a better view. Corbin had ordered the trial to be held open to the public. He must have known that the ordinary folk of the Convergence would find the humiliation of one of their betters an irresistible entertainment.

Miranda had debated at university, but never before common people and the sounds and even the smell of the rowdy crowd made her feel small and insecure. She told herself that such insecurity was unworthy of a master, took a deep breath and prepared to fight her way through an assault course of gropes and pinches.

Adrian Lavety stumbled from the swirl and pointed a be-jewelled, accusing finger at her. In the entire universe, at that moment, she could think of no person she wanted to see less.

"I know exactly what you've done," he said.

Miranda wasn't sure to which of her recent wrongdoings he was referring.

"Not now, Adrian, the trial is about to begin." He grabbed her roughly by the shoulders as she tried to step around him. It was only then that Miranda noticed his eyes were bloodshot and bulging with fury. He was shaking.

"The meeting of the Convocation. You've made some kind of deal with Gleame, haven't you? What did you promise him?"

"Let go of me this instant." Adrian seemed frantic, out of control.

"Why didn't you talk to me about it first?"

"Because it has nothing to do with you."

"What about our discussion? My plans?"

"Unhand me." She looked around for a guard, or anyone else who might be of help. "I don't care about you or your stupid plans!"

"Miranda, you must learn to obey me better."

Miranda slapped him across the face as hard as she could. Her blow landed perfectly; the sound alone was painful. It turned more heads than just his. Adrian stepped back and clutched at his reddening cheek. He looked as if he might cry.

"Her Grace said you would wait," he said. "There was talk of marriage. Everything was being arranged."

Miranda's teeth locked in fury. Her tongue took on a life of its own.

"You think you can scare me with your stupid tricks and lies? Well, it didn't work last time and it won't work this time either. Now get out of my way, you talentless prick!"

The words shocked her as much as him. Miranda had never spoken to a gentleman so crudely before, certainly not in public. She felt her face flush and stepped back, expecting him to strike her.

"What are you talking about?" Adrian looked genuinely confused. The crowd had turned to face them. They seemed to be enjoying the sideshow.

Realistically, there were two choices now: apologise, or run away. Miranda straightened herself, righted her face and dived into the crowd.

"Miranda, wait!"

The air between the bodies, slippery with sweat and breath, caught in her throat. Her mind pulled in two directions, worrying about what she had just done, and imagining the trial ahead.

She emerged from the mob between aisles packed with demi-masters, scribes and alchemists. Only the masters and those who might be called as witnesses had seats reserved for them. She hurried down an aisle and took her place in the front row.

The cold white light of the immense candelabra had been set to painfully bright. It drained the stage of colour. A podium affixed with a justice bell waited ominously at its centre, and beside that, a walnut table. Her spine stiffened as the presence of a man filled the seat next to her. She saw it was Somney and relaxed, glad of his company. He looked at the arrangement on the stage with open disgust.

"An open trial is not a requirement of the law. Corbin is making a show of this."

"The staff seem pleased."

Somney grunted. "What are you doing here anyway?"

"I might be called as a witness."

Somney stared at her. Miranda turned her attention to the congregation behind, and tried to feel the mood of the room. Excitement, anger, alarm. She guessed at the audience's sympathies. For some, the trial would be a vicarious entertainment, for others a reminder of past oppression. As she waited, the glow-stones flickered wildly overhead and a shower of magic fell from the lights like a mist of golden dust. Nobody else seemed to notice.

There was a bustle around a side door, some shouts and catcalls. Heads turned. Corbin strode into the room in his freshly pressed uniform, either oblivious to the attention or deliberately ignoring it. Daniel, also in his blues, trailed behind the prosecutor. A cloth sack bulged uncomfortably over his shoulder, and a vermilion book was clutched in his free hand.

Gleame's guards sealed the doors.

Daniel's eyes searched the crowd. When he spied Miranda, he smiled and frowned in rapid succession, then stared at his feet, blushing. An icy pulse of satisfaction ran through her. *The pillow knife cut true,* she thought. *The fool is love-struck. She observed Daniel closely as he followed* Corbin to the stage. He glanced furtively at her, twice more before he reached it, and once again as he took up his position at the walnut table. *He can't help himself.* The thought pleased her more than she liked to admit. She pursed her lips and presented him with her most kittenish face.

Corbin rang the justice bell almost carelessly, like a lord summoning supper. The trapdoor in the stage opened and Bolb was elevated slowly into view.

Bolb's shoulders were hunched, but he did not appear frightened, more distracted, as if he imagined himself dreaming. His belly bulged under the grey gown of an accused man. Miranda knew of the special methods her mother's agents used in interrogations, the bending of limbs and sinews, but she could see no subtle signs of injury upon his body. A heavy chain weighed down the iron shackles that bound his wrists. There were murmurs of opprobrium from the crowd. Miranda could not discern if they were directed at the master or his imprisonment.

"That is unnecessary," Somney said angrily.

He was half right, Miranda thought. The idea that the chubby master would attempt to flee was absurd, but this was the first time Miranda had seen Bolb out of his chiming finery. By dressing the master in the trappings of guilt, Corbin had diminished his authority. The prosecutor added to the effect by ignoring the appearance of the master as studiously as he did the crowd, which now waited expectantly upon on his word.

His attention remained fixed on his papers, which he shuffled with a look of intense concentration on his face.

Once he had arranged them to his satisfaction, he turned to the items on the evidence table and examined each in turn. Some caused him to nod thoughtfully, as though reminded of their significance. Others he inspected closely, as if to confirm some tiny yet important detail. He triumphantly held Bolb's metal hand above his head, so that all could marvel at its intricacy and wonder at its meaning.

It was all a ritual, as precise and calculated as an act of cunning, designed to demonstrate, even before the trial had begun, that the evidence Corbin had assembled was complete and incontrovertible.

"He's enjoying this," Somney muttered.

Corbin looked up and scanned the audience. He seemed to notice everyone. Miranda shifted uncomfortably in her seat as his piercing grey eyes paused momentarily on her.

With a few practised words, Corbin introduced himself and established the legitimacy of his jurisdiction. Finally, he allowed his passionless gaze to descend upon the shackled master.

"Master Pendolous Bolb, born Martin Stead of Thurlowe, you stand before me accused of crimes against property, crimes against person and crimes against the state." He displayed a sheet of velum to the crowd, and then picked words from the page as if they were mere examples from a vast compendium of villainy. "Theft. Conspiracy. Attempted murder. Murder."

The chatter of the crowd grew louder as each charge was read. Corbin waited for the hubbub to subside. Then quietly, as if the word itself were shameful, he made his final accusation.

"Treason."

There was uproar. Corbin shouted over the pandemonium, "How will your confession be entered into *The Book of Inspection?*"

Miranda's gaze alighted involuntarily on Daniel. He was writing as quickly as his hand could bear, used the brief pause to flick cramp from his fingers.

"With a clean conscience." Bolb spoke loudly enough, but his voice could barely be heard above the crowd. He turned to face the throng and practically yelled, "I am innocent of all charges."

"You seek to deny every facet of this investigation?" Corbin's expression was incredulous. The crowd quietened to listen.

Bolb spoke boldly. "Facts are facts. My argument is with the prosecutor's interpretation of them."

"Your power and wealth make you arrogant. Perhaps you think that you can hide your guilt through some trick of the tongue, or intellect?"

Bolb's rueful laughter silenced the room.

The leading question was obvious, Miranda thought, but in avoiding it, Bolb had fallen into a trap better hidden. The tone of Bolb's response had indeed been arrogant.

"Corbin does not merely wish to condemn," Somney whispered. "He wants to see Bolb despised."

Bolb was astute enough to sense the error in his disposition. His voice turned soft, gracious and reasonable.

"Let me explain my circumstances and my innocence will soon become clear," he said.

"You have much to explain," Corbin confirmed to the audience.

Without a jury, there was no need for a summation, so Corbin immediately turned his attention to the first of the charges.

"The least of your crimes is theft."

"I am a wealthy man. I have no need to steal."

"I will now list the many items missing from the Convergence's inventory, which our investigation discovered concealed within your chambers. There are so many that I am able to display only a small selection." Corbin took in hand a thick sheaf of papers and wielded them theatrically in the direction of the walnut table.

He called out the names of many mechanical parts. Each item was of little value alone, but the reading of them all, bolt by wire, took several minutes. Bolb attempted to interrupt but Corbin rode over his objections. By the end of it all, through the strength of accumulation, it seemed, even to Miranda, that Bolb had indeed taken a great deal. The master was unsettled. A sour look pinched his face.

"I admit that I took many things from the inventory. Maybe I was remiss in my recording of them. However, the borrowing of parts is commonplace in the Convergence. If every item had to be formally accounted for we would never get anything made." There were a few murmurs of agreement from the crowd, which drew a raised eyebrow from Corbin. Sensing encouragement, Bolb elaborated, "Would you see us made scribes?"

Why does Bolb play to the audience, Miranda wondered, *when they can do nothing to help him?*

"I call Chairman Gleame as my first witness," Corbin said. The hall fell silent as Gleame, previously obscured from Miranda's view by the stage, rose to his feet. He made a gesture to the hall, as if to reassure them that he could salvage the situation through strength of reason. Despite that, Bolb flashed him a look of pure hate. Corbin's eyes narrowed a fraction. "Chairman, am I correct in believing that the Honourable Company of Cunning has by-laws specific to the maintenance of its inventory?"

Gleame coughed.

"The laws of the Convergence are complicated and frequently revised. There are several relating to its inventory. Master Bolb is not lying when . . ."

Corbin slapped the side of the podium with his hand. "Chairman Gleame," he cried, "your conjecture regarding Master Bolb's veracity was not requested. I deem that comment unconfessional. Strike it from the record." Corbin watched and waited as Daniel amended *The Book of Inspection*. "My question is simple. Does the Convergence maintain rules that require its stores to be kept safely? Or am I to understand that any vagabond or foreigner can freely take his pick?"

Gleame frowned deeply at the insinuation, but if he was angry with Corbin, he was clever enough to keep it from his voice.

"We have good laws," he conceded.

"Would you say that those laws are written clearly?"

"I wrote them."

Corbin produced an ancient scroll from the podium. "Would you like me to remind you of them?"

"No." Gleame pinched his brow. "There is no need. The forty-fifth amendment of the Company's constitution states that all items taken from an arcane inventory must be signed for by the master, or the one acting in his place, under the observation of a quartermaster. Any master seeking to invest magic in a device must obtain prior approval, and its form and properties must be recorded in the Convergence's register. These things are well known." Miranda could hear masters muttering uncomfortably all around her.

"Thank you, Chairman. That is all." Gleame hesitated for a moment, weighing further comment. Corbin motioned for him to sit, and, after a brief consideration, he obeyed.

"Master Bolb, do you wish to amend your confession?" Corbin said. Bolb's pate was crowned with heavy drops of sweat that sparkled under the cold light of the glow-stones. His face was contorted with anger. Miranda leaned forward in her chair. Surely, he wouldn't contest what had been proved beyond a doubt.

He spoke with extreme reluctance. "On these points of law I was ignorant. My ignorance has no bearing on the justice of it. I must accept that my conduct was irregulatory."

"Irregulatory? Later we shall discuss what you did with these stolen parts. What devices you made and the perverted uses you made of them."

Bolb ground his teeth. "There is no need. In this matter I change my plea to guilty."

"Louder," Corbin insisted.

"Guilty," Bolb called out. There were grumblings from the other masters in the hall. A slight smile played across Corbin's lips. He addressed the hall with open arms.

"Finally, we are afforded a little truth."

He made a signal to Daniel to record the admission, and returned to shuffling his papers. The chatter of the crowd grew loud as he prepared for the next charge.

"That's a small verdict, resolved by a burn on the thumb and the payment of a fine," Somney said.

Miranda knew. "He should never have contested it." Somney nodded in agreement. Corbin rang his bell again.

"Master Bolb, do you intend to change your confession in regard to the other matters?"

"Of course not."

Corbin shook his head sadly, as if he were trying to help, and that Bolb's obstinacy was the true cause of the master's torment. "Let us turn to the charge of attempted murder." The crowd was intrigued. "Is it not true that you have attempted to take the life of Brother Miller on no less than three separate occasions?"

Corbin singled out Daniel with an outstretched finger.

"I thought the boy was a common thief," Bolb protested. "All men have the right to defend themselves."

"When resisting arrest? What about your attacks upon Albertus and Chairman Gleame?" He picked the victims out of the audience as he spoke. "I make no mention of myself, for it is the duty of a prosecutor to put himself in harm's way to defend justice, and I do not wish to rely upon my own testimony."

"I did not know that I was being arrested. That was later. The situation became confusing." Bolb became defiant again. "No fair warnings were given."

"On the occasion that my assistant overheard you conspiring with that most dreadful villain Riven Gahst, who recently escaped justice by taking his own life . . ." There were gasps and cries from the audience. ". . . did you not set your machines against him?"

"You weave a web of lies," Bolb shouted, and Corbin smirked. *That was a bad mistake*, Miranda thought, to accuse a censor of lying.

Daniel was called as a witness. He recounted, briefly and in plain language, how he had followed Bolb into the catacombs beneath the Convergence, overheard the conversation between Bolb and a person then unknown, and fled from Bolb's mechanical assailants. Entranced by the story, the audience did not see Miller for the scoundrel that he was, or protest his spying within the Convergence, but chose to see him as a brave and honest soldier. Miranda had no doubt that those listening would take his word over Bolb's.

"There was no way you could have known who was behind that door, who it was that you set your poisonous machines against. What if it had been an unfortunate maid or engineer, without the martial skills of my young colleague?"

"My mechanicals were armed with paralytics, not poison!" Bolb protested.

"Then you admit that you set your creations against my colleague, not for the last time, and that you meant him harm. You admit that you met with Gahst. That you conspired with him."

Bolb turned to face the audience. "This young censor is unharmed. That boy, who lived amongst us like a spy or a thief, is unharmed. You can all see that. I am a master of the Convergence. If I wished him dead, his flesh would be scattered like leaves on the wind. I admit to two offences only. Theft and assault. I did not conspire. Rather I was misled by Riven Gahst in many matters. I am no traitor. Let me speak my part."

Boos and catcalls came in reply. It seemed to Miranda that everything Bolb said brought the Convergence into disrepute, irrespective of the words he used.

"He admits assault," Somney said dolefully. "Now he has lost the arm that was to be burnt. Maybe he doesn't understand the penalties. If conspiracy is proved, his tongue will be pulled."

The trial was not going well for Bolb. Miranda could feel the crowd's hostility growing. Nobody wanted to side with a loser. Some would now be thinking that it would be better for the Honourable Company if Bolb were simply gone, and the scandal with him. *They are so wrong*, Miranda thought, and felt the upset power of the Convergence convulse and groan beneath her.

Corbin returned to the podium. "Your admissions are purely a matter of record, irrelevant to the facts of justice. Nonetheless, I am interested to hear your story. Please explain how you were 'tricked' into conspiracy. That is not a defence I have heard before."

"I took mechanical parts in secret. I admit to that — I stole them, if you must — to make the hand you now possess. Gahst tricked me into making it for him. He told me it would carry a message to the Wise Council. If I had known his true purpose, of what would happen to Brother Adelmus, I would never have helped him."

"Why the secrecy? What was it that required concealment?"

"Gahst told me that the work we do here is harmful. Out of control. That the Hidd . . ." Several of the masters stood, and Bolb stopped himself. "That we have overstretched our powers. Taken too much. Given too little."

There were hisses from the crowd. Corbin paced the stage.

"I have heard similar from the mouths of Freeborn, and renegade godsworn. You say he convinced you of that. Your conspiracy led to the death of Brother Adelmus. Of that, we are certain. Nevertheless, you say you claim to have acted to save the Convergence from itself. That you are not a traitor, but a hero."

"Yes, well, not a hero, but . . ."

"You expect me to believe that Gahst convinced you that the work of the men sitting around us is a danger to the Unity?" Corbin gesticulated at the crowd. "Yet you did not resign, nor even slow your work? I can see from the records that in the last month alone you have fulfilled orders for a steam battalion and a ballroom's worth of amber dancers. For these orders alone you received more than ten thousand pounds."

"What else was I to do?"

"Did you ever raise your concerns with Chairman Gleame or the Convocation? Did you use your powers as a master to challenge the Convergence's practices?"

Bolb shook his head mournfully.

"I call as my next witness Miranda, Ward of the Duchess."

The summons came without warning, landed in her lap like a grenado. The crowd gasped in surprise. Miranda rose to her feet and saw Lavety staring at her suspiciously from across the stage. She instinctively looked to Daniel for reassurance and hated herself for it.

At Corbin's direction Miranda related her finding of the hand in the dunes of Seascale Bay, and her examination of it.

She omitted many details — her delay in bringing the hand to Gleame, her tryst with the miller — but Corbin did not press her on those points. Compared to his demeanour with the other witnesses his tone was pleasant — serious but also courteous.

"What did you make of the hand and its contents?"

"The hand carried information."

"What kind of information?" Miranda glared at Daniel, the bastard who had dropped her into this mess in the first place. He was staring at her in puppy-eyed wonder. It was pathetic.

She raised her voice for the crowd. "An inventory of all the devices manufactured at the Convergence and a summary of the magic invested in them. It also contains a calculation of how much magic the Honourable Company has invested."

Corbin silenced her. "The hekalogical details are unimportant. This list you describe, does it include descriptions of all the weapons and mechanicals that the Convergence has delivered to the military powers of this land, for our mutual defence? Their power and abilities."

"The list is complete, without exceptions. Everything's listed."

"Including the military devices. Do you suppose that information would be of benefit to the enemies of the Unity?"

Miranda felt cold sweat on her brow. *I am not helping Bolb's case*, she thought, *I am making things worse*. She coughed to ease her tightening throat.

"I am no expert in military affairs," she said. Someone in the audience laughed. Baldwin, probably.

"Indulge me. I am interested in your opinion." Corbin looked at her knowingly, as if he had her at an impossible advantage. *Daniel has told him everything*, she thought. *Even our act of loving is described in that red book of his, to be laughed at and ogled over.* She boiled with humiliation. The pillow knife was not enough, she decided. She would curse Daniel. Devise a spell so powerful it would shrivel his balls into tiny black turds.

"I imagine so."

"That is all."

Miranda fought the urge to sit down. Her testimony had been ruinous for Bolb, but the relief of her dismissal was hard to ignore. Corbin attended to his papers.

"Prosecutor Corbin. If I may," she called out.

"You are dismissed," he replied unconcerned. Something in her snapped then. She was tired of being told what to do by men.

"The information in the hand. It could be interpreted as a warning, if you believed Master Gahst's theories." There were sounds of amazement from around the hall. Gleame stood abruptly, to the confusion of the masters and guards that surrounded him, and stared at Miranda, eyes ablaze.

"Lady Miranda," Corbin said gently, and looked pointedly in Daniel's direction as if to warn her. She dug her nails into her palms and met his gaze with steely eyes. Then Corbin noticed that Gleame had risen, and that a tension had arisen in the theatre that was not of his own making.

"Who am I to deny a lady? You say that you understand Gahst's theories. What is it about these that you want to tell us? Have you uncovered some great secret?"

The world froze in anticipation of her answer, even Somney, down by her side. Corbin's eyes goaded her on, dared her to continue.

She thought she saw something then, something hidden deep within his gaze. A righteous light, like the cleansing flames of a tar barrel awaiting a heretic, or the light of a hot iron waiting to be pressed into bare flesh. The unalloyed certainty of a fanatical mind. *Is that what he really wants? To bring down the*

Convergence? To end its entire works and to make a bonfire of those who have performed them?

That was a lot to read into a stare. Maybe it was only her imagination. Maybe it wasn't.

"I meant only to say that I can see how Bolb could have been fooled."

"By Gahst's theories. Because there is some merit to them?"

"No. None at all. They are gibberish."

"Believable?"

"The works of a madman."

Corbin smiled a peculiar smile. "A madman or a man who wished to be seen as one. I thank you for your service." He spoke to the entire audience. "A maiden's gentle temperament is inclined towards pity, which is only natural, but Miranda's sympathy is misplaced. You may think me severe, but this is what you do not know: the Brotherhood of Censors has apprehended a secret shipment of gold bound for the Convergence. That gold was carried by agents of the Evangelicy. It was meant as payment for master Bolb's hand."

There were cries of outrage from the floor. Miranda flopped back into her chair like a discarded puppet.

"I am no traitor," Bolb pleaded. "I thought the message was for the Wise Council. I realise now that I have been played for a fool — by a madman."

"After all that has been said, do you believe that there is a single person in this room who would take you for a hero?"

"I am no hero."

"Then why did you participate in this plan? What did you hope to achieve?"

"A scandal. I thought that our beloved chairman would be forced to resign, that I might take his place." There were cries of "Shame" from the audience. Bolb turned angrily on the crowd. "The Convergence would not exist if it were not for me. Nobody has brought the company more profit. I am becoming an old man. When will it be my turn?"

The room grew angrier as Bolb ranted. Catcalls, crumpled balls of paper and shoes were flung in his direction. Corbin allowed himself a self-satisfied smirk.

Gleame stood again, and though his face was clouded, he spoke calmly.

"Prosecutor Corbin. You have handled this trial admirably. The misdeeds that you have uncovered are terrible and lessons must be learnt. The Honourable Company will be eternally grateful — but I ask you to consider mercy. Dealing with the arcane can corrupt the minds of the noblest men. Bolb has served the Honourable Company and the Unity faithfully for many years. He is like a son to me, my greatest apprentice. Punish him as you must, and I assure you that he shall never work magic again, but please — if he is a traitor he is one by accident, not design."

Somney held his face in his hands. "No. This is exactly what he wants," he whispered.

"Take his arm — take his tongue if you must," Gleame continued, "but Bolb's death would serve no purpose. I beg for clemency."

"Kill him," called voices from the crowd. "Mercy," cried a few others.

Miranda stood again. "Please, let him live."

"The man is a disgrace to the Honourable Company; he should feel the full force of the law," Adrian shouted imperiously, drawing applause from across the room. He stared at Miranda as he said it. Maybe he suspected her pleading was part of some deal with Gleame. Maybe he'd said it just to spite her. In the end, it didn't matter either way.

"Silence," Corbin shouted. "Enough of your sentiments. Such talk is an affront to justice. Now hear my verdict." He took up his longsword and moved to the front of the stage.

"I was called to the Convergence to investigate a murder; the killing of Brother Adelmus. I knew the man well. He devoted the whole of his life to a single cause: the preservation of the law, the maintenance of the peace and order that you enjoy. He was a man willing to risk his life to defend any one of you, from any crime, no matter how unworthy of his protection you might be."

His gaze travelled across the audience of masters, demi-masters and those who served them.

"Without law and order there could be no Convergence, no Honourable Company. Without the Brotherhood of Censors, men would know nothing but chaos. You might have thought that you were safe, here on your island, with all of your wealth and all of your power. These things can sway a man's mind; make him believe that he lives beyond harm, by different rules. Now you know differently."

Even as he trembled in fear, Bolb looked at his colleagues accusingly, as if they were responsible for what would follow.

"I came to the Convergence to investigate a murder," continued Corbin. "I will leave having achieved something far greater, something that would make Adelmus proud. I will have reminded you that you are not beyond harm; that laws do not bend for the powerful; that there is no greater force than justice."

With that, he rapped the pommel of his longsword hard upon the stage. "Master Pendolous Bolb, you have shown yourself to be a base villain. A man who thinks only of himself. You may not have intended to be a traitor, but your actions have made you one. They have threatened the security of not only this place, but the entire Unity. Furthermore, your crimes led directly to the death of Brother Adelmus. You are found guilty of all charges. The punishment is death."

There was a roar from the crowd and a fist-fight broke out amongst the demi-masters. The masters sat in shocked silence. Bolb fell to his knees and wailed like a demented child.

ABATTOIR BLUES

The rope trailing behind Jon switched like a rat's tail, chafed a layer of skin from his wrists every time it caught on a piece of rubble or refuse. Peacock and the Sharks made him walk ahead, like a slave, or a prisoner of war. He kept his head bowed and prayed to the All-seeing that the blood and bruises that swelled his face would spare him from the shame of recognition. The Sharks look impassive, bored even. Matthew marched triumphant, his blunderbuss loaded and readied. Jon could sense it trained vaguely at his back.

"Where are you taking me?" he asked.

"To meet a friend," Peacock said. "Keep moving."

"What does this friend of yours want?"

"That's up to him."

"Then what?"

"Then I will return to my brand new mill and attend to some unfinished business." Peacock's bravado lacked enthusiasm. He had always enjoyed the chase more than the prize, Jon thought.

He imagined Gilbert Gordon coming at his balls with a pair of scissors and surreptitiously increased his pace, looking for an alleyway to dive into as the Sharks marched mechanically towards their destination.

His arms were wrenched backwards and he was forced to a halt in blinding pain. Peacock had planted his heel on the rope.

"There's no point in running, Jon. After what you've done, the censors would catch you anyway, as certain as your next birthday."

"More certain," rumbled Big Shark.

"A point well made," Littleshark agreed.

"Settle," Matthew snapped. He wasn't in the mood for joshing.

"You're turning me in, then? Not taking me to Gordon."

"The brothers have got a book with your name on it. They want to make sure they know everything about . . . about everything they need to know."

Jon nodded and they began to walk again, more slowly.

"Once you're on the books you never come off," Littleshark said.

Jon knew that already, Daniel had explained it to him many times. There was no prison in the seminary, only stocks, branding irons, chopping blocks and scaffolds. You were received. They took your confession. You were judged. Punishment or freedom followed. Mercy did not enter into it. According to the censors, mercy was a betrayal of justice. *Do I even deserve mercy*, Jon wondered, *after all I've done?*

Peacock kicked a discarded bucket to the edge of the kerb. "I still can't take you for a rebel. Bombing the Bell Jar; that's a thing of wonder to me. You might even have got away with it all if you hadn't fallen for that tart. Still no man can choose who he falls in love with." He sucked air through his teeth.

"True," Big Shark said.

"I used to think about that a lot when Anna was sucking on my prick."

Was it true? Had she done that to keep Matthew at bay? To save the mill? Maybe when she was supposed to be at temple. Jon stopped his mind. He didn't want to know. He wasn't even angry. None of it mattered any more.

"Look after her, if she comes back," he said.

Matthew didn't nod. He didn't make a joke either.

The streets to the north of Turbulence had taken the worst of the rioting. The charred beams of the houses looked like the stumps of a forest cleared by fire. Remnants of families, soot-faced, coats peppered with ash, collected their broken pottery and burnt sheets from the rubble and piled them into barrows and carts. Peacock's militiamen claimed anything of obvious value in return for safe passage.

"This isn't the way to the seminary," Jon said.

"Not to worry," Matthew replied.

"Not far now," Littleshark offered.

They passed through the edge of the city into the desolate countryside beyond. Jon didn't venture there often; he was surprised how empty the highway was, how barren the fields. There was nothing but road dust and insects. They walked under a pallid sun for half an hour, and then turned down a narrow lane that circuited a field. It was edged with stinging nettles and a rickety fence overgrown with blackberries. Peacock picked a handful and passed one to Jon. He burst it between his teeth and let its sweet juice pool under his tongue.

The path led to a small hut, thatch-roofed and wicker-walled, sheltered by a broad oak that had mysteriously escaped the woodman's axe. Its door was chained, which was a joke — a grown man could kick it through in seconds.

The Sharks untied it and bundled him inside. The Peacock followed a moment later, and closed the door behind them. It was hot and dark despite the gaps in the wicker walls, which allowed thin beams of light to enter. There was a musty smell. Hooked chains hung from the ceiling. This place had been a slaughterhouse once, or a slave pen. Its rough earthen floor was littered with segments of chain, stained black with the blood of past visitors.

Outside a crow cawed.

"What now?" Jon asked.

"We wait," Matthew said.

A soft voice issued from a shadowed corner. "No need to wait."

"Magistrate Lang." There was a nervous edge to Peacock's voice. Jon peered into the dusty gloom, saw the jagged outline of a man.

"Colonel Peacock, have you done as I commanded?"

Matthew cleared his throat. "The raid was victorious. The man who claimed to be Barehill is dead. And I have taken his lieutenant prisoner."

"Who?"

"Jonathan Miller, a very wicked man."

"Present him to me." The Sharks pushed Jonathan forward. Now he could see to whom they spoke. The man wore a shepherd's cloak, huge and grey, a peek of midnight blue underneath the rags. It made him look like a child in adult's clothing.

There was something odd about the man's stare, Jon thought. His eyes flitted from side to side and when his gaze held it seemed too intent, as if his point of focus was just behind Jon's eyes. Lang inspected him, questing for something, and Jon imagined a cold breeze wending through the crevices of his mind. Lang's lips curled in detached amusement. Jon sensed that he had recognised something in him, but he could not imagine what he saw.

"Wicked indeed," Lang said, "and captured by these rugged-looking gentlemen, the famous Sharks."

"Barehill was my work; I struck the fatal blow," Matthew said.

"Of course." Lang addressed the Sharks directly. "You are the gentlemen who served me in the North."

"Yes," Littleshark said.

"And you have told nobody of your actions."

"Not even Gordon," Littleshark said.

"You should have told us he was a censor; I nearly got caught out," Big Shark drawled. Littleshark hissed at him to be quiet.

"Be patient. Your reward will be forthcoming. Now let us deal with the matter at hand, the infamous Mr Miller. Gentlemen, please untie him, but hold him fast, just in case."

Am I to be judged here and now? Jon wondered. The Sharks cut the rope from his wrists and forced him to his knees. Each held up one of his arms, twisted it up behind his back so that he was pinned down. Lang raised his arms into the air and the sleeves of his cloak rolled back to reveal a pair of long pistols, double-barrelled and brass-hilted.

"Jonathan Miller, you now stand trial. I accuse you of the murder of Brother Nielsen, of acting as quartermaster to the traitorous Freeborn, of orchestrating the massacre at Bell Street. Will you make your confession?"

Jon nodded. Lang lifted Jon's chin with the barrel of a gun and stared deep into his eyes. He felt the cold draught in his mind again, but stronger this time, as if Jon's memories were a storybook and the gods were turning the pages. Lang released his chin. The drop of his head jolted him back into the room.

"How do you plead?" Lang asked.

Jon stared at him defiantly. "I did what I had to do."

Lang levelled his guns at Jon's forehead. "As do we all, and you will pay for your actions. I pronounce my sentence."

I'm sorry, Anna, Jon thought, *for everything*. He heard the double click as the pistols' hammers fell, then the deafening roar of their discharge. The small hut was engulfed in blinding light.

Jon fell to the ground deafened, clutched his hands over his ears. Big Shark landed beside him, his face mangled, grey eyes no deader than before. Littleshark fell across his legs.

Matthew brought up his blunderbuss and fired wildly in Lang's direction. The shot tore a hole through the wicker wall the size of a fist. Sunlight poured into the hut. Matthew blinked in confusion. Jon saw Lang standing behind him, outlined in the smoky brilliance.

Lang pressed the barrels of a pistol to the back of Matthew's head.

Peacock's body went stiff with fear. The smoking blunderbuss slipped from his trembling hands. Jon watched his lips move.

"Please," he seemed to say, then he spoke some more, but Jon could not follow the words for the ringing in his ears. A tear rolled down the Peacock's cheek.

There was another flash, and Matthew tumbled forwards. His body landed heavily and his brains spilt out across the floor. Jon watched mutely as Lang moved calmly around the room, crouching to check that each man was dead. After a couple of minutes, he felt ready to speak.

"What did you do?" Jon said.

Lang stood, satisfied with his work. "I take no pleasure in killing. The death of even the wickedest man weighs heavily upon my heart. I do only that which is necessary for justice to prevail."

Jon got to his knees. His ears still hurt, but strength was returning to his arms. Lang levelled his pistol at Jon.

"If you have been keeping count you will know that I have one shot left. I'm afraid it is meant for you."

With a leonine growl, Jon leapt forwards. His roar was drowned out by the discharge of the pistol.

It hit his head with the force of an anvil. *I've been shot*, Jon realised, as his body spun around. *Am I dead?*

Engulfed in a wave of pain, he awoke with a gasp, lying on the ground. Lang was leaning over him, slapping his face with somebody's ear.

"You should be more careful, Jonathan. You nearly caused an accident. But the gods smile on both of us today." Jon focused on the ear. There was a scrap of skin hanging from the side of it, a tuft of blond hair. He tried to think who the other blond in the room might be. He put his hand to the side of his head and the delicate touch swamped him with nausea. His hand came away wet with blood. "You would be bleeding less if you had held still," Lang said. "But you'll live."

The magistrate offered his hand, and Jon took it reluctantly. The man was half of Jon's weight, but he pulled him to his feet with ease. Jon surveyed the massacre all around him. The week before, it would have shocked him.

"Why didn't you kill me?" he asked.

"Because justice has need of you. If you prove half as capable as your brother you will serve me admirably." Jon could not suppress a laugh. It made the whole of his face roar with pain.

"You call this justice?"

"A path to justice." Lang pointed his ornate pistols at him, checked their mechanisms and the alignment of the barrels, then flipped them around and held out the stocks. "These are yours now. They're good pieces, worthy of a hero of the Freeborn." Jon took them. "You defeated the Peacock and the Sharks single-handed. When you return to Turbulence, you will be a hero of the Freeborn. Every radical and malcontent will want to share his or her secrets with you. You will allow it and, in turn, you will pass those secrets onto me."

"What's the point? Barehill's dead."

Lang shook his head sadly. "Every unhappy city in the Unity has a man who claims that name. If there really is a Barehill, if he is anything more than an idea, and of that I am uncertain, he is definitely not the man who died at your mill."

"Dan's alive then."

"Your brother prospers. You will see him again, no doubt, but that is not your immediate concern." Lang drew his shepherd's cloak close around him. "You have had a lucky escape, Mr Miller. Understand that if I ever have cause to shoot at you again, you will not live."

Lang stepped out.

Jon looked at the corpses that lay all around him. He spat on the Sharks, took their coin purses. The key to his mill hung from Matthew's belt. He took that as well. The Peacock's red beaver hat lay crumpled under his body. He straightened it out, closed the Peacock's eyes and placed it over the remains of his head.

"Goodbye Matthew," he said.

Lang was right. It was time to go home.

JUSTICE

Daniel slung his travelling sack over his back and made his way to the Convergence's tall teak gates. The individuals he passed moved aside and stared. Groups huddled and whispered comments. He felt no nostalgia. The strangeness of the Verge no longer provoked wonder in him, only a mild distaste, and his mind was already on Bromwich and his family. The only thing he would miss was Miranda.

She was waiting for him by the wicket door. At the sight of her, his breath caught in his throat. She was still dressed in the black and red gown that she had worn at the trial. Not a hair was out of place on her beautiful head, but she looked worried. It was clear that she meant to speak to him one last time before he left for good. He halted before her and dropped his baggage to his feet.

"Direct to Bromwich?" she asked.

"There has been rioting there, some kind of crisis. My family might be in danger."

"So that's it. You were going to leave without a word."

"I didn't think you wanted to speak to me."

For a moment, he wished that he could still be Edmund Sutton, the adorable oaf. He sought the words to make things right, to make her understand that his loving hadn't been an act, even if he hadn't realised it at the time.

"I'm sorry, Miranda, about what happened. How it happened, not that it happened. I will treasure that memory forever."

Her expression was impossible to read.

"What about the final matter?" she said. "Corbin left with Bolb an hour ago."

"He went to administer the lesser punishments, said it was a mistake to try to do everything the first time."

Miranda's eyes opened wide with shock. "Corbin means for you to do the killing?" Daniel tried to stand tall. He looked out across the bay towards the dunes.

"He thinks that I'm ready for it."

She took his thick-gloved hands in hers, and drew him close. "If there is anything you can do to stop this madness, do it." Her emerald eyes bore deep into his own. "Do it for me, your family, for everyone."

It was so like her to try to save Bolb's life. Her head might be in the clouds, but her heart was gentle and caring. It pained him to be the one to disappoint her.

"There's nothing that can be done," he replied sadly.

"Bolb isn't a traitor."

"He might not have intended treason, but that doesn't change what he did. You saw the mood at his confession. If we hadn't taken Bolb away, someone would have lynched him there and then."

He wished that she would stop thinking about the case. It was such morbid talk. What he wanted was the opportunity to say exactly the right words to make her understand how he felt without making himself look foolish. He smiled and shook her hands to change the mood.

"You will prosper here, I can tell. You'll be a master the next time I see you." He pulled off his glove and showed her the livid scar that ridged his left hand. "I will remember you every day, whether I want to or not. Will you speak to me in Bromwich as you promised? If I can't use a hekamaphone, you could write to me at the seminary. I really can read, you know."

She ran an elegant finger down the length of the wound, and looked at him strangely, as if she knew all the answers already, and that he could not begin to imagine what she understood. She was probably right.

"Maybe I have hurt you a little more than you deserved," she conceded. "But what's done is done." She smiled at him a little more sweetly and he saw a glimpse of what he had been praying for in her eyes. She stood on her toes to kiss him. He shut his eyes and readied his lips. She kissed him on the cheek.

"Good luck, Miller. The gods know we both need it."

He watched her walk into the bustle of the atrium, to be swallowed by the stream of panniers, porters, scribes, artisans that flowed through its gaps and passages. Her stride was poised and businesslike; people parted before her as if she was every inch the master she hoped to become. He waited for her to look back at him, one last time, but she didn't, and then she was gone.

●

A stiff wind scoured the dunes of Seascale Bay, sent eddies of sand twisting across the beach that forced Daniel to shield his eyes.

Corbin led Bolb by a rope. Daniel brought the horses close behind. Corbin had cauterised the master's wounds with a hot iron but not well enough to prevent the blood from soaking Bolb's chin and turning the grey cotton of his gown black, beneath his missing arm. His empty sleeve flapped like a pennant in the breeze.

The slope towards the cross of the sky burial, which had once carried Brother Adelmus's bones, was a gentle one, but the old master was struggling. Daniel wondered if it were the wounds or the fear that slowed his path to destiny. Every time Bolb stumbled, Corbin dragged him back to his feet and kicked him in the back. He made no sound, not even the plaintive moan for which men who have lost tongues are famous.

A small crowd of spectators had gathered at the foot of the beach.

"The audience is smaller than I expected," Daniel said.

"I told them to keep their distance. There will be others watching from the Convergence, through lenses."

"Why didn't you order a public execution?"

"This work is not an entertainment for the ignorant. We do only what is necessary."

They reached the crest of the hill and Corbin pushed Bolb onto the barren, windswept turf. Bolb, insensible with pain, knelt on his haunches in front of the wooden cross. His breath heaved raw. The master was going nowhere. Corbin dropped the rope and tethered the horses to the cross.

"It is quite a thing, to kill for the first time," Corbin said.

"My brother once told me that killing should always be done with a heavy heart. Even killing a mouse."

"Sounds soft, your brother. Pray he never sees a battle." It was true, Daniel thought, Jon was soft.

His throat was dry. He went over to his horse, the fine white gelding, and took a swig from the flask that hung by its side. The water tasted brackish, though he knew it was fresh. He spat it onto the grass.

"My brother's good in a fight. They used to call him the Lion."

"I mean no offence. Not all men can be killers."

A killer. Is that what I have become? Daniel drew his sword and weighed it in his hand. Its guard glowed softly in the weak, low light. This was not what Daniel had in mind when he had dressed up in a cape made of sack and pretended to rescue Dahlia and Anna from monsters in the mill.

He tried to remember the sister who had been stolen from him, to imagine Bolb as the monster who had taken her. To conjure from his melancholy a sense of vengeance.

"The first time is hardest," Corbin said, "but remember, this is no ordinary death. You are avenging the murder of a brother. That's enough justice for a lifetime."

Daniel nodded and positioned himself besides Bolb. The condemned man looked up at him. There were white blotches around his eyes and nose. *This is what true fear looks like*, Daniel thought. *Mortal fear.* He would not forget it.

Corbin tore a strip from Bolb's nightgown and folded it into a blindfold. Bolb shook his head. Corbin kicked his thigh. "It's not for your benefit," Corbin said, and slipped it over the master's head.

"It's better not to see the eyes," Corbin explained, and rolled Bolb forwards into a bowing stoop.

Daniel stared at Bolb's neck and the back of his head. The master didn't look like a monster. He looked like the fat baker who had tried to rip off his brother. Did he deserve to die? Better men died in Turbulence for less every day. He raised his sword above his head and remembered Miranda's plea to stop the killing. She was right. It was madness. He imagined how awful what he was doing would look from the outside. At that moment Daniel hated Corbin and justice far more than he hated Bolb. He wanted to curl into a ball, be somewhere else.

Was there any way to stop it?

He pictured running away, running at Corbin with his sword, a frantic duel amongst the dunes, sparks flying from the edges of their blades. Fantasies as stupid and impossible as his childish role play in the mill.

"You can use this if you want. It might make things easier." Corbin's hand was resting on the pommel of his longsword.

Daniel shook his head. The sabre Lang had given him was more than up to the task.

Corbin stepped back. "The gods are watching," he intoned.

Daniel brought his blade down with a sudden slash. Bolb's head thudded on the ground. Corbin mounted his chestnut mare, wheeled it around.

"I was wrong about you. I will send Lang a commendation of your work."

I was wrong as well, Daniel thought, and nodded gravely.

"Back to Bromwich, is it?"

Daniel nodded again, and thought of home.

"Good luck."

THE MASTER

Miranda observed Bolb's execution through a curved lens mounted on the edge of a wall walk, tormented by her vertigo but unable to resist. The bird-like view from hundreds of feet above the bay, gave her a sense of distance, but did not lessen the horror.

She gasped as Daniel's blade descended, raised her hand to her mouth.

She was still in shock as Corbin galloped north towards the highway. She watched Daniel as he stood motionless, contemplating Bolb's corpse. When his thinking was done, he turned to face the Convergence and seemed to stare straight at her. He leapt smoothly into the saddle of his white horse and then he was gone too.

It was done. Now there was no turning back.

The small crowd of gawkers who had gathered on the beach dispersed rapidly, disappointed with the show. Bolb's body lay unattended where it had fallen. His head rested in the scrub a few feet away. Miranda wondered if Gleame would send porters to collect his remains later in the day. Maybe after nightfall.

She closed her eyes and listened to the magic.

Already it had begun to twist and scream in confusion. Whatever the damage that Gahst's death had caused, Bolb's death was far worse. Hundreds of the gossamer strands that arced above her head, the conduits that linked the Convergence to the arcane devices that had been created there, began to peel and fray.

Magic was in her blood now, and she could feel a gouging in her stomach, as if the baby of a monster fretted inside her, but she was learning how to control these waves of pain, how to live with them. She pushed the feelings away.

It was all very ironic, she thought. Gahst had been right all along, yet it was his concern that had triggered the crisis he feared, and in a roundabout way, Bolb's mechanical hand had delivered exactly the warning that Gahst had intended.

It had fallen to her to fix the system from within. To do so would take every part of her intellect and her will. She would work with Gleame, learn his secrets and then combine them with her own. In doing so, she could become the greatest master the world had ever seen. It was her destiny.

●

Her handmaid's delicately scented hands trembled as they tied the black velvet choker around Miranda's neck, fixed a diadem, a peaked cobweb of black coral and pearls, to her hair with small silver pins. The mirror on the vanity was set low; Miranda could not see the expression on her handmaid's face but she could tell that she was afraid.

Whom does she fear? Miranda wondered. *Them or me?*

"That jewel was a New Year gift from Mother. At the time, I thought it quite dreadful. Now I realise that I like it. A touch more kohl above the eyes." A little brushwork and it was done. "Go now. I'll wait for them alone."

The handmaid bowed, paused as if to say something, and then walked backwards from the room. *Do not worry, my little finch*, Miranda thought.

She stood abruptly and the lines of her black and crimson dress snapped into place. Miranda twirled once, made the colours of her hem flash like the dying embers of a fire. She was feeling calmer now, bathed and powdered. She had followed Gleame's example, protected her room with a simple construct to give her peace to think. Now the tension she felt was worry, pure and simple.

What if I cannot find the solution? What if it's all too late? Before she knew it, her mind was sucked into a whirlwind of theories and calculations, experiments that had to be tried, and practices that should be restricted.

She was still enraptured when the knocking rattled her door. She realised that she was pacing, biting on her knuckles. She unclenched her fists, stood as tall as she could and unsealed her chamber. Two men stood before her, unidentifiable in purple robes and hoods.

"Do you accept the call?" they asked.

"Gladly," she said, and knew it was not a lie. They grasped her, not roughly, and spun her around until the world became a dizzy blur.

●

It was not until the initiation was over that Miranda could reassemble its fragments in her mind. She remembered seeing the world inverted as she was pulled backwards down corridors, held by her arms and elbows, her heels dragging along the floor, her artificial leg scraping on the stone. The men in purple took her down and down, descended to the dark lake that lay beneath the Convergence by secret, empty ways.

When she arrived at the chamber of the henge, the sound of engines was absent and the huge basket lanthorns that normally illuminated the standing stones had been extinguished. She could see the torus unaided — it rotated slowly and uncertainly, as if the magic caught and ground against itself like floating sheets of ice torn and crushed by opposing currents.

She thought, *It seems to be in pain.*

Before each of the stones that ringed the sacred lake, except for four that were unattended, stood a man wielding a firebrand. The light of the torches was doubled in the still surface of the water.

Four empty stones, Miranda thought. *Two for the men who carry me. One for Gahst. One for Bolb. Two masters dead; two new masters to replace them.* She could have slapped herself then. Now she understood why Lavety had said what he had at the trial. *I will not be the only one promoted to master tonight*, she thought, and had a premonition of Lavety in a newly made robe, the colours of a rainbow.

The masters removed their cowls in unison. Miranda recognised Somney, Essossilam, Nirmeen, all of the masters. Even Talon was there, upright in his gurney with his teeth set in a rictus. Those who had supported her promotion and those who had sworn to oppose it stood side by side in silence. Gleame waited on the opposite shore in his robes of pure white. He stepped forward, to the edge of the water, and in a booming voice asked for a password to be given. The men who held Miranda's arms each gave one before removing their masks. *Baldwin and Bohapemetys* — she might have guessed.

She was turned to face the lake and they left her side, took places by the stones, leaving her alone at the water's edge. Though she was deep underground, gusts of cold night air caressed her face.

Gleame demanded her given name and she called it out proudly.

"Miranda, Ward of the Duchess."

"Do you promise to serve the Honourable Company in good faith, to keep no secrets from us, to lend us the whole of your trust, and to accept no other ruler?"

"I do."

"And do you swear to preserve the mysteries of the Convergence, against the penalty of having your throat cut across and your tongue torn out by the root and buried in the sands of the sea?"

That last bit seemed terribly silly to Miranda, but she knew how much the men loved secret rituals, so she answered gravely.

"I do."

"Have you chosen the name by which you will henceforth be known?"

"Master Miranda Solitaire." The jumbled echo of her new name was chanted from the stones.

"Now say unto us the name of that thing which binds you to this earth, that which you must discard to become truly free. Speak truly or suffer the consequences." Something in Gleame's voice warned her that the threat was no joke. She knelt at the water's edge.

It seemed to her that the lake had become a night sky. Far deeper than the stars are set in the firmament, she could see distant cities and the pale shadows of figures, vast and shambling, under the water. She wondered if it were some trick of the light, but could not shake the impossible feeling that these beings saw her also; that in all the vastness of the universes revealed to her, they observed her precisely, just as she saw the stars and comets that passed around them.

"Her Grace," she said. "That is what binds me to this world. My loyalty and love for my mother." The distant figures nodded imperceptibly and then faded from view.

"Step upon the water," Gleame commanded. Miranda reached out her foot, the metal one, and stepped out, expecting to plunge. The surface of the lake was as firm as obsidian glass. She walked slowly to its very centre.

"The moment arrives, so you must decide," Gleame announced.

The masters who ringed the lake stepped forward and lowered their torches, touched the flaming heads against the hard water. Gouts of flame leapt up where they connected, and the lake was encircled with fire.

Miranda became afraid. All she could see was the magic of the torus arcing above her head and the angry flames around her. The surface of the lake bubbled like oil. Her mind screamed at her to run, and she turned, but there was no escape.

All of a sudden, she felt a strong wind. It turned the whole of the lake into an enormous pyre. The flames rushed towards her, and for an instant, she felt the skin of her face sear in the heat. The hem of her skirt caught fire, and then the ground gave way beneath her feet and she was plunged into brackish, icy blackness.

She felt hands clawing at her shoulders, and she tried to fight them away. The weight of her dress pulled her deeper into the water. She seemed to sink for minutes. The world became utterly black. She closed her eyes.

She opened them. Baldwin and Bohapemetys held her by the arms. She stood by the side of the lake where the ceremony had begun, dry and unblemished. A triumphant cheer arose from the men around the stones. She did not need to be told that she had become a master. She knew it. The faltering power of the Convergence coursed through her veins.

A HOMECOMING

The yellow grass that lined the country lane was noisy with the chatter of insects. Wind played through the hedgerows like a falconer's whistle. Jon was far enough from the city limits that highwaymen and vagrants would not fear a censor's patrol, but no sane man would dare assail him. He walked, fangs bared, his guns tucked into the top of his breeches, exposed for all to see — one set against his stomach, the other flat against his back. The manner of his walk assured his safety. He was unafraid.

The sun was setting. To the south, Bromwich lay golden at its feet, the gilded peaks of domes and spires shining brilliantly in the dying light. The silhouette of familiar roofs, jagged like the teeth of a broken jaw, guided him home. As the town drew closer into view, Jon saw it was wreathed in smoke. Not the normal wisps of chimney smoke that rose unsteadily in lazy air, but towering black pillars that blotted out the sun. There were fires burning everywhere, many more than before, all across the city. Not rebellion, he thought, something different.

He passed through the ruins at the edge of town, to the streets that had names, and then to those he knew well. Up Pinfold, left onto Peek Lane and up towards the mill. He passed censors and guardsmen by the dozen, fighting fires, helping men and women to salvage goods. He did not hide his weapons, yet he travelled without challenge.

As he climbed Peek Lane, he felt the wind strong against his face, as it had been before the cunning had changed it all.

At last, the mill came into view. It stood solid, though fire had taken the loading-bay doors and left black smears above the windows. One of Peacock's orange-men, in a helmet and breastplate and clutching a pike, stood guard outside the loading bay. He guessed the others were inside, waiting for the Peacock to return.

So was Laila, terrified and desperate.

Laila knew where Anna was hidden, if she was still alive. She had to be alive. He would know if she wasn't. The gods would have given him a sign.

There was a crashing noise from within the mill tower, a sound like fighting. The guard turned his back on Jon and stared upwards, aimed his pike towards the ruckus as if the mill tower were a giant and he were a valiant knight. Jon crept up behind him, grabbed his helmet and broke his neck with a savage twist.

Planks cracked overhead and the street was showered in wood and plaster. A hole had appeared halfway up the tower, as if an enormous cannon had blasted out the wall from within. The carousel horse landed in the middle of the street, ablaze with lanthorn oil. It hoofed at the ground, scraping cobbles from the earth. Jon stared into its dull, moronic eyes. Those red stones betrayed no thought, but there was something new in them, a wildness that was impossible to describe. The blazing horse seemed to smile at him, although its mouth did not move, then it jumped over his head and cantered into the city.

Jon was beyond amazement. He went to the mill door and listened. He could hear men arguing. No more than three or four. He had a bullet for each of them. He drew the pistols from his breeches and made sure they were properly loaded.

He heard a noise behind him.

A small gang of men emerged from the ruined house across the street, wielding pitchforks, cleavers and jagged strips of wood. The remnants of the Freeborn.

"The Lion," one said in wonder.

"How did you escape?" asked another.

"By the grace of the gods," Jon replied.

They nodded solemnly. "What should we do?"

"Say your prayers, ready your weapons and prepare to follow me."

Continued in Book Two of the
Thrice~Crossed Swords Trilogy

'THE PILLOW KNIFE'

A REQUEST FROM THE AUTHOR

In the world of 21st-century publishing, the opinions of readers are worth far more than those of any critic. If you have enjoyed reading *The Censor's Hand*, and wish to help others discover it, please consider leaving an honest review on Amazon or Goodreads.

Subscribe to www.amsteiner.com for news, special offers, short stories and updates on *The Thrice~Crossed Swords Trilogy*.

ABOUT THE AUTHOR

Adam M. Steiner grew up in Highgate, North London, a place of wild forests and ancient graveyards. He spent his schooldays raiding the local library, immersing himself in role-playing games and paying attention to his teachers when they were talking about ancient gods.

Later in life, he travelled the world, had many adventures, and learned a great deal about the murky worlds of business, politics and magic.

When he is not writing dark fantasy novels, Adam fences épée and longsword. He recently returned to Highgate to raise semi-feral children with his perfect wife.

ACKNOWLEDGEMENTS

Creating a book involves far more people than you might suppose. Thanks are due firstly to my family, without whose belief and support *The Censor's Hand* would not have been possible. Next, to Pat Sumner, for her wonderful editing. To John Jarrold, for his advice and encouragement. To Helen, for her wise reading. To Patrick Knowles and Sergey Zabelin for their evocative art. Lastly, to the many wonderful authors and film-makers who proved to me long ago that if something can be said, it can be said better in fantasy.

Proof

Made in the USA
Columbia, SC
11 May 2017